BEHIND
THE LIES

A Montgomery Justice Novel

Robin Perini

Published by Montlake Romance
P.O. Box 400818
Las Vegas, NV 89140

ISBN-13: 9781611098853
ISBN-10: 1611098858

In loving memory of my wonderful great-aunt, Lillian Bailey, the original storyteller. For special moments filled with spicy tacos, a warm feather bed, and fairy tale after fairy tale. Though I lost you too soon, your generous and beautiful heart gifted me with the love of story and the belief I could tell one. I love you, Aunt Daddee. Each word in my stories is laced with your inspiration.

Prologue

The last time Sergeant Patrick Montgomery had seen his third-oldest son, Zach had been on the cover of a tabloid cavorting with five naked women.

Every twenty-seven-year-old male's fantasy, perhaps, but between those pictures and the rumors of wild parties, alcohol, and God knew what else, even Zach's brothers had voiced concern, not envy. Last night they'd finally revealed the location of Zach's favorite blues bar to Patrick. A sure sign they were troubled by the daredevil brother who had scaled the imaginary mountain peak of Hollywood and now dangled on a zip line over a crevice of jagged temptation. If the rope frayed any more…no one could save him.

Patrick's steps thudded across the cracked concrete in the war zone in downtown Denver. His hand settled over the Kimber 1911 tucked in his pants. He'd walked this beat as a street cop plenty of times, but unease tightened his trigger finger.

Could it be the sense someone was watching? Or could it be his wife's strong grip on his arm just before he'd left home? Even though Anna had spent countless nights in silent tears over the troubling tabloid articles, she hadn't wanted Patrick to go out tonight. One of her infamous *feelings*.

She was never wrong, damn the woman.

The streetlamp above him flickered, its fading light reflecting off the tequila in the liquor store in a glimmer of enticement. Sirens squealed down the block. The smell of old booze and urine permeated his nostrils.

A small grunt sounded from a darkened alley to his right. Patrick didn't hesitate. He clasped his weapon and whirled around, ignoring the twinge in his hip where a twenty-two-year-old bullet was still lodged.

"I've got the time, sugar. I could rock your world."

A hooker. Patrick's hand released the gun as he made out the crow's-feet around her eyes, the desperation in her gaze. A woman trying to look a decade younger than she was, and not succeeding.

She hitched her spandex-covered hip and did her best to smile. "You're a handsome guy. I'll do you for half price. Tonight only."

Patrick raised his left hand and tilted the gold band at her. "Sorry, honey. I'm taken."

"Most of my customers are," she muttered with a drawn-out sigh. "Suit yourself." She lifted her chin, stuck out her chest, and strutted on four-inch heels to the sidewalk's edge with a fake smile and clenched fists.

He could've pulled his badge and run her in, but what would be the point?

"There's a shelter down the block," he called out as a Lincoln pulled up next to her.

She flipped him a third-finger salute and slid into the vehicle. The luxury car sloshed through a puddle, spraying oil-laced water on Patrick's boots, then passed by. She stared out the window at him, her expression sad and haunted.

Nothing he could do. She'd made her choice.

Just like Zach. His son had come to town for his latest B-movie publicity junket. He hadn't taken the time to see the family—whether he was embarrassed or just didn't care, Patrick didn't know. He feared he may have waited too long for this conversation.

His son had run away. From home, from his family, from his faith, from his soul. Only one thing to do when a black sheep lost its way—and it wasn't throwing a welcome-home party.

Call it an intervention, call it a kick in the pants.

Which was why he was heading toward a bar he had no business being near instead of cuddling with his wife in front of a roaring fire, enjoying a shot of whisky, and maybe even getting lucky. Not that Anna would have needed much persuading. Even after nearly thirty years of marriage, his blood ran hot for his wife whenever he saw her pretty ginger hair and piercing green eyes. She felt the same. His heart warmed at the certainty. They'd had their rough patches over the years, but these days... no man could ask for a better life. A fulfilling job as a cop, the love of a woman, and six strong sons.

Most of whom were on the right track.

Patrick crossed the street and settled in just outside a small convenience store. Zach would show up at the blues bar eventually. From what Patrick had seen in the tabloids, his wayward son couldn't resist booze, smoke, and sex.

"Hey, Pops. You Sergeant Montgomery?"

Patrick turned and studied the teen who stood in an open stance at the corner of the building. A large birthmark stained his face. Thatch of black hair. Tattoo on his arm. A pretender's Special Forces tattoo. Nothing like the one Patrick had had removed. He labeled him quickly. Punk.

Make that...scared punk.

The kid's hands shook.

He held a gun.

Patrick grabbed for his 1911.

A hot blast from behind pelted his back. Where the hell had that come from? He sank to his knees. The .45 caliber slipped from his hand.

His head dropped and he stared down at his front. Blood pooled over his chest, soaking his shirt.

The kid ran, but he'd been a distraction. Who...?

Patrick keeled over on his side, his forehead slapping the concrete sidewalk. The sounds of the city muted. He couldn't move. Couldn't breathe.

He tilted his head and blinked. White spots circled his vision.

A cold but familiar face stared down at him, a gun in hand. He'd seen the man once. That last confrontation. Damn it. He hadn't believed they'd go this far.

"Why?" Patrick whispered.

"You know too much."

The figure melted away.

Far-off screams barely penetrated his mind. His phone rang. He couldn't pick up. His body tingled, then went strangely numb. And he knew.

"Aww, Anna. I'm sorry, my darling."

Each breath turned into a struggle. A gurgling bubbled in his chest.

"Dad?" His prodigal son's voice shouted from the darkness.

Strong hands grabbed him. "Oh, God, Dad. Someone call an ambulance!"

"Zach," he whispered, struggling to form the word.

"What are you doing here?" Zach choked.

Patrick's strength poured from his chest, but he rallied his heart and forced his eyes open. His boy stared down, in that moment looking so much like Anna. Her hair, the shape of her eyes. He looked up into his son's face.

Tears streamed down Zach's cheeks. Bloodshot eyes laced with fear...and regret. He cradled Patrick close, but Patrick could no longer feel his son's touch.

"Hold on, Dad. Please."

It was too late.

"Tell...Mom. Love her," he gasped. A gray cloud closed in on him, washing out life's color.

"Don't do this, Dad." Zach clutched him, rocking him back and forth. "Please. Caleb said you were looking for me. God, I'm sorry. I'll make this right. Somehow."

"Robbery," a voice shouted from nearby. "We got him."

Patrick clutched Zach's neck.

"Lies."

Patrick wanted to say more. To tell his son the truth. So many secrets. Too many secrets. They'd killed him.

His eyes fluttered closed. He wanted air. Needed air. He tried to breathe. Something huge and horrible clamped down on his chest.

He panted. He tried to speak.

Then an odd warmth flowed through him. The pain twisting his insides vanished. He wished he could tell Zach it would be all right. He didn't want to leave his family, but he had faith. In his family, in his wife, in his children.

They would be OK.

He and Anna had done their job.

And Zach. Zach *would* find his way.

Chapter One

Five Years Later—Istanbul, Turkey

HIS WORLD WAS NO MORE THAN A FAÇADE.

Zach Montgomery strolled across the intricate parquet floor of the Dolmabahce Palace. The Ottomans certainly knew their opulence. Gold ornamented the nearly forty-foot-high walls and molding on either side of him. The crystals of the gargantuan chandelier winked as if knowing all of his secrets as he passed under the baroque dome.

A sea of well-groomed, preening penguins milled around him. They were the beautiful people, too perfect to be real.

Zach tugged at his bow tie. The supposed Armani tuxedo did look damn good. Of course, like his surroundings—like Zach himself—nothing was as it appeared.

"Action," the director shouted.

Zach picked his way through the crowd, focused on every blocked step, every movement. The timing had to be perfect. A glimmer of metal shimmered to his right. His muscles tightened like a puppet string pulled taut.

A gun's barrel pointed directly at him.

With a quick shift on his right leg, he twisted his body and shoved his sleek, blonde costar to the floor. He covered Anastasia and tugged the fake Sig Sauer from his waistband, the gun's weight perfectly balanced in his hand.

Two quick shots and the movie's villain smashed into the champagne fountain. Blood pooled on his white tuxedo shirt. Under his weight, the huge gold structure crashed over, its sparkling liquid turning into a waterfall.

Screams ripped through the elegant mansion. The flock of extras dove toward the exits, sloshing through the amber liquid, avoiding the predator.

Zach tucked Anastasia to his side and maneuvered through the panicked throng. A dark-headed man grabbed at her with a scowl. Zach didn't hesitate. He shoved his elbow into the guy's nose. Synthetic blood spurted. Howling, he fell away.

Zach grabbed Anastasia and slid under a silk-covered table, with her nestled against him. He jumped to his feet, reached one of the prefabricated panels that protected the palace walls from the movie's more destructive special effects, and shoved it open, ducking them inside.

"Cut!" the director shouted.

Anastasia sagged against him. Zach smiled down at his costar. Her eyes couldn't hide the relief. She hadn't mastered the acting craft, but at least she had a soul blazing from her eyes. Unlike so many others in his plastic Hollywood world.

He softened his smile and tilted her chin up. "You all right?"

She stared at her Christian Dior dress, now soaked with fake champagne. "I just hope we don't have to do that again."

"Don't bet on it, but it'll take a while to reset the stage."

"We go again in three hours," the director yelled.

Zach chucked Anastasia's chin. "You better get to hair and makeup, honey."

She blinked her baby blues at him then licked her lips. "We could spend part of the break…together. They gave me a private trailer. It's in my contract."

The come-hither words might have been tempting at one time. Five years ago, he'd definitely have taken her up on the offer, but these days…she was too young. Too innocent. An oxymoron in the movie business, but everyone was too innocent for Zach. "Thanks for the offer, Ana, but I have a call to make."

"Girlfriend?"

"Not hardly," he chuckled.

She raised a brow. "Boyfriend?"

He didn't bother to respond. One more false rumor about his lifestyle might piss off his brothers and disappoint his mom, but it kept him alive.

Anastasia flipped her hair and pushed through the door where the director oohed and aahed over her performance.

Zach just snorted. He skirted around the corner toward the series of rooms the film crew had taken over as dressing areas. He threw the Armani suit at one of the gofers and slipped into black leathers and a jacket over a white T-shirt.

"But, sir," a young intern squeaked. "You have hair and makeup soon."

Zach shrugged. "I'll be back. Have a small errand to run," he said, and winked at the guy. The kid's eyes grew wide. He probably thought Zach was going out for a bang in a back alley… or maybe a line.

Let them think what they wanted.

He exited the nineteenth-century Turkish palace on the opposite side from the Bosphorus Strait, though the blast of salt and sea still hovered in the air. The water would have been a stealth exit, but he didn't have the time. He hit the velvet lawn in a run, his feet sinking into the sod after the unusual afternoon rain. The palace glowed golden in the dusk, illuminating his path—and him. He had to get out of sight. Quick. He dodged behind a nest of foliage before tugging a small beeper out of his coat pocket. *Damn. Less than thirty minutes.* It'd be tight.

Under cover of the trees, he pulled a kit from beneath his jacket and quickly donned his disguise. With one last look in the small mirror, he frowned at Zane Morgan, with his goatee and scar on one cheek. Ten years in the movie business had taught him how to make himself into a man who would never be connected to Zach Montgomery.

The skill came in handy. The disguise kept his family safe, but these days Zach found it increasingly difficult to maintain the façade of his alter egos. Zane Morgan, CIA operative; and Zach Montgomery, B-movie hack.

The movie business did provide Zach the perfect cover. He could travel into the most sensitive countries in the world with very few questions. Once he entered as Zach, once he'd played his part, he could get down to his real job—becoming Zane Morgan, a spy who could filter into a location, gather information, and leave unnoticed. Most of the time.

Minutes later, he reached the edge of the palace estate and eyed the high stone wall. They'd clearly landscaped the place for looks and not protection. Not unless armed guards patrolled—which they normally didn't these days, except for show. Zach eased along the rough wall's edge, past the empty guard post, until he reached a locked gate. He snagged one of his cooler toys from his zippered pocket. With a quick snap, he picked the lock.

Man, what he wouldn't have given to have this gadget when he was a teenager sneaking in and out of the house for a night on the town. Trying to avoid his dad had probably been the best training he'd ever had. The guilt embedded in Zach's skin like a splinter rubbed raw, exposing a sorrow he could never shake. He couldn't do anything about the past...or gain his father's respect, but he still might be able to save the man who had risked his life to expose a terrorist.

Pendar had wanted a better life, particularly for his daughters, so the Afghani had come to Zach and volunteered to provide information. On his own, Pendar had infiltrated a group that dealt closely with Khalid—a leader known only by one name, but that name struck dread in so many. Pendar had recognized the mass murderer must be stopped. Despite Zach's concern that Pendar had been in over his head, Zach had admired his contact's courage. He'd allowed the situation to develop. Now Pendar, along with his family, was missing. They'd vanished four months ago. Too long. Zach had no one to blame but himself.

He made his way to a large hedge just beyond the palace's perimeter. Behind it, he found the motorcycle he'd stashed there earlier. He snagged the helmet and pulled out his phone and earpiece before starting the engine.

The bike roared to life between his thighs, and Zach steered the machine onto the road. He tapped his earpiece.

"I'm en route," he checked in over the rumble of the engine.

"You're late." Theresa's silky-smooth voice caressed the phone.

How was it she could make getting chewed out sound like foreplay? On the other hand, Theresa had black belts in two martial arts disciplines. She'd trained Zach. Taught him how to kill and how to hide his identity.

"I told you this director has his own timetable," Zach snapped. "You should have given me more leeway."

Theresa laughed. "I know better. Besides, our pigeon is high maintenance."

Zach rounded the corner and leaned into the curve, twisting the gas and ripping through the narrow city streets. "How does a Turkish informant have information about Pendar? When was your contact in Afghanistan?"

"He *says* they were still alive as of a month ago. He claims he saw Pendar and his family brought into a militant training camp run by your favorite terrorist."

"Khalid." Zach's grip tightened on the gas. "Khalid is why you got me on this movie so quickly. It's an A-list job, and I can't believe Matt just bailed. What did you have to do, Theresa?"

"Do you really want to know?"

Zach urged the bike forward. "I guess not." Sweat beaded on his upper lip. "So, is the information credible?"

Theresa didn't say anything for a moment. Zach knew the truth. She believed that Pendar, his wife, Setara, and their two daughters were dead. Khalid's group had a reputation for kidnapping for hire—resulting in beheadings, not ransoms. Zach's assignment had been to discover the group's location so a smart bomb could take out the man responsible for over one hundred deaths—that they knew of. Pendar had been a godsend.

Until he'd disappeared.

"What does this guy really want?" Zach muttered. No one bargained these days without a major favor in mind.

"He made enemies. He needs asylum."

"Can we do the deal?" It wasn't always possible.

"The boss wants to take out Khalid any way we can. He's willing to take the risk."

The motorcycle whipped down the brick-covered streets, the uneven ground vibrating his back teeth. He flew past shop after shop, a hint of spice and smoke still in the air from the final hours of life at the street market. Finally, he shifted around a last corner to a part of Istanbul that no tourist should frequent. He turned into the sunset, and the glare blinded him momentarily. Zach blinked and pulled on his sunglasses as the landscape shifted. Fewer buildings, more trees, much more remote.

"Almost to the rendezvous point." The area was deserted. Zach eased on the gas, his breathing steady, his hands itching to hold his weapon. "I need to find Pendar, Theresa."

She sighed again. "It wasn't your fault. He got careless."

"He wouldn't have put himself in that position if I hadn't twisted his arm."

A figure stepped into the darkening road.

He aimed a submachine gun directly at Zach. The bullets would rip through Kevlar like butter and explode inside him. If they landed true.

"It's a setup."

Theresa spit out an unladylike curse.

Zach had no choice. He gunned the gas, leaned back, and forced his bike into a skid, his thousand-dollar leather pants taking the brunt of the slide. The motorcycle slid into the guy, undercutting his legs before he could get off a shot. He fell back with a loud roar. Before the bike slid to a stop, Zach shot to his feet, his father's reliable Kimber 1911 in his palm. He ignored the pain shooting down his right leg. Warm liquid bathed his skin, but he raced toward his assailant. He had more than a few questions.

A van screeched to a halt. Five men jumped out.

With a harsh expletive, Zach spun around. His legs pumped hard as he dove for cover in a grove of trees at the side of the road, hidden in the shadows, the black of his clothes blending him into his surroundings.

The men scattered, their weapons at the ready, shouting in Turkish.

He didn't make out all the phrases, except one. *Kill Zane Morgan.*

Zach shifted. A woodpecker sounded an indignant call and took to the skies.

The men whirled toward the sound. One raced at Zach.

Shit.

Five against one. Not good odds.

The barrel of the submachine gun pointed just to his right. The guy let the bullets fly. Zach took one shot. The bullet hit true. His assailant fell to the ground.

The four men left shouted out and started his way. Zach picked off two more.

The remaining assailants raced back to the van using curses that definitely weren't part of his original lessons in Turkish. Nothing like on-the-job-training to expand the vocabulary. The men climbed into the vehicle and screamed away.

Zach fell onto his back and tapped his earpiece. "Three dead. I need cleanup."

His contact sighed. "Can't you go anywhere without leaving a mess?"

He didn't joke back. "How'd they know about the meet, Theresa?"

"I don't know. I'll get back to you."

Zach didn't like the worried tone in her voice, but she'd figure it out. She had his back. She always did.

He shifted and his leg burned. Zach studied the damage. "Damn it. I'm going to be late for the next take."

———————————

Chippendale furniture and Waterford crystal didn't matter if you were dead. Jenna Walters knew she wouldn't be leaving her house alive. Not if she stayed another hour.

Standing in the elegant bedroom where her dreams had been created—and shattered—she dialed a well-rehearsed number with shaking fingers, a number she'd *believed* was her salvation. After the last few months, she didn't know if she could believe in anything or anyone anymore.

She tucked the phone under her chin and opened another drawer from the priceless mahogany antique.

"FBI," a formless tone answered.

"Agent Fallon, please." She cursed her quivering voice. If betrayal could drive away fear, she would've been the bravest woman on earth.

She studied the smashed FBI listening device in her hand. The trembling hadn't stopped since she'd discovered it. He knew. Brad knew what she'd done. What she'd tried to do. There was no other explanation. He was playing with her, like he had for the seven years she'd known him.

She shoved aside the truth of what her husband could do to her as quickly as she pushed the drawer closed. The television rumbled on the news channel in the background. She glanced over at the distraction. The breaking announcement at the bottom of the screen made her still. The phone dropped to the floor. She stared at the words, desperately praying they would change, but of course they didn't. She stared at the phone on the ground, her lifeline. She scooped up the receiver and stuffed two more nondescript shirts in the duffel. If she'd had any doubts before, they were gone now. No regrets. No more designer gowns. She had to disappear.

She'd give the FBI one last chance.

"Fallon." The crisp voice on the other end of the phone didn't calm her as it had in the past. In fact, he sounded shaken.

No more out of sorts than she. "He knows."

"Jenna?"

"One of the bugs is in pieces. I'm telling you, he knows. I've got to get out of here. Now. I don't know why he hasn't already killed me. Probably because he couldn't find a babysitter on such short notice." The forced laugh didn't hide the panic in her voice.

Who was she kidding? She shoved underwear into the bag and yanked open another drawer.

"Wait a minute, Jenna. Let's think this through. We can salvage the operation." He didn't sound like himself. Something was wrong. The gut instinct that had abandoned her when Brad had swept her off her feet revved into overdrive.

For months after her dad had died, she'd survived on the streets, instinct and desperation her only allies. At fourteen she'd kept herself safe by trusting her gut.

Right now, every fiber in her being told her that the man on the other end of the phone was lying to her.

She couldn't afford to doubt. Besides, why should she be surprised that another person she'd trusted was a liar?

Fallon had blown his last chance.

Her comfortable existence might be gone, but she *would* scrape a life together. She had reason to. "*You* think. I'm out of here. His flight's already landed. He's an hour from home."

The breaking news flashed on the television screen a second time. The caption scrolling across the bottom said it all. *San Francisco. Joseph Romero, primary witness for the prosecution in extortion trial, murdered while in protective custody.*

"Brad was in San Francisco," she said, her voice wooden and way too calm.

"What are you talking about?"

Another lie. "I can hear the wobble in your voice, Fallon. You're not that good." With a quick tug, she zipped closed the surplus store duffel. "It just flashed on the news. Brad killed Joseph Romero, didn't he? He goes to a city. Someone dies. Isn't that the pattern?"

A sharp curse exploded through the phone. "Look, Jenna. We believe Brad got to Romero. We don't know how, but it doesn't change anything. We can still protect you."

"Is that what you told Joseph Romero?"

"Damn it, Jenna. You need us."

"I can't trust you to protect us. I should have known better. I'll be in touch when we're safe. Maybe."

She slammed the phone against his shouts of protest and hung her head in her hands. What was she going to do? How in God's name was she going to protect her son?

"Mommy? Are you all right?" Sam's tentative voice filtered across the room.

She pasted on a cheerful smile before she lifted her head. She clasped the locket dangling around her neck, the locket her father had given her, and squeezed it tight. She met her son's troubled gaze. His green eyes—so like hers. Nothing like his father's.

Her five-year-old's presence stiffened her spine. She was doing this for him. He'd given her the strength to fill out the divorce papers and the courage to call the FBI. He'd give her the strength to protect him and the strength to abandon everything she'd believed she wanted.

Now she knew the truth. Her dream was based on a lie.

"Sure, baby." Moving a shaking hand under the edge of the bed frame, she searched until her fingertips encountered the bundle of cash she'd taped there while Brad had been barricaded in the office on the phone. Arranging one more of his "deals." Now she knew that "deal" had been murder for hire.

Sam jumped on her bed and tugged at the duffel. "Are we going on a trip?"

"A quick one, Sam. Go grab one toy you want to take with you."

Oh, that hurt. Her throat thickened, but she swallowed past the regret. She didn't want to limit Sam. He was giving up every-thing, too, but they had to travel light until she found a place for them to be safe.

"But Dad's coming home today. And he's taking me to a baseball game soon. He promised."

"Change of plans. It's a surprise." She forced a big grin. "You'll love it. I promise."

Eventually. Maybe. *But at least you'll be alive, and safe. Not the son of a man who kills people for a living.*

She glanced at the bedside clock. Not enough time to think about any of the memories she had to leave behind. They were false anyway. All except one. She snagged a set of photos of Sam from the dresser. It would have to do.

One look at his mutinous pout and she sighed. Except for her eyes, he looked *so* much like his father. "I'm not playing around, Sam. Grab your stuff or leave it here, but we're in the car in five minutes."

Stomping shoes and a slamming door calmed her a bit. He was mad, but he'd do it. Thank God. Her little boy still minded. Most of the time.

She turned toward the closet filled with boundless clothes, a plethora of shoes, and all the trappings she believed had made her life complete. She'd believed in Brad, her Prince Charming. She'd been wrong.

Jenna hitched the bag onto her shoulder and hurried down the stairs. She set the duffel by the door to the garage. She and Sam would start over. Everything would be fine. It had to be.

Her heart pounded and a niggling skittered up her spine. "Let's go, Sam," she called up to the second floor, trying to keep her voice steady. She could do this. A few more minutes and they would be free—then she'd have to figure out how to get out of this mess. But she would—for him.

He sulked down the stairs, his chin dropped, holding a baseball glove and ball in his hand.

Not subtle at all.

"Good choice," she said with a smile. At least she could speak the truth about one thing. Sam could play baseball anywhere. They would find a new life. Somewhere.

The sound of the automatic garage door opening slammed shut the hope. It couldn't be. He hadn't had time to get here from the airport. Unless he'd taken an earlier flight. Stupid, stupid.

"Sam."

His eyes widened. "What's wrong, Mommy?"

She grabbed his shoulders. "I don't have time to explain. Someone bad is breaking in the house. We've got to run. Don't make a sound."

She'd thought he would argue, but the panic in her voice must've gotten through to him. She'd scared him, but hell, she was terrified. If Brad found her, she was dead. Then what would happen to Sam?

She took one last glance toward the hallway leading to the garage. Her duffel sat there waiting. The money. Their future. But she couldn't risk going for it.

She clutched Sam's hand and ran to the back entrance.

"What about my ball and glove?"

"There's no time." She struggled with the doorknob. She sucked in a deep breath.

For Sam.

She opened the French doors leading into their large, elaborate backyard. She twisted the lock and closed the door behind them.

A waterfall trickled to the side, hiding any noise they made. Maybe...just maybe...she tugged Sam across the grass, behind a grove of trees, into what her son had termed "the jungle."

Thank God for the dense pines.

A door slammed open. "Jenna!" A voice bellowed from the back porch. "Get in this house. Now!"

Her entire body stilled, resisting the urge to follow his orders. She'd gotten into the habit of obeying to protect her son. No more. This wasn't how life should be.

"Daddy?" Her son peeked between the leaves.

Jenna tugged him back. Anxiety had darkened his expression.

She swallowed and knelt in front of Sam. "Listen to me, honey. I need you to help me. I'm afraid. Do you believe me?"

His gaze returned to where his father raged, kicking the patio furniture around, and nodded.

"For now, can you just trust me?"

Brad's fierce scowl didn't resemble the man who'd swept her off her feet. This man was definitely *not* Prince Charming. And he wasn't father of the year, either.

Her son stared at his father's expression. "Daddy can be mean sometimes."

She kissed his forehead as Brad peered through the darkness. With a violent curse he disappeared into the house.

She had to move. Now. He'd already seen the duffel by the door. He knew she was on the run. He would search everywhere and use his contacts at the bus station, the airport, the train station. Without the stash of money or clothes, she'd have to be even more creative than she'd imagined.

Laughter filtered from the party next door. Jenna rubbed her temple. No help there. She couldn't risk anyone knowing she was leaving. Brad could be very persuasive. She needed to disappear. Somewhere her husband would never guess.

She had no one to call. No real friends. She'd never been very social, and Brad had plucked her off the streets when she was so young. She was truly and utterly alone, except for her son.

A searchlight from the house behind theirs flickered on. Eight on the nose. Zach Montgomery's automated security lights were like clockwork.

The actor's house was empty. At least she could get out of sight for a few hours. Figure things out.

"We have to leave Daddy alone, don't we?" Sam said, his voice so sad her heart wept.

"For a little while. Let's go, baby."

She guided her son another twenty feet through the designed chaos of their landscaping to the back wall. It was high, but they could climb the tree and drop into Zach's backyard.

"Come on, buddy. Up and over," she whispered.

"How long is Daddy going to be mad?"

He scampered up the wall. She'd answer his questions later. She was just thankful he believed her for now. Because if Brad found them, she was dead, and her son would be raised by an assassin.

Chapter Two

THE GULFSTREAM'S ENGINES WERE TOO SILENT. IF ONLY THEY'D roar so Zach didn't have to listen. He'd never returned to the set. Theresa had ordered him to the airport, not even giving him time to pack.

He hunkered down in the private plane's butter-soft leather seat and glared at the communication screen in front of him. His entire body vibrated with fury. His knuckles had turned white. "Do you have any idea of the problems you've caused? How are you going to explain my disappearance to the movie's director?"

"I'm not," Theresa said. Even on the video call, he recognized the pained expression on her face—and the guilt.

Oh man. Zach tilted his head back and groaned. "*You* ordered me to take that gig. I told you I'm better off taking bit parts. This was an A-list movie, Theresa. You knew that. Going AWOL will tank what's left of my acting career. I may never get another part. You do realize that if I become too flaky an actor, there's no more cover, no more entry into sensitive countries? You lose me as an asset."

Like he cared about the acting. He *did* care if he had no more reason to go to Turkey or Iraq or Uzbekistan.

"We may have lost you anyway," she whispered, glancing around.

The crystal glass with two fingers of scotch stopped on the way to Zach's lips. "Whoa. Wait a minute. What the hell are you talking about?"

"A classified file about your last mission is missing. After the blown handoff, we're certain your identity's been compromised. So are the powers that be. It's not looking good for you to continue your double life, Zach."

He stilled in the seat and his gaze narrowed on the woman who'd been his handler for the last five years. This couldn't be happening. She'd taught him to kill, to lie, to cheat, to steal...all in the name of justice.

Funny thing was, he'd discovered he'd been born for deceit. And for this job.

Zach tossed the rest of his drink back and slammed the crystal glass on the elegant table in the middle of the cabin. "Find a way to get me back into the game, Theresa."

He kept the desperation rising within him out of his voice, but he needed the Company. She didn't know how much. The thought of losing the only value he had to offer—his entire body went cold. He hadn't felt such a chill since he'd held his dying father in his arms.

His talent agent had called the day after his father's funeral offering him a location shoot no one else wanted. In Iraq.

At that moment he'd known what he had to do. He might not ever earn his father's forgiveness, but Zach intended to keep his promise. Even if his father had called him a liar.

Zach had phoned his brother Seth. The rest had been easy. Seth's black ops contacts had put him in touch with the CIA. They'd been looking for someone who could get into Iraq and other sensitive countries without suspicion. Who better than a third-rate playboy and has-been actor who could be convincing in one role in public but become someone else in thirty minutes or less?

"Theresa, don't tell me you can't find a way. You can make anything happen." He prayed she couldn't see the panic that clawed up and down his insides.

She frowned, the line between her eyebrows deepening. "I'm working on it, but unless we determine who took the file…"

She couldn't stop the pitying look on her face.

"I'm toast." Zach could see his entire existence slipping past like the insubstantial cloud outside his window.

"Pretty much. Look, find a place to hide off radar. I'll be in touch. Just stay out of sight. If they know who you are and tell the wrong people…"

"I'm dead."

"Pretty much."

"Thanks for the positive energy, Theresa."

"Anytime, sugar."

She ended the video call, and Zach let out a slow sigh. He stared out the plane's window, fighting the suffocating wave of uncertainty—not the adrenaline-rushing good kind either. No, this was an oppressive, paralyzing emotion. The kind he'd avoided for five years.

He wouldn't go there. He glanced at his watch. They had to have crossed into California by now. To the false life he'd created with money he'd earned after *Dark Avenger* topped the box office. Had it really been a decade ago?

His house in La Jolla had cost millions. Theresa had found it for him, and he'd paid cash, wanting a place to call his own, needing a place to disappear away from the endless Hollywood parties and temptation. But the property taxes. How long could he keep up the façade before he'd have to crawl back to Denver and prove everyone right? That he was a screwup.

He shoved the possibility aside. No way would he face his family even more of a failure.

Most of the time Zach had no problem feeding the ne'er-do-well image. Then, once in a while, one of his brothers would call, worried about him. He'd laugh off their concern. When his mom called—that was another story. Anna Montgomery would shift between blunt Irish mom and softhearted worrier. At the end of every conversation, Zach's gut would twist with regret. He'd pushed his family away. And none of them had an inkling as to why—except Seth, who'd never give the truth away. Seth understood the risk. Not only to Zach, but his mom and brothers.

If he could find the leak, find the file, maybe, just maybe he could get back to the movie before his acting career was completely destroyed. Blame his absence on an accident—he had the scratches to prove it—or food poisoning, the flu, anything that sounded halfway reasonable. Rumors would fly over the Internet, but he'd maintain his access to Turkey.

He hated to admit it, but he needed Theresa and the Company to need him.

Zach couldn't give up the life. The only thing worth living for.

An unusual tingling fluttered through his hands. He squeezed the leather arms on the chair then straightened his fingers. Strange. What was going on? He stared at the nail beds. They were tinged with blue. The last time he'd seen that effect he'd climbed above fourteen thousand feet in the Kazakhstan mountains.

One look out the window showed the sun dropping low in the sky. The plane had turned south toward Montgomery Field. The name always made Zach chuckle. How apropos that the Company flew him into Montgomery Field. He'd always wondered if he had a long-lost relative with tons of money. Not hardly. Christmases had been chaotic enough with the Montgomery clan of eight. A bunch of cousins would have been plain irritating.

Odd how his mind had wandered to the past. He blinked his eyes and shifted his gaze to the Kevlar-lined cockpit door, barricaded shut. The gray steel grew fuzzy.

He inhaled. His head ached, he longed to close his eyes and sleep. Just sleep.

Oh, hell.

He had to…his mind wandered. Forcing himself to focus on his seatbelt, Zach struggled with the flap. After several tries he finally released the buckle. He shifted his weight to stand, but his legs shook beneath him. His head spun. He clutched the back of the chair, stumbling from one chair to the next down the wide aisle of the plane.

He recognized the oxygen deprivation symptoms from a training session in an F-16 for *Dark Avenger.* He glanced up to the ceiling. The masks should have come down.

One more step and he keeled over. Spots circled in front of his eyes. He tried to breathe but could feel his energy waning.

Think, Zach. Think.

Oxygen. Tanks. When the pilot had placed Zach's jacket in the coat compartment…

The pilot. Was he conscious? Zach didn't register any unusual downward trajectory of the plane, but he could barely focus. He needed air.

He dragged himself to the closet.

What was he trying to do?

He squinted at the metal latch holding the closet closed. Right. Something in there he needed. He propped himself up. Surely he could open it. He lifted his hand. His fingers were fuzzy. Thick and clumsy. He struggled, his breathing more and more shallow, like a steel band had tightened around his chest.

He needed to breathe.

Out of time.

The latch opened. With a final heave, he shoved aside the door. The momentum flung him to the floor. He turned on his back and stared at the ceiling. He blinked. He panted. His breathing slowed.

He didn't want it to end this way. He'd expected to die young. But not lying on the floor helpless.

He tried to take one last deep inhalation, but all he could manage was a pathetic wheeze. He turned his head and pawed at the strap from the green oxygen canister. He clawed it to him. The mask tumbled beside him.

He used all his energy to turn to his side. His stomach cramped. Sweat beaded on his forehead. He turned the knob of the canister. A hissing sound gave him hope. He slammed the mask on his face.

He breathed in, hard and deep. His hungry lungs gobbled the oxygen. For a few seconds he just lay there, his chest expanding and contracting. His mind cleared a bit.

Thank God.

That had been way too close.

He scanned the empty forty-foot-long cabin. There were only three of them on board. Zach and two pilots.

None of the oxygen masks had deployed.

That meant only one thing. Sabotage.

He had to get to the pilots. If they weren't already dead.

He adjusted the mask over his head and clasped the oxygen tank in front of him. He struggled to his knees and crawled a few paces. He braced himself and tried to rise. His legs folded under him. He fell to the ground. The oxygen tank tumbled toward the main cabin. He rolled over and reached for the canister.

The cockpit door clicked open behind him. Thank goodness. Someone was still alive. The pilots must have had time to don their oxygen masks.

Zach tried to turn over, but his body wouldn't move. Not yet. He tried to slow his breathing, let the oxygen do its work.

A pause. A deep voice mumbled. Zach strained to listen.

"Worked…Montgomery…dump…body…"

No way.

Zach stilled.

A setup. All along. His mind whirled. Only the Company knew he'd been taken out of the job.

His cover really *had* been compromised.

Footsteps headed toward him.

Zach tensed. He had to keep perfectly still. He sucked in more of the healing oxygen.

The man stopped. Every muscle in Zach's body contracted to the ready. He had to time it perfectly for his air-starved body to have a chance.

A foot nudged Zach's back. He let himself be shoved forward, further hiding the oxygen canister from the traitor's gaze. If the guy didn't notice the elastic holding the mask to Zach's face, he might…

A hand grasped Zach's shoulder.

Time was up.

Zach flipped over.

The pilot's eyes widened. Zach yanked off the man's oxygen gear, snapping the elastic. He stumbled away. Zach lunged toward him and grabbed his feet. The pilot pitched forward with a shout. Zach didn't let go.

He pinned the man's legs to the ground and pressed his forearm against the guy's throat. His lips started turning blue. "Who ordered my death?" Zach growled.

The pilot shook his head. "Just kill me."

"You die anyway if I don't let you put the mask on."

The man lay motionless. Zach didn't ease his grip. No one gave up that easily.

The pilot arched up, the sudden movement shifting Zach off the man's body. A knife slashed at Zach's oxygen tubing. He twisted out of the way, but the blade sliced through his shirt diagonally across his chest, drawing blood.

He hissed at the burning of the cut. He wasn't going down from this traitor's actions.

The pilot dove for the oxygen mask. "He's awake," he yelled. "Get out here or we're dead."

The captain scrambled from the cockpit, a mask on his face.

Zach backed up a step, eyeing both men. "We don't have to do this," he said, behind the thick plastic.

They didn't respond but stepped forward as one.

"Shouldn't someone be flying the plane?" Could the autopilot land the Gulfstream?

Zach shifted his weight, testing his strength and balance. He couldn't move with the bulky tank. He heaved in a last breath, dropped the oxygen, and threw the mask to the ground. He launched himself toward the men. He shoved his boot straight into the windpipe of the copilot. The man's head whipped back and he slumped to the ground, neck tilted to one side, eyes wide open.

Lungs burning, Zach whipped around to the captain. The man drew a gun. *Hell, no.* Zach recognized the resolve in the pilot's eyes, but saw no regret. No emotion. Zach was just a job.

So be it. Zach did jobs, too.

He shoved his shoulder at the guy's chest. They went flying. Zach landed on top of him, grabbed him in a chokehold, and stared into the captain's eyes.

Zach wanted to breathe. Strange how everything sort of faded to gray. Strange how this man wanted to kill him. Too bad they didn't have Irish whiskey on board. Zach had a fondness for a nip.

Wait a minute. He shook his head, trying to clear the odd thoughts. He had a mission. Stay alive. Out of time. He needed air.

Zach ripped off the captain's life-giving air and slammed it against his own face. He sucked several breaths then met the captain's gaze.

The man's eyes bugged. Zach didn't loosen his hold.

The weapon slipped from the man's fingers.

"Who gave the order?" Zach demanded.

The captain clutched at the mask, but didn't say a word.

The plane shifted underneath them.

"You'll die, too," the man gasped. "Unless you can fly this thing."

He sagged forward, his eyes closed. He'd passed out.

Zach took several deep breaths and raced to the cockpit. He scanned the panel. There it was. The outflow valve was open. Slowly, so he wouldn't blow out his eardrums, he restored cabin pressurization.

He took in several deep breaths to clear his head and strode back to the main cabin. The pilot stirred and moaned. Zach didn't waste any time. He wrapped the man's hands and feet with plastic tubing and shoved him into a seat, then secured the tubing to the chair. He'd interrogate the guy when they landed.

First things first. He had to find a way to survive landing a jet.

He circled his neck to ease the tension and walked to the cockpit, adjusted the pilot's seat for his six-foot-three-inch frame, and tucked on the headset. He'd been flying since the age of sixteen. His dad's doing, though he'd probably regretted the gift. Zach had gotten a taste for excitement. Skiing, skydiving, mountain climbing...and risk taking. The kind that seduced you to Hollywood's so-called glamorous life and lured you into being a spy.

He'd never flown anything quite this big, though.

He glanced at the sophisticated screens and panels. Like something out of *Star Trek*. A hell of a lot more involved than the small Cessna he'd learned on or the Huey he'd flown in his last movie. Methodically he scanned the dials. Altimeter, heading. And yes... autopilot. On.

Thank goodness.

A crackling sounded in his ear. "Camelot three-two-nine. Fifth time I tried to call you. Respond or an F-16 will be escorting you in and you won't like the reception," an irritated voice snapped.

OK. Clearly someone had noticed the pilotless plane. Los Angeles Center sounded pissed.

Zach took a deep breath. "This is Camelot three-two-nine. Go ahead." At least he hoped he was Camelot three-two-nine.

"Camelot three-two-nine, Los Angeles Center. Did you enjoy your nap?"

Yeah, the controller was in a mood. Zach glanced at the altimeter. Thirty-nine thousand feet. And he was only ninety miles out of La Jolla. Shit. This was going to be a wild ride.

"Descend immediately, maintain flight level two-four-zero," the controller ordered.

Straightening his shoulders, Zach focused on the videogame-like screen. He knew what he *should* do. He *should* have someone talk him through the landing. Except he couldn't reveal his identity or the true situation. He had a dead body on board. The airport would pull out all the emergency vehicles. It would be a circus.

And if word got out he was alive…the fewer people who knew he was still breathing the better. No. He had to make this work. He'd flown planes before. Like riding a bike.

"Los Angeles Center, this is Camelot three-two-nine. Request lower altitude."

"Descend to twenty-four-thousand feet. What, were you joining the mile-high club?"

Yeah, funny guy. The controller barked out instructions. Zach set the altimeter and heading, then sifted through the captain's flight bag and found the aircraft operations manual. "At least I have step-by-step instructions," Zach muttered.

His head ached at the number of pages. He didn't have much time. He skimmed the section on normal operations. Like this was normal. Reading the manual the first time twenty minutes from landing made even the adrenaline junkie in him sweat.

"Camelot three-two-nine, descend to twelve thousand feet, turn left, heading three-two-zero," the voice sounded through his ear.

Zach entered the change in direction and let the autopilot do its thing. He had about fifteen minutes to figure out how to land the plane.

He'd flipped through the section for the fifth time when his earpiece crackled.

He tossed the manual into the copilot's seat and waited for the handoff to another controller.

"Camelot three-two-nine, Los Angeles Center. Contact SoCal approach on frequency one-two-four point three five."

Zach confirmed, and on the new controller's instruction, he descended to three thousand feet.

He scanned the horizon for the private airport. Just where it was supposed to be. He narrowed his focus, shoving aside any uncertainty. He wouldn't let them kill him. Not like this. "This is Camelot three-two-nine. Airport nine o'clock. Ten miles."

"Camelot three-two-nine, clear for the visual approach twenty-eight right. Contact Montgomery tower one-one-nine point two."

After he was cleared to land, Zach pulled the throttle to reduce air speed and extended the flaps. He lowered the gear handle and aligned the plane with the runaway. Steady. Not too slow.

His memory trailed back to the first time he'd flown. The first time he'd landed with Ace by his side. His dad's buddy had been a military pilot. He'd flown scads of Libya missions back in the day. Knew his stuff.

Zach could almost hear the guy's final advice in his mind. *You're a natural. If you doubt, trust your gut, kid. It'll never fail you. Don't think. Do.*

Trust his gut.

Zach eased the yoke back to stop the descent.

Don't think. Do.

The runway loomed closer and closer.

The ground rose to meet him.

Zach held his breath.

The gear hit hard.

His body jerked. He clutched the wheel. The plane bounced, pulling to the right. Zach gripped the yoke tighter and added a bit of power. Finally, the Gulfstream slowed and settled on the tarmac.

Zach's head fell back against the seat.

His heart restarted.

A good landing is one you walk away from. Ace's voice filtered through his mind.

"Amen."

With a long, slow sigh, Zach steered toward an out-of-sight hangar. His hands and legs shook with each move of the pedals and tiller. Adrenaline. He used to love the feeling.

Not quite so much these days.

He shut off the engines, set the parking brake, and threw down the headset. Now for a little talk with the captain before anyone realized that the plane that just landed ended up in the wrong hangar.

He shoved aside the sliding door separating the cockpit from the cabin and stared at the man tied up in the seat.

Make that two dead bodies.

Something white foamed from the captain's mouth. In his hand he held a small syringe. Zach strode to the body, sank down, and studied the captain, his face screwed in agony. Who had so much power the guy would kill himself in such a horrible way?

Clearly, the same someone who wanted Zach dead.

He checked the identities of the pilots, storing them in his memory, then rifled through the electronic equipment and clothes in his duffel. He shoved it aside. Nope. He'd leave everything here. He needed to disappear. And he needed information.

He emptied his wallet of cash, then scanned his passport and driver's license looking for anything unusual, even a microdot that could track him. Nothing.

He stuffed them in his pocket. "Welcome home, Zach."

Perched in the tree at the back of her large yard, Jenna peered at the embedded glass protruding from the top of the cinder block wall. Zach Montgomery didn't want visitors, that was for sure. She eased her jacket off and swung it over. She pressed her hand down, testing the cushion. Enough to protect Sam. She shifted her weight and surveyed the actor's yard. The automatic strobe lights illuminated the huge swimming pool holding center stage. A quick scan revealed a hot tub, tennis court, half a basketball court. All a playground for an overgrown boy.

Not different from most of the actors in this neighborhood. Their big breaks usually came with big purchases. Cars, boats, houses.

A lot of them lost everything soon enough.

She'd thought she'd been so lucky, falling for a man with money who had a *normal*, but very well-paying job.

She couldn't have been more wrong.

Sam tried to wriggle away.

"Don't move, honey."

"I don't like it up here," he said with a frown.

"You see that swimming pool? The Dark Avenger swims in that pool."

Sam's eyes grew wide and his mouth opened in awe. "The *real* Dark Avenger?"

"The one and the same."

Sam had happened upon the B-movie about six months ago and had become obsessed with the superhero.

Jenna hadn't known having a neighbor who was famous might come in so handy. Even though Zach Montgomery hadn't hit it big recently, he still worked in the movie biz and was gone for months at a time.

At a cocktail party just last week, a neighbor told her that Zach had been seen in the tabloids with his newest young starlet, all comfy-cozy on location in Turkey.

Sam leaned forward. "Is the Dark Avenger home? Can we meet him?"

"I think that's a great idea." Guilt flashed through her at the false enthusiasm, but Sam just gave her a big grin.

"He likes kids," Sam said, his voice certain.

She chucked his chin. "And he'd love you."

Sam smiled and Jenna studied the ground below her. Fifteen feet. They could do this. She held out her hands to Sam.

"Hold on to me. I'm going to lower you down."

He bit his lip. "OK, Mommy."

That look was so trusting, so believing. How long would it last when he realized they weren't coming back?

Another roaring yell pounded over the huge wall.

Sam stared at the lights streaming toward them from their house, his eyes growing wide. "Daddy sounds really mad. He needs a time-out."

A permanent time-out. She couldn't go back. Not now. Not ever. She hugged him close. "I know, baby. Let's find the Dark Avenger."

She took a deep breath and lowered Sam as far as she could down the wall. The drop looked way too far.

A strobe light swept toward them.

"OK, Junior Avenger," she said, desperately trying to keep her voice calm despite the panic prodding her, causing her heart to gallop. "We're escaping the jungle. Can you jump down?"

He gave her that rolling eyes look—the one he used when fear took a backseat to common sense.

"It's easy, Mommy. Watch."

His hands slipped from hers. Suddenly, he landed on the ground and stared up at her. "You can do it, Mommy. Don't be afraid."

His small face gazed up at her. If her boy could do it...she took in a deep breath. She shifted her leg over the side. Her foot slipped and glass gouged into her calf. She hissed in a breath to keep from crying out. What was a little cut compared to Brad's reaction if he caught them? She eased her legs over the wall and hung there, fingers gripping the edge. With a small prayer, she clutched her jacket and dropped next to Sam. She fought to smile. "Nothing to it."

Sam crouched by her leg. "You're bleeding."

She looked at the deep, bleeding scrapes. A line of blood sprinkled to the grass. "It's just a few scratches. I bet the Dark Avenger has a first aid kit."

Taking Sam's hand, Jenna led him to the back door. She peered inside. A blinking light flashed on a security panel. She rested her head against the door. It looked like the same brand as hers. Brad had picked it out. State-of-the-art. Without the code, she couldn't chance breaking in.

She bit her lip and studied the backyard. A pool house stood vacant. "Come on, Junior Avenger."

"Where is he?" Sam asked.

"He's not home right now. Come help Mommy take care of her leg."

Sam nodded and followed her to the small building. Once inside, Jenna released the blinds to enclose the pool house's interior then turned to the refrigerator. Darkness made it difficult to see, but she couldn't risk turning on the lights. She opened the door. Alongside the expected beer was a large array of water bottles, juice boxes, and applesauce cups. Not exactly what she'd expected.

But at least the light from the refrigerator gave her just enough to see.

She grabbed two juice boxes, left the refrigerator door open to illuminate the room, then sat on one of the lounge chairs. Grabbing a fluffy white towel and bottled water, she dabbed at the scrape. She hissed at the tender skin. Red blotted the towel, but the bleeding soon stopped. Antibiotic ointment would have been nice. Maybe...

Jenna rose and searched through the cabinets. She found some snacks and protein bars that might come in handy. She snagged a few, then in the last cabinet she hit the lottery. A small first aid kit.

She pulled out the spray disinfectant, gave her leg a few squirts, and closed her eyes against the burning.

Sam's lip trembled. "I don't like that stuff. It stings."

"Yeah, but sometimes we—"

"—gotta do things we don't wanna," Sam parroted. "Like picking up toys."

She pulled him into her arms. The strobe lights from their backyard had gone out. The light of the refrigerator bathed the pool room in a dim glow.

Even though Brad was only yards away, for the first time in the months since she'd called the FBI Jenna's heart didn't race in unending panic.

She toyed with Sam's locks. She'd make certain he grew up without fear. She wanted him to be secure like she'd been, before her dad died. Before she'd been forced to fend for herself. She had to find a way.

"Tell me a story, Mommy," he whispered. "You haven't told me a story in a loooong time."

"What about last night, Sam?"

"That was forever ago. Tell me about the Dark Avenger again."

She listened. The sound of summer crickets circled the pool house. No threats floated in from her backyard. She settled Sam against her, wrapping him close. She kissed his hair. "Once upon a time—"

A bright light exploded in Zach Montgomery's backyard.

Jenna gripped Sam tight. *Oh God.* Had her husband found them?

Chapter Three

THE AFGHANI WIND HOWLED IN WARNING THROUGH THE HID-
den pass. Sweat beaded on Farzam's upper lip as his captor removed the blindfold. The jagged rocks surrounding him
loomed upward, and the scraggly junipers growing out of the
stony landscape reached out as if to yank him from rounding the
next bend in the barely visible path.

He wished he could run, but he had no choice.

His gun-wielding escort shoved Farzam forward. He stumbled and hit his knees. Stones sharpened with eons of desert
wind dug into his skin. He winced but didn't cry out. A show of
weakness meant death. Of this he had no doubt.

He could feel eyes watching him from the crevices to either
side. His loose-fitting pants hid his shaking legs, and he stood,
forcing himself not to cower.

For his family.

The guards had broken into the hovel he now called home
and dragged him from his bed. Many never came home after
disappearing in such a manner. His beloved sister Setara, along
with her husband and their two daughters, had vanished in a
similar fashion four months ago.

Farzam swallowed down the bile rising in his throat. If he
didn't return, would his in-laws take his family in, or would his

own dishonor infect what little remained of his life? Farzam's only hope was that his wife and son hadn't been taken, too. Maybe he had a chance to survive.

The guard pushed him through a chasm. Farzam slipped on the crumbling rock and rounded a large outcropping. He sucked in a breath at the sight before him. A narrow crevice opened into a gap housing several traditional buildings formed from mud, some embedded into the edge of the mountain.

His escort nodded to the armed guards standing at the narrow entrance. Farzam swallowed and stepped past them. Would he leave here alive?

He paused in front of the largest building's open doorway. A man stood before him, his bearing haughty in a way inappropriate for his traditional attire. The guard clasping Farzam's arm bowed his head and forced Farzam to follow suit.

"I am Khalid."

Farzam swallowed deeply. He recognized the name of the vicious tribal leader.

Khalid smiled. "I see you have heard of me."

Farzam nodded.

"You are brother by marriage to Pendar, the traitor?" Khalid asked.

Farzam's entire body sagged. They knew of him. They probably knew he and his brother-in-law had been educated together as well. He was dead.

"Respond," Khalid ordered.

Nothing could be done but acknowledge the truth. Farzam nodded again.

"Come. You shall witness the punishment."

Farzam's throat tightened, his mouth and lips dry, but he couldn't hide the relief that blew through him like a hot desert wind. A witness existed to report events. If he was only an observer, maybe he would find his way home to his family. Maybe Setara and her daughters would leave with him.

Khalid led them through an open doorway.

Farzam gasped. His sister stood, head bowed, hair uncovered, against a rock face littered with bullet holes. A firing squad faced her.

Beside her, a man so beaten he was unrecognizable struggled to rise.

The man raised his chin, his expression defeated, sorrowful, dead. "Farzam," he choked. "Forgive me, brother."

The slurred words carved at Farzam like a pulwar, the traditional sword of his people. Pendar was barely alive. Then Setara turned her face.

He bit back a shocked cry. Her cheek had been sliced open from her eye to the corner of her mouth. Dirt caked the wound. Bruises mottled her jaw. Her chadri had been sliced, leaving the skin of her arms and even her torso exposed. She wrapped her arms around her body and averted her gaze.

Farzam's hands tightened into fists. He wanted to rush to her, but he couldn't move; his feet stayed still, as if cemented with clay. He said nothing. Shame burned through him with the sting of a viper's venom.

"For treason against the tribe, for consorting with the enemy, the United States, we condemn Pendar Durrani to death. His wife, Setara, for conspiracy."

"No, please! I beg of you," Pendar pleaded with a weak croak. "Let my wife and daughters go."

Khalid's gaze narrowed. He looked with deliberation at Farzam and cocked a brow.

Farzam couldn't speak. Where were his nieces? His tongue wouldn't move. His throat closed off.

"So be it." The man nodded at the firing squad.

Bullets sprayed his beloved sister's body, tearing her flesh. She fell to the ground.

Pendar cried out, his anguish echoing through the camp.

"Fire," Khalid said, with no emotion, no caring in his voice.

Bullets pelted Pendar until he went silent, though his eyes continued to stare blankly at Farzam, even after his body lay limply on top of his wife.

Farzam said nothing.

Two squeals of horror from behind him penetrated his skull with the force of the bullets that had just murdered his family.

"Mother! Father!"

Farzam whirled around. His nieces' eyes were wide with horror. Failure sliced at his soul, shredding the last of his dignity. He had failed them. He had failed his sister. He had failed his family.

"Take them away."

Farzam could feel his mouth opening and closing, but nothing escaped. Even now.

Khalid stared down his nose at Farzam. "You wish to speak?" he said, his voice quiet.

Farzam shook his head in shame.

"I thought not."

"May I bury them?" Farzam whispered.

"They deserve no honor. They will become a reminder." Khalid stared down Farzam. "You worked with your brother. You studied in the United Kingdom. You share his views?"

Farzam swallowed. "No, sir."

"Very well."

"His daughters?" Farzam asked.

"You care for Pendar's children?"

"It is my duty." Farzam refused to let him see how much he cared.

"It is their duty to serve. If they do well, perhaps they will be returned. Perhaps not."

Khalid waved his hand, walked back into the building, and closed the door. Two guards pulled Setara's screaming daughters into what looked like a men's barracks.

They would be unable to wed after being held here. Of this, Farzam had no doubt.

His eyes burned as he stared at his sister's torn and shredded body. She had been so smart, so beautiful. His father and mother had dressed her as a boy so she could attend school. Her education had been her downfall.

He let his gaze fall to his brother-in-law. The fool. The idealist. He had believed the CIA goon who had convinced him they would be safe, that Pendar and his family would be welcomed in the United States. Zane Morgan had caused this calamity.

He had brought dishonor and tragedy on their entire family.

Farzam would never be welcomed back at the university as a professor. His entire life had been ruined already. Once Pendar's fate was learned, any hope of salvaging the life he had lived was gone. Khalid would see to that. His influence went well beyond the borders of the tribal lands.

The guard shoved him toward the exit. He was leaving this place. He had half expected to be taken before the firing squad as well.

He was alive.

The guard blindfolded him and led him back through the pass, through twists and turns, thoroughly confusing Farzam. Finally, the guard removed the covering over Farzam's eyes.

"You can walk from here."

"Water?" he asked softly.

Surreptitiously, the guard glanced from side to side. He shoved a small bottle at Farzam. "Make it last. It will be dusk soon. I wouldn't be on the road after dark."

Farzam started toward Kabul. Step by step he left the bodies of his family and the ruined lives of his nieces farther behind him.

Zane Morgan owed their family. He would pay.

An eye for an eye.

On his honor, Farzam would make the American suffer and die as Pendar and his sister had.

There would be no reprieve. Except in death.

———————

Zach scanned the street, searching for anything out of place before stepping out of the taxi in front of his La Jolla mansion's privacy gate. Behind the tall iron entrance lay the refuge Theresa had discovered for him six months ago. The ocean breezes swept across his face, the bite of sea air and salt nipping the tip of his tongue. Good to be home and not at the wrong end of an Uzi... or a knife...or suffocating.

He hadn't almost-been-killed this many times in one day since the *Dark Avenger* movie—if his luck held.

Which was why he couldn't stay. He had to outfit his truck and get to his Colorado safe house before anyone found him.

With a twist, he slipped a few bills from his wallet to pay the cab driver. The movement tugged at the cut across Zach's chest. A drip trickled down his skin. *Great.* He'd reopened the wound. He needed a few butterfly bandages before making the trip.

The taxi revved and pulled away.

He dug his keys out of his pocket then scanned the front of his home, checking for signs of any intruders. The vehicle gate was closed. He eased closer. The infrared sensor positioned at the entrance didn't indicate any tampering. Zach checked the settings. A bit of movement, but the gate hadn't been opened from the inside or outside since he'd left months ago. Wind, a dog, a cult fan trying to get in perhaps.

He reset the sensor and pushed through the small, hidden door at the side of the driveway. Once at the front door, with practiced fingers, he ran the tips around the doorjamb and perused the sensors hidden in the hedges on either side of the threshold.

No sign of intruders.

So far so good.

He pushed inside the house and closed the door behind him. A loud beep sounded from the security system. Zach hit the code and scanned the log. No one had tripped the system.

Safe, for the moment.

Zach kneaded the muscles at the back of his neck in an attempt to stave off the building headache. First things first. He crossed the tile and headed straight for the bar. He placed his 1911 on the marble, pulled a longneck bottle out of the small refrigerator, and slammed a swallow of cold brew down his throat. With a flop he landed in a large leather chair and rubbed at the stubble on his chin.

Maybe he'd let it grow out. Fewer people would recognize him that way.

Another swig and he sighed. A beard wouldn't stop his enemies. He couldn't stay here. Too many people knew about the address. Hell, he was on the B-movie-star tour of fame.

He tapped the half-empty bottle and hit the remote for the large-screen television. A scan of the national and local news revealed nothing about the abandoned airplane or two dead bodies at Montgomery Field. No locking down of the San Diego airport. No security concerns.

Someone had to have found the plane by now, which meant Theresa had done a thorough cleanup job. Now he had to do his part.

Thank God for his backup plan. Under an assumed name, he'd purchased a small piece of property hidden on the western edge of the Holy Cross Wilderness in the Colorado mountains. Just in case.

He'd always hoped he'd never need it unless he retired there.

Zach placed the bottle on the coffee table and stood. He stretched his back and made his way to the rear door. Could he afford the time for a soak in the hot tub to ease the aftereffects of oxygen deprivation?

With a flip of the floor and ceiling dead bolts, he unlocked the glass door. He slid it open. The strobe light flooded the pool and hot tub with light. Quickly, Zach shut it off. He didn't need to advertise his presence.

He looked longingly at the water. One switch and he'd be in heaven. He tugged at his shirt and stepped into the backyard.

A loud buzzer sounded from the security panel.

Zach tensed. The front gate. He could ignore the summons. He filtered through the possibilities. He needed to know how close his enemies were—whoever they were. And truthfully, anyone really wanting to kill him wouldn't announce their presence, they'd simply attack.

He reentered the house, crossed to the security panel, and glanced at the screen on the wall. A lone man stood at the gate, peering inside.

Zach pressed the button. "Yes?"

"This is your neighbor, Brad Walters. I need help. My wife and son are missing."

Zach stilled. He recognized the name. He'd requested a scan of his neighbors when he'd first moved in. Nothing out of the ordinary had appeared on the initial report. Damn it. He'd hoped to come and go completely stealth, but he couldn't turn the guy down. His family was missing. Zach pressed the code. The gate swung open. "Come in. The gate will close behind you."

The man hesitated, then walked in. Alone. After he passed through, Zach entered the code to lock the gate.

He set the bottle on the bar, stuffed his 1911 in the back waistband of his jeans, and strode to the front door.

He peered through the peephole. The grainy view from his surveillance camera hadn't lied. A nondescript man stood outside. Someone who would fade into the background. Not a typical look for this neighborhood with most faces either perfect from birth or sculpted to look that way.

The guy could be anyone...including the man sent to kill him. Zach would know the truth before Walters left. Poised for an attack, Zach eased open the front door, his hand gripped on the weapon.

"Thank you for answering," the man rushed, rubbing his hands over his face. "Our backyards connect."

He was nervous. Really nervous. And relieved.

Or a really great actor.

Zach studied his so-called neighbor. Zach rarely socialized. A few parties to keep up the appearance of his actor identity, and not much else. The guy really was forgettable until you looked at his suit. The cut reeked of money. It would have to, living in this neighborhood.

But there was more than worry in the guy's eyes. Intelligence, awareness, and something a bit cold. Before Zach could even process the dichotomy, Brad flashed up a picture of a woman and child.

Zach's heart tripped like a faulty detonator. The woman's dark hair was pulled back into a chignon, elegant and just asking to be mussed. Her emerald eyes peered out from the photo, a smile teasing their depths. She looked happy. Achingly beautiful and happy.

A hint of mischief bubbled from the expression on the boy at her side. He looked to be a bit older than Zach's precocious niece, Joy. Maybe four or five.

The man's expression narrowed. "You know them."

Zach examined the photo again. He couldn't help it. He didn't want to look away. "Your wife looks familiar, but I don't believe we've met."

"But you *have* seen her. Today? When?"

Something wasn't right here. A flash of caution ignited in Zach's gut. First off, he didn't like the coincidence. A neighbor showing up right after he arrived home. Second, he didn't like the slight hitch of the man's jacket on the right side.

A holstered gun could do that.

If nothing else, Zach trusted his instincts. They'd kept him alive for the last five years. The one time he ignored them…well he'd have to find another way to get Pendar and his family to safety. If they were still alive.

For now, he wanted Brad Walters away from his house.

Zach cleared his throat. "I just returned from a trip. I haven't seen anyone today except the cabby."

Brad's eyes flashed from worry to irritation. "We live behind your house. Do you mind if I check your backyard?"

The request tightened the knots already tensing Zach's shoulders. With a quick shift of his body to keep Brad at a disadvantage, Zach tilted his head, analyzing his neighbor's expression closely. "You think your wife and son climbed into my yard? It's a fifteen-foot wall embedded with glass at the top. It keeps the paparazzi out."

Brad looked away. When he turned back and met Zach's gaze, the irritation had vanished, his eyes now dark with concern.

Yeah...an actor. This guy was playing a part. The question was why.

He shuffled. "My wife is a bit...high-strung. She had a rough childhood. I don't want my son hurt."

In short, my wife is crazy and has taken my son. The woman in the photo didn't look insane, but then again, Zach had seen some expert actresses over the years, and not all in the movie industry.

Something didn't quite jibe with this guy, but Zach couldn't come up with any factual reason to refuse a look in the backyard. To complicate matters, if the guy was telling the truth, Zach didn't need the cops at his door questioning him. He *had* to stay off the radar.

Weighing the alternatives, Zach tightened his grip on his 1911 and moved aside. "Of course." He led Brad through the house, studying his every move. One misplaced step and the guy would be on the floor with a .45 caliber at his head, except he didn't make one false move...which in itself increased Zach's suspicions. Brad was sure-footed, confident. He scanned the layout of the house but didn't attempt to touch anything.

He didn't plant bugs, or listening devices, or explosives. Could the guy just be worried about this wife?

Either way, Zach wanted him out. Fast.

His entire body at the ready, he cursed the situation. If he hadn't been forced to come back for the truck, he'd never have returned home, never would have had to deal with anyone.

He opened the sliding glass door, escorted Brad into the yard, and flipped on the light.

"I saw it come on earlier," Brad commented. "Maybe—"

"I was having a beer after a long trip and contemplating the hot tub," Zach countered just as he caught a flash of movement out of the corner of his eye. He shifted and drew Brad's attention.

His neighbor sighed in frustration. "Jenna and I had a misunderstanding. I don't want her to do anything rash. You have kids?"

"No. Too busy traveling," Zach muttered, aching to get rid of the nosy guy. "I wish I could help, but I'm off again tonight. I won't be back for a while." He wanted anyone who asked to get the word he was gone. He didn't need more unexpected visitors.

For the next few minutes Brad searched every inch of the backyard. Finally, he strode to the pool house and tugged at the door. To Zach's surprise it didn't open, and the blinds had been closed. Interesting.

Zach never locked it.

Brad's jaw tightened and he extended a stiff hand. "Thanks for the help."

Reluctantly Zach shook it, still not certain of the man's motives. He trusted his gut, and instinct said Brad Walters had something to hide. "I hope your wife and son are safe."

"Me too," Brad commented. "Can't be too careful. So many crazies out there these days."

Still on guard, Zach escorted his neighbor out and through the front gate. He reengaged the locks and strode back to the bar. He snagged his beer, took a long, last swallow, and grabbed a prepaid cell phone out of the bottom drawer. Four other phones lay scattered there. He pocketed another. He couldn't be too careful.

Zach headed to the pool house, where he'd seen the flash of movement. Anyone climbing over that wall had to be extremely determined. He tested the door. Unlocked now. A bottle of water lay on its side and a towel was crumpled in the corner. He raised the terry cloth. Droplets of red. The glass had done its job.

A five-year-old alone hadn't been this quiet.

"I hope you're OK, lady," Zach muttered. "And not crazy."

He tapped on his phone to access the Internet. Soon he had confirmation. Brad and Jenna Walters lived behind him. They had a five-year-old son. Brad worked for a computer corporation as a salesman and troubleshooter.

He traveled a lot. Sometimes to sensitive countries. Strange, that hadn't shown up in the preliminary investigation. Zach didn't like the gaps in the Company report.

The entire visit could have been a surveillance activity.

Except anyone in the business would be too smart to bring their work this close to home. Unless the money was that good.

Zach tapped a few more buttons.

Still nothing unusual being reported out of Montgomery Field. Theresa would have planted a Zach Montgomery story if he'd been safe, which meant he had a target on his back.

It made getting out of La Jolla and to the cabin more imperative than ever.

He didn't know if Brad was a player. For all Zach knew, Walters's gorgeous wife was helping him. This entire situation could be an elaborate setup.

If it wasn't...Zach unfolded a thousand dollars out of his wallet and placed it in the pool room. He didn't like Brad, had a bad feeling about him. If Jenna Walters wasn't involved, and she came back, the money would give her a choice.

Knowing he'd done all he could to help—if the woman was innocent—Zach locked down the backyard.

He had one chance to survive. Get to Colorado. Find the traitor, and pray to God he could save his life without anyone else sacrificing theirs.

Jenna mentally thanked Brad for distracting her neighbor.

One thing in the last eighteen months she could thank him for.

She held on to Sam as she pulled him into a pantry off Zach Montgomery's kitchen. The place was spotless. All canned items aligned. In alphabetic order for goodness' sake. Dry items together. Everything in perfect order. Did he even live here? Ever?

She'd heard the actor say he planned to leave town for a while. Maybe they could stay here now that they were inside. Once Brad left she could sneak back into their house and grab their money and clothes.

Except for the security system...how could she get around that? She rubbed her temple, fighting off the dejection. There had to be a way.

Sam tugged on her lightweight sweater. "Can we say hi to the Dark Avenger? He looks nice."

"Looks can be deceiving," she said softly.

"What's 'd'ceeving'?"

What your father turned out to be. The perfect gentleman. A man who would love her forever.

A killer.

She shivered slightly.

"A liar."

Sam stuck out his lower lip. "The Dark Avenger *never* lies!"

"Shhh," she said, kneeling down. "I'm sure you're right, Junior Avenger. Just like you never lie, right? Say...when I ask you to clean your room?"

Sam scuffed the toe of his tennis shoe against the floor. "But I'm not the Dark Avenger yet. I'm just a little boy."

He refused to meet her gaze. Jenna ruffled his hair, then put her finger against her lips. "Stay here, Junior Avenger. Don't move. I'll be right back. Promise you'll be very quiet? Truth?"

He nodded and sat in the corner, arms wrapped around his legs, and placed his small finger against his lips.

Her heart swelled with love for him. She prayed she could protect him. "Good boy."

Shoving down the tension pulsing through every muscle in her body, Jenna cracked open the door and peered into the darkened kitchen. A slice of light cut across the floor.

A door slammed, followed by a muttered curse.

Zach Montgomery wasn't happy about something.

Footsteps came her way. She ducked behind the island in the center of the large room and held her breath. A loud thud sounded in the hallway. The steps came closer and closer. He headed toward the closet where her son hid. Fool. Why had she left Sam alone?

Please don't come out, Sam. Please.

Her son wanted *so* much to meet the Dark Avenger, and she didn't want to ruin his childhood fantasy. Too much of his innocence would be stolen over the next few weeks.

Zach veered right and headed through another door. She caught sight of a truck's hood as the door closed behind him. The garage.

Was he leaving?

She held her breath, then crawled from behind the corner of the island.

The door squeaked open.

She dove back behind the butcher block.

Zach muttered to himself and raced up the stairs, two at a time.

She had no time left. As soon as he disappeared off the landing, she ducked into the pantry, a desperate plan formulating in her mind. They had to find a way to get out of the state unnoticed. She couldn't walk away from the chance.

Sam sat there, still as can be. "I was quiet, Mommy. Can we meet the Dark Avenger, now?" he begged. "Please."

This time, she took stock of the shelves more carefully. Canned Vienna sausages, juice boxes. A kid's dream. Odd. She filled a grocery sack with some of Sam's favorites and set them beside him.

"Wait here."

She didn't have much time. Zach could come down the stairs any minute. She darted into the living room and snagged an afghan and pillow off the sofa, then headed back to her son.

"What are you doing, Mommy?"

"We're taking a little trip, Sam."

She grabbed the supplies and blanket and opened the door to the garage. The room was huge. Her stomach dropped. Four vehicles. A Range Rover, a Corvette, a small Jeep and a pickup.

A quick scan of the cars revealed a layer of dust on all of them. Then she noticed the swipe near the truck's door handle.

An itch to reach under the steering wheel, tug a few wires, hotwire the car, and make a run for it tingled in her palms. It would be too easy. Those years of hell after her father had died might actually be worth something now, except she couldn't risk it. Not with Sam by her side. Her chances of getting through Zach's security system, off the property, and out of the city before the cops tracked the stolen car were slim. Especially with GPS. Zach's car would have been outfitted with all the bells and whistles. He didn't skimp on the luxuries—that was for sure.

She couldn't go back. She'd burned her last bridge with Brad. She had to be smart. Get as far away from her husband as possible. Then she'd figure out what to do next.

The vehicle had a black cover over the bed. She wrestled with the latch and peered inside. A toolbox, a tarp, and not much else.

No time to debate. She had to take a chance. Pray Zach didn't look in the back before he left. Pray he'd leave California far behind and she could sneak out before he ever knew they were there.

Jenna grabbed Sam's hand and helped him into the truck. She tucked the blanket around her son then climbed in after him. She poked a straw into a juice box, handed it to him, and slid the cover back into place before throwing the tarp over them both.

The world went dark.

"Mommy. I don't like this game." Sam squirmed against her.

She settled him in the crook of her arm. He snuggled in. "I know, honey. But we're going to be fine."

"Hasn't Daddy been in time-out long enough? I wanna go home. I want my house, and my baseball mitt and my Dark Avenger movie."

The door to the garage slammed open. The truck shifted under Zach's weight as he got in.

She'd guessed right.

And he hadn't looked in the back. Was her luck finally holding?

"Shhh," she said, kissing Sam's cheek. "See how quiet you can be, Junior Avenger."

She couldn't make out his expression, but her son sighed and cuddled against her. The fear around her heart didn't ease. Her heartbeat raced as she focused on the sounds around them. Relieved Sam couldn't see the apprehension on her face, she held him tight.

The garage door opened. The truck roared to life and started forward.

Almost there. Almost on the road.

The truck drove down the driveway and paused. They must have reached the gate.

She held her breath.

The purr of the engine accelerated, then stopped.

"Wait!"

The shout punched Jenna in the belly. Her stomach roiled.

"Daddy?" Sam whispered.

Chapter Four

ZACH'S HEADLIGHTS SLICED ACROSS THE SHOUTING FIGURE. He slammed on his brakes and curled his finger around the trigger of the 1911 before pressing the window control.

The smell of burned rubber filtered over the glass. The gate behind him whirred closed, clicked, and locked into place.

The streetlight illuminated Brad Walters. He crossed his arms, his intense gaze sweeping the interior of Zach's truck.

"Are you crazy? What do you think you're doing?" Zach snapped.

"Someone climbed over our fence into your yard. I saw blood."

Zach schooled his features into a skeptical expression that was a lie, of course. He didn't have much doubt Jenna Walters had sneaked into his house. A pillow and afghan had vanished from the sofa. Some canned goods were missing from the pantry. His jaw tightened in irritation. Brad Walters and his missing wife were a distraction he couldn't afford.

He gunned the gas on the truck.

"Look, I'm sorry about your wife and son, but I can't help. You looked yourself. As to the blood, it happens. Paparazzi, fans seem to think they have the right to snoop. File a missing persons report."

Mostly truth. Jenna Walters was probably long gone, along with the guy's son. Zach's final scan of the security system hadn't detected any heat signatures inside the place.

"You know something. I feel it," Brad snarled. He slammed his fist against Zach's window. "I want to look again."

He didn't need this. "Then climb over the backyard and knock yourself out. But I have somewhere to be."

He shoved the truck into gear and swerved onto the street. He wasn't staying in the open for a second longer.

A quick glance in the rearview mirror solidified his decision. Brad's face had turned red under the streetlamp. The guy needed an anger management class. Any guilt about not revealing that Jenna had probably been in his backyard and even inside his home washed away like the golden sands of the nearby beaches.

So much for a completely covert escape. Brad Walters was an irritant, though, and Zach had more dangerous predators after him. He still wasn't sure he could reach his safe house in Colorado in one piece.

On high alert, he gripped the steering wheel. He checked his mirrors over and over, watching for signs of anyone tailing him as he headed south on La Jolla Shores Drive.

When he was certain no one followed, he took a side road and shifted direction toward the freeway. West and north.

Toward the Colorado cabin only one of his brothers knew about. The place that housed the secret life he could never reveal. To anyone.

Sixteen hours.

Zach kneaded the back of his neck. He'd stopped a few times to buy gas at the most out-of-the way stations he could find, paying cash each time, tugging a ball cap over his face to prevent anyone from recognizing him.

Now he was wired from one Red Bull too many as Fools Peak loomed in the distance.

He didn't stop to consider the irony of his cabin's location—situated two miles high in the mountain chain better known for Aspen or Vail, magnets for the rich and famous. He negotiated curve after curve, going deeper and deeper into the forest. Pine and aspen lined one side, a steep rock face lined the other.

He'd fallen in love with the spot the moment he'd seen it. Three years, a plethora of machinations to cloak the transaction, and a barrelful of cash later, he had the perfect base. State-of-the-art security and toys in the middle of nowhere. Mountain climbing galore, gorgeous lakes. Who could ask for more?

And no one knew.

He squeezed back the twist of loneliness. He'd never brought anyone here. And he never would.

He rubbed at the grit in his eyes and blinked back the burn. He hadn't slept for three days. Probably why he'd become so introspective all of a sudden. He needed to recharge, then log into the secure computer and try to figure out who had betrayed not only him, but the country.

The only good news. He hadn't been followed.

With a last turn, Zach pulled up to the large cabin, its solid wooden walls and isolation finally easing the tension in his neck.

He needed some real food, a soak in the hot tub, and sleep, in that order. He grabbed his duffel from behind the seat and shifted it onto his shoulder.

June had finally brought spring to the mountains—except at the peaks that still held a dusting of snow. He caught sight of a few tufts of daffodils against the bright blue Western sky. The hardy flower fought to survive. At this elevation, though, even in summer, a slight nip hung in the air.

A small sigh escaped Zach. He'd hoped to come here for a vacation away from the press, not as a haven to save his life. Though, truth be told, he'd built it for just that reason.

He even had a plan in place to disappear.

He didn't want to have to do that. His mom…Zach closed his eyes. She loved him, even though he'd disappointed her. Even when he'd sat in the hospital covered in his father's blood… she'd loved him.

Zach didn't deserve her.

He unlocked the cabin and stepped inside. Dust had settled every-where. He tossed his duffel on the sofa and walked out back to check the helipad. The chopper was still there. He'd ditch the pickup in the garage and use the Range Rover. The vehicle's ownership had been buried so deep even Theresa wouldn't be able to uncover it.

A loud rumble sounded from out front.

His truck.

He ran around the cabin. A woman's very curvy backside stuck out from the door. A small boy's face peered at him from the backseat.

The woman rose. When she spotted him, her face turned milky pale. He knew her. He'd recognize those emerald eyes anywhere. She sucked in a breath, dove into the truck, and slammed the door.

He raced toward her, but she ground the gears and peeled out down the road. He skidded to a halt and stared in stunned disbelief.

Jenna Walters had just hot-wired his truck.

———————————

Jenna clung to the steering wheel of the large vehicle. Her knuckles whitened when she squeezed tighter, forcing her shaking hands to still. The truck's powerful engine rumbled beneath her and she pressed down on the gas.

One glance over her shoulder had her swallowing back a lump. Zach Montgomery looked stunned…then really, really pissed.

Her internal alarm rang, making her hands shake. Zach could have been a mirror to Brad when his frustration built to the point where he would burst into a yelling fit. Maybe all men but her dad were the same, ready to explode at the first challenge instead of finding a way around the problem. Well, she refused to live in a state of constant tiptoeing. Not anymore.

"You took his truck without asking, Mommy," Sam said. "That's bad."

And how did she explain this to a five-year-old? "Sometimes—"

He frowned at her. "You stole from the Dark Avenger." Sam crossed his arms, his lips tightening in a stubborn line, his eyes glaring at her from the backseat.

Jenna couldn't answer, but she could distract him. "Put on your seat belt, Sam."

With a grunt he did as she asked. At least her son knew right from wrong—unlike his father.

She'd make it up to him. Once they were safe. She'd lost the luxury of choice once she'd made her deal with the FBI. Now she had to live with the mistake she'd made. Jenna focused on maneuvering the large truck. She turned out of the long driveway and headed down the mountain road.

She used all her strength to force the vehicle into the middle of the road. The winding stretch and tight hairpin turns made her want to stop and walk. She stared unblinking at the white line down the center of the asphalt.

Another turn and she caught a glimpse of the true danger she found herself in. The trees on the driver's side melted away revealing a sheer drop down. She gasped. It had to be a thousand feet. No guardrail to protect her. Her stomach rebelled. Now she understood why she'd nearly lost it during the last hour of being stuck in the hot bed of the pickup. Each turn had sent her insides roiling.

Bile rose in her throat, though not just from the twists on the road. She glanced at her son, still mutinously silent behind her. She'd jumped out of Brad's dangerous life into a mountainous torture chamber. What had she done in the name of protecting Sam?

A loud honking sounded from behind her.

A Range Rover ate the distance between them. As the black vehicle drew closer, the windshield framed Zach Montgomery's determined face.

This couldn't be happening.

She pressed down the gas pedal as much as she dared. She hadn't expected him to care if she took his vehicle. After the small car lot she'd found in his garage, she knew the man owned more than any person needed and could have called for help to get down the mountain.

Why had he followed her? Where was the spoiled actor she'd expected who wouldn't fight for something as mundane as a car?

She had to get away from Zach. She had no doubt that if he found her he'd turn her in to the cops. If that happened, she was dead. And Sam, no telling what Brad would do to her son. At one time, she'd thought her husband loved them—or at least loved Sam—but that man had vanished eighteen months ago.

With a firm grip on the black leather steering wheel, Jenna refocused. She recognized the unwavering resolve. It mirrored the backbone she'd found when she decided to turn Brad in. She pressed down on the gas. The truck sped up and headed toward the mountainside. She turned. The tires squealed beneath them.

Sam whimpered in the seat behind her.

A glance in the mirror revealed the truth. She'd taken the risk for nothing. Zach Montgomery knew how to drive. He'd picked up speed and had closed the distance between them, tailgating her. His face livid, he rode the horn for all it was worth.

Her heart raced as the next turn approached. She had no choice. She had to slow down. Her foot mashed in the brakes. The car veered toward the rock face.

The truck's side scraped against the jagged rocks jutting out, riding the granite. Metal sparks flew, and her hands shook in her effort to control the wheel. A lump of terror closed off her throat. This couldn't be happening.

Another sharp turn.

The nose of the truck edged down, racing toward a huge boulder that blocked the middle of the road.

Oh God.

On the way up the mountain in the dark back of the truck, there'd been that sudden jerk causing Sam to slide into her. Now she knew why.

She yanked the steering wheel, but too late. The right side of the truck shoved at the boulder. The tire blew and she barreled toward the tree line.

Jenna fought against the wheels, forcing them toward the rock face, but the truck wouldn't veer.

She'd lost control.

"Mommy!"

She couldn't let anything happen to Sam. She wouldn't.

Praying, and with strength she didn't know she possessed, Jenna shifted the vehicle's direction. After miles of no protection, a guardrail appeared at the side of the road. If she could just reach it.

She pumped the brakes. The truck lurched forward. Sam cried out in fear.

Sheer momentum shoved them toward the pine trees and barricade. Her stomach twisted, and with one last desperate plea, she skidded into the barrier.

Metal creaked and tore at the side of the truck. The scraping clawed at her ears. The tires squealed. The edge loomed closer and closer.

She held her breath, her knuckles went white, her nails bit into her hand.

The guardrail ended and the car hood shoved into the top of a huge pine tree.

The air bag blew out.

Her head whirled. Spots darkened in her eyes.

Then she knew no more.

———————

Zach watched in horror as the small boy in the backseat stared at him, his eyes wide with fright. The truck rocked toward the edge, the front left wheel hanging off the mountain, the other tires precariously balanced on the edge.

With a quick maneuver he'd learned while doing stunts on an Indy racing television film, his Range Rover skidded to a halt and he jumped out. The little boy twisted in the backseat. The truck teetered.

"Be still, kid!" Zach yelled as he raced to the truck. "Don't move. Can you do that for me?"

The child bit his lip, but he didn't panic. He froze.

Brave little guy—or in shock—not that Zach cared, as long as the boy didn't move. Zach ran to the side of the vehicle. Jenna Walters didn't stir. Blood dripped from her head onto the deflated air bag.

He had to be careful. Any movement could send the vehicle plummeting hood first down a hundred-foot incline, with only piñon trees and a grove of thin-trunked aspens to stop its descent before it dove into a thousand-foot chasm.

Zach knew these mountains well. They didn't let a man get away with a mistake.

Jenna had made a big mistake running from him when all he'd wanted to do was help.

He moved to the driver's-side door. Carefully, he squeezed the handle. Locked. He tugged the keys from his pocket and pressed the button. The locks clicked free. He moved his hand to the metal and pressed. No luck, it didn't budge. The door had jammed. Zach rounded behind the vehicle. He tried the passenger door and let out a small breath as the latch clicked. The door unhitched. He eased it open. With caution, he flicked the lever. The seat back shifted forward.

The boy remained frozen in the seat behind his mother.

"What's your name, kid?" he said softly.

"S...Sam." The boy's eyes went wide. "You're the Dark Avenger."

Zach sighed. Another fan, but perhaps he could use the kid's belief to his advantage. "I need your help."

"I can't. I'm not big enough. Please help my mommy. She's hurt."

"I'm gonna get your mom, but I need you to do what I tell you. Unbuckle your seat belt and crawl toward me real careful. Can you do that?"

The boy nodded. He looked at his mother and bit his lip.

"I'll get her. I promise." Zach prayed he could keep that vow. The truck could plummet any minute.

"You're the Dark Avenger. You don't lie, do you?"

Not about anything except my entire life. Zach steeled a confident glance at the boy. "I don't lie to little boys."

Until today, that is. Sometimes it paid to be an actor.

Sam clicked open his seat belt, took one last glance at his mom, and scooted toward Zach.

The truck inched forward.

"Stop, Sam," Zach said, his voice hushed.

The boy's eyes widened, but he froze.

The truck steadied. He was less than a foot away from Zach's reach.

"OK, start scooting again. Slow and easy."

Time seemed to stand still. Zach held his breath as Sam crawled toward him. Zach leaned in and plucked Sam off the seat.

The truck teetered. The rear wheels no longer hugged the road at all.

Zach hugged Sam to him and backed away several feet.

"Mommy!" Sam leaned away from Zach and reached out toward the truck, his small fists opening and closing as if willing his mother to come with him.

The truck didn't obey. It started the evitable slide and shoved into the trees.

No time to lose. "Heads up, Sam." Zach tossed the boy toward the safety of the cliff face, hearing him grunt has he hit the road. The bruises would heal, but if Zach didn't get to the woman, that boy would be motherless. Within seconds he'd scrambled down the incline. Piñon trunks had bent in a U-shape over the roof, keeping the vehicle from going headfirst down a thousand feet.

No telling how long they'd hold. And snagging an active five-year-old's fifty-pound body out of a seat was different than an unconscious woman's hundred-and-twenty-pound deadweight.

The loud crack of a breaking trunk echoed through the forest. The truck groaned. No time to think. He had to move fast, but easy. Any transfer of weight could break the last of the trees that cushioned the truck. He leaned in as far as he could without touching anything and snapped the seat belt free from its latch.

Jenna shifted. The truck shuddered. Zach had to pull back.

He let out a long, slow breath. He'd have one chance at this.

He had to gain leverage. Throwing any hesitation off the ragged mountainside, Zach stepped on the running board. The truck tilted his way. He reached in and grabbed one of Jenna's hands. He dragged her toward him and clasped her under her arms. In a single motion he pulled her across the seat and out of the vehicle.

Just as her weight came free, the piñon trees holding the truck gave way.

The vehicle sped down the incline then disappeared over the cliff. Metal crunched and squealed. Finally a huge crash echoed from below. Zach lay back on a bed of pine needles, Jenna draped over the lower half of his body. He stared at the blue sky above.

Too close.

Jenna's soft curves pressed against him. He liked the feel of her in his arms, but he shouldn't. She was a whole different kind of trouble that he couldn't deal with right now. Even if he offered to help her, she'd only run from him. Again.

He sat up and shifted her into his arms before he stood, trekking up the twenty feet to the road.

When his feet hit pavement Sam ran over, his small face streaked with tears, his eyes bright. "You saved her!"

He beamed up at Zach then stared at his mother. Sam reached up with a tentative hand and touched her bruised face. "She's hurt."

"I'm sorry I had to throw you, kid."

Sam looked at his scraped hands and wiped them on his jeans. Zach winced. Tough little guy, though.

"We'll get you fixed up." Zach probed the deep cut just above Jenna Walters's espresso-colored hair. "We'll get you both fixed up. It looks worse than it is," he lied. Head wounds could be trouble.

He settled her soft frame against his chest and carried her to the Range Rover. He placed her into the seat beside him. She hadn't budged, hadn't regained consciousness.

He turned to help Sam into the backseat.

He fought against a gasp. The boy stood, peering over the side of the mountain. Much too close to the edge.

No sound filtered through Brad Walters's house. Eerie actually—and pleasant. His wife's joyous laughter grated when she lavished all her attention on Sam. He should have found peace in the silence, but his well-ordered life had tumbled into chaos. All because of her.

Disbelieving, he stared for the third time at the stash of items dumped in the hallway.

He couldn't believe Jenna had possessed the guts.

He'd taken her off the streets. She'd had nothing. No one. He'd made her into a lady, given her everything. And this was how she repaid him.

He walked through each room, once more searching for anything out of place. He'd identified all the listening devices. Luckily, he knew better than to discuss business in his home.

This house had been one piece of his well-orchestrated cover. His two worlds had never collided.

Or so he'd believed.

He should've killed Jenna already, but he had to know how she'd discovered his secret. Besides, he had to make arrangements for Sam. The kid couldn't survive without someone watching over him.

He made his way to the back door. It had been her only way out. He picked up the flashlight from the patio table where he'd left it after his last foray and walked the yard again, this time more deliberately. With Montgomery gone, he could take his time to do a proper study of her movements.

Sam had left the signed baseball tossed in the middle of the yard. He needed to take better care of his things. Jenna had always been too easy on the kid.

His son was coddled and spoiled. That would change. Once Brad eliminated Jenna, order would return. Then he'd make sure the boy learned self-control.

Brad's father had taught the lessons well. Control must be maintained at all times. It was the only way to succeed. To win. To be someone.

The ball could rot. The boy would pay for a new one when Brad got his son back.

Brad ran the beam of light across the back wall, skimmed across the blood. They'd climbed into Zach Montgomery's yard. He didn't care what the actor said.

The man was a bum. No discipline. No control. Ever since Zach had moved in, he'd watched the guy come and go on a whim and then perpetually make the cover of the tabloids.

Anyone who let themselves show their weaknesses in public was a fool.

With a quick move, Brad vaulted to the top of the wall. He studied the drop. Far, but not too far for Jenna to help Sam down. At least his son showed some athletic prowess.

Brad scanned right, then left. It was the only way down. He could always predict his target's movements, but Jenna had surprised him. He didn't get it. His wife was a coward. She wasn't a risk taker, which is why he'd chosen her. She had been exactly what he wanted.

The first time he'd seen her, Jenna was nothing but a street rat picking pockets. She'd been foolish enough to target him. He'd considered breaking her hand as punishment. One squeeze at the right point and she'd have been begging for mercy, but then he'd seen her eyes. He'd recognized the potential. He'd wanted her.

After one date, he'd known she was vulnerable, that he could mold her. He'd paid her uncle enough money not only to wash his hands of her but to make her life hell on the streets.

With nowhere to go, she'd been putty in his hands.

She'd been his perfect wife. A woman who would question nothing.

Until now.

Brad didn't like the unexpected.

So, what had changed?

With a quick swing, he dropped into his self-indulgent neighbor's yard.

The man was never here. A waste.

The space appeared different from this angle. What would Jenna see? What would she do? He put himself in tracking mode and studied the surroundings carefully. A house with a security system. Similar to theirs, but Jenna knew nothing of electronics or surveillance. She'd barely graduated high school.

She would have needed to check her or Sam's injury from the wall. Brad's gaze stopped at the pool. Towels, perhaps bandages.

He strode to the small building off the flagstone deck. The door had been locked.

This time when he tried the knob, it opened easily.

There, on the stone, a drop of blood pooled on the uneven surface. An empty water bottle and juice box had been tossed in the trash can.

Apple.

The same apple juice that Jenna kept in the refrigerator.

He slugged the wall; his fist broke through, leaving a hole inside the building. She'd been inches from him all the time.

His gaze lit on the cash lying on the table, and he stilled. He thumbed through the money. Over a thousand dollars. Thrown down as if it were nothing.

Not his Jenna. She grew up scraping by.

Zach Montgomery's face filtered in his vision. The bastard had known.

He was an actor. He lied for a living.

No one else would have left the money here. The truth sliced through Brad. Had he underestimated his neighbor? Brad pulled his cell phone from his pocket. He pressed a key.

"Johansson."

"Find out everything you can about Zach Montgomery."

"The actor?"

"I want the data tonight." Brad ended the call. He had other research to do. He had to figure out whom Jenna had contacted, and what she knew.

His identity had been compromised. He would plug the leaks and then begin again. He'd done it once.

His son...he hadn't planned on that small wrinkle. But he could find another woman to raise his son. And do a proper job this time.

A simple plan. Once he found Jenna and the evidence his FBI mole had warned him about, she would have to die.

His phone rang. He glanced at the number. His eye flinched with the tick that only appeared when one person called.

The moment he'd agreed to the first job, he'd regretted it. Too many loose ends. He'd been right. Until today when Jenna had left him, this client had been the only person over whom he had no leverage.

"Walters."

"I have another job for you. There's been a development."

"I'm booked." He peered into Montgomery's house. He would search the premises.

"A follow-up to the Colorado job from five years ago. Questions are being asked. I want them silenced. I want you in Denver tonight. Your target won't be easy."

"That's what you said about the last one."

"Well, this is a SWAT captain. John Garrison."

"My price just went up fifty percent. Half now. Half on completion."

"If you can do it within the week, I'll double the payment."

Brad flicked his thumb against his pinky. It was a risk, but the fat paycheck would help his transition to his new identity. He couldn't allow questions to remain about the Colorado job. He had a reputation. Besides, Jenna's betrayal had made him vulnerable.

"Done. Send the particulars to the same location."

"No mistakes."

Brad chuckled and brushed imaginary dirt from the perfectly pressed cuff of his shirt. "I don't make mistakes or leave a trail that can be followed."

"Don't challenge me too boldly, Walters. You wouldn't want me for an enemy. I would think the last eighteen months had taught you that."

The call ended. Brad's fingernails bit into his palm.

Too many loose threads. Not enough control. Unacceptable. He could hear his father's voice berating him from the grave. *Fool, pathetic weakling, wimp.*

He would trim all the loose ends. He'd use every set of skills to make sure no one would be left who could identify him.

No one except his son.

Chapter Five

SAM!

Her son's name filtered into Jenna's foggy mind. She blinked. Pain from the bump on her head dug into her like a knight's sword.

Where was she? She cracked open her eyes. The sun burned into her through the car's windshield. She couldn't stand the light. The supple leather of the luxury seats cradled her body, yet the interior pressed on her heavy with heat. What had happened? Whose car was this?

The memory slammed into her. The truck. The cliff.

Sam.

Her pained gaze found his slight frame hovering far too close to the edge of the road.

"Don't move, Sam." Was that her shaking, weak voice?

Her heart stuttered. She had to get to her son. Jenna rolled to her side, but her entire body felt weighted down. She reached out her hand toward him. "Sam," she called, her voice barely working.

Then she saw him. Zach Montgomery. Sam's Dark Avenger raced across the road.

In one fluid motion, he scooped Sam up and away from the drop-off. Jenna's throat closed off as Zach, his eyes closed and his chin lifted to heaven, hugged her boy tight. The emotion painted on his face made Jenna swallow to avoid a sob escaping. His shoulders sagged and he carried Sam to the car.

Jenna fell back against the seat, boneless in relief.

"Don't wander off without an adult," Zach's firm voice counseled Sam. "You could get lost. Or fall."

"Like the truck."

"Just like the truck."

"It got smashed," Sam said as he scrambled into the backseat. "I wanted to see." The door closed.

Jenna shut her eyes. Her son was safe.

They were both safe.

For the moment.

Except now Zach knew about them.

If Brad ever found out...she'd discovered in his records exactly what he did to people who crossed him. Had she made Zach a target, too?

She tried to shake her head and groaned as the throbbing behind her eyes exploded.

"Mommy!"

Her son leaned into the front seat of the Range Rover. His small hand touched her face. She couldn't move her head, but his cool touch reminded her why every sacrifice would be worth it.

The car door opened and a warm body leaned over her. "Jenna. Can you open your eyes? Look at me."

She focused on lifting her lids. Such a small thing, but her body rebelled this time. She just couldn't seem to compel her muscles to obey.

A large hand folded into hers. "Can you squeeze my fingers?"

She gripped him tight, holding on to the strong hand as if clinging to a lifeline. He'd saved her son. Saved them both.

"Good girl."

His fingers tightened around hers, his strength frightening and calming at the same time. She didn't want to let go.

Her son's small sniffles filtered from behind her. "Why won't she wake up, Dark Avenger? Make her wake up."

"Don't worry, Sam. I'm taking your mommy to the clinic. The doctors will get her all better."

She gripped his arm, her fingernails digging into his skin. "No, please," she whispered. "No doctors. He'll find us."

Zach leaned closer. The lingering scent of lavender and shampoo made something inside of him shift.

"Your husband?" he whispered.

She nodded, then winced. "Please." She clutched his hand harder.

"You have a head injury. You may need a CAT scan."

"No one can know," she whispered. She opened her eyes. His icy-blue ones stared back at her. He studied her for a moment, his pointed gaze probing, searching for the truth. His thumb touched an area on her forehead. Even his gentle stroke made her wince as a shard of pain burrowed into her head.

He let his finger follow the line of her cheekbone to her chin. "Rest, Jenna. Nothing will happen to you. I promise."

She shouldn't believe him. He didn't know about Brad. Her husband appeared to be a nonthreatening, mild-mannered traveling computer expert. Zach Montgomery was no match for a killer. He might be the Dark Avenger in movies, but Jenna knew the truth. Zach Montgomery wasn't a real hero, only a professional pretender. He couldn't help them.

She tried to push away from him to sit up, but her body betrayed her again. With a groan, she sagged in the seat. She couldn't afford faith, but here she was, relying on a man she didn't know, who could very well be another disappointment.

"Just don't let Brad find us," she whispered.

The Hidden Springs medical clinic sat nestled at the base of Fools Peak, in a small valley with a few fields and a sparkling spring nearby. Luckily, the small town housed state-of-the-art equipment, mostly due to the numerous mountaineers going after the surrounding thirteen- and fourteen-thousand-foot peaks. Jenna would get the best care here, even though she'd tried to refuse the CAT scan.

Now, he and Sam just waited for the results. What was taking so long? Zach scratched at the cut across his chest. It had started to itch. Healing, he hoped. Maybe he could palm some more butterflies off the nurse.

A woman whispered to her husband across the waiting room. He nodded slightly and she smiled tentatively at Zach.

Damn. He'd spent too much time sitting, too many chances to be identified. He normally wore his Zane Morgan disguise into town, but with Jenna hurt, he hadn't taken the time. It wouldn't take long for word to get out Zach Montgomery had been in Hidden Springs, Colorado. He'd blown his secret, and he really liked his cabin. If he survived the next few weeks, he'd have to sell.

Zach shifted his gaze away, hoping they'd get the hint.

Within a few minutes, a nurse escorted the couple out, but the knot at the base of Zach's neck didn't ease. Hopefully he could get Jenna and Sam back to the cabin and away from small-town questions soon.

The little boy beside him squirmed in his chair. Zach looked down at Sam. "How are those scratches?"

Jenna's son sat cross-legged in the chair worrying his jeans. He flipped over his hands and stared at his palms, reddened but now clean and doctored with antiseptic. He straightened his back and looked up at Zach. "I didn't cry. I'm a big boy. My mommy said so."

Zach quirked a smile. "I can see that."

Every so often Sam would get up, but for the most part he'd just stayed next to Zach, unmoving and not speaking—unlike Zach's four-year-old niece, Joy. That worried Zach more than anything. Weren't five-year-olds much more…lively and prone to trouble?

Sam was too polite.

"Why can't I see my mommy?"

Sam gazed up at Zach with eyes just like his mother's, not only in color, but in the apprehension simmering behind the golf-course-green pools.

Zach ruffled Sam's hair. "The doctor is looking at her. I'm sure we'll be able to see her soon."

Sam bounced his leg up and down, clearly nervous.

"She doesn't like doctors," he said, his voice so low Zach had to bend closer to hear him. "My daddy made her go to a lot of them. She gets hurt a lot."

Zach's lifted his gaze to the ceiling so Sam wouldn't see the fury simmering behind Zach's eyes. Why couldn't his gut have been wrong? His hand itched to grab Brad Walters by the throat and give him payback for everything he'd ever done to Jenna.

Then the disgust turned inward. Zach had lived next door and hadn't known what was going on beyond the walls protecting him.

Walters had given off a noxious vibe. If Zach had taken the time to meet him, he would have known something was wrong in the house behind him. When had he lost sight of the world around him?

Even tonight, Zach had been focused on his own problems—he did have someone out to kill him after all. Walters had never been after Zach, though. He'd been after Jenna. The idea of the bastard laying a hand on someone as fragile as her... Zach tightened his fists, and his teeth ached as he gnawed over the truth.

Vulnerable and gentle. With no one to help her.

That would change.

A small tug jerked him out of his contemplation. Zach cast a sidelong glance at the small boy twisting his fingers.

"My mommy needs me."

Zach picked Sam up and stood him on the floor. With an unswerving gaze, Zach looked the kid square in his wide-eyed gaze. "Do you know what a lie is, Sam?"

"When you make up a story to get out of trouble. Mommy won't let me lie."

"I need you to tell me the truth. Does your daddy hurt you? Does he hit you?"

Sam bit his lip and bowed his head, avoiding Zach's gaze. "Not really. Sometimes he yells a lot. That's when Mommy and me go away, 'cause he's in time-out. That's where he is now." Sam scuffed his feet. "But after he's bad, he plays ball with me or takes me to a baseball game. I like that."

Zach had his own suspicions about what happened between Jenna and Brad behind closed doors.

The clinic's double doors swung open. "Mr. Smith?" The doctor gave Zach a secretive smile. One more person who clearly knew his identity. He stood and Sam jumped up with him.

"Your *wife* has a concussion, but the CAT scan doesn't show any other concerns." He frowned slightly. "She's a stubborn woman and refuses to stay overnight. I hope you can convince her."

Zach nodded. "I'll do what I can."

He took Sam's hand and together they followed the nurse to the end of the hallway. The nurse shoved aside a curtain.

Sam dropped Zach's hand and bounded across the room to his mother. "Mommy!"

He jumped on the bed.

Jenna clutched Sam into her arms, closing her eyes in relief. She kissed his forehead. "You all right?"

"The Dark Avenger saved us," Sam said.

Jenna struggled to sit up and pasted a smile on her face, but her complexion matched the white sheets.

"Whoa, there," Zach said, hurrying across the room and pushing her into the pillow. "Now I can see why they want you to stay."

"I can't." Jenna's gaze fell on her son, but she lowered her voice. "He'll find us."

"Mrs. Smith?" the nurse said.

Jenna didn't answer, she just gaped at Zach, her vulnerable gaze tugging at emotions he'd thought he buried.

"Mrs. *Smith*?" the nurse repeated, giving Zach a long, questioning look.

Zach lifted her chin and sent Jenna a pointed stare. "*Darling*, the nurse is speaking to you."

Jenna blinked once. Her eyes widened with understanding, and she glanced at the nurse, clearing her throat. "I'm sorry. I was so relieved my son wasn't hurt in the accident, I didn't hear you."

The nurse held out papers for Jenna. "The doctor reluctantly signed your release forms. You're free to go once you provide your signature."

Jenna nodded and winced, putting a hand to her head. Zach took the papers.

The nurse sighed. "Call if you need anything." She gave Zach one last worried look, then left.

"You should stay tonight," Zach said, even though he would rather get them both up the mountain.

Jenna ignored him and eased her feet to the floor. She stood up and swayed.

Zach let out a sharp curse.

"You said a bad word, Dark Avenger," Sam muttered from his mother's side.

Zach flushed and steadied Jenna.

"Clothes," she whispered. "Please."

With a shake of his head, Zach handed her a pile from the chair. "Come on, Sam. Your mom needs to get dressed."

He jumped off the bed, and Zach closed the curtain. "I'm not moving from this spot. Call if you need me."

There was silence. Sam stood waiting, and Zach listened. A clatter sounded.

Zach threw open the curtain. Jenna stood in a pair of underwear, her shirt halfway on. Her long legs went on forever, though one was lined with a crisscross of barely healing cuts. Zach studied the injury before the truth slapped him. Cuts from the glass on the top of the wall surrounding his home.

She let out a puff as she struggled with her shirt. She'd tangled the material around her. At the flash of her full breasts, Zach held his breath and walked across the room. He shoved her hands aside and righted the material.

A blush rose up her cheeks.

The awareness between them crackled like the latest Colorado wildfire. Zach shoved the feelings aside. He didn't get involved with married women. Period.

It was the one line he didn't cross. She tempted him, though. Boy did she. He snagged her jeans from the chair and held them out.

"Put your hands on my shoulders," he said.

She hesitated.

He met her gaze. "It's either this or your ass stays in the hospital tonight," he said under his breath, sending a sidelong look at Sam, who had poked his head around the curtain.

"You don't get to tell me what to do," Jenna whispered. "No one does. Not anymore."

She jerked the jeans away from him and shuffled over to a chair. She sat down and slid the denim on. When she pulled them over her knees she stood up, braced herself, then lifted them over the scrap of lace she called underwear.

Zach hovered near her while she glared at him, motioning to her son. She grasped Sam's hand. "We're leaving, baby."

Sam stared up at her. "You're hurt, Mommy. You need the Dark Avenger."

Jenna took a shuddering breath. She placed her hands on her knees. "We can make it, Junior Avenger. This is our adventure."

He crossed his arms.

Stubborn little guy with a good head on his shoulders. Zach stepped in. "Buddy, I think you should come with me. Your mommy needs someone to watch her tonight. Is it all right if I take care of her?"

Sam looked from his mom to Zach. He nodded his head.

Jenna glared at Zach, but he just shrugged. If he let her out of his sight, she'd keel over.

Her flitting focus measured the distance to the door. Zach narrowed his gaze at her. He bent down, his mouth near her ear. "Don't try it. Not until you can stand for five minutes without falling over. If not for you, for Sam."

Her confidence wavered.

"Look, stay with me tonight. Doc said you should be much better tomorrow."

Jenna rose, her legs still shaky. Zach steadied her, but she shrugged his touch away. Stubborn woman.

"You don't know what you're getting involved with."

Zach shook his head and chuckled. "Honey, I could say the same thing." He tilted her chin up. "I'll make you a deal. Come home with me. Tomorrow, I'll spot you the cash you need to go wherever you want."

She stared up at him, her expression stunned...and suspicious. "Why would you do that?"

"Let's just say Brad isn't on the top of my favorites list." Zach glanced pointedly to Sam.

Jenna let out a long sigh. "I need to regroup," she admitted. "Just for tonight." She clutched his arm. "You won't tell anyone where we are?"

"No one for me to tell."

She nodded, then winced, pressing her hand against her forehead. "Just for tonight. Then you can forget you ever saw me or Sam."

Zach pushed her dark hair away from the white bandage on her forehead. "I doubt I'll forget this day anytime soon, Jenna Walters," he said, his voice soft.

Taking Sam's hand, slowly, steadily, she walked out of the room, refusing the wheelchair the nurse brought in.

Zach hovered near her. He admired her grit. And her stubbornness. She'd be fine. Zach could counter Brad Walters's money advantage. And before she left, Zach could make certain Jenna could defend herself. He refused to leave her without the skills to make a new life. If he could strong-arm a friend or two—given he still had them—Brad Walters might conveniently lose his job jockeying computers and be forced to leave Jenna alone.

Still, the sooner he got her and Sam on their way, the better. It wouldn't be long before his enemies caught up with him. They had more tools at their disposal than he did. He couldn't let Jenna and Sam be caught in the middle.

She swayed, and Zach wrapped his arm around her waist, unable to ignore the soft curves pressed against him. Not silicone, not fake. A real, live woman with a heart and soul and strength.

She might have made a wrong choice, but she possessed the courage to change things. It couldn't have been easy.

Another time, another place, Jenna might have been a woman to tempt him to settle down.

Too bad by the time she and Sam started their new life, Zach would probably be dead.

Jenna didn't want to lean on Zach Montgomery. She didn't want to rely on anyone. Not again. She had to find the scrappy kid she'd hidden away when Brad had found her. The girl who could pick a pocket without her target having a clue; the girl who could hot-wire a car in thirty seconds, not the minute it had taken her to start Zach's truck; the girl who'd survived on her own for two years, carelessly overseen by an uncle whose best friends were paid to break kneecaps. Until he'd vanished, leaving her homeless and hungry.

She clutched at the hood of the Range Rover to steady herself. As much as she wanted to walk away, she couldn't take care of Sam. Not like this.

And her son clearly idolized the man. She prayed Zach wouldn't disillusion her son. He didn't need any more disappointments.

Zach's strong hands settled on her waist. He helped Jenna into the vehicle, his touch lingering on her back. She shivered. Try as she might to not be impacted by him, he was more handsome in person than on the big screen. His pecan-colored hair, highlighted with strands of ginger, glimmered in the billowing light of dusk.

He'd been younger when he'd played the Dark Avenger, but she'd fallen for that mischievous glint in his eyes that made the superhero oh-so-sexy.

She didn't admit it to Sam, but she'd relished watching the movie as much as he did. She'd thought him harmless eye candy. Had believed she'd married her very own superhero. Not the supervillain.

As with every time she remembered all of Brad's lies, nausea rose deep within her. If her husband had risked searching the neighborhood, he was desperate. Just because they were sixteen hours away from La Jolla didn't mean they were safe. Ever since she'd approached the FBI, they'd drilled Brad's skills into her. According to law enforcement, her husband had avoided detection by both American and international police for over a decade. That meant he not only knew how to fly under the radar, he also knew how to manipulate systems.

He didn't just have money. He had powerful connections.

She sent a sidelong glance to the man who hadn't hesitated to help. He had money, but he was still just an actor. She couldn't let herself mix up the hero he played on screen and the real man. Even if he'd saved her life.

Still, something didn't quite fit. Those instincts from her childhood had started pinging. With everything in the press, she'd thought Zach Montgomery was a soft playboy who looked good. Now, studying the hard line of his jaw and his intelligent gaze, she recognized she'd made too many assumptions. The story of her life.

She let out a small sigh.

"Are you ready to talk yet?" he said, his deep voice smooth as milk chocolate.

She glanced at Sam, who stared eagerly at the back of his hero's head. How had her life gotten so complicated?

"Why steal my truck?" he persisted.

"I would have left it for you somewhere," she said. "I'm no thief."

"I have a perfectly good vehicle in pieces at the base of a thousand-foot cliff that says differently."

"I'll pay you back."

"I'll take a check."

She blanched. "Someday."

"You're running," he said.

She looked at Sam. "Later," she pleaded.

"Fine," Zach said. "Once you're safely at the cabin."

Jenna placed her hand on her temple. "We'll never be safe," she muttered.

In another half hour, Zach pulled into the front of the house. He opened the car's back door for Sam then walked around the vehicle to help Jenna out. He stuffed the car keys in his pocket. "I'm going to trust we don't have a repeat. I really like the Range Rover."

She flushed and slid to the ground. Zach swept her into his arms.

"What are you doing?"

"Keeping you from falling on your face," he said.

He marched up the steps, Sam trailing behind like an eager puppy, awestruck by every gesture, every word, every movement Zach made. Too much like Sam's reaction to Brad at one time. Jenna's gut lurched with concern. Sam had idolized his father...when Brad was home.

Until the last few months, Jenna had been able to protect Sam from seeing the darker side of her husband. *She* hadn't seen the darker side until the last eighteen months.

She'd thought he'd been having an affair.

She couldn't have been more wrong.

Her son didn't know it yet, but he'd lost his father today.

She'd lost her Prince Charming the moment he'd hit her for the first time. She'd taken a bite of the apple the moment she'd discovered she'd married a killer.

Zach jostled her a bit and she wrapped her arms around his neck. Brad had never carried her this way…not since he'd carted her over the threshold. It was part of the honeymoon—part of an act, she recognized now. After one night and day of bliss, he'd received a phone call and left for a job. She'd been disappointed, but proud. He was her provider.

What a fool she'd been to believe in him.

Zach cradled her securely as he walked through the living room and down a hallway. The walls were made out of logs, and the large stone fireplace took up an entire wall. If you dreamed of mountain cabins, this would be the one.

He pushed open the door to a large bedroom and gently laid her on the quilt. "You're staying in here tonight."

Sam skipped behind her holding a football in his hand. "Look, Mommy. Can I play ball with the Dark Avenger?"

Zach winced at the name but didn't correct Sam. The kindness warmed Jenna from the inside. Clearly the role that had made Zach famous also made him uncomfortable, and yet no matter what Sam said or did, Zach was nothing but patient.

"Tell you what, buddy," Zach said. "How about I put on a movie for you?"

"*The Dark Avenger?*" Sam's eyes were wide.

"I think I can arrange something," Zach muttered.

He left the room and within a few minutes Jenna heard the TV blaring from down the hall.

She tilted her head, testing the pain. Pressing her hand against her temple, she sighed, resigned to spending the night with the Dark Avenger. She found it easier to think of him as a movie star. She had enjoyed him holding her way too much, and his profession made him untouchable.

"How many times has he seen it?" Zach asked from the doorway before returning to her bedside.

Jenna shoved her musings away and shifted in the bed. Her heart sped up as his large frame filled the room. Why did the room seem so much smaller, the oxygen so much thinner?

"I stopped counting at twenty," she choked, cursing her nervousness. "And that was the first week we bought it."

With a grimace Zach sat in the rocking chair by the bed. "Sorry about that."

"It's a good movie. You were good in it."

"Good special effects. I had nothing to do with that." Zach propped his boot across his knee.

"You're wrong. It's not the explosions that make the movie special. It's you, Zach. *You* gave the Dark Avenger soul. *You* make the audience understand honor and justice. That's why I let Sam watch it so many times. He needed a real hero. Especially recently."

Zach started to protest, and Jenna clutched at the quilt. "Please. Let me get this out. I need to thank you. You could have turned me in to the police. You've been very kind...to me and to Sam."

"You did a hell of a quick job hot-wiring the truck," he said. "Besides, natural curiosity dictates I have to find out how you gained such an...unusual skill."

"I'm not as good as I used to be." Jenna smiled for the first time since she could remember.

He quirked a brow. "And that's not a statement I'd expect from a woman in our neighborhood."

Jenna looked away from his speculative glance. How could she explain where she'd come from? How her life with her father had been so wonderful, only to have it ripped away—the same thing she was doing to Sam now. This time, though, she'd make sure Sam had a foundation of security to hold on to.

Zach leaned forward in the chair. "Look, I have to know what's going on. Your husband stopped me as we were leaving. You may have heard him. He told me you have...challenges." Zach's jaw tightened. "Sam told me he gets angry. What's the truth, Jenna?"

Jenna bowed her head. "Brad yells. He...loses his temper sometimes."

"Did you ever call the police?"

Shamed, Jenna toyed with the quilt's stitches. "He always apologized. He hasn't always been this way. I hoped he'd turn back into the man I married." She let out a sharp laugh. "I had no idea who I'd married. That's the scary part."

Zach rose and sat on the bed next to her. He covered her hand with his. "You're obviously terrified. I could take you to the police station now."

"I can't. I'd be dead before they could help me." She scooted away from him and rubbed her chilled arms with her hands.

He moved in closer, his face just inches from hers. He tilted her chin up, his gaze holding her captive. "What are you leaving out, Jenna? Convince me not to get the cops involved for your own good."

She let out a slow sigh. "My husband is more than a computer salesman. He's an assassin."

―――――――――

Anna Montgomery sat on the sofa in her house checking the clock once again. She twisted the pearls around her neck and stared up

at her husband's picture, right next to his favorite piece of art—
nothing fancy, nothing special, just the one she'd sketched of their
cabin in the mountains near Kremmling. Where they'd made love
on their anniversary. Where Zach had been conceived.

Five years Patrick had been gone. Five long, lonely years
since she'd felt her heart beating.

The doorbell rang. Her pulse skipped and she rose, smooth-
ing her skirt as she walked to the door.

She stared through the peephole.

It was him.

"You can do this, Anna. Just because you're a grandmother
doesn't mean you're dead."

She opened the door.

John Garrison stepped inside. Her son Gabe's former captain
smiled, the crow's-feet crinkling, his hazel eyes warming at the
sight of her.

"Anna," he whispered softly.

"I wasn't sure if you'd come," she said. A tingling sensation
prickled at her temple. The warning sense she'd always heeded.
Zach had called it her *spidey sense* during his superhero phase.
She'd known exactly when her kids were in trouble—or lying.
She stared up at John. Maybe her intuition was warning her she
wasn't ready to take this step.

"I've been hoping for this invitation since that barbecue
three years ago," he said.

Her cheeks grew warm. He made her heart and belly flutter
like a schoolgirl. She hadn't felt this way since...Patrick.

John strode into the living room. She closed the door. She could
do this. She'd been working up the courage since that same barbecue, when he'd brushed his hand with hers and a spark of some-

thing had flared deep inside. He'd fanned the flames, slowly, gently, taking special care. Sharing a meal at a family picnic, a waltz at Luke and Jasmine's wedding. Then just nine months ago at the hospital while Gabe was recovering, something had shifted in Anna; the spark no longer flickered, it began to glow. She recognized the truth. John was always there. She wanted him there. Still, it had taken months to call. Peeking after him, she watched Patrick's oldest friend move about the room. He stopped at a photograph.

He picked up her wedding photo. "I remember this day. You were a beautiful bride."

"Thank you." Anna swallowed. "I better check the roast."

She hightailed it into the kitchen and leaned over the stove. She couldn't do this. It was too soon. How would she explain to her boys, especially Zach? They'd all adored their dad, but Patrick's death had stolen a piece of Zach's soul. Would he think she'd betrayed Patrick's memory?

A pair of warm hands touched her shoulders.

John turned her toward him.

Her breath caught as she met his gaze. This had been coming for a long time. She knew it. So did John.

He traced the curve of her cheek with his hand. "You're nervous."

The low timbre of his voice made her body tremble in a way it hadn't in such a long time.

She tried to bow her head and look away, but John tilted her chin up. "We don't have to do this. We can keep things the way they've always been. Old friends. Good friends."

"Is that what you want?"

"You know it's not." His voice dropped to a husky whisper. He pressed his body against hers. Though she knew she still had ample time to escape, she didn't want to. In her heart she knew Patrick wouldn't have wanted her to give up her life.

"I'm afraid," she whispered.

"Anna Montgomery. The Irish terror of Arvada, Colorado?" he teased. "The woman who raised six sons and never blinked an eye at Gabe and Luke's crazy antics. Not to mention Zach's frequent stays in the Jefferson County jail."

She smiled up at him. "You know them well."

"Patrick shared more than one story."

She sighed.

"It's Patrick, isn't it? You still love him." John's face closed off, and he looked as if he were waiting for a blow.

Anna gently eased from his arms and went to the sink, staring through the kitchen window into the night. "I'll always love him."

John grabbed her hand and pressed his lips against her palm. She shivered at the pressure of his soft touch against her skin.

"I know that, Anna. Is it too much to ask for a small piece of that heart? We've been dancing around each other for years."

John straightened and toyed with an errant strand of hair. Then his expression grew dark, his gaze narrowed. He stared past her shoulder. "Stay here."

She recognized the awareness of a warrior, the stance. So like Patrick. Too much like Patrick. The tingling in her temple screamed in panic. "What did you see?" She followed him to the back door. "It's probably just a stray cat—"

"Shit!" John grabbed her hand and tugged her into the yard. "Run!"

Anna didn't hesitate. She sprinted toward the back fence. John followed her.

She reached the perimeter and looked back.

The house stood, untouched.

"I don't understand," she panted.

"I heard the timer," John muttered. "I know I did."

She put her hand on his arm. "It wasn't a flashback?"

He glared at her.

"Patrick told me about the post-traumatic stress disorder," she said. "He worried about you. He knew no one else had any idea."

"We're keeping it that way," John muttered and gave her his cell phone. "Call nine-one-one. I want the bomb squad out here now."

Anna dialed. John eased closer to the house.

"Nine-one-one. What's your emergency?"

A blinking light flashed where the gas line entered.

"John!" she screamed.

A loud explosion rocked her body backward. Plumes of fire shot to the sky. Rain of fiery metal and wood pummeled against her body.

A huge piece of siding flew toward her.

She raised her arms over her head as the metal slammed her to the ground.

She lay there stunned. *Oh God.* She rolled toward the house.

John lay there. Unmoving in the darkness.

She couldn't have lost another man she…loved?

She loved John Garrison.

She struggled to her knees and crawled to him. Her head pounded; her ears rang. She touched his forehead. Blood ran from a wound near his scalp.

Somehow she'd held on to the cell phone. She raised the receiver to her ear. No sound came from it, only a high-pitched squeal inside her head.

Another explosion erupted. Fiery heat slammed into her temple.

"Oh Patrick," she groaned. "Help us."

Chapter Six

ZACH STILLED ON THE BED NEXT TO JENNA AND STUDIED HER flat expression.

Brad Walters was an assassin.

It made sense. Those inconsistencies in Brad's demeanor... Zach could see the man pulling a trigger—just for business. Still, he needed more. "You're certain?"

She tucked her legs up and wrapped her arms around her knees. "He made you believe him, didn't he? Made you think I might be crazy."

"It's not that, Jenna—"

She grabbed his hand, her determined gaze capturing his. "He murders people for money, and he used me and his son to pretend to be a normal man with a normal job. He's a professional killer and liar. He can make anyone believe anything."

Ouch. A chill skittered down Zach's back. Like him. An actor *was* a professional liar. And his job with the Company... yep, he was a killer, too. Her disgust at Brad's life hit a target in Zach's conscience.

"You asked why I ran." She let out a small laugh. "This is why. Who's going to believe a mild-mannered, very rich computer salesman is an assassin? I didn't believe it either." She rubbed her temple and winced. "Not for a long time. He was the perfect husband," she whispered.

At the heartfelt truth in her words, Zach's gut churned with mixed emotions. Jenna had clearly loved Brad, which was more than Zach had ever experienced or even witnessed, except between his parents. But he hated that she'd loved Brad, hated that her husband had betrayed her, hated that he couldn't stop wondering what it would be like to be loved by her.

"He was charming and considerate after he came home from traveling." Bitterness crept into her voice. "The first five years were great. He was attentive. Even when we fought, he simply turned cold and reserved. Then about a year and a half ago he changed. He grew even more distant, except with Sam. He was gone more often." She swallowed. "He couldn't control his temper any longer. Looking back, I think his façade cracked. Suddenly, I saw the man I married, a man who could kill, a man who could hurt the same person he claimed to love."

She rubbed her forearm. Zach moved her hand away. A fading bruise in the shape of four fingers colored her pale skin. Gut-burning anger boiled in Zach's belly. "He did this?"

She covered the offending mark. "It doesn't hurt that much anymore."

"He's hurt you worse."

She refused to meet his gaze, and bile erupted into Zach's throat. "What about Sam?"

"You have to believe, Sam came first. I protected him. Always," she said, clutching his arm. "But he knows his dad gets mad sometimes."

Zach could hear the embarrassment in her voice. "Jenna—"

"I was stupid, OK? I thought it was me. Everything was so perfect for so long. I thought it was me."

She buried her face against her knees, hiding from him.

"You know that's not true," he said. With gentle strokes, he caressed her ebony locks, all the while forcing his intense desire to kill Brad Walters into that cold, still place in his heart he never allowed anyone to see.

"I stayed," she choked out. "I stayed too long. I couldn't let Sam see any more than he'd already seen. Brad's temper, the screams. Sam started acting out, hitting the kids at school. I had to do something. I had to know why Brad had changed."

"So you started asking questions."

She raised her head and swallowed. "God, no. He blew up the one time I tried to get information out of him." She pressed her hand against her cheek. "I wasn't risking him losing control again. I snuck into his office. I wondered if business was bad...or if he'd met someone else."

Zach wanted to ease her pain, kiss her cheek where Brad had hurt her, but he knew he couldn't. "You found something."

"For the first month I denied the truth. It had to be a mistake. All the secrets; all the lies. All the strange phone calls and hang-ups." She picked at imaginary lint on the quilt. "An affair would have made divorcing him easy."

Zach didn't quench the spark of hope that flickered within him. "You're divorced?" He edged closer.

"I have the paperwork ready to be signed, but I never gave it to Brad because I found a ledger, some notes. I searched the Internet and I pieced together the truth. Brad's trips almost always coincided with someone newsworthy being killed. Accidents, explosions, kidnappings. A few suicides."

"It could have been coincidence."

"Not when I discovered the bank accounts. Millions of dollars. A ledger with dates. I had proof. I went to the FBI."

She'd made all the right moves, so how had everything gone wrong enough for her to end up terrified, stowing away in his truck with no money and no plans?

"Did they arrest him?"

"Agent Fallon listened to my story. He believed me. All I wanted was a divorce and a new identity for me and Sam. In exchange, I would give them everything I had."

"You were like manna from heaven," Zach said. "Fallon must have kissed your feet."

"He wanted more. They asked me not to start divorce proceedings until I gathered more proof. Now I wonder if Brad has a spy at the FBI. Maybe the whole thing was a ruse so I could have an *accident*. That would take care of all his problems, wouldn't it?"

"The feds asked you to *stay*?" Zach couldn't keep the shock from his voice. "With the evidence you gave them already wrapped up in a neat, tidy bow?"

"Not complete enough, evidently. Not after a decade of trying to catch him. They wanted a sure thing. They gave me listening devices to hide in the house."

Zach could see the cliff a mile away. She'd been set up. "You agreed, and somehow, Brad found out."

"I was dusting, making certain when Brad came home this time the house looked perfect and nothing was out of place so he had no reason to…"

Her voice trailed off and Zach had to fight the growl growing in his chest. He struggled to maintain control. He didn't want to frighten her. She'd been through enough.

She cleared her throat. "Anyway, one of the bugs had been tampered with. He didn't allow anyone else in the house. I knew he'd caught me. I had no choice but to leave."

"Why not go to the FBI? Wouldn't Fallon help?"

She twisted her finger, and the platinum-and-diamond wedding band glinted in the light of the bedside lamp. "I can't trust anyone. Not the police, not the FBI."

"Not me."

The words shouldn't have hurt, but they did. A lot.

"You don't understand. Brad knows things. I wasn't sure if he found the bug by accident or someone told him." She swallowed. "The guy in witness protection, Joseph Romero, the one gunned down in San Francisco yesterday? That was Brad. Romero was in protective custody and Brad still killed him. How can you fight that? How can I?"

Zach folded her hands in his. "What was your plan, Jenna? When you ran from your house—when you hid in the back of my truck—what did you think you would do?"

Jenna lifted her impossibly long lashes. Her emerald eyes shone with determination. "Disappear."

"Do you still want to vanish?"

She bit her lip and nodded.

Zach took in a deep breath. He had the means, he could help her, and it wasn't really even a question. He would help her. He had no choice. "OK, then, listen to me. I'd made plans to start a new life if I had to. I can help you disappear. I have everything set up. Fake identification, an unidentifiable car, a house bought and paid for."

Her eyes widened. "Why would *you* want to disappear? You have everything you could ever want."

"My life is a bit more complicated than it seems. Let's leave it at that."

Her forehead wrinkled in confusion. "I don't understand."

"You don't have to. The point is, I can give you a new life."

She tugged her hands from him and shook her head. "You've already helped us enough. I can't let you do any more. I'll take care of me and Sam from here."

"Really?" he challenged. "Where are you going? How will you get there? How will you avoid Brad if he's as wired in as you say he is?"

"I've survived before," she said, tilting her chin.

"And Sam?"

She winced. And there was her soft spot. Her son. As it should be.

"I can take care of him."

"He still loves his dad."

"I know." Torment laced her eyes. "He doesn't truly understand."

"Are you going to tell him you're running because Brad hurts you? Or he's a bad guy?"

"I don't know," she snapped. She lay back against the pillow. "Can I rest? I'm tired."

She closed her eyes and feigned sleep. She really was a terrible liar.

Zach rose and touched her delicate cheek. "Don't let your pride interfere with accepting my help. If not for you, for Sam."

Her lips tightened, and Zach sighed, closing the bedroom door until the slight snick indicated the latch caught. She needed help. She'd never be able to avoid Brad on her own. But she needed more than just money. She needed skills.

Before she left, Zach would have to teach her a few things about living under the radar and protecting herself. Her and Sam's lives were about to change. At least until Brad Walters was caught and prosecuted.

Zach would make certain that happened.

He walked down the hallway and paused at the entrance to the living room.

Sam stood in front of the television acting out the long, drawn-out action scene in the middle of the movie. The kid had every move down. Zach shook his head and walked past the living area to the basement stairs, hoping he could carve out an hour before the movie ended.

Once downstairs, he strode past the pool table and dartboard to a huge bookcase. He flicked a small switch and the bookcase swung away from the wall. Very James Bond, if he did say so himself, but a necessity to keep the classified information he accessed on a regular basis protected.

Because of the sensitive equipment and data, Zach had been forced to tell Seth about his hideaway. His brother's black ops experience made him the obvious choice. Seth had the clearance and the knowledge. He would be able to disassemble the room if anything happened to Zach.

He stepped into the high-tech setup and sat in front of the computer terminal. He booted up the system, opened his eye for the retinal scan, and placed his thumb on the fingerprint reader.

"Zane Morgan," he spoke into the microphone.

"Identification authenticated. Proceed," the computer's voice droned.

Why not begin with a simple search of police records involving Brad?

The machine whirred, connecting through the secure server. Zach drummed his fingers, his frown deepening. The search was taking way too long.

"Access denied," the computer voice chirped.

"What the hell?"

He reentered the request.

"Access denied. Connection terminated."

This was so not good. Someone had blocked him, and he'd alerted them to his presence. At least his Internet addresses bounced through numerous servers all over the world. Whoever had monitored his access would have to follow hundreds of false leads before finding him. It would take days, and he and Jenna would be long gone by then.

Zach switched his computer to a normal browser and typed in Brad's name.

A ton of results popped up, but none for a computer salesman from La Jolla.

Weird.

He searched the local California television stations. Surely Brad would have reported his wife missing by now.

No news stories. The man was invisible. No business articles, no record of him in the local chamber of commerce. Everybody had some mention on the Internet. What kind of man chose to be this invisible? Answer: a man who had something to hide.

He reconfigured the search for Jenna's name.

Several items popped up. Events for a preschool. A birth announcement for Sam. Not much else. The Walters gave a new meaning to "low-key."

"Is this your secret hideout?" Sam's voice piped up from the doorway.

He hovered. Zach could tell the boy was itching to enter. With a quick swivel, Zach faced the awestruck boy.

"Do you like it?"

Sam nodded and shifted from foot to foot.

"You wanna come in?"

Sam's eyes widened. "You'd let me? My dad never lets me near his stuff. One time—"

The boy paused and looked down at his feet.

Zach leaned toward Sam. "What happened?"

"He yelled. Really mean. Then Mommy yelled back." Sam lifted his gaze to Zach's. "I don't like when they yell."

"Sometimes grown-ups yell, Sam."

"I know. But I still don't like it."

Zach ruffled Sam's hair. "Do you like video games? I've got some cool ones upstairs."

Sam nodded. Zach turned off the system. If he wanted information about Brad, he'd have to find another way.

The question remained, who'd removed his access to the secure systems?

Farzam entered his cramped Kabul home after bouncing over dirt roads up the hills surrounding the city. He shouldn't be living in this pigsty. He was a scientist. An educated man. But he'd fallen mightily over the last six months. From a well-respected member of the community to practically a beggar. And all because his brother-in-law had been stupid enough to deal with the Americans. Their CIA had promised Pendar the world.

Look what it had gotten him and his sister. A spray of bullets, and their daughters taken as slaves.

A loud knock sounded on the door.

Farzam's entire body shook as he turned to the flimsy barrier. What if he didn't answer? Would they go away?

The next pounding shook the door on its hinges. He had no choice. He swallowed and slowly opened to the outside.

A man with an AK-47 shoved two filthy girls at him. "Khalid sends his regards. They're yours now. They've done their duty."

The guerilla fighter grinned, and his nieces fell to the floor in front of him.

He lifted the chin of Aliya, the older daughter. He winced at the shamed expression in her eyes. She'd been used, fully and painfully. She would never have a husband now.

"Uncle?" the girl whispered, using one hand to cover the torn clothes. "Please, don't turn us away."

"Go to the kitchen. Your aunt will care for you."

The older girl held the hand of her sister and led her out of the room. His wife let out a shocked scream.

Farzam turned so as not to reveal the sting in his eyes to the man who had delivered what was left of his sister's family. They had been on the cusp of something wonderful. Now she was dead and he was left to clothe and feed her two daughters along with his own son. His nieces would have no life. Even if they recovered from this abuse, word would disseminate. They were ruined.

"You have a son," the gun-wielding intruder snapped. "Bring him."

His wife gasped from the kitchen. "No, Farzam. No."

"Khalid wishes to be certain of your loyalty."

Farzam bowed his head. "I am loyal."

"You were educated in the West. Your words mean nothing. Khalid wants proof."

Proof? What could Farzam possibly offer? He no longer had funds, or a decent job, or access to equipment and information from any of his Western contacts.

Twelve-year-old Hamed walked into the living room, his hand in his pocket, his chin held high. "I am here, Father."

Farzam closed his eyes. He could see the beginnings of the man his son could become. If he lived that long.

"The boy has more courage than his father. Come. If your father proves his worth perhaps you will return to this hovel. Unless you find your calling with us."

Hamed followed the man from their house down the dusty road, the shacks and hovels framing his son's brave figure. In triumph, the guerilla looked back at Farzam. Hamed raised his chin, but Farzam recognized the fear.

He slammed the door and kicked at the flimsy chair in the corner. The thing shattered into pieces at his feet.

He blamed Pendar, but truthfully, his brother-in-law had simply been a fool. The true cause of everything happening he could name. One man had caused his family to lose everything.

Zane Morgan.

Proof.

If Farzam killed the CIA operative, maybe he could buy back Hamed's life and soul. Of course, Zane Morgan had disappeared in the way of all lying devils, but Farzam would find him. There had to be a way.

His wife came out of the kitchen, tears rolling down her cheeks, disappointment in her gaze. He had failed her. He wouldn't fail his son.

Slowly Farzam conjured a plan.

"Get me a traveling bag," he ordered his wife.

In silence, she complied.

Slowly, he packed a change of clothes and what little money he'd managed to hide away. He knew what he had to do to succeed in his quest. Bargain with those he despised, those who cared nothing for life. He would find Zane Morgan, and the man would pay just as Farzam's family had paid. With his life. And his soul.

———————————

Jenna hadn't intended to sleep. She glanced at the window, but no light trickled between the shutters. Darkness had fallen on the cabin. She fingered the bandage on her forehead. How long had she been out?

She swung her legs over the side of the bed, her feet warm on the heated floor. Zach Montgomery spared no expense for his creature comforts.

Zach. The man made her flutter with conflicting emotions, and she refused to acknowledge the strange attraction haunting her. She felt safe with him, and she couldn't believe she'd revealed so much to him. She still couldn't understand why he wanted to help them. Who did that for someone he'd only just met?

Jenna rose from the bed and took a survey of her body. Sore, but steady. The ache in her head had muted into a dull throb, and nausea no longer gurgled in her belly, threatening to rise to her throat.

Which meant she would leave tomorrow. Into the unknown. With her son.

Swallowing down the trepidation, Jenna padded toward the kitchen. Sam's laughter trickled out to her, the sweet voice yanking on her heart. When was the last time she'd heard her son giggle quite that way?

A low belly laugh followed and she pressed open the swinging oak door. Sam sat on a stool and threw mushrooms into a big pot. Spaghetti sauce laced with oregano wafted across the room. Her stomach rumbled.

Forcing herself to smile despite the awkward way Zach had left her room, Jenna stepped to the stove, peering into the simmering pot. "So, a man who can cook, too? Are there any more surprises?"

Zach gave her a wicked wink. "None with a G rating."

This was a different man from the one she'd met—he was a charmer and a flirt. Zach's gaze slowly scanned her T-shirt and jeans. Heat rushed to Jenna's cheeks. Nothing was sexy about this outfit, except that Zach seemed to pause on each and every curve. Jenna crossed her arms in front of her and focused on her son, anything she could do to keep her attention from the man who seemed to compel her gaze toward him with every movement.

She flicked the hair off Sam's forehead. "What are you doing, baby?"

"The Dark Avenger is making *sketti*, Mommy. I'm helping." Sam tossed in a few more mushrooms.

"I can see that."

"Do you feel like being a sous chef?" Zach asked. "We could use a salad."

Jenna nodded and walked over to the counter where fresh lettuce and tomatoes waited on the counter.

"Did you go to the store?"

"As a distraction while you were in the CAT scan. Sam here said spaghetti was your favorite."

"Oh, he did, *did he*?" She nuzzled her little boy's cheek. "It couldn't be that *someone* here decided I liked spaghetti, because it's *his* favorite food."

Sam gave Zach a sheepish look. "It's really *my* favorite."

"I got that." Zach grinned and sprinkled in a bit of cheese.

So strange. A family cooking together. Like evenings she'd spent with her father after her mother had died. She'd wanted this with Brad, but she'd learned that first week of their marriage that Brad had very specific ideas of her role as a wife. At his beck and call. A hot meal when he chose to come home. She'd shoved the disappointment aside in exchange for her so-called *perfect* life. And yet, today, a movie star in a cabin in Colorado made her feel more a part of a family than her husband ever had.

Jenna finished putting together the salad and set it on the table. "Anything else I can do?"

"You must be feeling better. How's the head?"

"Could be worse."

A timer rang.

"Grab the garlic bread from the oven," Zach said. "The basket's on the table."

Jenna tried to align the man she'd imagined to a man who had a bread basket. She quirked an eyebrow.

"My mother. She gave all of us one for Christmas a couple years ago. Said since the only dish my brothers and I knew how to make was pasta—despite her desperate tutorials in the kitchen—the only way we'd get a girl to stay past one night was if she thought we were halfway civilized."

Jenna would love to meet the woman who clearly held the power in the Montgomery clan. "I think I'd like your mother."

"Everyone does," Zach said.

"Do you see her often?" Jenna asked as she carried the bread to the table.

"Not enough." His face fell a bit. "After my dad died. Well, it was hard."

Silence spread between them. Jenna could only offer the standard sympathy. "I'm sorry about your dad."

"Yeah, me too."

Zach's mask fell away. For a moment, Jenna caught sight of something she hadn't expected. Real pain. Real suffering.

An uncomfortable quiet settled over the kitchen, with the bubbling of sauce and Sam's quiet humming the only sounds.

Jenna cleared her throat. "I lost my dad, too. When I was fourteen. Car accident."

Zach touched her arm. "That must have been tough."

His hand was warm and comforting against her arm, but she couldn't let herself lean into him. She had to be as strong as she'd been then. "I survived. Just like I'll survive now."

Zach nodded, a speculative expression on his face, then he directed his attention to Sam. "OK, buddy. Time for dinner."

Sam yelled his approval then shot across the room to the table while Zach drained the pasta. He mixed in the sauce, then carried the steaming bowl over and set it next to the Romano cheese.

Without comment, he pulled out Jenna's chair for her and she slipped into the seat. His mother had definitely taught her son manners.

In the next half an hour, Jenna laughed more than she had in years. Zach told her story after story about strange and unusual happenings on movie sets and location shoots. None of which answered the question of why he would have an elaborate escape plan ready. Should she ask him? Brad had taught her to be careful about questions.

Dampening her aroused curiosity, she pushed her chair out. "First we do the dishes, then it's time for bed, Sam."

"Aww, Mom."

"I mean it."

He bit his lip. "Where do I sleep?"

"You can sleep with me," she said, at the same time as Zach chimed in, "Down the hall."

She was dubious. "I don't think—"

"There's a room with bunk beds. If Sam wants—"

"Yes. Can I, Mommy? Please?"

"Clean the dishes and no lip."

She'd never seen her son more eager. After helping with so much enthusiasm that several puddles had to be mopped, Sam brushed his teeth—with the toothbrush Zach had purchased because he really *had* thought of everything.

Jenna tucked her son into bed and settled down beside him. She toyed with his hair.

He gazed up at her with not-completely-innocent eyes. She hated that he'd lost some of his childhood because of

Brad's temper...and that he'd lose more innocence once their life changed.

"A story," he pleaded. "Please."

She kissed his forehead. At least she could give him the gift of her father. Stories and dreams. She glanced over her shoulder. Zach wasn't there. She let out a long breath. Searching for inspiration, she noted an outline of an iron bear hanging on the wall. "Once upon a time, in the forest of a magical land, a boy lived with his mother..."

But not with his father.

She'd barely gotten to the bear winning his magical powers from the wicked wizard when Sam began to snore softly in her arms. Quietly, Jenna rose, turned on the hall light, and left the door cracked open.

She glanced around the living room and recognized the outline of Zach's broad shoulders on the porch that surrounded his cabin.

He sipped from a mug. She hesitated. Maybe she'd be better off just going back to bed. Her head still ached a bit, despite the ibuprofen she'd downed. Not so much because of the accident. Maybe more because of the uncertainty of tomorrow.

She couldn't stay. Brad would eventually find her. Of that, she had no doubt. She had to cut the last line between them—Zach.

She eased open the outside door. Zach's back stiffened a bit. She paused. "You want to be alone."

"Not really," Zach said. "Sam asleep?"

"It's been an eventful day. He couldn't stop talking about your secret room," she said, her voice full of questions.

Zach shrugged. "Just a computer room with some way-too-expensive toys." He faced her and leaned back against the wooden railing. "I ran a quick search of the news websites in California. Brad hasn't reported you or Sam missing. He doesn't want the publicity."

"What does that tell you?" Jenna asked.

"That your life is in danger. And you need me. You have since you hid out in my pool house."

A chill raced up her arms. "You knew I was there."

"I'm an observant kind of guy," he said. "I saw the towel and the empty water bottles." He tucked a lock of her hair behind her ear. "I didn't know you'd stowed away in the truck, though. You surprised me, and that doesn't often happen."

She stared at him as if he were an alien. "Who are you, Zach? Why do you say you can help me disappear? What's the truth?"

"I play a superhero on the silver screen," he said. "You pick up a few things here and there."

She reached out a hand and laid it on Zach's arm. His muscles tensed under her touch, but she didn't let go. "You're...not what I expected, Zach Montgomery. Why get involved?"

"Everyone needs choices."

His warm, strong hand covered hers. Her breath stuttered at his hooded gaze. She still couldn't get over the truth that he'd tried to help her when he didn't even know her. Who did that?

A hero?

A *real* hero?

Not a fake. Not a man who lived a lie. Not a man like her husband.

Her husband.

He lifted a finger to her cheek and trailed down the softness of her skin. She leaned into his touch.

"You're beautiful," he said, his voice dropping low and husky.

"Not like the women you know."

He raised her chin.

"You're real, Jenna. You have courage and guts. That makes you more beautiful than you realize."

His gaze dropped to her lips. Jenna's body stilled, wanting to deny what he said. She'd been a coward for far too long, but she couldn't speak. He held her captive with one look. The heat generated between them entangled her, wrapping her entire being in temptation.

"I wish—" she whispered.

"So do I," he muttered quietly. "More than you know. But it can't be."

She took a shuddering step away from him. Her entire body grew cold and chilled. She rubbed her arms. "I'd better go back inside. Before I do something…"

He clutched her. "Jenna." His gaze softened. "Tomorrow we'll find a way out of here for you."

She wanted to throw her arms around him and hug him, but she knew if he ever held her in that way, she wouldn't want to let him go. And she had to let him go.

"Leave," he ordered softly as if reading her mind. He touched her shoulder. "You're too tempting to me, and we both know giving in to temptation leads to disaster."

She nodded and backed away. He turned, the stillness in his body almost eerie.

She'd found a man who didn't take everything he wanted. Who did the right thing.

Zach Montgomery might be an enigma, but she believed in him. She'd seen him for who he was. But could she trust herself? She'd been fooled before.

She shuffled down the hall and checked on Sam.

She'd believed Brad, too.

A shiver quaked through her. How could Zach help her? Really? If Brad wanted to find her, all the money in the world wouldn't stop him.

Jenna sat on the bed and wrapped her arms around her knees.

For a moment, in Zach's presence, she'd felt hope. Hope for the first time since she'd recognized the lie her marriage had become, and the dangerous man with whom she'd entwined her life.

In the silence of this room, she couldn't stop the beasts of uncertainty from clawing at her memory. Betrayal lurked everywhere. But in the still, small space within her heart, hope glowed bright.

Maybe this time. Maybe this time she could believe.

Brad watched the ambulance pull away from the curb. *Damn it.* He should have known this assignment would be a disaster. John Garrison was a SWAT captain, but he'd seen better days. He should be dead.

Instead, he was alive.

More importantly, Brad didn't like the smell of the assignment. He knew this house.

Knew this street.

Knew this woman.

Five years ago. Five years of jobs that had grown steadily more and more risky. During the last eighteen months his client had become even more unmanageable. Brad had lost control of the situation, and now he'd screwed up. Alerted his target of the danger.

The job would be that much harder.

His phone rang.

He cursed, but knew he couldn't avoid answering. His deadly customer had too much power. Too many connections.

He regretted the day he'd ever agreed to that first contract.

"He's not dead," the filtered voice accused through the phone.

"Stating the obvious, are you?"

"You've lost your edge, Mr. Walters." Fingers drummed against the phone, each sound skewering Brad's brain with irritation. "Should I remind you once again what you have to lose?"

"You didn't tell me Garrison was dating Montgomery's widow."

A small gasp made Brad smile. Perhaps his employer didn't know everything.

"I'll get the job done," Brad added. "And I have a bone to pick with the Montgomerys, so just back the hell off."

He ended the call and watched as the house fire blazed on.

Brad didn't like coincidence. The moment he'd realized who Zach Montgomery was, he should have moved. But moving attracted attention. Caused records to be created. He'd played it safe.

Too safe.

He pulled one thousand and fifty dollars from his pocket and thumbed the bills—the money Zach Montgomery had obviously left for Jenna. Proof of his lies. And a potential lead to his traitor wife. Brad needed to question Zach.

Perhaps this awkward situation would work out for the best. Zach Montgomery would care that his mother had been hurt. He'd come home. He could have a lead on Jenna.

Brad's phone rang again. He cursed at the number and didn't pick up.

A huge risk. And another loose end.

Brad flicked his thumb over his pinky. Yes, if Montgomery cooperated, Brad might be able to tie up his loose ends sooner than he'd expected.

Chapter Seven

*A*BOVE ZACH, THE STARS GLEAMED. A HERMIT THRUSH TRILLED from the pines surrounding his cabin. Crickets chirped a farewell to Jenna as she left him standing alone in the night.

Zach glanced over his shoulder and sighed at the sway of her hips as she disappeared into his haven. He couldn't deny the attraction. His entire body thrummed with want, but Jenna Walters wasn't an affair kind of woman.

She was the forever kind.

Something he could never have. Even if he survived the next few days.

He leaned forward against the pine rails. Knots from the hand-carved wood pressed into his palms. The crispness of snow tickled his throat. He couldn't see the peaks through the surrounding forest, but he could feel their snow-covered majesty. If they could only hide him from the world, he might very well follow Jenna back into the house and beg her to stay.

A week ago, he wouldn't have doubted his next move; he would have called the Company. But the cut across his chest remained a grim reminder of betrayal on that airplane. Once he made a phone call, no matter how secure his connection, they'd track him eventually. He could route through numerous towers to delay the tracking dogs, but he couldn't hide forever.

A second bird joined in with the thrush, maybe a blackbird. The two very different species had quite a dialogue going on before one went silent. Not unlike him and Jenna. Two birds passing each other in flight, yet destined to travel alone.

Zach wished he didn't care. He shouldn't. She'd stolen his truck, run from him…tempted him in ways she shouldn't. But he did care. He wanted her and Sam to be safe. To accomplish that, he needed information on Brad.

To get the data he needed, Zach had to hang in the wind—a big target nailed to his naked ass.

With a last look at the one place on earth he'd felt completely secure, he turned his back on serenity and walked inside. After locking the door, he did a quick check on Jenna and Sam before heading down the stairs, his footsteps heavy on the wood floors.

He entered the communications center, booted everything up, and connected his cell to the relay program.

A flurry of tones sounded after he entered in his access code. This should be interesting.

"Where have you been?" Theresa shouted through the phone, more concerned than he'd ever heard her.

Zach pulled the receiver away from his ear. "Lying low."

Not exactly the truth. The trip to the clinic and being scoped out by tourists wasn't exactly covert.

"They've cut you off," she said tensely. "They discovered you were going through files you weren't authorized to access, but I don't know who ordered the block. You're not helping me keep your job, Zach."

He leaned back in his chair. His father's files. About nine months ago, Luke had told the family that their father hadn't been forthright about his military service. Zach had wanted to know why. He'd needed to know. He'd thought he'd been careful.

"I didn't compromise national security, Theresa. And I already figured out someone cut me off. I tried to get into the system."

A sailor's curse escaped her. "You need to come in. If you stay AWOL too long, I can't protect you."

"I need a bit more than reassurance from the Company. Who got to those two pilots?"

He allowed the words to settle between them.

"I don't know," she said after a long silence. "I haven't been able to discover who leaked your location in Turkey or who paid off the pilots, but I'll keep pushing. It might go high up, Zach. I'm just not sure."

He didn't like the doubt in her voice. A few clicks sounded on the phone. He recognized them. Someone was listening. And not on his end. "Don't say anything else," he muttered and cleared his throat, a signal between them from way back. "What would you think if you were me?"

"I wouldn't trust anyone," she said, her voice understanding his hidden signal. "Not even me."

She tapped a few keys and a small hum sounded. "Clear," she said.

"I need information. Brad Walters. Who is he? I want deep background. ASAP."

Silence lingered over the phone, and with no comforting birdcalls or quaking aspens in the background, only busy office mumblings. She muttered under her breath, phrases with so many four-letter words it would've caused his mother to rinse out her mouth with soap. The click-click of typing sounded. Zach smiled. Finally he'd get what he needed.

"What a white-bread guy," Theresa mused. "Barely a blip. Which in itself is—"

"Suspicious." Zach shoved his hand through his hair. "Dig deeper. I need to know who this guy's contacts are, what he does for a living, his bank balance, and what he likes for breakfast."

"You don't ask for much. How long do I have?"

Zach glanced at his watch. "Nine in the morning." Even Theresa couldn't cut through enough red tape to arrange for transportation, get from DC to Denver and then to his cabin that quickly—*if* they'd been able to follow his signal. He studied the communication center's control panel. He still showed green... meaning he hadn't been tracked yet.

"What are you into, Zach? You're not asking for information on who's out to get you. This guy's name comes from nowhere." Her voice lowered. "Have you picked up another stray kitten? That could be as dangerous for your new pet as it was for Pendar."

Ouch. She knew just where to hurt him, and she'd done it on purpose. She'd been part of his evaluation team when he'd twisted Seth's arm into getting Zach into the Company. She knew his buttons. He wouldn't mention Jenna. He'd keep her invisible until he could get her out of his life. "I'm not taking the bait. Just run Brad Walters."

She sighed. "I can't guarantee your safety. I don't know who ordered the hit, but I can find out. Let's meet. You give me the time or the place. I'll be there."

"I have business to deal with before I put myself out in the open as bait. First, find out who Brad Walters is, and then we'll talk."

The clicking of keys sounded through the line. With enough time, Theresa could uncover everything there was to know about Brad Walters.

"You took a big risk calling me," Theresa acknowledged. "Hope she's worth it."

He didn't say a word, just ended the call. Damn she was good.

The smell of fresh coffee could wake a dead man. Even one dead tired. Zach didn't open his eyes. He sensed the light through closed lids, knowing the early morning rays would have created a pattern on the quilt his mother gave him. The smell of dew permeated the room and the soft mattress made him not want to move. He hunched to drag the quilt over his head when the door creaked open. His hand slid under his pillow and palmed the 1911. He didn't move, didn't reveal he'd heard a thing.

A small tennis shoe squeaked on the oak floors in a failed attempt to be quiet. Zach released his grip on the weapon. He rolled over and opened one eye, nearly bursting out laughing as Sam froze into place.

He quirked a brow at the small intruder.

"Mommy's cooking breakfast," the boy whispered loudly. "I'm s'posed to ask if you like pancakes, but I'm not s'posed to bother you."

"Pancakes are worth bothering me for," Zach said, with a groan in appreciation. How long since he'd had a home-cooked meal? Since he'd gone home. At his brother's wedding almost a year ago, maybe. "Tell your mom I'll be right there."

Sam ran from the room. Zach sat at the edge of the bed and tugged on jeans and a black T-shirt. He rubbed his hands through his hair and yawned. Morning had come too early. He'd searched all the databases he could hack into without using his clearance. The phone call had been risky enough. Brad Walters was too much of a mystery. Assassin, computer salesman. Both? He needed details.

With his eyes half closed, he tugged open the nightstand's drawer, drew out another of his spare phones, and dialed the classified number. The tones repeated in his ear, each series clawing his nerves like a cricket stuck in the walls.

A message came on. "Zach, I have to leave the country. I didn't finish…" She paused. "…your request. I will. Be careful."

"Damn it." Zach didn't have time to wait for information about Brad. Jenna and Sam could wind up in the crossfire between him and whoever wanted him dead. By afternoon he needed Jenna and Sam to be gone, and he'd follow their lead—in the opposite direction.

Depressed, he padded barefoot into the kitchen, assaulted by the heavenly scent of bacon along with the dark roasted coffee he kept in the freezer. "Java and bacon. I may have to marry you," he said, breathing in the scents, letting them tickle his palate and revive his mind.

"My mommy belongs to Daddy and me," Sam said, his voice sharp. "You can't have her."

Zach's eyelids snapped open. The boy crossed his arms and stood in front of his mother, legs apart, mutinous as a five-year-old warrior.

"I know, buddy," Zach said. "But she sure can…cook. I just wished I could have someone cook for me like that all the time."

Jenna glanced at him over her shoulder. Her face flushed and she placed a plate on the table. "Eat up, Sam. We have to wash your clothes from yesterday."

Zach poured a cup of coffee and wrapped his hands around the hot mug. One taste and he moaned, the smooth flavor bathing his mouth in ecstasy. "What did you do to my coffee maker? It never creates ambrosia like this."

He lifted his gaze to Jenna and the blush crept all the way to her ears. He shoved back a rough oak chair and sank behind the table, taking another sip of heaven. "I don't want to, but we need to go to town later. For a change of clothes and whatever you need for your trip."

Jenna turned the bacon over in the skillet. "Is it safe?" Grease crackled as she pushed around the strips with a meat fork.

"It won't get safer, and I'm not ordering anything delivered here. You're leaving today."

Sam struggled to pull out the chair next to Zach. He sat down and frowned. "But I like it here."

"So do I, buddy." Zach ruffled Sam's hair. "But sometimes—"

"We gotta do what we don't like." Sam stuck out his lower lip. "I know."

"How about after breakfast we find you a movie while your mom and I do some grown-up stuff."

"Mommy does grown-up stuff with Daddy a lot. She lets me watch *Dark Avenger* when they hide in their room."

Jenna dropped the meat fork onto the plate where she'd doled out the bacon. Bacon catapulted off the plate. She raced to the sink and tugged a paper towel from its holder to clean up the mess.

Zach jumped up and grabbed the precariously balanced skillet from her hand and set it in the sink. The hot pan sizzled when it hit the water. With a sidelong glance he studied

Jenna's mortified expression. His entire being urged him to comfort her, even as the images of Brad and Jenna curled together slithered through his brain like deadly serpents. As much as it turned his gut, he prayed Brad had taken her to bed and not used the privacy to create more of the faded bruises he'd seen on her arm.

He shoved aside the jealousy he had no right to feel and pasted on a fake and shallow smile. "The movie's in the player in the living room. Give me a half hour to shower and shave and we'll meet downstairs." He snagged three strips of bacon and bit down hard. "Man, that's good."

"What are we going to do while Sam's watching your movie?" she asked, her voice slow and cautious.

He could smell the caution lacing her words; he abhorred the fear in her eyes. He'd like to castrate Brad Walters just for that. "I'm going to teach you a few ways to crack my balls—and anyone else's."

Jenna hovered at the top of the stairs in trepidation. She glanced over her shoulder. Sam mimicked the Dark Avenger's moves in front of the television, his little body twisting and kicking. His tongue stuck out in concentration. The familiar expression tugged at her heart. Focused, and without fear. When he tumbled onto his backside, he laughed, stood, and kept right on going. She could learn from her son.

"Are you just going to stand there, or do you have the courage to venture into my lair?" Zach challenged, using a line from his movie.

"I have the courage," Jenna countered. "Do you have chocolate ice cream?"

He laughed and looked up the stairs at her. "Not bad. You could be an actress."

At his words, she paused at the bottom of the oak steps. "I've learned to lie and keep secrets for the last year. I didn't like it."

Zach's smile faded away. "You'll have to get used to it. Lies can be wearing, but they can also save your life." The form-fitting black T-shirt hugged Zach's torso. He didn't have an ounce of fat on him. His muscles rippled. He had to spend hours a day working out.

He crooked his finger at her from the doorway of a room with blinking lights and toys. He did have a superhero's lair down here. She crossed the spongy mat he'd laid out on the floor.

"How's your head?" he asked, probing at the cut just beneath her hairline.

Surprised that his touch didn't hurt, she pressed against her wound. "I thought I'd have a headache, but I didn't even need a pain pill this morning."

"Good," Zach said with a prying gaze. "I don't want to hold back."

She shifted in discomfort. As a distraction, she pointed to the desk, littered with electronics. "What is all this stuff?"

"A few toys."

He pulled out a folder and slapped it down on the wood. "Before we start, are you certain you want to disappear, Jenna?"

"Do you have a better idea?"

"The best option is for you to give me the proof that Brad Walters is an assassin. I'll find an honest government official and Brad goes to prison for the rest of his life."

The words sounded good, something from a happy ending, but she knew better. "I tried that with Agent Fallon. I trusted him, but he lied to me. He's acted really strange ever since they tied Brad to the Chameleon."

Zach stilled and faced Jenna. "Your husband is the Chameleon?" He shoved his hand into his hair.

"That's the same reaction Fallon had. That's why he wanted me to stay with Brad until they had proof."

Zach kneaded the back of his neck. "Holy hell, Jenna. That guy's on every agency's wanted list from here to Istanbul. No one's been able to catch him. They don't even know how many people he's killed. He's *that* good. He has no regular modus operandi. The man is an encyclopedia in methods to murder."

"I know," Jenna said, swallowing the churning her stomach. "And he's killed one hundred and seventy-eight people in the last decade."

A long, low whistle escaped from Zach. "You have names, dates, the works?"

She shook her head. "I have dates, initials, and dollars. A few travel receipts."

"And they didn't run the bastard in." Lines narrowed on Zach's forehead. "Right. No FBI." He faced Jenna, his expression troubled. "You were right not to trust them, Jenna." His hand stroked her cheek. "If I had more time, I'd work this differently, but I don't have a choice. Come here." He reached for a small electronic gadget on the table. "You'll need communication. Use prepaid phones. Switch them out once a month." He turned the small device over in his hand. "Hook this to the power source when you're making a call. It will jam any tracking."

Zach set down the phone attachment and picked up a small box. "This will turn your phone into secure Internet access without you ever having to sign up."

"That's not possible," she said.

"Really?" He quirked a brow.

Heat rushed into her cheeks. "How'd you get all this? Brad loves his gadgets, and I've never seen anything like these," Jenna said, turning over the items in her hands.

"Being in high-tech movies gets me access to lots of gizmos," Zach said, meeting her gaze with his own steady look.

She recognized the unflinching, deceitful stare, and she hated it. She'd seen it too much after her father died, and now realized how often Brad had pulled it on her, but she'd been too in love to notice. No longer. She placed the items on the table. "You're lying. Please, Zach. Don't lie to me. If you can't tell me, say so, but don't lie."

He tilted his head and studied her. She met his look unblinking, her chin raised, determination vibrating through every cell.

"You've got good instincts," he said finally, not denying the accusation. "Trust them, no one else."

"Not even you?"

"Especially not me."

Then what was she doing here, with him, alone in his basement?

He took her hand and pulled her to the mat. "You only have to remember a few things. Pay cash for everything. Don't fill out any forms requiring an address for at least a year. Lastly, know how to defend yourself and run."

"I can't even rent an apartment without signing my name and allowing a credit check."

"You won't have to. I've taken care of everything, Jenna. You'll have a place to live, money, and food. But be guarded. Always." He nodded toward the white packet on the table. "It's all in that envelope. I'll go through it later. For now, we work on self-defense. Have you taken any classes?"

She shook her head. "I tried a year ago. Brad found out. He wasn't happy." She rubbed her arm. The bruises had taken days to heal that time. "I had a few practical lessons when I was fourteen, though. I can handle myself."

"Really?"

Zach grabbed her by the waist and threw her down to the mat. He pressed his foot against her throat. "You're dead."

Jenna swallowed and gripped his sneaker. She shoved him away. "I wasn't ready."

"You have to always be ready. Get up."

She stood and backed away, her legs shaking.

"Don't show me fear. I don't care if you're scared out of your mind, don't show it. Never show it."

Zach didn't give her time to think. He lunged at her again, his hands moving to her throat. She stumbled back, lost her balance, and hit the ground. Even with the mat, the blow jarred her entire body. She slapped her hand on the vinyl. "Crap."

"You're afraid of me."

She glared at him. "You're bigger than I am."

He held out his hand and pulled her up. "Size matters. I won't say it doesn't, but you can use it against me. When I come after you this time, cover your head with both hands and duck. Then ram me with your head and shoulder. Use your entire body weight to knock me off balance."

Zach charged. Jenna ducked and pushed at him.

He twisted and had her flat on her back in seconds, his forearm at her throat. "You're dead because you held back." He glowered at her. "Never, ever hold back, or you and Sam won't survive."

She sank into the vinyl foam gasping for air. She gripped his arm and heaved at it. "Get off me," she shouted.

"That's it. Be angry. Show me the woman who hot-wired and stole my favorite truck."

She bounced up and planted her feet. "Do it again." Energy rushed into her muscles. Everything slowed down. This time when Zach pounced at her, she ducked and covered, then used all her strength to push him.

He stumbled back, a big smile on his face. "That's it. I'm off balance. So, what do you do now?"

"Run."

"If he's injured or if you have time, run like hell. What if he's like me? I stumbled, but I can trip you."

He swept a leg under hers. She fell to the mat.

She glared at him.

"Remember this, Jenna. Whatever happens before you severely injure the guy doesn't matter. Just like in a boxing match, the first ten rounds don't matter if the guy who's getting pummeled lands one lethal blow." He leaned over her, his gaze intense and deadly. "If he's hitting you, hurting you, punching you, and you can still fight, you have a chance. Don't give up. That's all that matters. One good blow to the eye, the groin, or the throat, you can take him out. That's all you need. One good hit."

"Eye, groin, throat," she repeated. "One hit."

Zach rose. "You're on the ground, you've got great leverage. Take your heel, kick me in the nuts."

She pulled back her knee and paused. "As hard as I can?"

"Do it."

Jenna closed her eyes and kicked out with all her strength. Her foot hit flesh.

"Never close your eyes," he growled. His hands clutched her heel. "Most attackers won't expect you to fight back when you're down. They think they have the advantage. Turn the tables." He pulled her to her feet. "Again."

Zach shoved her to floor. Jenna twisted and kicked with all her might. He jumped back, hips first, just in time to avoid her heel in his groin. She frowned, but Zach smiled. "You're a natural."

She couldn't stop the pride rushing inside her. She faced him. "What if he grabs me?"

Zach took her through three more moves. She didn't know how much time had passed when she finally stared in triumph down at Zach. Sweat dripped off her face, her entire body ached, but she'd tripped him.

"Yes!" She punched her fist in the air.

Zach grinned up at her. "You got it."

She smiled back, then a horrifying thought raced through her mind. "What if Sam's with me? He can't run that fast. What if I need to really hurt Brad to protect Sam?"

Zach bounded up and put his hands around her throat. "What are the three areas?"

"Eyes, throat, groin," she repeated.

"If you hesitate, you die."

She nodded.

"Push your hands between his arms. Stick him in the eye with anything sharp. A pin, a stick, but visualize it going to the back of his head. Don't hold back. Blind him." Zach took one hand in his and folded her fingers at the second knuckle. "Make the attack surface small. He's less likely to block you. Shove your knuckles at his Adam's apple as if you're punching straight through his neck. Put all your body weight behind it. You'll break his larynx. He won't be able to breathe. If he can't breathe, he's dead. That's your death blow. There's no halfway."

She closed her eyes. No halfway. Could she do this?

His warm hand cupped hers and showed her the move, past his neck, even with the back of his throat. "Lean forward. Feel it?"

"My weight follows my arm."

"Exactly."

"If you go for his balls, you won't kill him, but he'll wish you had. At your size, the target should be within easy reach. Grab as much tissue as you can, then squeeze, twist and tear with everything you've got." He twisted his wrist, mimicking his words. "Say it."

"Grab, twist, tear." She wrinkled her nose at the gruesome image.

"How do you think I feel? But don't consider the damage. It's him or you. Pull the rocks off him. No hesitation. Even through clothes you'll hurt him. I guarantee he'll fall to his knees."

He lowered her hand to his groin. She didn't even have to bend her knees to reach the vulnerable part of his body. Her hand brushed against him. His body quivered. Zach sucked in a breath.

She dropped her hand and stepped back.

Zach stared her down, his face unreadable. "Like I said, it's a tender spot. Do it again."

"What?" she squeaked.

He winked at her. "While I'd love to have you explore me to your heart's content, we both know that's a bad idea. I meant, let's try the chokehold again. Last move. Then we head to town."

"Come at me," she ordered.

Zach charged. He grabbed her neck.

"Mommy!"

Sam ran into the room and jumped on Zach's leg, pummeling him. "Stop. Stop. Stop," he screamed, crying.

Her heart broke at her son's desperation. She'd stayed with Brad too long.

Zach knelt to the ground and grabbed Sam. "Quiet, Sam. I'm not hurting her."

Sam shook his head back and forth, closing his eyes, shoving his fists into Zach's chest.

Jenna put her hand on Sam's back. "I'm fine. Zach was helping me."

Sam slowed his punches, then opened his eyes. "Really?"

He squinted at Zach, his look hopeful, and way too suspicious for such a little guy. Jenna swallowed down the regret.

"Your mommy needs to know how to fight off bad guys, don't you think?"

"Like the Dark Avenger." Sam bit his lip. "Yes, but so do I."

Jenna opened her mouth to protest. Zach shut her down with one look. "You want to be a Junior Avenger?"

"Please." Sam nodded his head so hard he could very well have shaken it off.

Zach straightened. "Stand in the middle of the mat."

Her son did and looked expectantly at Zach.

"If a bad guy comes after you, Sam, there's one place that you can hit him that will really, really hurt."

"Where?"

"Before I tell you, you have to promise me something. Deal?"

"I promise." He crossed his heart.

"If someone tries to hurt you or your mommy," Zach said, his voice serious, "you need to run away."

"I won't leave Mommy."

"Until you're a grown-up, you need to find someone bigger to help, Sam. Someone you trust."

"Like you, Dark Avenger."

Zach ruffled Sam's hair. "Like the Dark Avenger." Zach planted his feet in front of her son. "If the bad guy comes at you, and you can't run, don't wait. Hit him really hard before he can even grab you, but not on his leg." Zach pointed between his legs. "Right here. As—"

Sam reached out and slugged Zach.

"Humph." Zach's face paled, and he bent over and cupped his groin.

"Like that?" Sam asked.

Jenna winced and squeezed her legs together in empathy. With eyes full of pain, Zach reached out for a high-five from Sam.

Who did that? Once again, he amazed her. He would make a wonderful father.

"Exactly like that," he coughed. "Good job. What do you do next?" he said, his voice breathless.

"Run away," Sam said, chest stuck out with pride.

"And go for help," Zach added.

Sam whirled around. "See, Mommy, I did it. I'm a Junior Avenger." He ran to her and threw his arms around her.

"Good job, baby." Jenna kissed his hair then met Zach's gaze. "You all right?" she mouthed.

"I'll live." The words came out slowly with a whoosh of air. He straightened, adjusted himself, then shook his head at Jenna. "Your son certainly knows how to ruin a mood."

———————

Jenna scanned the discount store aisle once again, her entire body tense. Even though they'd done nothing to attract attention, she couldn't stop the edginess that had settled over her. Her muscles ached after Zach's workout. She wished she had another week with him, but they only had a few hours left together.

The melancholy she'd been fighting since they arrived in Hidden Springs tugged at her. She'd only known him a day, and yet somehow Zach Montgomery had wormed himself into her life. She wouldn't forget what he'd done.

She'd never forget him.

Zach grabbed a bottle of baby aspirin from a shelf and dumped it into the cart. The mound had exploded into a mountain.

"It's too much," she argued.

He turned on her and crossed his arms over his chest. "Haven't we covered this already?"

"You went overboard," she muttered, her jaw tightening.

They passed by the toy aisle, and Sam paused, peering at the overflowing selection of sports toys.

"Want something, Sam?" Zach asked.

He knelt in front of her son, and Jenna sighed in appreciation. Zach's jeans cupped his backside in all the right places.

She'd spent two hours this morning touching most every inch of him. Those muscles weren't airbrushed. Granted he'd thrown her down and choked her, but in the process she'd explored every definition of every muscle. She couldn't stop staring. He was gorgeous, but she'd met drop-dead handsome men before. Her old neighborhood had been full of them. None of them had tempted her like Zach. He was sigh-worthy, all right. And not just because every woman in America wanted him.

Because he cared. He refused to tell her why he had an escape plan for himself, but she recognized he was sacrificing his arrangements to give her and Sam a shot at a new future.

His soul tempted her much more than the eye candy of great pecs and abs.

Besides, she couldn't deny the wicked grin and mischievous expression in his eyes didn't hurt. Neither did the concern with which he looked at her son.

Sam eyed the baseball mitt with a longing that couldn't be missed.

Zach picked it up. "You want the glove?" he asked.

Sam bowed his head. "My dad plays ball with me. We were going to a game. What's today, Mommy?"

"Friday, June twenty-ninth."

"Daddy's taking me to the baseball game on Saturday. Is that why we're leaving?"

Zach met her gaze over Sam's head.

"He may not be able to take you this time," she lied softly.

"But he promised." Sam crossed his arms. "Is he still in time-out? He's been in time-out a really long time already."

"How about you and I play catch at the cabin when we get back?" Zach tossed the ball from hand to hand.

"I don't want to." Sam stuck his lip out and threw down the mitt. "Besides, we're leaving today. You don't want me." He stalked down the aisle.

"Sam," Jenna called out, her cheeks flushing with as much embarrassment as regret.

Zach picked up the mitt, snagged a ball, and set it in the cart. "Just in case."

"I'll be back," she said, and took off after her son.

Sam plopped down on the vinyl floor and kicked at a large toy car sitting on display, his arms folded.

Jenna walked down the hallway, frustration warring with sympathy. The last two days had been hard, emotionally draining, and Sam didn't have any idea how their lives would change in the next few hours. Still, that didn't justify his behavior. "What do you think you're doing, Samuel Walters?"

"Why did you say Daddy won't take me to the game? He *always* takes me after he's been in time-out."

"Your dad has to work," Jenna lied again, biting her lip, hating herself, praying Sam would understand someday.

"Last time, you promised I could go to the game. You *lied* to me, Mommy."

Man, her kid knew how to dissect her heart. How could she make him understand? "Grown-ups sometimes make promises they can't keep," she whispered, pushing back his hair. "I'm sorry you can't go to the ballgame, but when you get big, sometimes you have to do things—"

"…you don't want to. I don't like being a big kid," he said with a pout.

She wrapped her arms around him for a hug. "Me either, Sam."

Her son sat stiff in her arms. She rose and held out her hand. He glared at her. She didn't budge, didn't flinch. She could stare her son down, as long as it took. After a full thirty seconds—longer than she'd expected he'd last—her stubborn boy finally blinked.

"I give." He rose to his feet.

"And…?"

"I'm sorry," he bowed his head.

"That's better. Let's go find the Dark Avenger."

A horrified expression twisted Sam's face. "He's going to think I'm bad."

She ruffled his hair. "I think he'll understand. I bet his dad—"

"The Dark Avenger didn't have a daddy," Sam said, knowingly. "It said so in the movie. Do you think he's lonely?"

"I hope not."

"Me too," Sam said. "Everyone should have a daddy who takes care of them."

Emotion clogged Jenna's throat at her son's words. They walked back to Zach, who had filled the cart even higher. She glanced down at the panties and bras…in just her size.

She flushed slightly. "You were…thorough."

"Is everything all right?"

She pushed Sam forward.

He scuffed his shoe on the floor. "I'm sorry, Dark Avenger, sir. I didn't mean to be bad."

"We all have our days, Sam. You're due yours."

Her son's brow furrowed, but Zach smiled and handed him the mitt.

"I can still have it?" Sam's eyes widened with surprise and joy.

"Every kid needs a baseball glove."

"Did you have one?"

Jenna studied the change on Zach's face, the flash of pain he couldn't hide. He sighed. "I wasn't the baseball type."

"'Cause of your daddy being gone?" Sam asked.

Zach stared at the boy, stunned. "What do you mean?"

"The Dark Avenger didn't have anyone to teach him to play baseball. Not a daddy anyway."

"Right." Zach cleared his throat. "Something like that."

Muscles throbbed in Zach's jaw. Jenna distracted Sam with his mitt, but kept her gaze on Zach. For only the second time, she saw him lose that glint in his eyes. Whatever his relationship with his father, Zach hurt, and missed him.

Once they were in the checkout line, though, he acted as if nothing had happened. He teased Sam and winked at her when he threw her unmentionables on the conveyer belt. Finally, the last item crossed the scanner. Zach pulled out a wad of cash.

Jenna grabbed the receipt from him and stared at the number. "Oh my goodness." She stared up at him. "I don't know when I can pay you back."

"Do I look worried?"

She stuffed the receipt in her pocket. "Well, I am," she said as they left the store.

Jenna walked beside him. He pushed the overflowing cart toward the Range Rover. Sam skipped behind them.

A fast clicking noise sounded off to the side. "Hey, Zach. Why are you hiding out in the middle of nowhere? Is that your kid?"

Chapter Eight

*T*HE PARKING LOT WAS AN OBSTACLE COURSE OF CARS, SHOPPERS, and carts. A paparazzo moved in closer. The clicking spree started again. Zach rounded on the photographer. With a surprisingly quick sidestep, the guy weaved between a plethora of parked cars toward Sam, camera pointed at the boy's face.

The guy cleared the hurdles between him and Jenna's son. He had a clear shot. Zach lunged toward Sam just as the little guy darted his way. Zach couldn't stop fast enough. He ran over his Junior Avenger and knocked him into the pavement.

The kid held his hand against the back of his head, tears stinging his eyes, shock on his face. One more way Zach had hurt the boy.

The photographer dove behind a vehicle, snapping pictures as if he'd won the lottery.

"Get your son in the car," Zach growled, careful not to use their names in front of the paparazzo. He shoved Sam into Jenna's arms, forcing himself not to think about the boy's tear-stained face.

The clicking rolled on like a machine gun.

Jenna snagged her son, flung open the car's door, and pushed him inside. Zach could hardly stand the fearful expression on the boy's face.

Zach pivoted toward the man now hiding behind a Jeep, snapping pictures of all of them. With one smooth move, he slid across the trunk and swiped his leg along the photographer's lower body. The man hurled into the hot asphalt. His camera skidded out of his hands. Zach scooped up the equipment and popped the SD card from its slot.

"You can't do that!" the paparazzo screamed.

"I just did," Zach said. "Now get out of here before I knock you out for invading my privacy."

"You're public property. Don't complain about getting what you wanted."

Jenna and Sam hadn't signed up to be on display, though.

"I object now." Zach tossed the camera across the parking lot, and it shattered into pieces. He let some bills fly at the man. "Clear out of here before I really get pissed."

The man ran to his broken equipment. "You'll pay for this," he shouted.

"Not if you don't find me." Zach glanced past Jenna into the Range Rover. Sam's eyes remained wide and terrified. Zach let out a slow rush of air. "Is he all right?"

Jenna flung open the door and Sam threw himself at his mother. She hugged him close. He whimpered when she explored the back of his head. "A bump," Jenna said, her voice soothing, "but you're tough, aren't you, baby."

Sam nodded and gave her a tremulous smile. She kissed his cheek, then turned.

Zach winced at the accusation in her eyes.

She closed the door on her son. "I promised him a movie while we pack. He's a little freaked out. So am I. That guy took our picture. What if Brad—"

Zach raised the SD card. "I got the pictures."

She kneaded the muscles at the base of her neck and met his gaze. "We can't stay here, Zach. Not with you."

The words were too true, and stung more than they should have. Zach rubbed his chest to alleviate the invisible pain. "I know." If he'd imagined that Jenna and Sam wouldn't have to leave today, the unrealistic hope had vanished in one click of the camera.

Zach scanned the parking lot. For such a small town, too many shoppers stood gaping. "We're attracting attention," he said, and pushed their cart toward the back of the vehicle. "Show's over, folks," he shouted.

At his confrontation, the looky-loos stared anywhere but at them and quickly packed up their groceries or disappeared into the store.

Zach thrust the first bag into the back of the Range Rover, taking his frustration out on the sacks of clothes and supplies Jenna would use when she left him for good.

Jenna passed him a sack from the cart. "How did the photographer find us?"

Zach took the merchandise and stowed it. "There was a couple in the clinic who recognized me. I'd bet on them." He shoved his fingers through his hair. "Let's get out of here. This paparazzo, singular, may just be the first wave of paparazzi, plural."

Zach stuffed the last of the supplies into his car, the cold fury at being caught reverberating through him when he slammed the tailgate. He paused; his neck tensed, the hairs standing at attention. He perused the surroundings. Suddenly, the parking lot was empty of people.

"What's wrong?" Jenna asked, her voice low and tense.

"Maybe nothing. Keep an eye out. I want to check something." He knelt next to the truck.

"Should I get Sam out?"

"Not yet, but be ready."

The instincts that had saved Zach's life more than he cared to admit sounded in his head. He scooted under the vehicle and plucked a small but powerful flashlight from his pocket. After a visual search, he ran his fingers along the rear axle feeling for tracking devices or worse. He let out a quick exhale. Nothing. He slid out and checked under the hood for the same.

"Let's go," he said quietly. "I want you away from here."

Zach tossed the new prepaid cell phone into the front seat and opened the door for Jenna. She grabbed the handle to heave herself into the tall vehicle when two men came out of nowhere. Before Zach could react, the leader grabbed her, pulling her close.

"You weren't hard to find, Zach," the man said. "You don't seem to truly understand what lying low means."

Zach froze. The same words he'd said to Theresa. His calls *were* being monitored.

"Come with us." The man opened his jacket and revealed an Uzi under his coat.

"Did you just walk off my movie set, Brutus?" Zach said with a smile, sticking his unknown adversary with a traitor's name.

"Nice try, Montgomery, but you won't learn my identity so easily. I thought you were supposed to be one of the best at the game."

Zach shifted his body, searching for a good angle. "Jenna, get in the car."

She tugged her arm.

"Don't try anything, lady, or you and your kid won't leave this parking lot alive."

Zach's body tensed, struggling not to react to the deadly weapon just inches from her. "Jenna, get inside and lock the doors," Zach ordered, raising his hands. "I'm giving her the keys. She has nothing to do with our...supervisors' *request* for my presence."

Brutus loosened his grip a bit.

Jenna's hand folded just like he'd taught her.

She wouldn't dare.

Zach stepped forward.

She pivoted on one foot and shoved her knuckles into the guy's throat.

She didn't follow through. *Shit.* Brutus growled and shoved her face to the pavement. He whipped out his Uzi, pointing the barrel at a terrified Sam. "This is on your head, Montgomery," he yelled.

"Duck, kid!" Zach yelled. Sam's head went down. Zach spun around and shoved his foot into Brutus's neck, shattering his larynx. He crumpled to the ground trying to no avail to suck in air. The gun clattered to the ground.

Brutus was dead.

Too late to save his comrade, the other man jumped into the fray.

His mistake was ignoring a still-downed Jenna. She cocked her leg as he stepped past her. She shoved her heel into the guy's groin. He doubled over with a grunt.

"Like I said, a natural." Zach pounced onto the moaning man, holding his 1911 against the man's temple. "Who sent you?"

The operative's red face twisted in pain, but he pursed his lips. Zach bent closer. "Listen to me, buddy. I could end you right now. You know it. So do I."

"You do, and you're rogue," the man said. "The Company wants to talk to you."

"Two of our pilots tried to kill me," Zach said, his voice flat. "Your friend here threatened to take out a five-year-old child. I'm not coming in until I know who ordered the hit. You tell our *supervisors* that."

The man's eyes widened.

"So, they didn't give you that little piece of information." Zach rose but didn't let the sight of his 1911 waver from the guy's temple. "Clean up this mess and don't bother coming back to Hidden Springs. I won't be here. Which ticks me off by the way, 'cause I really like this town."

"What am I supposed to tell them?"

"That they trained me well. I won't die easy."

The man lugged Brutus's body over his shoulder and stalked off while Zach covered him. He committed the license plate to memory as the guy drove off. It wouldn't matter. The plate would be untraceable.

Zach held out his hand to Jenna. "You lost your follow-through with Brutus, but the other guy, you nailed him. Good job."

Her hand shook as he lifted her to her feet. "Who are you really?" she whispered. "Because I know you didn't learn that on a movie set."

"I could have."

"You killed him," she whispered.

"It was him or Sam," Zach said.

"I'm a basket case; you didn't flinch." Jenna tugged her hand from his and stepped away. "Please. Who are you?"

He hated the fear on her face, but perhaps it was for the best. "Do you want me to lie?"

She shook her head.

"Then don't ask me again."

He clasped her arm and opened the car door so she could slide in. "Everyone buckle up. I'm taking you to the cabin and getting you and Sam on the road as fast as I can. It's no longer safe here."

"Are...are you coming with us?" Sam asked, his voice small. "Please come with us, Dark Avenger. I'll be good. I promise."

Zach looked at his Junior Avenger, so vulnerable in the backseat.

The boy's entire body shook. "We need you."

He was a good kid. With a touch of innocence that would be lost before too long.

"I can't. I'm sorry."

Sam flinched, avoided Zach's gaze, and scooted as far away from the driver's seat as possible.

With a sigh, Zach closed the car door, rounded the Range Rover, and slid in. Jenna's hands trembled each time she tried to pull the seat belt across her body to buckle it. Delayed reaction, most likely. She'd tried to kill a man, then she'd watched him die. Zach didn't know which sent the adrenaline pumping through her. It didn't really matter.

Gently, he moved her hands aside and snapped the belt closed. He leaned close to her ear. "You're going to be fine."

"I'm sorry, I—" She held out her fingers in front of her. "I can't seem to stop shaking. I thought I could do this. I thought I could protect Sam," she hissed under her breath.

"You did," Zach said.

"Brutus...he could have killed Sam. I screwed up," she whispered. "How do you live like this all the time?"

"You learn," Zach said, his hand gripping hers until the trembling eased. "You made a mistake. If you'd followed through, he would have gone down, Jenna. You had him right at the Adam's apple. You'll do it next time."

"I don't know if I can."

Zach tugged at a small curl of hair that had escaped from behind her ear. "You will when you have to. You've got the guts to protect *both* of you." He tucked the strand away. "If things were different—"

She pulled away from him. "Like you said, it's for the best."

He shifted into gear and headed toward his mountain.

"You'll be fine, Jenna," he said with a sidelong glance.

She didn't respond, but looked out the window, creating a disconnect between them. The separation scraped at something deep within Zach. A little piece of his heart flaked away as he stared at the distance growing larger and wider between them.

For the first time in a very long time, his heart and head were at war.

She was right. Separating was for the best.

He had to believe Jenna and Sam were better off without him.

―――――――――――

Jenna's heart stuttered when the crumpled guardrail came into view. She clutched the armrests, digging her fingers into the expensive leather in the Range Rover. She wouldn't miss these hairpin curves.

She wished she could just fly off this mountain instead of driving down again. At least it would be for the last time.

Her surreptitious glance swept Zach's cold and calculating expression. So devoid of emotion since they'd left Hidden Springs, so much like Brad; a quiver prickled the base of her spine. She couldn't get over the change in his demeanor. As if he were another person entirely.

Too much like her husband.

She missed the mischievous twinkle in his eyes. Jenna shoved aside the regret, the might-have-beens. She glanced at Sam. Her normally talkative son hadn't said a word the entire drive.

The vehicle pulled in front of Zach's cabin. A haven, she'd hoped. Now, just another place to say good-bye to on their road to oblivion.

He turned off the engine and rotated in his seat. "Let's get you guys packed." Zach circled the vehicle to the tailgate.

She unbuckled her belt and slid to the ground. The nip of chill stung her cheeks. How could snow lace the air in June? Weird.

She stared at the mound of purchases. Guilt overcame her. It was hundreds of dollars, but could have been millions. "I may never be able to pay you back."

Overladen with bags, he simply shrugged. "Just keep yourself safe."

Zach hauled the loot into the house. Jenna opened the back door of the Range Rover.

Her son sat mutinous on the backseat. "What's going on, Sam?"

He thrust out a stubborn chin—a lot like hers. "I don't wanna go. I wanna stay here."

His small legs swung against the seat.

"I know, but Zach has to leave, and we do, too."

"Make him come with us. Please, Mommy." He worried his T-shirt, twisting the material until she wouldn't have been surprised if he wore a hole in it.

She gripped his small hands. "What's the matter?"

The haunted look in his eyes tore at her heart. "Those bad men came after us. We need the Dark Avenger to keep us safe."

"I can protect us." Zach had given her the tools. She had to believe she could use them on her own.

"That man was going to shoot me, Mommy. He knocked you down. We *need* the Dark Avenger."

Her son's lack of faith tore at her confidence. How could she argue? "We can't take him with us, Sam," she said, finally. "He has other business." An utterly lame excuse.

"Then I want to go home. Daddy can take care of us. He's big like the Dark Avenger. And then I can go to the baseball game, too." Sam crossed his arms in front of him and stuck out his lower lip.

She shouldn't be surprised. He hadn't had a lot of sleep, he'd been in a car accident, he'd slept in a strange place. She couldn't reason with Sam when he was like this.

The burden of her choices sank on her shoulders. She sagged with its weight. "Go inside, Sam. Now." She used the mom tone on him. It usually worked.

Indecision screwed up her son's face, deciding how far to push her. Jenna didn't possess the reserves to deal with him. "I mean it."

He shoved his foot into the back of the leather seat and hopped out. He ran through the front entrance with a slam.

Zach stood inside the screen door and watched her son vanish down the hallway.

"I take it the conversation didn't go well?"

The tension in Zach's body had dissipated. The chill in his eyes had warmed a bit—in sympathy at least. Maybe because he was getting rid of them.

"Temper tantrum. He doesn't know where to put all the emotions." She scratched the heel of her palm. "He misses his dad." Jenna raised her gaze to Zach. "How am I supposed to explain to him that he's never going to see Brad again? He won't understand."

Her words trailed off as she rubbed her still-sore wrist. All she'd wanted to do was protect her son, and by doing so she'd made it impossible for him to comprehend the hard choices she'd had to make. "Am I doing the right thing?"

Zach pulled her hand in his and gentled away the ache with his touch. Jenna's pulse skipped, then raced.

"The Chameleon is a cold-blooded bastard who kills for money. No one's been close to identifying him as long as he's been on my radar. I've seen the sheet on him, Jenna. He can't afford to be caught. He'll do whatever it takes to protect himself. No matter who gets hurt."

Zach's gaze followed Sam's path.

The certainty in her bones when she'd packed her bags— was it only forty-eight hours ago?—returned. Jenna clasped his forearm. "Thank you for that."

He studied her hand on his warm skin. The cobalt flecks in the depths of Zach's eyes flared with something Jenna hadn't recognized in far too long. Desire.

She swayed toward him, but he closed off his expression and held her shoulders. "I wish we had more time," he whispered.

She reached up and placed her hand against his face.

"Or maybe I'm relieved we don't. You could tempt a saint, Jenna Walters."

"McMann," she whispered. "Walters belongs to an assassin. My name is McMann as of today."

"Well, then, Jenna McMann. You go inside and pack. I left a couple of suitcases besides the bags. Raid the kitchen. Take anything you need. I doubt I'll be returning here anytime soon." He glanced at his watch. "I want you and Sam down the mountain before dark."

With a sigh she entered the house behind him. He veered to the stairs and she walked down the hall to the bedrooms. Sam had flopped onto the lower bunk where he'd slept, his head buried.

She touched his back. "Sam."

He stiffened, attempting to feign sleep. She knew better. She sat on the bed next to him and drew his stiff little body into her arms. "I know this is hard. I know you're scared."

"If we can't stay here, why can't we go home? Daddy can be nice to you. I'll ask him."

She pushed away the hair on his forehead. "Sometimes we can't—"

"Have what we want." He turned away from her and huddled in the bed. "Go away."

She sighed and rubbed his shoulder. "I'll come get you when we're ready. Everything will be fine. I promise."

She left the room and went into the kitchen where the sacks were piled high next to two suitcases, just as Zach had said.

He'd thought of everything.

She unpacked the shopping bags, stunned at the items Zach had filled the cart with when she hadn't been looking. Clothes, toiletries, even toys and a portable DVD player for Sam, along with copies of a dozen movies for Sam and several books for her. Jenna's eyes burned as she organized the items in the suitcases.

How could one man be so thoughtful? This would last her months. Long enough until she found a way to generate an income.

Hiding for the rest of her life wasn't the future she wanted for Sam, but perhaps she could contact a different FBI office. Maybe—

A shadow crossed her plane of vision. She whirled around, her fist clinched.

"Pretty good reaction time," Zach said. He clutched a white packet in his hand. He sat it on the table and opened the clasp. Two familiar blue booklets, several cards, and two pieces of paper slid out, along with a rubber-banded stack of documents.

Hand shaking, Jenna shifted through the papers. Her entire being stilled.

Social security cards and birth certificates with new names. Gennita and Zan McMann. She opened the authentic-looking passport. A photo of her stared back. She couldn't tell when it had been taken. It resembled her driver's license a bit. Same quality, but something…then she recognized the shirt. The one she wore today.

Her mind tried to wrap itself around the quality of the documents. "How?"

"I tried to keep them close to your real names without being obvious," he said.

Emotion shut off her air passage. She swallowed past the realization of Zach's gift. He'd provided them a lifeline to a future.

He tucked the items back into the envelope. "There's a deed to a house in Georgia, paid for free and clear. A bank account with enough money to see you through a few years, I'd think." He handed her a second envelope. "This is five thousand dollars, proof of ownership, insurance for the Range Rover, and a New Jersey driver's license."

Jenna's legs shook at the magnitude of what he'd done. She sank into the oak chair before she passed out. She opened the envelope and pulled out the driver's license. Perfect. Just like everything else he'd done for her. "I...I don't know what to say." She stared open-mouthed at him.

"It wasn't hard. I just changed a few names on the forms." He nodded toward the suitcases. "Those ready?"

Her mind awhirl, she nodded. He walked over to the bags, and the truth slapped her in the face. Everything she'd seen. The high-tech room, the gadgets, his ability to fight, his secretiveness. She seen enough of his heart to know he wasn't like Brad. But he did hide his true job. Maybe he was a spy or a secret agent. But he was in danger. That much she knew. And he'd created a new identity to keep himself safe. He'd sacrificed his plans for her and Sam.

"If you give me all this, how will you disappear, Zach? How will you protect yourself?"

He shrugged and crossed to her, dragging his knuckle down her cheek. "I'll land on my feet, Jenna. I always do. I still have resources I can tap."

She sucked in a slow breath and leaned into his cheek. "Are you certain?"

"Of course."

His gaze was steady. She couldn't tell if he was lying.

He ran his hands up and down her arms. She shivered under his touch. What might have been.

Zach stared down at her with a gaze so intense, her entire being felt the pull toward him.

He shook his head as if to clear the electricity sparking between them. "Well…" His touch lingered for a last moment, then he straightened. "Let's get you on the road."

He loaded the suitcases and returned to the kitchen. "What else do you have?"

"That's it. That's enough."

He cursed under his breath, disappeared down a hall, and returned with a box topped with a folded quilt and two pillows. He stalked out of the kitchen and shoved it into the back end of the car. She followed, moved the bedding to one side, and peered into the cardboard container. Food, lights, tools, first aid.

"An emergency kit," he said.

She'd lose it completely if he kept doing this. She pressed the heels of her hands against her eyes. "I'll never be able to thank you enough."

He paused and took out a piece of paper with a phone number written down. "I can't give you a number to reach me, but if you get in real trouble…this is my brother's number. Seth. He has connections—"

"No! I can't risk involving your family."

"Call from a pay phone or a prepaid cell. He can help."

She nodded, knowing full well she'd never use it. Zach had done enough. He'd given her a new start. Now she had to learn to stand on her own two feet. She'd have to listen to the stories she told Sam. She'd have to be her own hero. Not rely on anyone else. It was the only way to protect them both.

Zach folded the note into her hand. "I can see in your eyes you want to throw it away. Don't. Keep it. You never know when you might need help. For you. Or for Sam."

Reluctantly, she shoved the paper into her pocket.

With finality, Zach slammed closed the back of the vehicle. He stood, staring at her, silent, watchful. Then his control slipped just a tad. Sadness laced his expression.

She wiped her hands on her jeans. "I guess this is it."

"I guess so." Zach looked down at her and smiled. "You'll be fine, Jenna. Don't forget, eyes—"

"Throat, groin." She shoved her hands in her pockets, then leaned up and pecked him on the cheek. "Thank you, Dark Avenger," she whispered. "You really are a hero."

She turned to the house, tears burning behind her eyes. Why couldn't she have met Zach some other time, some other place?

She glanced back, and his intense gaze followed her. Her steps faltered.

Slowly she faced him. She couldn't stop herself. She ran back to him and into his arms, hugging him tightly. "I wish…"

"Things were different," he finished.

She gazed into his eyes and placed her hands on his shoulders. "I know I shouldn't," she said softly. "But I'll always wonder…"

She stood on her tiptoes and pressed her lips to his. He groaned, his mouth still against hers. Finally, with a harsh curse, he took her lips.

His arms enfolded her and she felt safe. She wanted to burrow herself inside of him and just be warm and cared for and, dare she think it, loved. Zach pressed her mouth open and tasted her. A hint of coffee tingled on her tongue. Her belly flipped, her legs turned to noodles. She moaned under the welcome assault. He tasted of peppermint and something more, something that lit a fire deep inside her heart.

She pressed closer. She wanted more. And she could never have it.

He rubbed his hands up and down her arms, lifted his lips, and gently set her away from him.

"You pack one hell of a wallop, Gennita McMann."

The blue depths of Zach's eyes turned deep cobalt. Her breathing came fast. Her chest rose and fell. She wanted more.

"Now I know how it feels," she said softly.

"Now we both know," Zach agreed, his gaze hooded.

"Maybe that's not such a good thing." An unarguable melancholy settled over her. Maybe it was better if she didn't know what he tasted like, that they fit together, that he had the willpower to stop them from doing something they'd both regret.

"You have to go," he said, looking at the sky where the sun had dropped lower, just over the mountain range to the west.

She touched his lips then disappeared inside the house. He was right. Jenna walked down the hall to Sam's room. She knocked softly and opened the door. "Time to go, baby."

The bunk bed was empty. She tried the bathroom door. "Sam!"

Nothing.

"Sam. No more games. It's time to leave."

Zach opened the screen door.

"Sam's not answering," she said, frustration warring with an underlying fear. *Where was he?*

"I'll try the basement. He liked my communication center."

Zach bounded down the stairs, returning in less than a minute, his forehead creased in a worried frown. "He's not there."

They searched from room to room.

Nothing.

Sam was gone.

No one noticed Brad. That was his gift. Being invisible. It came in handy while waiting for the shift change at the Denver hospital. He'd make his way unobserved to the medical floor, take care of business, and leave, just as unnoticed.

He sat in the institution's coffee shop, his placement just out of sight of the surveillance cameras. He'd researched the security system. Amazing what information his FBI contact, Johansson, could provide. Once John Garrison was dead, the cops would pan through hours of footage, but they'd never see his face.

His smart phone beeped. He stared at the results and fumed. No sign of Jenna. Not on planes, buses, trains. She'd simply vanished.

He sipped the institutional coffee. He could've used a belt of whiskey to hide the bitterness. No more sour than the scent of failure.

His fingers drummed the table until the doctor sitting next to him glared. Brad forced himself to silence the unusual fidgeting. He didn't like the symptom. He refused to let his body's nervous habits overcome his mind. The thing was, he just didn't get it. Jenna wasn't smart enough to completely disappear. Not without help.

His phone rang. He glanced at the screen. An unknown number.

"Walters," he snapped.

"Daddy?" Sam's tentative voice filtered through the line.

"Sam?" Brad made his voice sound worried and concerned. "Thank God. Are you all right?"

"Tomorrow's Saturday," he said.

Hell. Saturday. Not the kid's birthday. Not Jenna's birthday. What then?

"I know. I miss you. When are you coming home?"

Sam sniffed. "I don't know. If I come home will you take me to the game? Please, Daddy?"

The damned baseball game.

Jenna had bought the tickets after he'd lost his temper a bit last week. He'd agreed in a moment of weakness, not because he wanted to go to the game with his son, of course. It looked good to see a father and son at the ballpark.

"I'd love to. I want to take you with me, Sam. What if I come get you?"

"Really?"

"Promise." Brad sucked in a deep breath. "Where are you, Sam?"

"I don't know. The Dark Avenger took us to his house. But now he's making us leave. Even though the bad guys are after us." Sam sniffed. "And he kissed Mommy. He's not s'posed to do that. She belongs to us."

Montgomery. Brad squeezed the coffee cup so hard, he was surprised it didn't shatter. *Son of a bitch.* He shifted toward the wall and lowered his voice. "Sam, I need you to look around. Where are you?"

"In the woods, but I can still see the Dark Avenger's cabin. I'm not lost."

"Good, good."

"The Dark Avenger had to beat up some bad guys. And they took his picture. He got really mad. I got scared." Sam choked back. "I want to come home. I want my toys."

"You'll have as many toys as you want," Brad lied, "but you have to tell me where you are."

His knuckles whitened. *Jenna was so dead.* Then Brad smiled. This could work to his advantage. Perhaps a murder-suicide. Zach Montgomery and Jenna were lovers, she ran off on him, and the drunken actor killed her in a rage.

No. It wouldn't work. The story would put Brad on the news. Something he couldn't afford. *Damn, Jenna.* Maybe a car wreck.

"We're in the mountains," Sam said.

Or Zach Montgomery could fall off a mountain. Brad would take Jenna home and the car accident would still work. No press.

The plan fell into place.

"Are you in California?"

"No. Mommy said we're in the Rock Mountains."

"The Rocky Mountains?" Brad asked.

"Yeah," Sam said, a smile of triumph in his voice.

"Good, good. You're doing great, buddy."

"Oops. I can hear Mommy yelling. I gotta go."

"Sam, don't let them take you from that cabin. You run and hide. I'll find you. I promise. I won't let the bad guys get you."

"OK, Daddy," Sam choked. "I gotta go. They're coming this way."

The phone went dead.

He dialed a number.

"Zach Montgomery's got a cabin in the Rocky Mountains. Find the location. I want it. Now. Check the news wires. Someone spotted him."

"There's a wall around the man, sir. I can't get past it."

Brad paused. "Security clearance?"

"And then some. I'll keep pushing, but it could take some time. Fallon is all over my case. He suspects something."

"That's not my problem."

"You're not the one risking his career."

"You made the choice, Johansson."

His mole sighed. "Montgomery is a nonstarter. His security clearance is untouchable. Which should tell you enough to leave the bastard alone."

A curse erupted from Brad. He wanted to slam the phone into the wall. The doctor next to him glared. Brad forced an apologetic smile, rose, and stalked out through the revolving door of the hospital. He breathed in the fresh air. At least he'd rid himself of the antiseptic smell.

"Don't fail me again, Johansson."

"Oh, I haven't failed you. I have a bit of news you might just want to hear."

The man's gloating tone made Brad's trigger finger itch in the worst way. Johansson was another of those threads that would be cut. Soon. Another car accident, perhaps. The traffic in southern California could be deadly. Or perhaps a natural gas line explosion. More perfectly planned this time. Everyone liked to blame the gas company for tragedies.

"You don't want to mess with me right now, Johansson."

"Fine. Fallon's beside himself. Your wife ran out on the investigation. Disappeared. Poof. And she refused to give them copies of the evidence until she and your kid were *safe*."

Brad burst out laughing. He hitched into his rental Jeep and turned the key.

"Johansson, you may very well have just saved your life."

The man choked.

"Find me Montgomery's address, and we'll know exactly where my lovely wife is hiding out."

Chapter Nine

ZACH CUPPED HIS HANDS. "SAM!" HE SHOUTED FROM THE porch, shoving down the worry. He scanned between the pines and through a grove of aspens that quaked in the late June afternoon. Several thrushes scattered with angry shrieks.

Jenna gripped the rough wooden post. "Sam!" she called, panic edging her voice.

They stood quietly, listening. Sam wasn't responding.

Jenna wrapped her arms around her body. Zach pulled her against him, hugging her tight, though he knew his touch offered little comfort.

"Where could he be?" she asked. "Sam!" she yelled again. "Do you think he's hiding in the house?"

"I can find out. Come on," he said, lacing his fingers through hers. With one last studied gaze into the wilderness, he led her to his communications center. He sat down at the monitor and activated the live cameras.

Jenna leaned forward when the high-definition pictures leapt onto the screen. She touched the monitor. "You used this to take our photos for the passports, didn't you?"

He nodded curtly and switched to views. "The playback will show us everything the cameras caught." He pressed the reverse button. Images sped past backward.

When their faces appeared near the car, Zach stopped and hit play. Jenna ran into Zach's arms on the screen. Their lips met. The world fell away.

The back of Zach's neck heated at the passion. He couldn't tell her how she'd felt so right in his arms that he never wanted to let her go.

"Oh, Sam. No," Jenna cried out. She gripped Zach's shoulder hard. "He saw us," she whispered.

Zach squinted at the screen. Sure enough. The small boy's face watched through the screen door as Zach kissed Jenna breathless. Hurt and anger twisted the boy's expression.

Sam spun around and ran toward the back entrance. Zach switched the camera view even as dread washed through him. Sam ran out the door, tears streaming down his face. The camera caught him disappearing on the north side of the cabin into the woods.

Zach cupped Jenna's devastated face. "It's not your fault."

She pulled away from him. "Of course it is. I kissed a man who wasn't my husband. No matter what's Brad's done, he's still Sam's father. Sam had every reason to feel betrayed." She bowed her head. "How will I ever regain his trust?"

"First, we find him," Zach said. He glanced at his watch. "It'll be dark before long."

Jenna's face paled and with desperation she scanned the room. "Please tell me something in your high-tech lair can help us find him."

Zach grabbed his handheld thermal imager.

"A video camera?" Jenna asked.

"Not quite. This will pick up Sam's heat signature. It's more sensitive than most. I can even track footprints up to about thirty minutes."

Jenna didn't pause. She rushed up the stairs, and Zach hurried behind her. He grabbed his emergency backpack from the closet and threw her a jacket before donning his own. He searched his pocket for his phone. Where had he left it? No time to look. He grabbed the last prepaid phone, stepped onto the porch, and scanned the sky, noting the sun sinking over Fools Peak. There wasn't that much light left, and a lot of ground to cover.

"The sun will set around eight thirty," he said. He led Jenna to the small clearing they'd seen Sam disappear into. He looked through the thermal imager's lens. A raccoon, a few birds, a couple of rabbits, but no footprints.

"He's so small the heat from his footprints dissipated too quickly."

Jenna glanced around and clutched at Zach's arm, anxiety driving her fingernails into him. "Which way?"

Zach scanned the ground, his vision catching some misplaced pine needles. "Over here," he said. They followed the trail for a good half hour. Shadows darkened the forest's floor. Fingerlike outlines clawed up the trees. A foreboding chill clung in the air.

Every few minutes he scanned the surrounding areas with the imager.

"Are you sure we're going the right way? He could have veered off in any direction."

The fear in Jenna's voice peppered Zach like a spray of bullets, but she had every reason to be frightened. Sam had been raised in California. He didn't know the first rule of hiking in the mountains—never, ever hike at night. He could walk off into nothing and not even know it.

Zach couldn't imagine Jenna would recover if they didn't find Sam alive and well. He paused, and Jenna halted behind him. He pulled her close and pointed to a tree. "See how the branch is bent. Sam walked this way."

"It could have been an animal."

Zach bent down near a bed of pine needles next to the tree. He outlined the edge of Sam's shoe. "Do you see it now?"

Jenna nodded, her eyes wide and wondering. "How did you learn how to do this?"

"My dad. Unlike my brothers, I could take or leave baseball or football, but I loved skiing, mountain climbing, flying. My family has a cabin a ways north of here, near Kremmling. He took me hiking there. Said if I was going to be crazy enough to run up and down the Rocky Mountains, I better know how to survive in case I got lost."

"He sounds like an amazing dad. He must've been proud of you."

Her misplaced words grabbed, twisted, and tore at Zach's heart. His father couldn't have been proud. He shoved the memories away. "We better get a move on."

He could feel her gaze boring into his back, but she didn't say anything. Thank goodness. The light had dimmed. He paused and rescanned the terrain using the imager.

Small footprints shone through the camera. "We got him," he said to Jenna. He refocused and followed the footprints leading off toward…crap…Sam was heading directly toward a dropoff of over three thousand feet.

He grabbed Jenna's hand and picked up his pace.

"What's wrong," she panted.

"Sam's heading toward a cliff."

"Sam!" Jenna called out, her voice frantic.

The sound echoed through the woods. Zach slapped his hand over her mouth. "He's hurt and angry. I don't want him running. We need to get to him before he reaches the edge. He won't see it coming. There's a line of trees and then...nothing."

"Oh my God." Jenna pressed the ball of her hand against her mouth.

Zach echoed the prayer that they'd get to him in time.

He stopped. Jenna plowed into his back, but Zach didn't budge. He raised the camera to his eye. Sam's footsteps had turned from a blue-yellow to yellow-red in color. "We're gaining on him."

Jenna bit her lip hard. They both scanned the darkening horizon. A glint of orange and purple reflected over the mountaintop. The shadows grew deeper.

Zach lifted the imager again. A faint shape ran away. A small figure. Sam.

"I see him," Zach said. "He's running. He's only a few hundred feet through those trees."

The yellow-red image glowed clearly then suddenly slipped out of sight.

Sam had vanished.

Anna Montgomery didn't want to leave the darkness. The lack of light soothed her, made it easy to forget. She breathed in, then out. She knew that smell. Anna hated the scent of hospitals. This was where Patrick had died, where her son Gabe had almost slipped away.

She opened her eyes and stared up at six sets of concerned gazes. She blinked. She should never have let the light in. It pummeled her mind. She squeezed her eyelids tight. Why did her head feel as if she'd been pounded with a meat tenderizer?

Memories beat through her, swirling, circling, like lumpy cake batter, incomplete and confusing.

A man. Not Patrick. Holding her.

A kiss.

She blushed.

Fiery visions exploded in her mind.

And she remembered.

"John," she whispered. "Where's John?"

"Don't talk, Mom," a voice choked.

Gabe. Her baby.

Someone squeezed her hand. "Open your eyes. Please, Mom," Caleb said, without any of the reserve his medical training had pounded into him.

His words, laced with worry, drove Anna to try again.

She forced her heavy eyelids open and blinked several times. The light made tears erupt, but she didn't give in. Not this time. She blinked again, her vision clearing. Her gaze moved from face to face. First to Jasmine, her daughter by marriage, a woman who had survived more hurt than Anna could fathom. Then Luke, who had healed Jasmine's soul with his love. Her second youngest was a good man.

Gabe, Seth, Caleb, Nick…

"Zach?" she whispered. "Where's Zach?"

Gabe's expression grew dark. "I'm sure he's fine," he said, patting her shoulder. "Don't worry about Zach. Focus on you."

Anna clutched the blanket in her hand. "He'd be here if he could," she said, wrinkling her forehead with an expression Patrick had called her stubborn face. "Make sure he's all right. Please."

Seth stepped forward. "I'll find him, Mom. I have ways. You rest."

Anna studied Seth. Everyone believed his job to be the most dangerous. He'd seen too much, and she recognized the torment he should never have known—too much like Patrick. But Zach, Zach had his secrets, too, and they rivaled Seth's.

She let out a sigh. "Please, find him." Her eyes drifted shut. "John saved my life. Tell him...thank you."

A small sniffle sounded. Anna refused to give in to the frisson of apprehension. John Garrison would come to her. She wouldn't consider any other alternative.

Jenna raced after Zach; the pine needles crunched under her feet. He jumped over a moss-covered stone and she stumbled after him. He grabbed her elbow but didn't slow down. With the imager tight in one hand, he tugged her after him.

"What did you see?" she panted.

He didn't answer, and Jenna's heart rammed into gear like a souped-up roadster. Her muscles pumped as the terrain flew under them. "Sam!" she couldn't stop the scream from escaping her lips.

This time Zach didn't hush her.

Oh God. What had he seen?

Zach skidded to a stop when he reached a small thatch of aspens. Darkness had begun settling over the mountain. The shadows made everything murky and indistinct. She squinted. "Is he here?"

"I hope so," Zach muttered, pushing through the thicket. He slowed down.

"Sam!"

She clutched Zach's hand. "Tell me," she whispered, her entire being shaking.

He turned to her and cupped her face. "Sam vanished off the screen."

Jenna's knees buckled. "No. This can't be happening. I'm supposed to keep him safe. That's why we left."

Zach grabbed her arms. "Listen to me. This is my mountain. There are holes and caves nearby. The cliff isn't for another fifty feet. Sam's here somewhere."

"Sam!" Jenna yelled. "Sam, can you hear us? Please, baby. Answer me."

They stilled, listening for any sound that didn't belong. Crickets chirped; chipmunks chattered; an owl hooted. A tree shuffled nearby.

But no voices save their own.

"Sam!" Zach shouted. "If you can hear me, call out."

A hole where Jenna's soul had been grew dark and empty, a void spreading that threatened to swallow any hope she ever had.

And then a sound filtered toward them over the chilling breeze.

"Heeelllppp!"

A boy's voice. Sam's voice.

Jenna closed her eyes, focusing everything within her on the direction.

The sound faded away before she could tell. She looked at Zach, his frustration mirroring her own.

"Sam, where are you?" she called.

"Mommmmmmmy?"

His voice sounded strange, echoing and far off. She strained to pinpoint the location, circling around and around in the small grove. "Where is he?"

"Get him to call out to you," Zach said.

She cupped her hands around her mouth. "Keep yelling, Sam. Don't stop, baby."

"Mommmy...Mommmmmy...Moooommmmmmmyyyy."

Zach shifted to his right, Jenna trailed after him. Little by little they followed Sam's oddly muffled voice. His calls grew louder and more distinct, and more scared.

"Pleeeaassseee. Save me, Mommy."

Jenna could barely keep a whimper from escaping.

Zach squeezed her hand tight, and she drew from his strength and his certainty. "This way." He pushed past a throng of pine trees and stopped.

A narrow ravine sliced through the landscape. Jenna swallowed down the bile rising in her gut. "Mommmyyyy!" Sam's voice rose from the chasm in the earth.

She lurched forward, but Zach shoved her back. "The ground has eroded," he said, pointing to the upturned dirt. "The earth just gave way, and Sam slid down. We can't get caught in the same trap."

With one hand clutching a long tree limb, Zach stretched out and peered into the crevice. "Sam?"

"I'm here!" he said, his voice cracking. "Where's my mommy?"

"I'm with Zach, baby. Don't worry. We'll get you."

Zach stepped away from the edge and slipped off his backpack. "Sam's down about twenty feet, but it doesn't look too bad. Some trees broke his fall. He's sitting on a ledge." Zach raised his gaze to the barely lit sky. "I'm going down."

He unzipped his pack and pulled out a long length of climbing rope and a rappelling device.

"What can I do?" she asked.

"Be ready to pull him up."

Jenna watched as Zach used an elaborate tie to secure the rope around a large tree with no hesitation whatsoever.

"You've done this before."

"I've climbed these mountains more than once." He tugged at the two lines. "Ready. Don't go past this point, Jenna," he said, indicating a boulder. "The ground's unstable."

She nodded.

"I'll yell when I have Sam secured. You pull him up."

"What about you?"

"Untie the rope from around him and toss it down to me. I'll climb up. Piece of cake."

He quirked a smile, but the clenching of his jaw and the intensity in his gaze spoke the truth.

Jenna clenched her fists and straightened her back. "I'll be ready."

He touched her cheek. "I know."

With a quick clip on his belt, he secured the line and eased toward the edge. Dirt sifted into the ravine. *Oh God*, now she understood the extent of the danger. The rim could give way at any time. He shifted his weight off the crumbling soil and planted his foot on solid rock. Picking his way, he maneuvered over the side, his silhouette framed in the reddening sunset.

"Red at night, sailor's delight," she whispered. She prayed the old saying would be true.

One last time Zach's gaze met hers. He winked, then disappeared over the side.

The climb was going to be a bitch. Zach couldn't believe he'd forgotten about the wide ravine. He avoided it on his hikes. He planted his foot on the crumbling side of the gorge. The dusky conditions made it difficult to see every nuance of the rock face. The soft sandstone crumbled under his touch. *Hell.* He balanced his weight between the rope and his feet and eased down.

With a quick glance over his shoulder he gauged the distance. Another fifteen feet.

Sam lay on a ledge, sitting up, staring wide-eyed at Zach. The boy's face was scratched, but he shifted his legs. At least he could move.

A tree growing straight out of the side of the ravine canopied Sam. The limbs must have broken his fall. *Otherwise…*Zach wouldn't let the thoughts go further. Sam was alive. That's all that mattered.

He tested the next foothold. His boot sent a wall of rock crumbling down.

"Cover your head, Sam!" he yelled.

The boy hunkered, and dirt sprinkled him, the biggest chunks missing the ledge altogether.

"What's wrong?" Jenna yelled from above.

"We're fine. Almost there," he yelled back. He hoped he wasn't lying.

A few more precarious feet and Zach hovered above the ledge. He studied the outgrowth. Granite, and not crumbling, thank God.

Zach lowered himself, giving enough slack to kneel beside Sam. "How are you doing, buddy?"

"I hurt my ankle," Sam said quietly, refusing to meet Zach's gaze. Streaks of dirt and tears marked the little boy's cheeks.

The kid didn't need a lecture. He'd learned his lesson, all too well. "I'm going to get you back to your mom."

The boy nodded. Zach unhooked the rope and created a cradle for Sam to stick his feet through.

With a quick tug he secured the double figure-eight fisherman's knot. "OK, Junior Avenger, your mom's going to pull you up. Just hold on tight. We won't let you fall again."

Sam nodded his head, then lifted his gaze to Zach. "I'm sorry I ran."

"You were mad, huh?" Zach said.

"I didn't want to leave, then I saw you kiss her." Sam bit his lip. "You shouldn't have kissed her. She belongs to me and my daddy."

Zach let out a slow stream of air. How to explain to a five-year-old, when he didn't understand it himself? He tried for as close to the truth as either one of them could understand. "I was kissing her good-bye, Sam. We're friends, right? Sometimes you kiss friends good-bye."

The boy bowed his head. "I guess."

Zach ruffled Sam's hair. "It's all right, but when you're upset, you need to tell your mom. Don't let it eat up your insides."

"Can't tell. If I'm bad, Daddy hurts Mommy. Then he has to go to time-out until he's better. It makes me sad."

Damn it. Zach didn't know what to say to that one. Jenna would be mortified Sam knew about her husband. How do you explain to a kid who loves his dad that sometimes time-out doesn't fix everything?

"Let's get you back to your mom." Zach cupped his hands. "Jenna, pull Sam up. Slow and steady."

Inch by inch the rope tightened. The line lifted Sam off the ledge.

"Easy does it," Zach yelled.

It took several minutes, but soon, Sam hovered near the top. Zach could barely make out his figure any longer. Most of the light had disappeared behind the peaks.

This is where it could get tricky.

Dirt filtered down, hitting Zach in the face. The edge crumbled under the pressure of the rope.

"Sam, see that rock to your right?" Zach shouted. "Can you grab for it?"

The boy reached for the outcrop, but he couldn't hold on. He swung away.

"Jenna, move to your left. Toward the rock! Sam, you can do this. Grab it."

Sam reached out his hands and this time clutched it and scrambled over.

"Run to your mom, away from the edge."

With the flexibility and resilience only a five-year-old could have, Sam disappeared.

"He's OK!" Jenna yelled, joy pouring from every tone.

Zach bent over, his hands on his knees. He let out the breath he hadn't realized he'd been holding. His entire body went slack. The kid was amazing.

A slight movement shifted Zach's attention. A sliver of remaining sunlight outlined a mountain goat. He stood on the side of the ravine, calm and relaxed, then cocked his head at Zach.

"Show-off," Zach muttered at the sure-footed animal that scampered across the rocks and disappeared behind a large outcropping and into the night. The animal had the right idea. Zach needed to get off the mountain.

"Untie Sam and throw the rope down," he called up.

Minutes later the lifeline soared to him, getting caught in the tree that had broken Sam's fall.

Could nothing be easy?

The rope hung about five feet away. Zach eased to the ledge and reached out his hand. Just a couple of feet too far.

He studied the suspect rock face. Too many opportunities for the surface to crumble away. He glanced up at the tree, grabbed a thin limb, and twisted and tugged until the green wood gave way. After several thrusts, the leaves caught the line and Zach slowly pulled it toward him.

He secured the tubular rappelling device and looked up. He could barely see the side of the mountain. Going by memory, Zach planted his foot against the side and began the climb. His movements careful, he eased up to only a few feet from the top. He squinted, but couldn't make out his target, consisting of a small island of hard rock surrounded by crumbling sandstone and dirt. Saying a quick prayer, Zach carefully placed his boot.

Rocks poured down like waterfall.

He tightened his grip and shifted his feet to the right.

Wrong choice.

The wall disintegrated beneath his feet.

Zach shoved away from the edge.

Time slowed down.

He couldn't stop the fall.

Chapter Ten

*J*ENNA CRADLED SAM IN HER ARMS AND STARED, UNBLINKING, at the shadowed cliff.

The line leading to the edge suddenly went taut.

She jumped up, her heart racing, the staccato beats thrumming against her chest.

"What's the matter, Mommy? Where's the Dark Avenger?"

"I don't know, baby. Stay there, all right?" Jenna dug into the backpack Zach had thrown next to the pine and pulled out a flashlight. Sweeping the beam across the area, she walked to the line still anchored to the tree. She gave it a small tug. No slack, just scarily taut. "Zach," she shouted.

"Stay back," his voice filtered from the crevice. "I'll be... right up."

She recognized the strain in his voice. Something wasn't right. The flashlight caught the line shifting, scraping back and forth against the rock. A rope would have frayed, but Zach's equipment was clearly high-tech.

Sam hobbled next to her and whimpered. "Where is he?"

She hesitated. "He's climbing."

"It's a long way down."

An arm reached up and over the rock. Red spots splattered his dusty sleeve. A grunt sounded. The other arm flung up.

Muscles strained. Zach heaved himself onto the granite, his chest and waist lying on the stone. He took in a deep breath. A two-inch cut slashed at his temple. Blood trickled down his check.

She started toward him. He lifted his head. "No! Stay away!"

Jenna skidded to a halt, every instinct urging her to go to him, to help him, but she fought the impulse. Sometimes brains had to overcome the heart. Now was one of those times.

Sam gripped her hand tight, sniffling.

Rolling to his side with most of his weight resting on his right arm, Zach crept from the cliff's edge. He looked like he'd been to war with the mountain. She shone the light on the ground to show him the way, trying to keep it out of his eyes. Finally he reached the large boulder. He stopped and collapsed onto his back, flinging his right hand over his eyes.

Jenna let go of Sam, lunged to Zach, and knelt at his side. "You're hurt. Let me see," she said softly, reaching into Zach's pack for the first aid kit.

Sam handed her the case.

"How you doing, buddy?" Zach asked, his breathing slowing.

Her son hid his face into Jenna's jacket. She propped the flashlight between two rocks so she could see what she was doing and dabbed at his cut with a bandage. "A twisted ankle and a new appreciation for the mountains." She couldn't stop the intense gratitude from rising into her throat. She wanted to throw herself into his arms and thank him, but there were no words, nothing she could ever do to repay him. "You saved his life. How can I even—?"

"Don't." Zach clasped the hand tending to him. "Anyone would have done the same."

"But not everyone could have." She turned his palms over, wincing at the scrapes and scratches on his hands. "You should see a doctor."

Zach sat up. "It's nearly dark. We have to find shelter. No way we're walking at night. Even with my imager."

He rose, groaning as he stood. In the eerie reflection of the flashlight, his left arm hung oddly at his side.

She reached out to him. "What have you done?"

"Banged myself up a bit."

She touched him. He winced and shut his eyes. His knees gave way and he collapsed onto the ground. "Damn."

"Dark Avenger," Sam cried out.

"Stay back, baby. Why don't you hold the flashlight for me?" Anything to distract him.

Sam nodded and clutched the plastic yellow tube in his hands, shining the beam on Zach.

"Not in his eyes."

Quickly Sam lowered the beam.

"You dislocated your shoulder." She should've seen it immediately. When she was about ten, one of the kids on her block had run to her house crying, his arm dangling at his side just like Zach's. Her dad had taken him to the hospital, then slugged the boy's father.

"We have to get you to the clinic in Hidden Springs," Jenna said, packing up the first aid kit.

"That's partly how we ended up on the side of this mountain," Zach muttered, sucking in a few deep breaths.

He didn't have to add if they hadn't been delayed, she and Sam would already be on the road to their new life, away from Zach.

"Just give me a second," he breathed. He rolled over onto his back. "I need you," he said softly, "to help me set the shoulder back into place."

Jenna swallowed. He had to have heard the gulp, but he didn't give her away.

"You're not going to run into a tree or something to shove your shoulder back into place?" she asked.

He quirked a grin. "Nah. That's in the movies. They aren't real, honey."

"The last two days feel like fiction."

"Ever hear that truth is stranger? Well, they were right." He let out a slow stream of air. "Raise my arm up to ninety degrees."

The beam of light dropped.

"Sam, keep the flashlight pointed this way, baby."

"OK, Mommy."

The illumination spread across Zach's torso, lighting his face. Jenna clutched his warm hand in hers and slowly moved him into position.

"Good. Now, turn my arm so my palm is facing toward my head."

She watched every facial expression as she turned the limb, but couldn't read a thing. He set his jaw and looked straight ahead, completely still.

He blinked once and bent his knee. "Now, I want you to put your foot where my collarbone is."

She shook her head. "I could hurt you."

"Right now it hurts. I need you to do this for me. Take hold of my hand and pull."

"Zach—"

"Brace yourself. Be firm, but do it slow and easy. You'll feel my shoulder slip back into place."

She followed his instructions. She couldn't help but wince when she practically stood on the bone. "Are you sure?"

"Do it," he ordered through gritted teeth.

She grabbed his arm. Slowly, she pulled. His arm moved. Nothing shifted. She eased her grip.

"More," he ground out. "Again."

She closed her eyes and heaved harder. Suddenly, the bone shifted against her.

"That's it. You did it."

His eyes cleared a bit.

"Position my arm as if I were wearing a sling," he said.

She removed her foot. With the greatest care she knelt next to him and placed his hand against his belly. He didn't move it. She let her hands linger on his arm and raised her gaze to his, gnawing her lip with worry.

He nodded with approval. "Not bad for the first time."

Her entire body sagged with relief. She bowed her head and sank closer. He caressed the back of her neck with his left hand. "Thank you," he whispered.

"Are you all right, Dark Avenger?" Sam said. "I didn't think you could get hurt."

"Everyone can get hurt, Sam. How's your foot?"

"Mommy told me I can't run around the mountains anymore 'cause I twisted my ankle."

"Your mommy is a very smart lady." Zach shifted and came to a sitting position. "Jenna, grab a long bandage out of the first aid kit. We need to immobilize my arm."

Within moments, he'd talked her through bandaging. He tested the ties. "Something else you're a natural at," he said. Zach rose and reached for the backpack.

"You might be indestructible in the movies, but this is real life, Dark Avenger. No way are you carrying anything heavier than Sam's flashlight after I nearly pulled your arm off." She shoved his hand away. "I'm carrying this."

He opened his mouth to argue, and she glared at him, giving him her best *I'm serious* look. It worked with Sam. Zach's brow arched. Jenna simply ignored him, heaving the pack with both arms. She planted her feet and gripped the straps tight. "Which way?"

"Fine," he said. "Can I have the flashlight, buddy?"

Sam handed it over.

"At least someone around here does what I tell them," Zach groused. "There's a cave a few hundred yards away. I've used it as shelter during a summer rainstorm."

Zach led the way, and by the time they reached the dark hole in the side of the mountain, the moon had risen enough to light their path a bit. "Get behind that boulder," he said, and stood to the side of the entrance.

Jenna pressed Sam to her side, peering into the inky blackness. Zach tossed a rock into the opening. It clattered inside and rolled to a stop. He repeated the action three times before motioning them out.

"No one's home," he said. "I'll go first."

He ducked his head and stepped through into the cave. The flashlight swept around. "It's clear. Bring Sam in."

Jenna helped her son through the darkened entrance. They picked their way into an eerie combination of dampened walls and a strangely glittering floor as Zach's beam of light sliced through the shadows.

"Look, the ground sparkles, Mommy."

"It's called granite," Zach said. "There are crystals in the rocks."

Sam crouched down and ran his fingers along the ground. "How did they get there?"

Zach stared at her son as if he were a strange alien, then let out a laugh. "I don't have a clue, buddy. Maybe you'll be a geologist when you grow up and teach me."

Sam scraped at the sparkling floor and Jenna set the pack down. She rubbed her hands together. "It's getting chilly."

"You wait with Sam. I'll get firewood."

"With one arm?" Jenna said.

"Sam needs you," Zach said quietly. "It's been a rough afternoon."

Jenna searched his eyes, recognizing the stubbornness. Reluctantly, she nodded.

"You'll come back, right?" Sam asked.

Zach knelt in front of her son.

"I promise, Sam. I won't let you down."

Each thud of Farzam's feet on the dusty road pounded another nail of hate into the coffin of his life. He held a bag in his hand, all that was left of his menial job.

Khalid and his terrorist contacts worked fast.

Farzam stood outside the hovel he called home. The wretched place would be too expensive now. He didn't know how he would tell his wife how far they'd truly fallen. He'd be lucky if she didn't leave him and beg her parents to take her back.

He pushed open the door.

His wife sat on the dilapidated couch and stared up at him, her eyes wide with fear. She blinked.

Farzam shoved away the panic that squeezed his lungs. He whirled around. A man stepped back, hands up in a peaceful gesture. "I am here to help."

His accent was unusual. As if he knew numerous languages but owned none of them. With a glance up and down the man's shabby clothing, Farzam let out a snort. "What can you possibly do? You're worse off than I am."

"Looks can be deceiving." He took a step toward Farzam. "You lost your position today."

His wife gasped, and Farzam glared at the man. "This is my business. Not yours."

A woman wearing a full *chadri* stepped from behind the man, her movement confident. The netting across her eyes hid their color from Farzam, but he could tell from her demeanor she was foreign.

"You've been asking about Zane Morgan," the woman said, her voice soft, but her accent clearly American. "Why?"

Farzam rubbed his tired eyes. He'd gotten nowhere in his search, and without any income, he wouldn't be able to buy information, let alone have enough to survive. His son was lost. His shoulders slumped under the burden. "If you're going to kill me, don't bother. We'll starve to death in a matter of weeks and save you the trouble."

The woman stood quiet and still, then tilted her head toward the door. Without hesitation, the man Farzam assumed to be in charge obeyed the silent order and left. Odd.

"Your son has been taken. Your job has been taken. Your sister is dead. Your life is over," she said.

"Get out," Farzam ordered. No way would he let a *woman* steal what little remained of his dignity.

"Zane Morgan caused your downfall," she said. "His death could rebuild your life, correct?"

Farzam paused. "Perhaps. If I could start again somewhere Khalid has no reach."

"That can be arranged."

Farzam stared at his fingers. No one gave something for nothing.

"What do you want?"

"I'm giving you a gift. Your heart's desire."

She pulled a poster from a bag she carried at her side. A flyer with a photo of an actor. Farzam read the words. *Zach Montgomery is the Dark Avenger.*

"What is this supposed to be?"

She took out a second poster and Farzam gasped. The hairstyle changed, a beard, a scar on his cheek. This man he recognized. "Morgan?"

She held the posters side by side. Now, Farzam could see. The same shape of face, the same eyes.

"Zane Morgan *is* Zach Montgomery. And I know how you can find him. I can even provide transportation to Colorado in the United States."

"Farzam, no. What will we do without you here?" his wife protested.

"Silence," he said. "I'm listening."

"I thought you might. I know about your brief but very interesting stint in your country's military. If Zach Montgomery dies, I guarantee you safe passage back and enough funds to provide you with a home, a job, and a new identity anywhere in the world."

Farzam's knees shook. He clutched the rickety chair. His grip broke the arm of the dilapidated furniture. He snagged the two posters and stared at one, then the other. Back and forth. Zane Morgan, Zach Montgomery. The world around him faded away: his wife, his nieces, his home. The images morphed until he met the eyes of the man who had seduced his brother-in-law and sister into betraying the family. The man who had ultimately cost him his son.

The man whose death would save his son.

He crumpled the papers. "How do I get to America?"

Very little could rival the night sounds in the Rocky Mountains or the crisp air. Zach just wished he had a few more supplies for a night on the side of the mountain.

An owl hooted nearby, and Zach bent over, shifting a small log onto his good arm. Jenna's place was with Sam, but it would take forever to gather enough firewood to keep all three of them warm for the night.

Jenna had really come through. If she'd been squeamish, she hadn't shown it. Not many could complete a shoulder reduction in the middle of nowhere. Jenna Walters—McMann—was a woman who had his back.

And Sam—well, that kid was something else. He made Zach think of his brothers, and the connection they used to have. A bond Zach had done his best to destroy over the last five years. He'd thought he'd made the right choices; now, he had to wonder. As his entire life slipped away—not only his acting career, but more importantly his national security work—he recognized for the first time how truly alone he'd become.

With the flashlight balanced in the V of his jacket, kindling and dried grass clutched in his bad arm, and a few logs propped on his left arm, Zach reached his limit. He made his way to the front of the cave and dropped his supplies.

Jenna looked up from where she'd laid out the space blanket, the protein bars, and the canteen from the pack. Fishing some matches from the side pocket of his backpack, he knelt at the mouth of the cave.

Sam stared at him, disappointment clouding his face. "Aren't you going to rub sticks together?"

Zach chuckled. "A good woodsman brings matches, buddy. Want to help?"

His young friend nodded and crawled to the entrance.

"We can't build the fire in the back of the cave. The smoke isn't good for us, so we'll build it at the entrance."

Sam nodded eagerly as Zach took him through the steps to place the logs where air would circulate to give the fire the best chance of catching.

"Did you chop the tree down?" Sam asked, his eyes wide.

"I'm using dead wood. It burns more easily."

With that, Zach struck the match. He took Sam's hand, and together they lit the kindling, blowing gently until the flames began to feed on themselves.

"We did it," Sam said, beaming up into Zach's face. "Look, Mommy."

"Good job." Jenna smiled gently.

"Now you're a wilderness expert," Zach said, ruffling Sam's hair. "You hungry?"

Sam nodded his head.

"We have two protein bars," Jenna said.

Sam frowned. "But there are three of us."

"Luckily, we're in the mountains in June. There's lots of good stuff to eat. I found some wild cucumber a few feet away from the cave, and I even came across wild strawberries.

"Watch the fire, Sam. But don't get too close."

Zach dug into his pocket for a knife. He snagged the flashlight and walked outside, turning back toward the cave. If he'd been alone he'd never have risked the fire, but Jenna and Sam needed the warmth. There wasn't much chance the flames would become a beacon to the wrong people. They'd traveled far into the wilderness. Only a fool would try to track them at night. And Zach didn't work for fools.

His mind plotted a route home to get Jenna and Sam on the road as quickly as possible. He wouldn't be able to carry Sam, so he'd need to take the easiest route for them. Zach crouched down beside the wild cucumber. Pine needles crackled behind him.

"Let me," she said, kneeling on the soft earth. "That can't be good for your shoulder." She took the knife from him and sliced through the stalks of the plant. "You're really good with Sam," Jenna said. "He likes that you don't talk to him like he's a baby," she said, through a smile. "He told me that."

"He thinks I'm a superhero," Zach said, holding another set of stalks so she could make the cut. "What's not to like?"

The firelight illuminated Jenna's features. "It bothers you."

"I'm not the Dark Avenger," he said. "I'm not anywhere close to being a hero."

She added the wild cucumber to the pile and laced her fingers through his right hand. Zach's body tensed at the voluntary touch. His chest tightened as if a vise closed around his heart.

"You saved my son's life. You outheroed the Dark Avenger, Zach. You can't run from that truth."

He refused to meet her gaze. She didn't understand. One saved life didn't make up for the tragedies he'd caused—his father's, Pendar's, probably others.

She scooted closer to him. "Why don't you see what I see in you?"

"Because you don't see the real me, Jenna. No one does." He stood, the darkness within rising up and taking over. "If you knew—"

"What? That you're human? That you make mistakes?"

"That I'm not who I pretend to be." He clasped her arm. "You just found out your husband lied to you for your entire marriage. You need to cloak yourself in skepticism, Jenna. For your sake and Sam's. You need to see people for who they really are. Even your son."

Zach weighed his words, and her need to hear the truth. "Do you know what Sam saw?" he asked.

Her hand dropped to her side. She backed away. "What are you talking about?"

"He saw your husband hit you. Sam saw you go back again and again. He believes Brad can change, that a time-out and 'I'm sorry' fixes everything. You and I know there are times when nothing makes it OK."

An itch rose on Zach's arm, the same sleeve that had been soaked in his father's blood. Sometimes sorry meant less than nothing.

"You can't let him believe in fairy tales any longer. Trust me, I know what I'm talking about."

Even in the dim light, Jenna's face washed out, completely devoid of color.

"I wanted him to have a father to look up to," she said. "Like mine. My dad gave me hope and a belief in the possibilities. I want Sam to be optimistic, to dream big."

"You can't afford for him to dream big, Jenna. He needs to be safe. Sam Walters could dream big. Zan McMann has to live under the radar," Zach countered. "While Brad is still out there, those hopes can't exist."

She turned her back to him. He tried to ignore the hurt fairly vibrating from her.

"Protect yourself and Sam, Jenna. You have to stop believing in superheroes," Zach said. "Especially me."

She rounded on him. "Why are you doing this?"

"For your own good. Go back to the cave. I'll finish here."

"Fine. I'll just go 'fix' what my son has seen. I may have made some mistakes, but you underestimate us, Zach."

He crouched to the ground, refusing to watch her return to their shelter. He sawed a few more wild cucumbers, trying to tear away the guilt at his harsh words. The clouds had hidden the moon, and the forest had grown black, save the littering of stars in the sky. The temperature had dropped. Zach told himself the chill settling in his bones had nothing to do with the truths he'd spoken and everything to do with the weather.

He made his way to the camp, shocked to hear Jenna's soft chuckle.

"Then what happened?" Sam asked, his posture eager as he leaned toward his mother.

"The warrior knew he had to save the princess…"

"And her son, the prince," Sam giggled.

"Exactly. He had a choice to make. To save himself and his own castle or to protect the princess."

"He had to leave his home?" Sam said. "Like we did?"

"Sometimes you have to leave things behind to move forward. What do you think he did?"

"He saved the princess and her son."

Sam's voice was so very certain. Zach leaned against the outside rock face and simply listened.

"What about the diamonds in the floor of the hideout?" Sam asked.

"Because the warrior sacrificed himself, the Queen of the Forest gifted him with the cave. He was able to take the diamonds and give them to all those who needed help. Until the end of his days."

She'd taken a few flecks of crystal in rock and incorporated them into a tale that mesmerized even him. And the message to her son couldn't be clearer. Sometimes the past had to be left behind—for the best.

"He did the right thing," Sam said.

"Sometimes doing the right thing is hard," Jenna said quietly.

Zach cleared his throat and entered the cave. She nudged her son, and Sam stood and faced Zach, meeting his gaze with unblinking courage.

"I'm sorry I ran away, Dark…I mean, Mr. Montgomery. I'm sorry you got hurt because of me."

Zach bent down to Sam. "It's all right." He held out one hand, full of green shoots and red berries. "I brought you something to eat."

Sam wrinkled his nose. "I don't eat green stuff."

"How about strawberries? Do you like those?"

Sam nodded.

"OK, then. We dine."

"Mr. Montgomery?"

He quirked a brow at Sam.

"If we need the Dark Avenger, will he come back?"

"All you have to do is call, Sam. I'll be there."

———————

Zach didn't sleep. He watched over Jenna and Sam through the night. They lay wrapped in the space blanket, covered with both jackets. They hadn't shivered at all.

Leaning up against the wall near the mouth of the cave, Zach recrossed his arms, taking advantage of his own body heat to warm the exposed skin. The hot coals simmered. His phone lay broken and useless on the floor of the cave, shattered by the slam against the cliff face. He considered topping the fire with another log, but the faded light of dawn eased toward the mouth of the shelter.

Their last night together.

Zach didn't like the emptiness in his chest at the thought. In just two days, Jenna and her son had snaked their way into his life.

His mind couldn't stop replaying Jenna's story in his mind. Or Sam's reaction.

He could understand Sam's faith. The boy was five. He hadn't had life rip the innocence from him. But Jenna. Jenna was different. She'd been betrayed.

And still, she believed.

A slight stirring captured his attention. Jenna shifted and stretched out her arms, her breasts pressing against her shirt. He could see every curve. He'd touched her just enough to imagine what those curves would look like. Soft, beautiful, comforting.

Like home. A home that would leave him in only a few hours.

He swallowed, unable to take his gaze away from the full pout of her lips or the upturned smile that seemed to always be just a moment away. Why did he always want what he couldn't have? He'd reached for the unattainable as a kid, as a young man, and he never learned. He was the definition of insane: repeating the same behavior and expecting a different result.

She turned to her side. Her emerald eyes fluttered open and the pools sucked him right in. He couldn't look away.

She slipped away from Sam and crawled over to him. "You've been up all night."

He didn't answer, but picked up his stick and stirred the coals, anything to avoid the temptation sitting next to him.

"You attacked me last night," she said. "On purpose. I want to know why."

Stunned, he flickered his gaze to hers.

"You hurt me."

"I know," he said quietly. "I'm afraid for you and Sam. I'm afraid you'll leave here and make yourself vulnerable."

Jenna hugged her knees to her chest. "I was fourteen when my father was killed in a car accident. Since my mother died of cancer when I was a baby, I was placed into foster care for a while. Then my uncle found me and took me in. He was nothing like my father. Uncle Sal was a dealer, but he was my only family.

He had no clue what to do with a fourteen-year-old girl. I went from being raised by a dad who loved me to taking care of myself. When my uncle was flush, he ordered pizzas; otherwise, we didn't eat. If I wanted to go to school, I had to find my own way. He got busted when I was sixteen, so I ended up on the streets for a while. When I was eighteen he kicked me out for good."

"I'd wondered where you learned to hot-wire my truck." Zach studied the woman who hadn't seemed to fit her image. Now he understood.

"While I was on the streets a mechanic taught me how to get any car running in less than thirty seconds. I think he felt sorry for me and gave me a job in a garage that doubled as a chop shop. That and picking a few pockets on the rich side of town earned me enough to eat without walking the streets."

Zach wanted to jump into her past and fight for the little girl who had no one. Her life could have turned out so differently. "How did you stay out of jail?"

"I was really, really good at what I did." She smiled. "I met Brad the summer I turned eighteen, when I palmed his wallet. I should have known then he was bad news. No normal computer jockey would have felt me lift that wallet." She picked the stick up from him and toyed with the coals. "Whatever you may think, Zach, I'm not a girl who believes life is all fairy tales and roses. My dad's heart broke when my mom died, but he never let it stop him from making sure I believed in the future. I won't let you or anyone else take the same dream from Sam. No matter who his father is."

She leaned back against the rocks. "The irony is, I forgot about my dad's lessons until I met you. You pretend to live your dreams, but you don't. So thank you for reminding me of the truth I want Sam to know."

She rose and walked out of the cave. Zach couldn't stop himself. All he wanted was to scoop her into his arms and hold her close. He'd seen more beautiful women. He'd made love to more beautiful women, but none compelled him to action like she did.

Zach glanced at Sam, but the boy was still sound asleep. He followed her into the wilderness and pulled her into his arms.

"What are—?"

He nipped at the lobe of her ear, and she shivered under his touch. Her hands roamed down his back and he wanted to purr.

"If I were a true superhero, I'd be able to resist you. Guess this proves I'm a mere mortal after all," he said softly.

His lips hovered over hers. His hand circled from her shoulder to her back, and she plastered herself tighter against him. She circled his waist with her arms, in a never-ending gift.

He needed to feel. She made him feel again.

She parted her lips.

His mouth pressed slowly to hers.

A loud explosion sounded much too close. The ground shifted under his feet.

Zach tore his lips from hers and jerked his gaze to the horizon. The sky had turned red with fire. He knew the location. His haven. His solitude. The last of his communications and equipment were a fiery ball.

They'd been found.

Chapter Eleven

*T*HE FIRE HAD CONSUMED EVERYTHING. HOURS LATER, ASH STILL floated through the wind, peppering the cove of trees and ground around Jenna. Nothing remained of Zach's cabin—his *home*. Family pictures had hung on the walls, unlike his La Jolla mansion. The California estate had been a movie star's show house—the one that appeared in magazines or on television shows. She'd believed the glass and stone to be a reflection of Zach's soul. Now, she knew better.

The powder prickled her nose, and a small cough escaped her. They'd watched from afar as the firefighters doused the blaze, then soaked the land around Zach's house. Wet cinder and twisted metal littered the ground.

The devastation choked her throat. She pulled Sam closer into her arms, holding him tight. She rocked him close, her eyes blinking back the burn. He stuck his thumb in his mouth, watching Zach's every movement.

Sam's Dark Avenger knelt at the edge of the structure where a small pipe emerged from the ground. He hadn't let a modicum of emotion or dismay show. He'd set his jaw and, after the firefighters finally disappeared on their trucks, he'd begun sifting through the little that remained of the cabin.

Zach dug in the debris. He pulled out a lump, then flicked the ash and dirt away. Jenna leaned forward, squinting. She couldn't quite make it out. *Metal, perhaps?* His face froze like stone. He clutched the item before picking his way back to them.

"The car's toast," he said, stating the obvious. "So is the helicopter." He tossed the metal gadget in his hand, then stuffed it into his back pocket. "Whoever did this was a professional. The detonator wasn't jerry-rigged."

"I'm sorry," Jenna said, tightening her arms around Sam. A detonator meant explosives. She *knew* who had destroyed Zach's house.

He shook his head. "No, *I'm* sorry. Once the paparazzo showed up, I should have gotten you two out of here. It was only a matter of time."

He knelt down in front of her and Sam. The icy-blue depths of his eyes held no blame, only concern and sorrow. He said nothing about Sam's escapade delaying them. Her gaze darted from his. They both knew the truth. If not for Jenna and her son, Zach would have been starting a new life, with everything he needed.

Now, he had nothing.

"We have to create new identification," he said, stuffing what remained of their supplies into his backpack. "Then we get you as far away from me as possible."

"I agree we should separate, but not for your reasons."

Sam whimpered in her arms. Jenna shushed him and met Zach's gaze, unwilling to flinch. The time had come to stop hiding the truth from her son, no matter how much it hurt. "Brad did this. When I researched his so-called accidents, he set explosives near gas lines. It fits."

"Whether Brad or my company set the charges doesn't matter," Zach said. "It doesn't change what we have to do." He slung the pack onto his good shoulder. "We can't hang around any longer."

Sam tugged at her shirt.

"Not now, baby."

He tugged again. "Did Daddy burn down Mr. Montgomery's house?"

Jenna winced and crouched down to stare at her son. "We don't know, Sam."

"He was mad when I talked to him," Sam whispered, burying his face in her shoulder. "I'm sorry, Mommy."

Sam's words drained the blood from her face. She lifted her son's chin. "When did you speak to him?"

He swallowed a loud gulp. "I was mad 'cause Mr. Montgomery kissed you. I called Daddy. I didn't mean to get the house burned down."

Jenna's hands clawed into the earth at her sides, the pine needles digging into her palms. She gripped the dirt in a futile attempt to keep her wits. "How did you get hold of him?"

"I stole Mr. Montgomery's phone," Sam said, head bowed. "Am I in as much trouble as Daddy?"

Jenna could do nothing but close her eyes and hold Sam close. "Oh, baby." She shook her head, her chin brushing his soft hair. She met Zach's somber gaze.

"Daddy's not a real bad guy," Sam said, his lower lip quivering, the uncertainty tingeing each hopeful word. "He just got mad. I'm sure he's sorry." Sam pulled the phone from his pocket.

The muscle over Zach's jaw pulsed. He let the pack drop off his shoulder and stretched out his hand. Jenna handed the phone to Zach.

"What did your father tell you, Sam?" Zach said, his voice calm and much too mild for Jenna's peace of mind.

"He wanted me to hide so we didn't leave."

Her son had obeyed his father. Because Sam loved his dad. Because she had betrayed her son.

A chill swept through Jenna's entire body. She scanned the perimeter with a shiver. "He could be here."

Zach met her gaze and shook his head. She recognized the reality. If Brad had them in sight, they'd both be dead.

With a quick pop, Zach opened the back of the phone. In seconds, he'd removed the battery and a chip and laid them on a piece of granite. He raised his arm. The sound of rock hitting rock smacked, the echo slamming through the woods. Zach had pulverized the electronics.

He knelt in front of Sam. The boy shrank back, and Zach sucked in a breath. "I'd never hurt you, Sam. No matter what you did or said. A man doesn't hit the people he loves in anger."

Her son's head cocked. "Even if they make you really, really mad?"

"*Especially* when they make you really, really mad."

Sam twisted his fingers in his jeans, his brow furrowed in thought. "That's right. I'd never hit my mommy because I love her."

Sam launched himself at Zach. "You're my best friend, Mr. Montgomery."

He wrapped an arm around Sam, holding the boy close. Zach's cheek rested against Sam's hair. He closed his eyes.

As much as her son's willingness to love Zach made Jenna's heart swell, guilt and worry choked her. He'd been right. Protecting Sam had endangered them all.

Shaky at the truth, she rose. "What do we do now?"

Zach set Sam on his feet, shouldered the pack, and took his hand. "We go into town, use my credit cards to get a car and some cash, and leave Hidden Springs for good."

Jenna walked beside them, their steps crunching against the burned pine and grass. When Jenna stepped on the sodden terrain, her feet sank down. The scent of the wet, scorched wood stung her nose. "They have to be tracking your credit cards."

Zach kicked aside some of the ash as they passed the blackened skeleton of his Range Rover. "Doesn't matter since they already know where we are."

They trudged down the driveway to the main road. Zach paused and veered to the side. "We'll have to stay out of sight as much as possible."

"You really think they're waiting?" she asked.

"I would be."

———

Zach had been wrong.

No one had been waiting on the road. No gunfire, no explosion, no attack. The unexpected development put his entire body on edge.

Dusk had settled over the mountains by the time they reached the edge of town. Zach shifted Sam's weight on his right arm, his left still immobilized against his body to protect his shoulder. The poor kid had conked out. His fifty-pound weight normally wouldn't have fazed Zach. He'd carried three times that amount on a pack he'd lugged into the jungle for reconnaissance nine months ago in South America.

Jenna's footsteps faltered.

"You all right?" he asked, tugging a few pine needles from her hair. They'd ducked in and around the road the entire way down. Had their circuitous route outsmarted their attackers, or were they just waiting around a corner?

She forced a smile. "Never better."

What a lie. He lifted his brow. She shrugged as if to say *what's the point in saying no.* They didn't have an alternative.

Zach paused and scanned the surroundings from their hidden position in a grove of pines just outside of Hidden Springs. The thick branches concealed their presence.

An abandoned building across the road would give them shelter. "Let's go," he said, and raced across the road, Jenna on his heels. He kicked open the door and lowered Sam to the floor. His shoulder was on fire. He needed some pain meds. A hot tub would've been great.

The graying wood had been eaten away by termites. Shots of light beamed on the floor in patterns from the bevy of holes in the walls. Still, they would be out of sight here.

Jenna lowered the backpack she'd carried after Sam had conked out. She spread the space blanket and laid Sam on it, covering him as best she could.

She stood and drew Zach away from her sleeping son. "He's exhausted."

Zach toyed with a strand of her dark hair, in such contrast to the pale fatigue on her face and emphasizing the shadows under her eyes. "So are you."

"I'll be fine."

The strength in her voice reminded him one more time why he admired the hell out of her. She had more grit than a lot of the agents with whom he'd gone into a firefight.

"Rest awhile," he said. He pulled his wallet from his back pocket. He'd used most of his reserves buying gas and food on the road to Colorado. His cash in the cabin—now ash. He fingered his last twenty. Enough to get Sam and Jenna something to eat and drink.

He slid out a credit card. "We're renting a car," he said quietly. He touched her face lightly. "Stay here with Sam. Don't show yourself. I'll be back with food and transportation."

"What if—"

"Jenna, I do have a plan. We still have choices. Believe me."

"I trust you," she said.

His heart swelled at the words he'd doubted he'd ever hear from her. Using side streets and alleys, Zach trudged into the mountain town. Soon enough, though, he had to walk down Main. He caught speculation in people's faces. His torn shirt and dusty jeans couldn't be hidden. Using most of his cash, he grabbed burgers for Jenna and Sam, a ball cap and some ibuprofen for himself, then hit the rental car company.

He tugged the hat over his eyes and walked into the garage that doubled as a rental site. The kid behind the counter nearly fell off his stool and snapped his cell phone closed, tossing it on the counter.

"Can I help you?"

Zach slipped his credit card across the counter. "I need a reliable car for a quick trip," Zach said.

The clerk pointed to a nondescript older Buick in the parking lot. Perfect. He would blend in easily. The kid studied Zach's clothes and face as he filled in the form using the La Jolla address. When the clerk ran the card, a strange look crossed his face, and all the color leaked out. The guy moved a shaking hand behind the counter.

Well, crap. Zach didn't hesitate. He grabbed the cell phone from next to the cash register, whirled away, and shoved through the door. Too bad the clerk hadn't pulled out the car keys yet.

Zach rounded the building and headed to an alley. Within seconds a siren screamed toward the store.

It only took a few minutes to race across town and slam into the abandoned wood shelter.

The room was empty.

"Jenna!" Zach shouted.

She creaked open a closet, the door hanging on one hinge. Her face was tight with strain, and she hugged Sam to her side.

"Those sirens are for me. My credit cards have been flagged." Zach handed over the smashed burger bag and palmed the ibuprofen bottle. Jenna sat on the floor laying out the pathetic picnic for Sam. Zach parked himself next to them, tilting the baseball hat away from his face. Wincing as he fought the childproof cap, he finally opened the lid and downed three tablets.

She paused as she fixed Sam his burger and looked up at him, her eyes shuttered. Zach hated disappointing her. It twisted his gut in a way he hadn't felt since his father spoke his last word.

"We can't stay," Jenna said. "Hidden Springs is too small and they know we're here. How far is the next town? Maybe I can find work and earn enough to get a car."

"In a year maybe," Zach said. He shoved his right hand through his hair. "We're out of options. We're going to Arvada."

Her face wrinkled in confusion.

"It's a suburb of Denver," he explained. "I'm out of tricks and people I trust. I don't want to, but we need my family's help."

He pulled the stolen phone from his pocket with its skull-and-crossbones skin.

At her questioning glance he frowned. "Don't ask."

Zach dialed a number only a few people knew.

"Montgomery." Seth's voice held a suspicious tone. He wouldn't recognize the number of a store clerk from Hidden Springs.

"Hi, Seth."

The phone went silent for a moment. Zach strained to hear footsteps.

"Where the hell have you been?" Seth's voice was a whisper.

"Incommunicado."

A door slammed. "You could have let someone know!" Seth raised his voice. "Why didn't you call us back?"

OK, he hadn't talked to Seth in months, but still…his brother *never* lost his cool.

Zach's entire body froze. "What happened?"

The last time he'd been out of touch on his recon mission in South America, his then three-year-old niece, Joy, had been kidnapped.

The only thing that could get Seth this upset was family.

"What's wrong, Seth?"

His brother took a shuddering breath. "It's Mom."

Zach's body went numb. If he hadn't been sitting, he would have collapsed.

"Is she—" He couldn't finish the sentence.

"She's going to be fine…" Seth hurried. "Captain Garrison might not be so lucky. He's still in a coma. When I find out who did this, they're dead."

Zach could almost see his brother pacing, his eyes narrowed in cold, hard revenge.

"Someone tried to make it look like the gas line near her house exploded," Seth bit out. "Coward attempted to make it look like an accident."

"Explosion," Zach whispered.

Jenna's mouth dropped open.

His eyes closed, the ash-laden clearing of his house flashing in his mind. He scratched the ball of his palm with quick, hard strokes. "When?"

"Two days ago."

Bastards. Three days ago, the organization he'd trusted had contracted a hit on him. Three days ago, Jenna stowed away trying to escape the Chameleon. Zach didn't care who had hurt his mother and Captain Garrison. They'd used his family.

They would pay.

"Seth, I may know who did it." Zach met Jenna's gaze, and she closed her eyes, her face turning a gray to match the nearly rotten wall behind her.

"Who?"

"It may be our mutual friends, but there is another option. You've heard of the Chameleon."

A string of curses pelted from his brother's lips. "What the hell are you into, Zach?"

"Sitting in a pile, brother."

"Then we get a giant shovel," Seth said matter-of-factly. "Mom wants to see you. Get here, Zach. Now that I know the stakes, I'll be more careful."

Zach rubbed his eyes with his fingers. This couldn't be happening. "What did you do?"

"Tried to find you," Seth said. "I called in a few favors."

"Not helpful."

"If my older brother kept in better touch—"

"Shove it." The ache behind Zach's eyes pounded in time with his heart. "I need transportation."

"Where are you?" Seth asked.

"Hidden Springs."

"I'll call you back."

Zach closed the phone.

"Explosion?" Jenna whispered.

"My mom and an old family friend were badly hurt."

She squeezed his good arm. For the first time since he'd witnessed his home explode, Zach had hope because of his family. They were damned good at what they did. *All* of them. He could count on them, but the idea of involving them made him nervous. Still, he had no choice. He hoped they'd understand. With Seth's contacts, they could get Jenna to safety while Zach and his brother dealt with Brad Walters. The Company—that was an entirely different problem. One he couldn't handle alone.

"Brad..." Jenna whispered.

"Maybe. Or it could be the men who are after me." This was why he'd stayed away from his family, and it hadn't mattered. *What a screwup.* He'd been selfish. As usual. His father hadn't been wrong about Zach. He wasn't a true Montgomery.

Zach shook away Jenna's touch. He strode toward a window frame, the glass long since broken, and stared across the valley toward the highest mountain visible. Fools Peak. The name had been a joke to him at one time; now it was simply descriptive.

A soft hand touched his back and he closed his eyes. He didn't want to find comfort in her touch. He didn't deserve it. Whether the Company or Brad had gone after his mother, the situation was on his shoulders.

Just like his father's death.

He stiffened under her caress, but she didn't take the hint. She rested both hands on his back and kneaded his muscles.

"Don't," he whispered, blinking away the sting that had settled behind his eyes.

She pressed herself against his back and her hands snaked around his waist. He looked down at the small hands and turned in her arms. Regret raked across her face. "I'm sorry I brought this onto you. If I knew where to run, I would."

Zach touched her cheek lightly and gazed into her green eyes. He could get lost in the moss-colored pools. They made him think of the forest, of better times. With his brother, with his family. With his father. "No matter who did this, I'll find a way to make sure you and Sam are safe. I promise you that."

The phone rang.

"Ace is coming for you. He'll be landing just north of Hidden Springs in less than an hour," Seth said. "Someone will meet you at the Rocky Mountain Metropolitan Airport."

"Thanks, Seth."

"Just get here, Zach. Then we'll kick some ass. Together."

That's what Seth thought. Once his brother got Jenna and Sam to safety, Zach would end this. The way he'd started it. On his own.

———————

Jenna sat against the fence overlooking a nearby field large enough for a plane to land. She cuddled Sam next to her. Her son had gone very quiet, watching Zach with a sadness and despair that broke

Jenna's heart. Did he finally understand that Brad had hurt Zach and his family?

No matter what Zach believed, Jenna knew Brad would do anything to get what he wanted. She didn't pretend he wanted her or even Sam. She was certain he wanted the evidence. *The irony*—everything she'd collected remained in California. She had no idea how she would retrieve it, or what Zach had planned. She wanted to talk with him, but he'd put up a wall after he'd hung up the phone. The man she'd grown to respect—and care for—stood alone, silhouetted against the western sky, searching, and he'd completely shut her out.

Part of her had wanted to fight him, but she had to face the truth. She and Sam had already caused too much trouble. Brad had hurt Zach's mother.

She swallowed back the bile rising in her throat. Zach was strong, but the best security in the world hadn't saved the people Brad had murdered. She shivered and rubbed Sam's arms. The summer Colorado air had turned cooler. Light was fading fast. What if the pilot couldn't land in the field in the dark? She didn't want to ask.

Sam sniffled. "Daddy won't find us, will he? He won't explode us, too?"

She hugged her son and picked up a dandelion, then blew softly. The seed heads scattered, floating as if magic on the air.

"Oooh," Sam whispered, instantly distracted, trying to grasp one of the white floating strands. "They look like fairies."

"Maybe they are," Jenna whispered. "What do you think they're doing?"

"That one wants to find his mommy. He's afraid," Sam said, kneading the knees of his pants. "He's all alone."

Jenna's heart ached and she tugged her son closer. "I bet his mommy is doing everything she can to keep him safe."

"What if he gets blown farther and farther away and she can't ever find him?" Sam asked.

Jenna didn't know how to answer. Sam's five-year-old mind was trying to process the strangeness of learning the truth of the man they had both once loved.

In the last three days, Sam's entire life had changed.

Zach stilled. He turned slightly and walked over, crouching in front of Sam. He held a dandelion.

"Is this the guy you were looking for, Sam?"

Her son squinted. "I can't tell."

"I think Zach found him," Jenna said softly, pointing to one edge of the flower. "Right there."

"Sometimes you can be lost for a while," Zach said. "But that doesn't mean you won't be found."

"Like when you and Mommy found me on the mountain."

"That's right."

Sam nodded and Jenna squeezed Zach's hand. *Thank you*, she mouthed.

He nodded, but his face had gone solemn, as if a light had been doused from within. She couldn't tell if it was concern for his mother or her and Sam, but she didn't know how to comfort him.

A buzzing noise drifted toward them from the east. A small plane glided, turned, then touched down lightly on the flat field.

"Let's go," Zach said. He picked up Sam and strode to the airplane.

"Zach," the pilot said. "Sorry to hear about Anna."

A man somewhere between fifty and sixty held out his hand then dropped it when he saw the makeshift sling on Zach's arm. "Seems like you've had an escapade," he said, crossing his arms.

A tattoo of an arrow crossed with a hatchet rippled over moving muscles. Zach nodded and set Sam down.

"I'm Ace," he said, tilting the brim of his hat at Jenna. "And who might we have here?" He knelt down to her son's level.

"I'm Sam," he said, his eyes wide as he stared at the tattoo.

"Sam, I am?" Ace winked.

Her son smiled for the first time since they'd left the mountain. "You're funny."

"I bet you've heard that joke more than once. So, young Sam, would you like a special seat in my plane?"

He glanced back at Jenna.

"Go ahead," she said with a smile.

She ran her hands up and down her arms.

"Getting cold?" Zach asked.

She nodded. "What happens now?"

"I go see my mom, and we find a place for you and Sam to hole up until I can collect new documents to start your new life. Then you leave."

She grabbed his hand and squeezed.

Zach pulled away. "Don't, Jenna." He led her to the plane and within moments the Piper Lance was airborne.

Sam stared into the sky. "Look at the stars, Mommy. They're sparkly."

The flight barely lasted an hour before Ace eased the plane onto a small runway. He turned back to Zach. "You need anything, you come my way. I owe your dad."

Ace exited the plane, and Zach followed. An SUV screeched to a halt near them. A man exited, limping toward Zach, his face none too friendly, but the square jaw was all too familiar. Obviously this was one of Zach's brothers.

"Stay inside, Sam," Jenna ordered.

She slid from the plane and cautiously approached the two men.

"Where the hell were you?"

"Calm down, Gabe."

"You bastard. Mom could have died."

"I'm here now."

Zach's face had gone as expressionless as a movie poster.

Gabe reared back and punched Zach in the chin. His head snapped back, but he didn't even raise his fist to defend himself. His brother's jaw clenched and he muttered under his breath.

"The least you could do is give me the satisfaction, not go all peacenik on me. You had everyone worried. Especially Mom."

Zach rubbed his jaw with a wince. "I don't have an excuse."

He met his brother's gaze, and Jenna recognized the pain in his eyes.

"How is she? Really?" he asked.

"Caleb can tell you better than me using ten-syllable words, but they say she'll make a full recovery. It was touch and go for a while." Gabe crossed his arms. "The house is gone. The pictures, most of Dad's stuff. Everything. She doesn't know yet." Gabe narrowed a dangerous glare at Zach. "Seth wouldn't say much, but I get the impression you know who did this. I want in. I have...connections. I can help."

Zach laid his hand on his brother's arm. "Listen to me, Gabriel. We almost lost you once. You stay out of this mess. It's mine."

His brother's jaw tightened. Must be a family trait.

"Crazy fan? Crazy girlfriend?"

"Something like that."

Jenna couldn't stop her open-mouthed gape at Zach. Why lie? Clearly the brothers loved each other, despite the punch. Still, she got the impression that Gabe didn't know Zach at all.

He gestured to her. "Jenna, this uncouth person is my youngest brother, Gabe."

The six-foot-three man took a careful step forward and tilted his head. "Are you the crazy fan?"

Irritation chewed at the nape of Jenna's neck. She wanted to defend Zach, but he squeezed her hand, giving her a warning look.

She cleared her throat. "Zach's been kind enough to help us. You might stop and look before you go off and slug him. He has a dislocated shoulder."

Gabe winced. "Sorry, Zach. I didn't notice."

"I'm fine," he said, frowning at Jenna. "She worries too much."

His brother stared at their entwined hands and cocked his brow. "Interesting."

Jenna felt a small tug on the back of her shirt.

"And who might this be?" Gabe asked.

Sam peered out and glared at Gabe. "He doesn't love Mr. Montgomery. I don't like him."

Jenna gasped at the same time Gabe turned pale. Zach stared at Sam, clearly shocked at her son's words.

"He hit Mr. Montgomery. People who love you don't hit."

Zach knelt in front of Sam. "My brother was just teasing, Sam. If he'd really not loved me, I would have slugged him back. I can hit pretty good, right?"

Sam chewed on his lip in thought. "You're confusing me." He straightened his shoulders and held out his hand to Zach's brother. "I'm Sam. But you still shouldn't hit. Mr. Montgomery told me so."

Gabe grinned. "You're right, Sam, I am," and shook the boy's hand.

Ace howled with laughter from where he'd secured the plane.

Zach groaned. "Can you be more cliché?"

"It was too irresistible." Gabe looked from Zach to Sam then back again. Jenna could see the speculation. Her cheeks flushed. She may have had a few fantasies about being with Zach in the biblical sense, but Sam belonged to someone else.

Unfortunately.

"Don't go there, brother," Zach warned. "You're climbing up the wrong mountain."

Gabe shrugged. "Joy showed up out of the blue on Luke's doorstep. I thought…"

"Well, you're wrong. I suggest you drop it." Zach's words made even Jenna shiver.

Gabe lifted his hands. "No harm, no foul. You ready?"

"Yeah." Zach picked up Sam and secured him in the back.

"Booster seat? Do you have kids?" Jenna asked, sliding in on the other side.

"I'm my niece's favorite uncle," Gabe said and slid into the driver's side. "Gotta be ready for the little munchkin."

"*I'm* the Dark Avenger. I'm Joy's favorite," Zach groused, getting in beside his brother.

"He *is* the Dark Avenger," Sam brought up. "He beats up bad guys. The Dark Avenger got two." Sam slugged his fist and kicked his feet. "Pow. Bang."

Gabe turned in his seat. "Really? Tell me about that, Sam."

"Once upon a time..."

Jenna could have stopped her son, but she didn't. She wanted Gabe to hear that his brother *was* a hero.

"...it was neat. He laid that one guy out flat. Then he saved me when I fell off the mountain. Mr. Montgomery is even *better* than the Dark Avenger."

Sam's face glowed.

"Sounds like you've been having quite an adventure," Gabe said, his voice speculative as he turned the key and the SUV roared to life. "Video game?"

"No, no!" Sam said, practically bouncing in his chair. "It was real. I promise. Then, the house blew up—"

"What?" Gabe shouted.

Zach gave his brother a deadly look. "Can we talk about this later?"

Gabe pulled onto the road and headed toward Arvada. "Fine, but you're going to be explaining a few things, big brother."

"I know," Zach said.

He leaned back in his seat. Jenna slipped her hand onto his shoulder. He stiffened, but then his shoulders relaxed a bit, as if he couldn't help himself.

Gabe's phone rang. "Yeah. I've got him."

He sent a sidelong glance to Zach. "Wanna meet at Luke's?"

"No," Zach said. "Nowhere that can be traced to the family."

Gabe raised a brow.

"I want Jenna and Sam unconnected to any of us. I'll explain later."

Jenna grimaced at the words, despite their truth. She wished she could be with Zach, but she knew in her heart it would never be. Her chest tightened at the thought of never seeing or touching him again.

"Hold on," Gabe said into the phone, lowering it. He twisted to Zach. "I'm bunking out in a small house behind the bar. It's safe, and the bar owns the house. If someone dug, they'd eventually connect you through me, but it would take a while."

Brad and the Company each possessed a lot of resources, and since they already knew about his mother, hiding wasn't realistic anyway. "Do it," Zach said.

Gabe placed the phone to his mouth. "Meet us at the bar. Twenty minutes."

"I'm going to the hospital first," Zach said.

"Mom's out for the count." Gabe glanced at his watch. "Visiting hours are over."

Zach stared down his brother. "Go to the hospital, Gabe. I won't wake her. I'll sneak in, but I *have* to see her."

His brother's face softened. "I hear you. We'll take a detour." He did a quick U-turn.

Jenna laid her hand on Zach's right shoulder and squeezed the tense muscles. He turned to her. "You need to duck down to protect yourself."

She leaned forward, her lips against his ear. "You're a good man, Zach Montgomery. Whether you accept it or not."

Heat rose up his neck.

Gabe let out a snicker, and Zach shot his brother a withering glance, but not before Jenna had had enough.

"I don't think you understand who your brother is. He's the most unselfish person I've ever met. You have no idea what he's given up for me and my son."

Gabe glanced over his shoulder, slack-jawed.

"So, before you go needling him, Mr. High and Mighty Montgomery, you might want to get to know your brother a little first."

Gabe shot Zach an irritated glare. "I might if he'd let me, ma'am."

Chapter Twelve

*T*HE LUXURIOUS AMERICAN PLANE LANDED ON A RUNWAY. Still under the watchful eye of his guard, Farzam looked out the side window at the mountain range, its tops dusted with snow. Through the opposite window, buildings stretched as far as he could see. No hovels, no decay.

This was an American city. Wealthy. Opulent.

So-called *freedom* existed here, but Farzam knew better. Appearances were deceiving. The shine of this grand place simply covered the decay beneath. The country had purchased liberty in exchange for its soul.

To survive, Farzam would have to be smarter than Pendar, smarter than the agents who brought him here.

The American woman emerged from the private room she'd vanished into as soon as the plane took off. His bodyguard stood. Farzam sneered at the respect. Another sign of weakness he filed away for later use.

The woman sat across from him, still appropriately covered in her *chadri*, the man poised at her side. "You are in Denver, Colorado," she said.

Farzam had heard of the city, vaguely. Somewhere in the middle of the large country, if he recalled. "Where is Zane Morgan?"

"Zach Montgomery," she corrected, ignoring his question. "Retrieve the bag from the compartment above you."

Farzam bristled at the order, but he could play her game. For now. He retrieved the satchel and unzipped it. A passport, a list of addresses, maps, and several weapons lay inside, along with a series of pictures including Zane...no...Zach Montgomery with several men who resembled him.

He flipped to the next photo—a house on a quiet neighborhood street.

The woman snatched the picture. "Don't bother going to his mother's home. Her house was destroyed."

"Did you do it?"

She didn't respond.

"Using a man's family is an efficient means of control," Farzam said through his teeth. "I should know."

The woman didn't respond. He studied the images. If he found the brothers, he would find—

"Don't get detained by the local police. If you do, your trip home won't be on this plane. I can't guarantee you won't end up in the hands of...a very different OGA."

"OGA?"

"Other government agency," she said tersely. "Trust me, you don't want to know."

"You mean I'm really going to be taken home?" Farzam asked, cocking his head.

"I keep my bargains," the woman snapped.

"Like you did with Zane Morgan?" Farzam said.

She stood. "Once Zach Montgomery is dead, your son will be returned to your wife. If you fail..." Her voice trailed off.

She exited the plane, her bodyguard following. This woman might wrap herself in the trappings of civilization, but Farzam knew the truth. She was more like Khalid than she knew.

———————————

Gabe maneuvered the SUV on the street in front of the hospital. Zach closely scanned the area. They hadn't been followed, but that didn't mean the building wasn't under surveillance.

If he'd been stalking a target, he'd set himself up on high ground near the hospital parking garage. "Circle the building," Zach ordered Gabe. "I need a safe way in. Maybe a staff entrance," Zach said, staring at the hillside across from the main entrance.

Gabe followed Zach's line of sight, his expression impressed. "Good spot for a sniper."

"Yeah." Zach continued his perusal.

"I recognize the advantages of the location because I was SWAT for five years. How do you? And don't tell me you learned during a lecture in Action Hero 101." Gabe straightened his shoulders, his gaze narrowed. "I'll find you the best entry point," he said as he perused their surroundings. "But, Zach, we're having a conversation when all this ends."

If it ends. Zach's teeth ground together. He didn't want to involve Gabe. His baby brother had almost died less than a year ago when a gang member's knife had sliced way too close to Gabe's femoral artery. He'd been forced to leave SWAT. He'd bought the bar and said he was happy. Zach wasn't too sure.

But now, he couldn't stop the avalanche. His family was being propelled down the mountain by too many unknown forces.

Gabe pulled the vehicle to a stop under a shade tree in the shadows. "See that door? Smoking area. We won't have to wait long before someone comes out. You can follow them in."

Zach gave his brother a nod. "Not bad, Gabe."

"I have my moments."

"Is everyone in your family a secret agent or something?" Jenna grumbled.

"Let's see." Gabe grinned. "I was SWAT…now, I own a bar. Luke and Caleb are former Army. Luke's a reporter, Caleb's a doctor, but the others…" Gabe gave her a wink. "If I tell you, I have to kill you."

"You can't hurt Mommy!" Sam yelled from the backseat. "The Dark Avenger will stop you."

Zach slapped the back of Gabe's head. "Good job, idiot."

Gabe turned to Jenna's son, his look pure chagrin. "I'm sorry, kid. I was just teasing—again."

"Oh." Sam bit his lip and looked at his shoes. "I didn't understand."

"That's because my brother isn't very funny, buddy."

Gabe shot Zach a dirty look.

He would have a few choice words for his brother after… A movement snagged his attention. The side door to the hospital opened. A guy in a white coat stepped outside and looked around. Then he held the door wider and a woman ventured out. The man tugged her into his arms.

"Great. Can't they get a room?" Gabe muttered.

The doctor's hands clutched her butt and he shifted her hips toward him.

Zach twisted in his seat, placing himself between Sam's view and the couple. "Buddy, I was thinking we could stay with Gabe while we're here. What do you think?"

"I don't know." Sam gave Gabe a suspicious glare. "He was mean to you."

Zach chuckled. "Sometimes brothers tease each other."

"I wish I had a brother," Sam said.

Zach looked over at Jenna. Her face flushed. He could picture her holding another child. A brother for Sam. A perfect family.

A dream that could never be his.

Gabe cleared his throat. "The heat's dissipating a bit. Out here, at least. Get ready, Zach."

He turned to Jenna. "I won't be long. I just need to see Mom."

She squeezed his uninjured shoulder. "Take as much time as you need."

Zach exited the car, his emotions swirling. He didn't like the link that had developed between him and Jenna. He'd tried to fight the feelings for so long. He was losing the battle. They barely knew each other and yet he felt more comfortable with her than with anyone he'd been with...in...maybe ever.

So not good.

Zach eased toward the hospital door, staying out of sight of the two staff members.

"You know I can't leave my wife," the doctor said softly.

"I can't do this anymore." The woman sniffed and cuddled against him. "I love you too much."

He cupped her cheek. "I love you, too." He pressed a gentle kiss against her lips.

"Maybe someday..."

Someday. The word reverberated in Zach's mind. Even if he stopped Brad, Zach's world would never be safe. There would be no someday for him and Jenna. She would be the woman he helped disappear.

The woman he remembered and dreamed about, wondering what might have been.

A beeper sounded. "Dry your eyes, sweetheart." He sighed. "Maybe I can find a way."

She went through the door, and the doctor ran his fist into the side of the building. "Son of a bitch!"

He slammed open the entrance and stalked through.

"You and me both, doc," Zach muttered under his breath. He blasted from his hiding place and stopped the metal from clicking shut before slipping into the corridor.

The scent of antiseptic burned his nose. He hated this place. He hadn't been inside since his father died. Gabe had spent a couple of weeks here last year, but Zach had been on assignment when his brother had nearly lost his leg.

He worked his way to the elevators and pressed the up button. The lobby was deserted since visiting hours were over, the flower shop closed.

His entire body tense, he waited until the steel doors slid open. Luke and his wife, Jazz, were locked in a hot embrace when the ding sounded.

Just what he needed: another up-close-and-personal view of what he couldn't have with Jenna.

His brother looked up, his eyes glazed, then just as quickly the satisfaction turned to irritation. "So, you finally decided to show up."

Zach shoved into the elevator and blocked them from leaving. "Stow it, Luke." Everything within Zach urged him to take his younger brother by the scruff of the neck, but he couldn't afford to let his emotions rule.

Jasmine leaned over to Zach and kissed his cheek. "I'm glad you're home," she said. "They were worried." She gave her husband a challenging glare. "They just won't admit it."

"Don't cut him any slack, Jasmine."

She studied Zach's face, and he squirmed under her penetrating stare.

"Look at your brother, Luke. Take a hard look."

As a sniper, Jazz's eyesight was keen, but for the first time Zach recognized how much more she saw than the obvious.

Damn her.

Luke let the elevator door close and leaned against the metal. Fighting to meet his brother's gaze, Zach ignored the twinge in his shoulder, crossed his arms, and faced the brother who had been through hell as an Army Ranger.

"Damn, Zach. What's happened to you?"

"I can't talk about it. If you're as good with the computer as you claim, though, I could use your help."

Luke couldn't hide his surprise. "You never ask for anything."

Zach rubbed his neck. It was the truth. For five years he'd pushed his entire family away. Now, to keep Jenna and Sam safe, he had no choice but to reach out.

"Brad Walters is a computer salesman from La Jolla. His property connects to mine. He's got another life as an assassin. Code name Chameleon. I need everything you can find out, but be careful. Don't do the research from home. Use whatever means you have to stay under the radar."

"Who do you think you're talking to, little brother? I can hack into most anything. I slip in and slip out. No one will know."

Zach clutched Luke's shirt. "Be sure. He has connections. Government. Probably FBI." Zach's glance went to Jazz. "Shit, this is a bad idea. You have a family. Forget it."

His brother let out a harsh curse. "Don't push us away, Zach. You wouldn't have come here if you had a choice." Luke's eyes flashed with pain. "And I'm pissed that it took you this long."

The elevator slid open. Zach shoved his hand through his hair. "Let me see Mom, then I'll explain what I can." He paused and met his brother's cautious gaze. "Protect your family."

"That includes you," Luke said to Zach, while gripping Jasmine's hand.

The words clogged Zach's throat. "I'll meet you at the bar."

Jazz plucked at his shirt. "Joy will want to see you. Don't leave before that. She's growing up so fast."

The thought of his little niece warmed Zach's heart. She was his biggest fan...except maybe for Sam. She'd probably already changed so much since he'd last seen her, he might not even recognize her except for the photos and videos Luke sent. Would she recognize him if he wasn't in his Dark Avenger costume? He cleared his throat. "I want to see her. As long as it's safe."

He tried to pull away, but Jazz clutched his arm, holding him close. "Don't go it alone. You don't have to. I learned that lesson the hard way."

He kissed her cheek. She'd been through worse than hell and had finally found a life with Luke and Joy. But shadows still lingered on her face. They'd probably always be there. Life drew lines that could never be erased.

A strong sniper with a soft heart. *Who would have thought?*

"Give your husband hell, Jazz. He needs it."

Zach stepped onto the ward, then turned and winked at Jazz as the elevator doors slid shut. The smile fell from his face as soon as he was hidden from view. Since Theresa hadn't called—which meant she was either dead or involved—Luke had to come through. For Jenna to have a chance at a normal life, Brad Walters had to be eliminated.

Zach followed the signs down the hallway and turned to his mother's room. His steps were silent from practice in more dangerous places, but all less important. He sucked in a deep breath and pushed the door open.

A curtain surrounded his mother's bed. Ever so slowly he eased around it.

Pale light bathed the bed in a spotlight. Even in the soft glow, he couldn't contain the gasp. Half of her face had turned mottled green, blue, and yellow, her complexion nearly matching the utilitarian sheets. Bandages covered one arm and her head, her cinnamon-and-sugar hair barely visible. An IV hung near her bedside. So small in the bed. So very, very hurt.

He leaned over her and gently kissed her temple, one of the only places that didn't appear battered.

"Zach," she whispered. Her green eyes blinked and opened. "You came."

"I'm so sorry, Mama," he whispered, and rested his forehead against the pillow next to her head. Burning pressed behind his eyes at the same time unfettered fury pulsed through his veins. He struggled to shove it aside. His mother could see through all her sons. It was one of the reasons he'd avoided coming home much since his father's death.

Her slight hand stroked his hair. "Shh. I'm fine. John saved me."

Zach lifted his head. "Captain Garrison?"

Anna's undamaged cheek flushed slightly. "He got me out of the house. He recognized the sound of the bomb."

"I'm glad he was there," Zach said, studying his mother's face. He hadn't realized Captain Garrison and his mother had become even closer friends. Zach's memories consisted of his dad and the captain taking him to task for every crazy stunt Zach had pulled. John had always had his dad's back.

Zach ran a light finger against the bandage on his mother's left side. He leaned toward her. "Did you see someone strange—"

She shook her head against the pillow. "We didn't see any-one. I've been through it all with the police. Let them do their job. I want to know where you've been." She clutched his hand. "You worry me."

The identical phrase she'd used five years ago.

"Mama—"

She flipped on a switch. Harsh light bathed the room. The bruises on her face stood out in sharp relief. Nausea twisted his belly at the truth in each contusion. She could have died.

"Look at me, Zach."

He lifted his gaze and she gasped. "Oh, my boy, what's hap-pened to you?" She placed her hand on his cheek.

He shook his head. "I'm fine."

"You're not. You're thin, you're pale, and your left arm is bandaged up. The last time you had that expression was…" Her voice trailed off. "When your father was killed."

"You don't have to worry about me, Mama—"

"Hush up, Zach." She squeezed his hand. "What are you doing here? Really?"

He shifted on the bed. "You're in the hospital. Why wouldn't I come?"

"Don't try to protect me, Zach." She let out a slow sigh. "You're as bad at it as your father was."

Zach pursed his lips, searching for a truth he could reveal. Anna Montgomery recognized every lie.

"Let me guess, your job got complicated. You don't know where to turn. You came home because you had no choice." She shook her head. "I recognize the signs. From Seth. From your father. You've been living a lie. Pretending to everyone. Even your brothers." She gripped his hand hard, hanging on tight. "And me."

Zach wanted to tug away from her knowing gaze, but he couldn't. He simply bowed his head. "How did you know?"

She quirked an eyebrow. "Please. You never could hide anything from me, Zachariah. You're transparent because you feel deeply."

"No one else thinks so." Except maybe his Jenna.

"Because they look with their mind, not their heart."

"A human radar detector." Zach smiled at his mother and a flash of insight hit him. "How many times did you tell Dad and John where I was?"

She shrugged. "I had a duty to protect you. I could see your struggles. You always believed you were different from your brothers." Her smile turned sad. "But you weren't, Zach."

"I appreciate the thought, Mama, but you know as well as I do they never understood." He didn't add his father hadn't either.

"If you'd asked, they would have gone with you on your mountain explorations."

"Everyone?"

She chuckled. "Well, all except Caleb. He hates heights."

Zach rubbed his eyes against the swirling of emotions. "I didn't think they wanted to go."

"Most see what they expect to see. I hope I see the truth." A tear slid down her face. "Just like I know John may not make it…even though no one has told me anything."

"He means a lot to you."

She blushed.

"Mama?"

For the first time Zach saw his mother as a woman, a woman who had been alone for five years. A woman who could feel, and grieve, and love.

"I loved your father. I always will, but—"

He patted her hand. "I understand."

"Now, you've surprised me. To think, I worried how you would respond more than the others."

"I've been thinking a lot about love and being alone the past few days," Zach admitted.

His mother's brow arched. "Really." She settled against the hospital pillows. "Tell me about her."

"I don't love her."

"Of course not."

Zach shoved his hand through his hair. "I can't love her, Mama. She and her son…we can't be together. My life…it's complicated."

"You can't ditch the subject. Not with me." Anna sucked in a sharp breath and winced.

Zach leapt to his feet, his heart racing in panic. "What's wrong?"

"Nothing." She pressed a button. "Pain medicine is wearing off. Burns hurt like the dickens."

Surprisingly enough, the nurse hurried in immediately and pushed morphine into the tube attached to Anna's wrist.

"So odd," she said, staring at her hand. "I can feel warmth moving up my arm and then going through my entire body."

Her face relaxed a bit from the pinched look that made Zach's heart clench. "Where were we?"

Her eyes fluttered.

"Don't worry about anything, Mama. I'll come back again."

He kissed her forehead. She clasped his hand.

"Don't let love slip away, Zach. It's too rare and precious not to fight for it."

She blinked several times, her eyes losing focus.

"Zach. Your father would be proud of the man you've become. Believe that."

Her words slurred, then her hand went limp and dropped to the bed.

Zach swallowed, clutching her small fingers in his. "I wish you were right, Mama."

He watched her breathe for several minutes just to make certain he hadn't lost her. She was an amazing woman. He should have known he couldn't hide anything from her. Jenna reminded him of his mom. She seemed to read him—all too well.

He'd thought he'd learned how to hide everything. Lies were second nature.

Had he been wrong?

He stepped back and stared at the woman whose unconditional love humbled him. He'd have to thank John Garrison for saving her. After he had a talk with the man about his intentions. John had been SWAT. They lived hard…and played hard if Gabe was any indication.

Before he spoke with John, though, he had to discover who had planted the bomb that could have killed his mother—and John. Whether it was Brad or someone connected to the CIA, they'd invaded his territory.

Mercy wasn't an option.

Brad Walters shrank into the shadows, his body disappearing from view. The last of the Montgomery family members had left the hospital. Finally.

The reporter and the sniper. An odd combination to be holding hands. He'd considered taking them out, just to prove a point, but he was too smart for that. Besides, there was no money in the deaths of Luke and Jazz Montgomery.

Brad glanced at his watch. Visiting hours had ended an hour ago. The glowing numbers moved too slowly. But he had learned to be patient.

The graveyard shift change would be his prime opportunity to complete the job. Part of him wanted to let the SWAT captain live mainly to annoy his most demanding client, but Brad's father's words rang through his mind.

Unfinished is failure.
Imperfect is failure.
To fail is to be powerless.

Nothing in his life resembled perfect these days. Brad's search for safety deposit boxes, mailboxes, lockers. Nothing had turned up in Jenna's name.

He had to find that evidence.

The phone in his pocket vibrated. He cursed at the number but didn't avoid it.

"Walters."

"Garrison isn't dead yet. You failed."

The staccato words tapped his mind like a perpetually leaky faucet. "He will be."

"Your performance is not up to par, Mr. Walters. I am not pleased."

A slight shiver scurried up Brad's spine. The words were businesslike, pleasant—and deadly.

"The job had a small hitch. Have I ever let you down?"

"Not yet. Which is why, instead of calling in other resources who are less, shall we say, fastidious, I am offering you an opportunity."

Brad didn't speak. He didn't want another job. He had to find Jenna and her evidence.

"By your silence, I assume you accept the assignment," the cold voice said.

"Of course."

"I'm glad you understand that you have no choice in the matter." Drumming sounded through the phone, the cadence scraping Brad's nerves. He fisted his hand, wanting nothing more than to slice off the fingers irritating him. "Kill Garrison, then stand by. Do not leave the Denver area. You will hear from me when you're needed."

The phone clicked.

Brad swallowed deeply. He didn't like being on the end of the puppet master's string. He gripped the phone. He hated not making his own choices.

Failure. Failure. Failure.

Brad stuffed his phone into his pocket and entered the hospital. He'd find a way to extricate himself from his client's hold. He just had to think and plan.

He excelled at planning. Despite what his father believed.

For now, he had a job to finish.

Chapter Thirteen

ERIE SHADOWS FILTERED ACROSS THE DESERTED PARKING LOT. Jenna stared at the door Zach had disappeared into. Separated for the first time in days, she missed his presence. Not a good sign. The side door of the hospital swung open, the jamb framing a large male figure. Jenna's heart skipped a beat in recognition. Zach.

He shoved a hand into his jeans and his shoulders hunched. His boots scuffed the asphalt in the parking lot. She slid closer to the window and placed her hand on the glass. He wasn't being careful enough.

When he strode under the parking light, she winced. The tension and worry painting his face hadn't eased with seeing his mother. The fingers of her left hand dug into her jeans.

Had his mother taken a bad turn? *Oh God. What if Brad had destroyed Zach's family?*

Her breath caught; she bit down on her lip hard.

"You care about him." Gabe's whispered voice echoed in the vehicle.

Jenna's focus stayed pinned to Zach, soaking in his suffering figure. "He's a good man."

"He doesn't take anything too seriously." Gabe let out a slow stream of air. "You seem like a nice woman, Jenna. Be careful."

She twisted in her seat and shook her head at the brother with whom Zach had traded barbs since their arrival in Denver. "I thought maybe this thing," she waved her hand in the air, "between you two was a brother deal, but you *really* don't know him at all, do you? How can you not recognize how much he feels?"

The car door opened and Zach slid in the front seat. He cleared the emotion from his throat. "Let's go."

"How's Mom?" Gabe asked, setting the SUV into motion. He maneuvered out of the parking lot and started down the road, but not without glancing at his brother time and time again as if he'd never seen Zach before.

Clearly, Gabe hadn't. Maybe none of Zach's brothers had.

"Bruised and battered." Zach bit through the words, his tone laced with a gruffness Jenna had never heard, a near break in his voice. Jenna leaned forward and rested her hand on his arm. He stiffened beneath her touch, and with a subtle movement avoided the contact.

Uncertain whether Zach had directed the rebuff at her or didn't want to make himself vulnerable in front of his brother, Jenna sank back into the supple seats. Her chest ached with disappointment. Either way, why would he need her—the woman who had brought a man like Brad down on his family.

"The cops are all over Mom's investigation—" Gabe began.

"They won't find anything," Zach said, staring into the clear night sky.

"It could have been an accident."

"Someone blew up my cabin this morning, Gabe. It wasn't an accident."

The SUV swerved. Jenna gripped the seat.

"What the hell—?"

"Seth really didn't tell you anything, did he?" Zach leaned his head back. "You're right, we have a lot to talk about."

"I'm hungry," Sam piped up, bouncing in his seat, oblivious or ignoring the strain pulsing between the brothers. "Can we have a snack before bed?"

Zach flexed his right shoulder and neck before turning to Sam with an indulgent smile. "You like hot dogs?" Zach asked. He glanced at his brother. "I'm assuming your favorite food group is still the only thing in your refrigerator?"

Gabe flushed. "Well, yeah. It's quick and easy. And the cook at the bar's restaurant…let's just say I could use a replacement."

Jenna studied Zach's smile. He could flip his emotions as quickly as the toss of a coin. If she hadn't been with him almost 24/7 for the last several days, she wouldn't have recognized the real pain flashing behind the blue depths of his eyes. She recognized the hurt hidden behind the glint of humor he shared with Sam. Jenna squeezed his right arm. His muscle stiffened under her touch, and she knew. His entire body had drawn tight as a stretched rubber band. But how much pressure would it take to break?

"Mommy is a really good cook," Sam said. "She makes yummy *sketti* and these really neat potato things with bacon and cheese." He smacked his lips.

"Potato skins," she offered.

"Really?" Gabe gave Jenna a speculative glance. "I don't suppose you're looking for a job?"

"As a matter of fact—"

"Not in Denver," Zach said firmly.

Gabe looked between the two them.

The small flicker of hope at the offer quickly died. Jenna sighed. "Not in Denver."

"Why is that?"

She leaned forward between the brothers and lowered her voice. "Because my husband wants me dead."

The hospital had gone strangely devoid of human sounds, similar to the mountains when a cougar stalked its prey. Anna Montgomery didn't know what had awakened her. Just a vague feeling. Only the odd collection of subtle noises filtered into range. Her eyelids cracked open. The morphine had knocked her out. She lay there, breathing, listening to her own slow inhales and exhales, then the soft whir of the IV machine. A variety of beeps echoed from down the hallway.

She clutched at the thin blanket covering her. Zach had come home. Over the last five years, she'd seen him transform from a shell of a man into a driven warrior—so much like her beloved Patrick. However, this evening, she'd seen someone nearly as vulnerable as he'd been the night her husband had died.

Unlike that horrific night, now she had hope.

Anna didn't know who had reignited the flicker within his soul. She hoped the woman's hands were strong and sure and worthy of her third-oldest. He deserved greater care and more love than he realized. Zach, more than her other sons, felt deeply. The gift—or the curse—made him a surprisingly good actor, but it brought him hurt that he didn't recognize, that most didn't understand.

When would her strong and brave sons understand that they needed even stronger women standing by their sides?

Luke had barely figured it out soon enough to win Jasmine's heart. Clearly his brothers hadn't learned from Luke's near fall.

Anna shifted in the bed. Her side no longer ached with every movement. The cuts and bruises were healing. She'd survived. John had saved her.

John. She was so tired of the avoiding glances and meaningless words. No one wanted to tell her the truth.

Well, she refused to wait any longer. She *had* to see John. For more than concern. A slow panic tightened her midsection. That feeling was back—the feeling from the night Patrick had died, the feeling from the day Gabe had nearly been killed.

Her body tender, Anna rolled to her back and sat up. An IV pump mounted on a wheeled stand stood next to her from her last trip down the hall.

John wasn't far away. She had to see him. *Now.*

She heaved her legs to the side of the bed waiting for the blood to flow into them. Her feet rested on the floor for several moments, then she slipped them into house shoes and stood. Donning the lilac robe Jasmine had brought her to conceal the hideous hospital gown, she fought for her bearings. It took a few moments to steady herself, but soon enough, she'd taken a few steps. Her head stopped spinning.

A plant in a glass vase rested on the window ledge holding her favorite—sunflowers. She needed to take them. She didn't know why, but she had to. They'd brighten any room. The rosemary sprigs had been Jasmine's touch once again. They had a nice scent. Even if John couldn't open his eyes, he'd know they were there.

She grabbed the glass vase—heavier than she'd realized—and started out the door. With care and quiet, she peered into the hallway. The sheriff's deputy who had been posted on her last foray around the floor had vanished.

Odd. At one point during her drug-induced haze she remembered her boys saying something about him staying indefinitely. Perhaps they'd changed their minds. Or the sheriff's office had.

Unease snaked around her heart, but Anna refused to give in to the caution. Unlike the night of Patrick's death, she would act on the wariness prickling in her mind. She sneaked out into the linoleum hall. The floor was strangely deserted. She'd never seen the place so quiet and glanced at the clock. Eleven. Shift change. That explained it.

She didn't attempt to walk past the nurse's station. Someone would be manning the location. Avoiding the center area, she crossed down the hall and detoured toward the room Jasmine had pointed out on their last excursion. Her daughter-in-law's sharp eyes had seen what all her boys but Zach hadn't. That John Garrison meant more than Anna had ever admitted. Even to herself.

Her arm quivered holding the weighty vase. She sped up her pace as much as she could. When she finally reached John's door, she pressed to open it.

Something got in the way.

Leaning against the swinging door, she pushed harder, shoving aside a heavy object.

She stared down. A man's shiny shoe attached to a uniform. The deputy. On the floor. Unconscious.

Her heart stuttered. She quickly looked up.

A man bent over John's bed. He wore a white coat, but he ignored the man on the floor.

She stilled. This was so wrong.

What to do?

She ripped the IV from her hand, clutched the vase, and tiptoed into the room.

"You won't be so hard to kill this time, Captain," the man said. He shoved a syringe into the clear plastic tubing.

Anna didn't think. She raced at the man and slammed the vase on his head. A loud curse erupted. He grabbed his bloody head and whirled around.

An ordinary man. A surprised man. An angry man.

He threw her to the floor and escaped from the room. Her head slammed against the metal bed. Mind whirling, Anna grasped John's IV and yanked it from his arm. Spots spun in front of her gaze. She couldn't see. She reached for the nurse's button and pressed.

Gray closed in on her. John's heart monitor sped up.

A shout echoed from the hall. Someone turned her over.

"Get security here, now!"

A man bent over her.

"John. Syringe. Murder," she whispered.

"Check the IV," the doctor shouted. "Anna. Can you hear me? Who did this?"

"Doctor." She lifted her eyelids. The doctor's concerned expression grew fuzzy. "Find my sons."

———————

The streetlights whipped past the SUV, the city's nightly glow reflected off the roads. Finally, Gabe entered Golden, the road on its outskirts nestled up against the hills west of Denver. He closed in on the Jefferson County Sheriff's Office. Zach forced his entire body to perfect stillness.

He'd have loved to cart Jenna and Sam to Gabe's former employers and put them in protective custody. If it were safe. Jazz might still be the lead SWAT sniper for the office, but Zach couldn't trust any law enforcement agency. Not with Jenna and Sam's lives.

The SUV swerved into the parking lot of Gabe's new endeavor.

"You've got to be kidding," Jenna said. "*Sammy's* Bar?"

Gabe winked at her and shrugged. "I didn't want to rename the business when I bought it. Sammy's has been an institution for years with a great location across from the sheriff's office. I guess your Sam was supposed to visit. A bit of fate taking a hand, maybe."

"It's *my* place, Mommy?" Sam asked with a huge grin. "Then I want something to eat."

Gabe maneuvered the vehicle behind the bar. The smell of barbecue hung in the air. The open lot with the basketball court made Zach uneasy. Too many places to hide. Gabe pulled up to a small house about forty feet from the back of the bar. Zach scanned the area.

A woman paced at the back door. "Who's that?" Zach said before Gabe had even turned off the engine.

He glanced at the lone figure. She bent over, hands on her knees, and took in several deep breaths before standing and stalking into the bar.

"That's Deb. She's all right, just a bit intense." Gabe's normally easygoing expression sobered. "She's the best chopper pilot in the state."

Zach paused, studying his brother's face. "Is she the one who flew you—"

"She saved my life and my leg," Gabe said quietly. "She's the go-to pilot for search and rescue *and* Flight for Life. She's scary good, takes risks no one else will."

"Someday, I have to thank her."

"Good luck getting her to say a word," Gabe muttered, exiting the vehicle. There was a story there, one Zach wanted to hear if he ever got his life back.

Gabe positioned himself a few feet away from the SUV, his body on alert. Once SWAT, always SWAT. Thank God. Zach unbuckled his seat belt and walked to the backseat. "Come on, buddy. Let's get you and your mom inside."

Taking Sam's hand, Zach helped the boy out. Jenna gave him a tentative smile, but he had a hard time returning the expression. His mother's words kept twisting around in his mind.

Don't let love slip away.

How had she known? Had he been so obvious?

How could he let himself feel anything?

And yet, as Jenna stepped into the cool Colorado night, his entire body tensed at the ready. He wanted to whisk her away, protect her, and take care of her. For now. Forever.

Searching for anything out of place, Zach peered into the night. A small man sprinted from around the bar toward them. He skidded to a stop, but not before barreling into Gabe. The man gripped his brother's collar. "You gotta hide me, Gabe. I got nowhere to go."

"He went this way," a deep voice yelled.

Pounding footsteps grew louder. Zach handed off Sam to Jenna. "Get inside the house. Now," he ordered.

For once she didn't argue or question. She carried Sam into Gabe's small house and slammed the door closed behind her.

Arms crossed, Gabe faced the mouse of a man. "You led them here, Ernie. I should beat the crap out of you. Get behind the truck. Stay out of sight." He glanced at Zach. "Follow your girlfriend in. I'll take care of this."

"The hell you will. Not alone."

Gabe shot Zach a deadly glare. "I can still take care of these yahoos—" Gabe's voice trailed off.

A man of at least six foot six thundered around the corner, his face red and twisted. Unfortunately, the giant's three buddies, who obviously spent most of their time in the gym as opposed to porking on pizza and beer, raced behind him.

"Shit," Gabe cursed under his breath.

"Ya think?" Zach muttered.

The giant stopped and folded his arms. "Lookie what we got here, boys. The gimp cop who's trying to horn in on the boss's business and a banged-up pretty boy. We get a three-for," the man snickered. "If you don't want to get really hurt really fast, send out the sniveling snitch and forget you ever saw him."

Ernie scrambled farther under Gabe's SUV and peered out, eyes wide, hands trembling. At least the man was out of harm's way. Zach edged slightly to one side to improve his angle. Even with his arm in the sling, he could take the three pretty quickly. They might be able to hold their own on the streets of Denver, but Zach had a few moves he doubted they'd seen.

Zach glanced at Gabe. His brother's knee remained an unknown. He'd never admit it, but that knife had done a real job on the muscles. No way could Gabe move like he had before the injury. Zach refused to see his little brother hurt.

"If you're smart, you'll mind your own business and let me take care of Ernie." The guy flicked open his knife.

Gabe chuckled. "You should've at least brought a gun, Tiny."

"Don't like guns. And I get my way just fine with this." He lunged forward.

With a quick step left, Gabe avoided Tiny, and Zach took his opportunity to take out Tiny's goons. He jumped in front of Gabe, swept a leg around, and shoved his foot square into the first goon's chest. One kick and the man crumpled. In a smooth move with no hesitation, Zach shifted and blasted his fist into the second guy's nose. He fell to the ground. Before the final man had even pulled back for a punch, Zach cut the guy at the knees, grabbed his hair, and slammed his forehead into the asphalt.

All three men lay at his feet. Unconscious.

Gabe's mouth gaped open.

Tiny took a step back.

Footsteps thundered toward them. Four Montgomery brothers raced out of the house to help. Tiny took one look at the Montgomery brothers and broke off running into the distance.

Ernie ran in the opposite direction.

"So much for gratitude," Zach groused.

His brothers skidded to a stop.

"What the hell?" Nick muttered.

"Ask Gabe." Zach frowned. "He's the one running a halfway house for petty criminals."

"I don't think Nick was talking about Gabe, big brother." Seth crossed his arms and eyed the three bodies still lying in the parking lot.

Zach shrugged. "I learned a bit of self-defense on set." He turned and strode to the screen door of Gabe's house. He didn't need the Montgomery family inquisition. Why couldn't they leave him alone?

Sam stood just inside the door, his eyes wide, his mouth gaping in awe. "You scared them away, Dark Avenger. Just like before."

Jenna placed her hands on Sam's shoulders. Her eyes twinkled with a secret knowledge. "How about something to eat?" She stared pointedly over his shoulder.

Zach turned around. His five brothers stood shoulder-to-shoulder, open-mouthed. *Great. Just great.*

He pushed into Gabe's kitchen. "I'd love something to eat."

"How's the shoulder?" she asked.

Zach shifted his arm. "Let's just say my little exercise class didn't help the healing process." He dug into his pocket and popped the last of the ibuprofen.

Jenna shook her head. "Men."

She opened the refrigerator and emerged with an armload of ingredients. Within minutes she'd dumped them into a skillet. Soon a whiff of amazing scents permeated the room and had Zach salivating. Bacon and spices wafted at him. His stomach rumbled. If only he could have a meal with Jenna and Sam and then hold her in his arms tonight and *not* talk. Just be. With no one after them, no knives or guns or explosions.

He sat down at the kitchen table facing the door, preparing himself for an onslaught, expecting any second his brothers to shove their way in. They didn't. "What do you think they're doing out there?" he asked Jenna.

"Talking," she said. "Wondering who you are, and if they're anything like you, trying to figure out the answers before they ask the questions." She bent to check the oven, then wiped her hands on a dish towel. "Why don't you go to them?"

He let out a sigh and rubbed his temple. He'd been the one to push them away; maybe he should make the first move. It had been much easier to avoid them, losing himself in the excitement of battling the bad guys, than reaching out.

Before he could decide, Gabe limped into the house. "You've got some 'splaining to do, my brother."

The rest of the Montgomerys filed in after Gabe. "Damn straight," Nick grumbled, tugging at the US Marshal badge clipped to his jeans.

"Kid," Zach murmured and ruffled Sam's hair. The boy sidled up next to Zach, complete trust in his eyes.

Jenna placed a plate in front of her son, then Zach. "Chili and cheese?" she asked.

"Yes, yes, yes," Sam hooted.

"You heard him," Zach said, thankful for the distraction. Anything not to look at the row of condemnation—too much like his father.

She ladled chili over the hot dog and sprinkled cheese on top. Sam eyed Zach and took a bite exactly when Zach did.

He groaned at the heaven hitting his tongue. "Jenna, you are magic in the kitchen."

Gabe's throat cleared.

Zach wiped his mouth and finally chanced a view of his five brothers. Gabe and Nick scowled. Caleb looked puzzled. Luke's and Seth's gazes had narrowed in speculation.

"What?"

"You're unbelievable," Luke said. "Fine, you want to play it this way, I'll start," He picked up a chair, turned it around, and straddled it. "Those moves weren't movie research. I recognize the training."

"And you all are just learning this?" Jenna broke in.

"Jenna—" Zach began.

"I've known you for three days, and I figured out you're some kind of secret agent guy. Even Sam knows. Why don't they?"

Zach glared at her. "Junior Avenger and I are eating. You need to eat, too. As for the rest of you," he stared down his family, "either join us or go into the other room to speculate, but quit hovering."

Sam glowered at them.

Luke raised his hands in surrender. "I'd love a hot dog."

The oven chimed. Jenna pulled a tray of hot slices of thick potato still in the skins. Cheese bubbled and bacon bits decorated the tempting morsels.

"Count me in. I've died and gone to heaven," Caleb said. He took a seat next to Zach and grabbed a plate.

One by one, the Montgomery brothers joined Zach at the table and shoveled down everything Jenna could put in front of them.

That hadn't been the plan.

He frowned at all of them as they ate, and Sam imitated his look. Luke choked on a bite of hot dog. "The kid could be your twin. We can't introduce him to Joy or we'll be ruled by two kids under the age of six."

All of the brothers stared between him and Jenna, then focused more intently on Sam.

"No," Zach said, his voice low. He couldn't keep the slight tinge of regret from his voice. He wished they belonged to him.

Caleb's phone broke the uncomfortable silence. "Doctor Montgomery." His face paled. "They're stable?"

As Caleb listened, his frown deepened. "I'll be right there. Have security call Detective Neil Wexler. He's in charge of the case."

He pocketed the phone. Silence held the room, a cricket from outside the only noise. Even Sam seemed to know this was no time to talk.

"What happened?" Zach asked through gritted teeth.

"They almost lost John. Someone dressed as a doctor put a stimulant in his IV and sent him into V-fib."

"English, please," Nick begged.

"His heart went crazy fast," Caleb said. "They were able to stabilize him because not enough drugs made their way into John's system." Caleb rubbed his beard. "Mom pulled out his IV just in time. She saved his life."

"What was she doing out of her room?" Zach jumped out of his seat. "When I left her she was zoned out on morphine."

"Obviously she woke up. She sneaked down the hall to see him and interrupted the killer."

The men rose as one, a wall of strength. This was what he'd missed. Being part of not just any family—but *his* family.

"She's all right?" Gabe bit out.

"Whoever tried to kill John shoved her down. She hit her head against the bed. She's still unconscious."

Zach paced the kitchen, his mind whirling. "It doesn't make any sense. Why John?"

Jenna cleared her throat and tugged at a nodding-off Sam. "Now's a good time for this guy to go to bed," she said, sending Zach a warning message. "Where should I put him?"

"Second door on the right," Gabe said. "Bathroom's across the hall. And Jenna, thanks for dinner. You rock," he added, wiping his mouth. "If you ever want a job—"

"She won't be calling you," Zach muttered.

Jenna took Sam's hand, but he jerked away. He ran to Zach and hugged his legs. "Will the bad men come back, Dark Avenger?"

Zach knelt down. "No one will get you, Sam. I promise."

"Not even Daddy?"

"Not even your daddy." Zach ruffled Sam's hair. "See those guys—all of them will help protect you."

"'Kay." He nodded, but his eyes were blinking hard. "Thanks, Zach. Mommy said I could call you that, 'cause there are so many Mr. Montgomerys." He looked around the table. "You all kind of look alike."

Luke swallowed back a laugh.

Zach chucked Sam under his chin. "Have a good night, buddy."

He followed Jenna out of the room. Gabe closed the sliding doors to shut off the kitchen from the rest of the house.

The brothers waited until they heard a door's lock click and water start to run. Then they pounced.

"What the hell is going on?" Nick demanded.

"What do you know about Mom's house?" Caleb asked.

Resigned, Zach sank into the chair and stared from brother to brother. They were all so different, but right now they shared identical determined expressions. Zach didn't blame them.

"Don't even try with the lies," Seth said. "This is Mom we're talking about."

"What I thought doesn't matter anymore." Zach methodically folded the napkin on his plate, half by half by half. "I had two theories since my cabin near Hidden Springs exploded just like Mom's, but neither one falls in line with an attack on John."

"Whoa, brother," Gabe said. "Start from the beginning."

Zach sank into the chair, then brought them up to speed. "I don't know what to tell you. If John hadn't been the target, I'd say that my...colleagues aren't very happy with me and they've gone way too far—"

"You think?" Seth muttered, shaking his head. "Your name popped up on the CIA's list of potential traitors. I assume that's who you've been working for. They're setting you up, big brother."

"Then why not just wait until he was in his cabin to blow it up?" Luke offered. "That's what I'd do if I wanted to get rid of him."

Zach grinned. "You've got an evil mind, Luke. Ditto."

"Except you don't just have the CIA after you, do you? There's also the Chameleon," Luke offered.

"Jenna's husband," Zach clarified at Caleb's confused look. "I planned to help her start a new life."

"Why didn't you call me?" Nick said. "I could have put her in touch with WitSec."

"I have two words," Jenna said, opening the door. "Joseph Romero. My husband killed him, and he was in WitSec."

"Why would your husband try to hurt Mom or John?" Caleb said, his face skeptical.

"I thought he might be using Zach to draw me out so he could take Sam."

"An assassin doesn't kill indiscriminately. It's bad for business," Seth said. "Unless he's gone psycho or it's personal."

"Zach's right about one thing," Nick added. "The speculation doesn't matter. We have two sets of targets. We need to split up until we figure out exactly what's going on. Three of us need to watch Mom. The others need to do a little...sensitive research."

"Agreed. Nick, Caleb, and I will head to the hospital," Gabe said. "Seth and Luke are the info guys. Zach...I'm guessing the news is wrong and you're not AWOL on your big comeback break and having fun with your *boyfriend* in the Bahamas, so you better hang with the spy guys on this."

Zach threw up a third-finger salute then rubbed his chin. "Let us know if there are any changes in Mom's condition."

The mirth in Gabe's eyes vanished. "Hopefully she'll wake up soon and can tell us who attacked her and John."

With an agreement on communication and weapons doled out, Gabe, Nick, and Caleb left. Zach locked the door behind them. The kitchen had closed in on him. He turned and faced Luke and Seth—the brothers who understood more than anyone exactly what he was up against. "First things first. I had a plan in place for Jenna and Sam to start over. I need to recreate all the documentation. Can you help me?"

Jenna laced her fingers through Zach's. He gazed down into her eyes, knowing once more they'd have to say good-bye. He couldn't ignore the twinge in his heart at the thought.

"Do you want to disappear with Jenna and her son, Zach?" Seth asked quietly.

"I can't until I stop whoever wants me dead," Zach said, struggling between what his heart longed for and what his head knew should happen. He scribbled down the addresses, bank account numbers, and the identification numbers of the new identities he'd created for Jenna and Sam. "I won't risk their lives."

"And I won't take you from your family," Jenna said. "They love you. We both know what has to be. Brad will never stop, not until he kills me and has the evidence. As my husband, if he ever found me and the location of the safety deposit box, he could gain access to it once I'm dead."

"Um, Jenna. That might not be quite accurate," Luke said, opening a file folder and flipping through the papers.

A small hitch of hope simmered within Zach.

"I dug into Brad Walters's life and found some very interesting information."

Leaning forward in his chair, Zach tugged the file from Luke's fingertips.

"Brad Walters isn't his real name. In fact, Jenna, your husband isn't who he pretends to be."

Jenna sank into the chair next to Zach. "What are you saying?"

"Brad Walters has no claim on you. You were never legally married."

Chapter Fourteen

F JENNA HADN'T BEEN SITTING, SHE WOULD HAVE KEELED OVER. She struggled to take a breath. A vise clamped around her chest.

Not married. Not married. Not married.

The words echoed in her head.

Her life with Brad had been nothing but a lie. A horrible thought occurred to her. "Did the feds know all along?"

Luke averted his gaze. "I can't be sure. When the FBI convinced you to stay to gather evidence, my guess is some cowardly prosecutor wanted a certain conviction. Brad can't argue against his own words."

"You mean, yes, they knew," Jenna said, struggling to stop the bevy of emotions from spilling all over the place. "So Sam and I were expendable—just part of a twisted game to catch Brad? They already had the evidence I'd given them. Why use us like that?"

"I'm sorry, Jenna." Zach lifted her from the chair next to him to his lap and pulled her close, cradling her, rocking her, hugging her against his warm body.

She sagged in Zach's arms, her entire body limp. "Get me out of here," she whispered. "Please."

"I will." Zach tightened his hold. "Seth, Luke, I want those documents ready. Get her and Sam a new life. Then we go hunting. For Walters and the truth."

Jenna had no idea how Zach's brothers responded. Her emotions swirled around her—battered, angry...and strangely relieved. She wanted the world to disappear. She buried her face into Zach's shirt and breathed in the pine scent of his clothes.

With her nestled in his arms, he walked her down the hall, cracked open an empty bedroom door, then shut them inside. He carried her to the bed and laid her down. She wrapped her arms around a pillow and hugged it to her chest.

"I can't stop thinking that I trusted the FBI to help us...and Sam and I could have been dead because I'm so gullible." She rubbed at her eyes.

Zach settled down next to her and pinned her close to his side. He wiped the tears from her cheek. "You got away, Jenna. You protected Sam. You're going to be just fine."

She scrubbed her face with her palms, scouring away the horrifying reality. "My life with Brad wasn't a fairy tale *or* a nightmare," she whispered. "It was just a lie."

Jenna sank deeper into the pillow and turned to her side, her back to Zach. She'd let herself be taken in by a man who never loved her. She'd been so eager to believe in love and happily-ever-after, she'd let him hide more than the truth in a veil of security. She'd bought into everything he'd sold her for so long, how could she ever trust herself?

She stared at the simple white curtains shielding the window from view. The fabric fluttered slightly when the air conditioner kicked on. The cool air blew across her face. She touched her wet cheeks. Nothing felt substantial or real anymore, only insubstantial and invisible as the circulating air.

Zach lay down beside her and she stiffened.

"Don't shut me out." He plastered his body against her, wrapping his good arm around her waist, throwing his leg over her, and pinning her close.

She lay quiet in his arms, her mind whirling, confused.

"I don't even know his real name," Jenna finally said with a sigh. "I don't know the name of my son's father."

"Does it matter?" Zach's mouth skirted her ear. "He's an amazing boy."

She shivered at the touch of his lips. She wanted to turn into his arms, but she couldn't stop the fear gripping her belly. "How do I protect him when I can't trust myself to see the truth? Brad used me as a shield. He even used his son—in more ways than I ever realized before this moment."

Zach scooted slightly away from her and tugged her arm toward him. She let him roll her onto her back.

"Look at me," he said.

His gentle expression tightened the knot in her throat. Pity, sympathy, and she couldn't understand what else.

"Brad Walters is an assassin—a professional con man and a killer. That hasn't changed. You followed your instincts and gathered evidence against a man no intelligence agency was able to touch, here or abroad." Zach cupped her cheek with his hand. "Jenna, don't doubt you *can* trust your instincts. Since the moment I met you, you've been right about so many things."

With a tentative hand, she reached to touch the brown and ginger hair. His blue eyes captured hers, their depth holding so many secrets—so much he didn't reveal to the world. "I was wrong about you. I thought you were a superficial actor with a harem at your beck and call."

He gave her a small smile. "You weren't wrong. I've been that man for a lot of years."

"Now who's not taking credit," she said. "I saw you take out those men in Hidden Springs when they could have killed us. I saw your super-secret room. I see how you've hidden your covert life from your brothers."

"And you thought you couldn't trust your instincts."

He tried to look away from her, but she refused to let him. She gripped his arm. "Why? Why did you push them away? Your family loves you."

"They love the boy they remember, but I can barely face them, Jenna. They don't know me or what I've done." Zach took a shuddering breath and closed his eyes. "I'm responsible for my father's death."

He shifted from her, moving to sit up, but she clutched at his shirt, refusing to let him go. "I don't believe you."

His eyelids snapped open. Anguish screamed from the depths of his eyes. She swallowed a gasp at the hurt he'd clearly buried. "Five years ago, he called me, wanting to meet. I was *exactly* the man you described. The tabloids weren't wrong. I was young, foolish, and going down a dark path. You name the vice, and I tried it more than once. I believed my own press, believed I was indestructible." He cleared his throat. "I learned the hard way that my biggest hero—my father—wasn't."

"If Sam were headed down that path, I'd do whatever it took to stop him," Jenna said, rubbing her hand back and forth on his arm. "That's what your dad did."

"My father was stubborn, that's for sure. Patrick Montgomery was more bullheaded than any of us." Zach smiled. "Except maybe my mom."

Jenna bit her lip. "Patrick Montgomery? The name sounds familiar."

Zach winced. "My father's death made national news. A decorated cop shot down in a convenience store robbery. No one knows the full story. Not even my mother."

Her heart aching for the agony in his voice, Jenna pressed close against Zach. "Tell me."

He closed his eyes. "He was waiting for me across from a bar where I was drinking myself into oblivion in a private VIP room. All because I wouldn't return his call." Zach lifted his haunted gaze. "He probably tried to stop the crime. He'd do that. Dad died in my arms. I promised him I'd make things right. He called me a liar. I was always the family's biggest disappointment. My screwup cost my father his life."

She wrapped her arms around him and laid her head on his chest. His heartbeat thudded beneath her ear, speeding up when she nestled into his arms. "You misunderstood your father, Zach. I've seen you and your brothers. Your father loved you. Just like mine did. You don't have to get yourself killed to prove yourself worthy of the Montgomery name."

He shook his head. "You don't understand. I robbed our family of a man who should be getting ready to retire and travel across the country with my mom in an RV. They'll never have that chance because of my selfishness."

She studied his self-loathing expression, and with a blast of insight recognized it mirrored her own. She'd wanted to disappear, too. She touched his face, her fingertips drawing down the stubble on his cheek. "Is that why you're letting your beard grow?" she asked. "A new disguise for your next dangerous mission—or to hide from yourself again?"

His jaw throbbed with unspoken emotion. "I have some unfinished business in Afghanistan. Since life as I know it is over, I better figure out who I'll be next."

A stark vulnerability had settled over him.

"I understand that, I do, Zach, but you know what? I think you've punished yourself enough. And so have I."

She framed his face with her hands. "The only good thing to come out of this entire mess is that I met you." She sucked in a deep breath. "I'm going to have to be strong for me and Sam in the future, but for now, can I just be free of the cage I've lived in? Will you help me do that?"

She wanted to be held, wanted to be loved.

She didn't want just anyone, though. She wanted Zach. "I...I want to be selfish. I want you to want me."

He caressed her hair, his touch tentative as he twisted the locks that fell over her shoulders. "I can't take advantage of you," he said, his voice full of regret.

"You wouldn't be. Unless...unless you don't want me?"

Part of her wanted to shrink away and roll over...until desire flooded his eyes.

He *did* want her.

And she wanted him. *Only him.*

He bit back a groan and shifted her hips toward the hardness that he couldn't hide.

"I want you, Jenna. I've wanted you from the moment I saw your cute behind and wide eyes when you stole my truck." He stroked her jawline with one knuckle. "But it can only be for one night, maybe two. My life is too dangerous. I won't put you and Sam at risk. Can you live with that?"

She placed her hand over his. "Yes, but can I ask you one thing? Will you tell me the truth? Will you be *you* and not live behind the lies for the rest of the time we're together? I've had enough deception. Just be real with me."

"I'll try," he whispered, his lips dancing on the smooth skin of her cheek. "You're worth facing a few fears."

Jenna clutched at him. "I regret everything about my time with Brad...except Sam. I don't want to regret any more. I'll take the memory of two nights over never knowing what it's like to lie in your arms."

He shivered at her words. A jolt of feminine power surged through her. She shoved aside the doubts creeping into her mind. She'd have tonight. With Zach. She'd make the memories last for the rest of her life.

"Help me forget, Zach. Help me forget everything."

She slipped from his embrace and pushed him to his back. She straddled his body, settling her hips on top of his. Her touch gentle, she fingered the bandage immobilizing his arm. "What about your shoulder?"

"Leave the bandage, but everything else—take it off," he said, his voice husky with acceptance, his gaze hooded.

She nodded and slipped her hand beneath his shirt until she encountered several butterflies against his skin. Carefully, she eased up the right side of the material and peered at the healing cut slicing across his chest with the strategically placed bandages holding his skin together. "How did this happen?"

"Occupational hazard," he shrugged.

She bent down, lowering her mouth, and kissed his ribs next to the injury. His blue eyes glazed over and a low groan escaped, starting deep and rumbling in his throat.

"You've sacrificed too much for me and Sam already," she said, gently caressing the mottled bruises over his chest. "And everyone else. Let me take care of you for a change."

Jenna could see in his eyes he wanted to protest. She didn't give him the chance. Leaning over him, she let her mouth hover over his. She wet her lips. A strangled groan escaped him. He reached up, claiming her, holding her captive with his kiss.

He tugged her to him, gripping her hair, and she let him take over. She fell into his embrace as he caressed her back. His tongue begged entrance and she gladly succumbed. Her hands roamed the strong muscles of his biceps, and Zach returned the favor, exploring her back, then slipping beneath her shirt.

His rough fingertips against her skin sent a shiver through her. His lips left hers and she nearly whimpered at the loss until he nipped at her collarbone, tugging at the shirt that scraped against her sensitive skin. As if reading her greatest wish, one by one by one he unbuttoned the cotton. She shrugged out of the top and threw the garment aside.

He cupped a silk-covered breast in his hand. With a flick he released the front clasp of her bra. He stared at her, unmoving, for what seemed like ages.

She squirmed under his unwavering gaze, shifted, and covered herself with her hands.

"Don't," he whispered.

Suddenly shy and uncertain, she lowered her gaze. "You've been with the most beautiful women in the world. How can I compete?"

His hand moved hers aside, then trailed down her curve, cupping its weight. "None of those women were real. Took me hours to make five minutes look easy, and, Jenna, none of those women made me shake with want the way you do."

She couldn't look away. Cobalt flecks of fire burned in his eyes, now hooded with passion.

"You're the most beautiful thing I've ever seen," he said, his voice husky.

"You promised not to lie," she said, unable to keep the hurt from her voice.

He clutched her waist, his gaze capturing hers. "You're strong. You fight for your son." At the dancing of his fingertips across her belly, a tremor fluttered through her. "You're unbelievably responsive. That makes you more than beautiful. That makes you perfect in my arms."

The muscles in Zach's neck corded as he strained his hips against her. His burgeoning length pressed against his zipper. "I've never wanted anyone more. I promise."

He pulled her down toward him and teased her nipple, triggering shocks of utter pleasure. She clutched his head closer. "Please don't stop," she gasped.

With a gentle push, he rolled her onto her back and unfastened the buttons of her jeans. Her body swelled in anticipation of his touch. His fingertips toyed with the lace encircling her hips.

His mouth skirted the shell of her ear and he nipped at the sensitive skin. "You want me, but not more than I want you. Can I have you, Jenna? Now? Tonight?"

She shivered at his low tones, and nodded her head.

With a groan, he slipped beneath the satin and found the center of her heat. Passion pooled low between her thighs, nerves begging for attention. He stroked her softness, toying, tempting, teasing the tiny nub of nerves. She gasped and her body hovered over a precipice. She held her breath, and then he backed away.

"Please, please." She nearly sobbed with want. She lifted her hips toward his touch. "Don't leave me like this," she panted.

"I have no plans on going anywhere anytime soon," he purred. "Lift up."

She didn't know how she made her quaking body obey, but within seconds, her jeans and panties had vanished and she lay open to him.

He kissed her belly, her hipbone, then tasted her center.

"Zach," she begged, straining for heights she'd never known. Her entire body quaked with want. "I need you."

"As you wish," he growled.

He struggled to remove his clothes. Hurriedly, she pushed his hand away, carefully unbuttoned, and lowered his zipper. He shucked off the garment, rose above her, and shifted between her thighs. She clutched at his shoulders, pulling him closer, shifting her hips to relieve the tension growing, building, wanting.

She scraped along his back and Zach groaned at her touch. "Make me feel, Jenna," he growled. "Make me burn."

Trembling, she reached down and took him in her hand, squeezing his hard length.

"Stop," he moaned. "I can't take it."

She stroked him, and he surged against her.

Her lips parted, and she nipped at the corner of his mouth. "Who's torturing who now?"

Shuddering in her arms, he bit back a cry and shoved her hands away. "No more."

He pressed her back against the bed and thrust into her. He filled her to the hilt and then stopped, his breath quick, his body slick with sweat. He throbbed inside of her. "Home," he whispered. "Home."

She wrapped her legs around him and bucked up against him. "More. I need more."

With a low groan, Zach moved against her, driving her to the edge over and over again. She clung to him, wrapping her body and heart around him.

He was hers, just as she belonged to him.

His movements quickened. She met him thrust for thrust. Her heat coiled around Zach, tight and straining.

An explosion of pleasure rocketed through her.

The entire world disappeared. Her heart slammed against her chest, and she gasped, stunned at the intense emotions pouring over her, wave upon wave, in time with the tiny pulses at her core. Somewhere inside, the soul that had been shattered at Brad's words and fists began to heal.

Zach sagged on top of her, his breathing sporadic. She cradled him close, stroking his hair. She'd never felt safer, warmer, or more protected.

He shifted, still buried inside her. She hugged him tighter. She couldn't let him go. Not yet.

A tear escaped down her cheek.

She felt complete for the first time in her life. It would also be the last.

Sirens screamed in the distance. Brad stumbled through the revolving door of the hospital, ignoring the shouts for him to stop. Blood dripped into his eyes, and he pressed the makeshift bandages he'd created against the head wound to staunch the bleeding.

His temple throbbed, but he pressed harder, using the pain to stay alert. He tripped over a cement barrier and slammed to his knees on the pavement. "Damn it."

Stupid boy. Get up and run.

His father's voice competed with the shouts from the hospital.

"Find him!" a voice yelled.

Quickly, Brad clawed his way up an embankment then slid down the other side to the abandoned parking lot in the doctor's offices adjacent to the hospital. He rolled the last few feet, coming to a stop on the asphalt. Sucking in a deep breath, he wiped away the sticky fluid pooling on his forehead.

His plan had gone to hell. He shoved himself to his feet, swaying slightly when the west wind whistled down from the mountains, and stumbled to his car. Brad tugged the keys from his pocket, opened the door, and slid inside.

He gripped the steering wheel tight and stared into the night. *Impossible. This couldn't be happening.*

He'd failed.

He couldn't fail.

He didn't fail.

Unacceptable.

"Bobby's got no smarts," his father screamed, shoving his wife against the stove. "He'll never amount to anything. Just like his stupid mother."

He punched her face until she curled up on the floor.

The words had seared themselves in Brad's mind. His mother had died for being stupid. Now Brad had let that Montgomery bitch hit him.

His blood was everywhere. They'd track the DNA. They'd find him.

He turned the engine on and eased toward the street.

Suddenly, a large pickup screeched past him into the hospital parking lot. He leaned forward and watched three large men race into the building. Part of the Montgomery clan. He hated that family.

His fists spasmed.

Cursing, he hit the steering wheel, then couldn't stop. He pounded and pounded until his hands hurt. He heaved in a breath, then another, then another until he regained control. He could do this. He had to maintain control.

The phone on the passenger seat rang. He glanced at the screen, but ignored the call from the puppet master.

He refused to play that game any longer.

He had to win his own battles.

He knew what Jenna wanted—her son. He knew what he needed—the evidence against him. Only one of them would be satisfied in the end. And it wouldn't be Jenna.

He picked up the GPS monitoring device from the seat. The southern California coast was outlined on the screen. A red dot pulsed in movement on the freeway.

Maybe his luck had changed.

Brad pulled a small device from his pocket. He zoomed in on the map. *A couple of miles ahead, the perfect spot.*

He dialed a number.

"Johansson."

"I need contact information for one of the Montgomery brothers. I don't care which one."

"You don't ask for much. I'm kind of busy right now."

"It's urgent."

"Fallon, it's the office calling. Give me a minute." His FBI contact's voice filtered through the car. A few seconds later, Johansson rattled off a number.

"Which one does it belong to?"

"Reporter," Johansson said, his voice short and staccato.

As if the man could hide his duplicity.

"I won't say it's been a pleasure, Johansson, but our association is over."

Brad pressed the button. Johansson shouted out. An explosion erupted. The phone went dead and the red dot vanished from the map.

One loose end obliterated.

He set aside the GPS tracker, picked up his phone, and dialed.

"Luke Montgomery," the voice barked.

Brad gripped the cell. "Tell Jenna that if she wants to keep the kid, she can have him, but I want the evidence, the tapes, everything. I'll be in touch for a meet."

He hung up. What a mess.

"Can't the kid even clean up after himself? All he does is leaves shit everywhere. Clean up his mess."

His father's voice echoed in Brad's memory.

There'd be no more messes this time. He'd make sure everything was perfect, then he'd vanish. He would become someone new. And stronger. And better. And perfect.

He'd start again. Not alone, though. Not this time.

He'd take his son and teach him how to do things right.

A chorus of crickets chirped their muffled song of joy outside the closed window. For one brief moment, Zach wanted to join in. Despite the chaotic world around him, he held perfection in his arms.

He *should* move, but he didn't want to let Jenna go. He eased his weight from on top of her, but she clutched at his shoulders.

"No. Don't. I want to remember," she whispered, and wrapped her legs around his hips.

God, so did he.

Her softness pressed against him and he groaned. He could get used to this. He kissed her temple.

If things were different.

They lay together until slowly her breathing evened and she fell asleep.

They'd have to talk, but he didn't want to ruin the moment. It would have to last a very long time. If this was anything like what his mom had felt for his dad, Zach didn't know how she'd survived losing her husband.

When Seth and Luke introduced Jenna to her new life, his own would become a colorless reflection of the possibilities.

A soft knock sounded on the door. "Zach. We got trouble," Luke said under his breath.

As quietly and quickly as possible, Zach slipped away from Jenna, slid on his jeans, and opened the door. He half expected some wiseass comment from his brother, but Luke's gaze didn't contain a glint of humor, only low-burning fury.

Zach shut the door behind him, and the click closed her away. He couldn't feel his heartbeat. "Mom?"

"No, we received a call from the Chameleon," Luke whispered, leading Zach into the kitchen. "He wants Jenna's evidence in exchange for leaving Sam alone."

"You've got to be kidding me." Zach rubbed his face in an effort to wake up to reality. "Why?"

"Mom knocked some sense into him when she bashed him with the vase?" Luke shrugged. "Hell, I don't know."

"A man doesn't go a decade as an invisible assassin and then just call up and say let's meet. No way. It's a trap."

"Of course it is." Seth propped his boots on one of the rough-hewn chairs. "I say we wait for his call and then treat him to a Montgomery welcome he'll never forget."

"Jenna has to be away from here before that happens."

Seth folded his hands behind his head. "I called in a favor. Her documentation is in the works. I'm impressed with what you already had in place, Zach. Not bad subterfuge for a has-been actor."

"Shove it," Zach countered. "As long as she's gone before we take care of Brad Walters."

Luke sat down across from Zach and cleared his throat. "When I researched Brad, I also discovered a few unusual details about Jenna. She has some pretty interesting secrets of her own."

Zach didn't like the look on Luke's face. Not one bit. "I know about her past, Jenna's a straight shooter. There's nothing that puts her in danger now that I can tell."

"I've seen how you look at her, Zach. Read what I found, then decide what to do." Luke slid the folder across the table.

Zach put his hand on the file but didn't open it. "When did Brad say he'd call back?"

A gasp erupted from behind them. "You've talked to Brad?"

Zach hit his feet and whirled around. Jenna stood, hovering in the kitchen doorway, looking sleepy and sex-tousled. Her lips were swollen, her body soft and appealing, except she couldn't hide the pain on her face.

"Jenna—"

She shook her head. "Don't." She raised her hand. "I'm going to assume—because you promised not to lie—that you *just* found out about Brad's call and you haven't been in contact with him the entire time."

Zach nodded.

Jenna swayed against the jamb. "Tell me what he said."

They relayed Brad's demands.

"No way. I can't give him the evidence," she said. "It's my only leverage to keep him away, to keep him from killing us."

Seth and Luke exchanged looks. "Jenna, we're not going to give him the evidence, but we're definitely going to use it as bait."

Red and blue strobes whirled and sirens shrilled behind Farzam, lighting up the interior of the rental car. His face flushed with heat, and he squeezed the steering wheel trying to plan an escape. Two sheriff's cars sped past him.

Shocked, he relaxed his grip. His breath took longer to return to normal. He watched the lights disappear in the distance. He squirmed in his seat. He didn't like the left-side steering wheel. He turned off the main road. *Less likely to attract attention that way.*

Farzam had seen more than one Uzi when he'd veered off course and driven through a few unsavory neighborhoods, though the danger of Denver's night streets didn't touch those of Kabul, particularly if a man was on Khalid's death roll.

He scanned the neatly typed list of addresses resting on the rental car's seat. He'd visited three already. The American woman had told the truth. One house had been burned to the ground. Perhaps the United States wasn't so different from Afghanistan after all.

Following the GPS, Farzam drove past a sheriff's office. He could see the tan vehicles with lights on the roof. All was quiet here now, however.

Farzam parked across from a bar. Alcohol. He knew about it. He'd been in his share of pubs in the United Kingdom. Not to imbibe of course, but Farzam understood the world. Its dangers and its temptations.

After a quick scan of the area, he exited the vehicle and strode to the swinging doors of the entrance. He stood in the doorway. Raucous men out of control. Women sidling up to them, flashing their flesh.

He ignored them, searching for one very particular man.

Two large men strode in from the back. One of them paused as his gaze crossed Farzam.

A warrior. He knew that look. Military.

In a move to conceal his face, Farzam ducked among a large group that had just entered the bar. He peered around the protection for a second glance. The soldier studied the figures surrounding Farzam, suspicious and alert.

He'd been seen, however briefly. Time to disappear. Besides, he had the information he wanted. He'd recognized the men from the photos the woman had provided. The soldier and his companion were both obviously Montgomerys, given their similar appearance, but not Zach Montgomery. Where there were two, Farzam might find more.

Since the men had come from behind the bar, Farzam's next stop became easy. The back rooms were definitely worth investigating. He slid outside, unnoticed.

Staying close to the shadows, he walked to the side of the building and worked his way to the rear, making himself as undetectable as possible.

"Jenna!" a voice shouted into the night.

Farzam skidded to a halt and sank deeper into the darkness, away from the lights.

He froze in the night, disbelieving as Zach Montgomery walked out of a house. There he was, the man who had caused Farzam's sister to lose her pride, her humanity, and finally her life. The man whose very existence had torn Farzam's son away from him.

The man Farzam needed to kill.

He reached for the weapon he'd purchased from a thug on a street corner. Farzam's hand shook, and he pulled the gun free. The time was here to prove himself a man, avenge his family, and liberate his son from Khalid's clutches.

Zach Montgomery walked over to a woman. Gently, reverently, he turned her toward him then pulled her into his arms, holding her close.

Stunned fury hit Farzam as he stared at the couple. His enemy loved, an emotion Farzam had never expected to see on the face of the man who'd so callously destroyed Farzam's family. He lifted his weapon and took aim.

An entrance to the bar opened and a sea of people exited, joking and laughing. They blocked Farzam's vision. When they headed his way, he lowered his gun to avoid detection. Seconds later, a spotlight illuminated the parking lot, showcasing a basketball hoop. The group set to a fierce game with shouts and catcalls.

Farzam cursed. He couldn't gun down Zach here. There were too many witnesses, too many chances to get caught. He couldn't risk making a mistake or he'd never get home. He needed his prey alone and vulnerable.

Montgomery tucked the woman to his side and walked her to the door, his touch tender and caring. They disappeared inside the house.

Farzam gripped the stock of the gun so tightly his fingers went numb. He stalked across the parking lot into the building next door. Struggling against his instinct to rush in after his enemy, he gulped down the rage. He'd bide his time. Soon enough, Zach Montgomery would make himself vulnerable, then Farzam would have everything he wanted.

His enemy would be no more.

His son would be returned.

He would have a new life.

If the American woman who brought him here kept her promise.

The screen door closed behind Jenna and Zach, drowning out the whoops and hollers from the basketball game. She sucked in a deep breath. Barbecue smoke and fried food wafted at her from the bar, but instead of making her hungry, the scents just stirred nausea in Jenna's gut.

Thankful Seth and Luke had taken off to the bar to give her and Zach a bit of privacy, she stiffened in his arms. "Brad always has a plan. He'll never just let us go," she said. The weight of her husband's skills terrified her. "I won't let him take Sam. I can't."

Zach turned her in his arms, the warmth of his body encompassing hers, but a chill settled deep in Jenna's bones.

"We'll catch Brad," Zach said. "He's making mistakes he never made before. His perfect disguise is slipping."

"Perfect," she spat, rubbing her arms. "I hate that word. Brad wanted his house, me, and Sam to be *perfect*. We're not, and

Brad doesn't react well to mistakes." She touched the cheekbone Brad had bruised the first time he'd hurt her. "I can't risk my son," she said.

"We won't let Brad near Sam—or you. We know what he wants."

Could she place her future in Zach's hands one more time? She met his strong gaze and took his hand in hers. "What's your plan?"

"That's my girl." Zach led her into the kitchen and pulled out a chair from the table. As she sat down a knock sounded at the door.

Seth peeked in. "Do you have a minute?"

"Yeah, get in here," Zach said. "We're going over the mission."

Seth and Luke entered, then hesitated just inside the door.

Zach frowned at them. "Something's wrong?"

"What happened?" Jenna rose.

Luke clutched his phone. "Was Agent Fallon your contact at the FBI?"

She bit her lip and nodded.

"I'm sorry. I just received a newsflash. Fallon and his partner," Luke looked down at the screen on his cell, "an Agent Johansson, were killed in a car accident on I-10 earlier today. No witnesses. Their car was found off the side of the road. It burst into flames."

Jenna went numb, and slowly sat again. "It's Brad." She closed her eyes. "Even halfway across the country, he can kill someone if he wants to badly enough."

Luke laid his phone on the table and placed his hands on the wood tabletop. "That doesn't mean he can't be stopped."

She kneaded the back of her neck. "How? He destroys everything he touches."

Zach knelt between her knees. "Don't give up, Jenna. You haven't let him knock you down yet. Don't do it now."

"What's the point? The evidence is in California. He'll be calling soon. He's smart, Zach. He'll find me wherever I run. Sam will never be safe."

"We'll stop him. Besides, there are always ways. I'll get Ace to fly us to La Jolla and we'll get the evidence. We can turn the rest over to the authorities and be back here in a few hours."

"What about Sam?"

"Seth and Luke can guard him. They'll protect him with their lives."

The two men nodded their agreement, but foreboding settled in Jenna's gut. Every time she let herself hope, the world came crashing down on her.

Sam's scream sounded from inside the bedroom. Jenna ran down the hall and slammed open the door. Sam was sitting up in bed, tears streaming down his face.

"Daddy!" he moaned, his eyes still closed

Jenna sat next to him and pulled him into her arms.

"Daddy, don't hurt her," Sam shouted, kicking and striking her blindly. Her heart hurt with each pound of his small fists on her arms and chest.

Zach leaned over Sam and clutched his shoulders. "Wake up, Sam. It's OK, buddy. We've got you."

"Zach?" Sam pushed away from Jenna and launched himself at Zach.

He tugged Sam into his arms. "You're safe. I've got you."

The little boy looked at the man holding him and immediately quieted.

Zach rocked him closely, each movement breaking Jenna's heart. Gently, she pushed the hair away from her son's tear-streaked face.

She had to end this. For Sam. She had to erase Brad from their lives or Sam would never heal. She headed for the kitchen where Luke and Seth huddled in a private conversation. Jenna scanned the table. There, Luke's phone in plain sight.

At the edge lay a folder labeled with her name. She grabbed it and slipped the phone under the manila file to hide her actions. With a deep breath she returned to Sam's room, staring at her terrified son, her heart aching.

"Jenna," Zach whispered, cradling Sam in his arms. "Where are you going?"

"He wants you right now, and I need to take a shower," she lied. "I…I need some time alone."

"Jenna, Sam didn't mean to hurt you. He just needs to be held right now."

"I know, and thank you." She smiled sadly at Zach and her baby. "As his mother, I know exactly what he needs."

"Have I overstepped?" Zach asked.

"No," Jenna said. "I just need a few minutes on my own. Please."

Zach nodded, his expression brooding while she walked to the bathroom, closed the door, and turned on the shower. She cradled Luke's phone in her hands, held her breath, and thumbed through recent calls. When she recognized the California area code she hit redial.

"That was fast, Montgomery."

The sound of her husband's voice made Jenna shake.

"I accept your offer, Brad," Jenna said. "I'll bring your evidence tonight. Where and when do you want to meet?"

Brad chuckled. "I knew you'd come through, Jenna. Don't try to double-cross me or else I'll take you down with me."

"I wouldn't dream of it." She clutched the phone and sent up a heartfelt prayer that her plan wouldn't fail. "If you give up Sam, Brad, you can have whatever you want."

She folded her fist at the second knuckle and tensed her hand. To protect her son, she would do anything.

Chapter Fifteen

*H*OT WATER DOUSED JENNA IN THE SMALL, UTILITARIAN BATH-room. The sheets of heat pounded into her, but she didn't linger. She couldn't afford to. Swirling steam cleared her head when she breathed in. She couldn't believe she'd agreed to meet Brad. She had no more chance of giving him the evidence in the next hour than she had of flying to the moon.

She slammed down the shower handle, grabbed a towel, and quickly dressed. She peered into the hallway, then skirted into the bedroom. She tossed the phone onto the bed and stared at the device. What had she done? Her legs trembled beneath her. The room felt colder than she remembered. Maybe it was the shower—or the thought of seeing Brad chilled her soul.

The crickets chirped a mournful song through the window. If she kept her meeting with Brad, she would never live to see her son again. She longed to go to him now, but she knew she'd break down.

A soft knock sounded at the door. "Jenna," Zach whispered.

She fell backward onto the bed, curled her body around the phone, and closed her eyes, feigning sleep.

A soft snick sounded as the door opened, then silence.

She focused on making her breathing slow and even.

A strange tension filled the room. She who had begged him for no more lies now deceived him. Her heart shattered.

Less than a minute later, the door clicked closed again, and heavy footsteps walked away. She squeezed her eyelids and a tear leaked down her cheek. She curled her arms around her abdomen and pressed tight, shoving down the shame and fears rising up into her throat.

No one could beat Brad, but he would never expect her to fight back. He'd cowed her for so many years. She would be the only one who might get close enough to surprise him—and stop him.

The longer she lay there, though, the more she doubted herself. Zach would be furious at her. He'd have gone in to meet Brad with his brothers—each armed with enough weaponry to kill ten men. She scraped her hands through her hair. What was she thinking trying to somehow surprise Brad enough to kill him with her bare hands?

She rolled onto her back and stared at the ceiling. She didn't want to die and leave Sam alone.

God, what a fool.

She knew what she had to do. She'd have to admit to Zach and his brothers what she'd done. They weren't going to be happy.

She groaned and sat up. Something crinkled beneath her. She tugged the manila file folder free and stared at her name, printed on the label. Her emotions were all over the place. This burgeoning sense of disaster hovered over her.

She should go out there and face Zach.

Instead, she removed the paperclip holding the documents together and opened the file. Several photos slipped out, including her engagement picture with Brad. The edge of the paperclip dug into her finger. She slipped it into her back pocket and nudged the image aside. Her hand trembled. Sure enough, her father's eyes stared back at her.

Beneath the newspaper clipping lay a mug shot. A prison photo. Of her father? But he'd died in an accident when she was fourteen. Maybe it wasn't him. This man had crow's-feet around his eyes. And the date. Only a few years ago.

It made no sense.

Her fingers trembled. She searched and found another document. A death certificate bearing her father's name and a date. *Oh God.*

Not over a decade ago. Two years ago. In prison.

She scanned the paperwork. In prison for fraud, tax evasion, assault, and battery.

The heroic image she'd held for so long exploded into sharp shards that pierced her heart. Her father had been a thug.

He hadn't died in a car wreck like she'd been told.

Another lie, but this one shook her to her core. She'd believed in him. Every cell of faith in humanity inside her came from him. And he had been a fraud.

Her stomach twisted. She gasped for air.

She'd loved her father. Believed in him.

Nothing about her life was real. Nothing. Not her marriage, not her childhood, not her life. She ripped the locket from her throat and dropped it on the floor.

Had Zach known?

She shivered again. She felt so cold. She glanced at the window. The curtains fluttered into the room, billowing.

"Mommy?" a small voice whined from the doorway.

Jenna turned her face from the window and scrubbed the tears from her cheeks. Sam tiptoed in.

"Hi, baby." She choked the words and struggled to stop her body from quaking. She needed the one person in her life who loved her unconditionally. "Can Mommy have a hug?"

"Don't cry, Mommy." He ran across the room and climbed into her lap, crinkling the file beneath her. She didn't care. She shoved the papers to the floor and clutched her son, praying he would restore the heart that had just been pulverized into oblivion.

Sam squirmed on her lap and faced her. He patted her cheek. "Everything will be OK, Mommy." He laid his head against her breast and she rocked him, holding on to the one real person in her life.

"Tell me a story, Mommy. It'll make you feel better."

Stories had been her father's way of driving away the pain, of giving her hope. The inspiration had vanished. "I don't have any more stories, Sam."

He sat up, his eyes wide. "None?" He gently kissed her cheek. "It's all right, Mommy. I'll tell *you* a story."

Tears burned her eyes. She lifted Sam and sat him on the bed. Her eyes flicked to the blowing curtains. *Oh, my God.* The window was open…and it hadn't been.

"Mommy. Are you all right? You're breathing really fast."

"I'm…I'm fine."

But she wasn't. She ran to the window and slammed it down. The screen was gone.

She turned around. "Run, Sam. Get out—"

Sam's eyes suddenly grew wide. His mouth gaped open. "Mommy!"

Something slammed against the side of her head and the room went black.

She'd made a terrible mistake.

———————————

Zach looked down the hall. Had he heard something? The television on the counter droned the local newscast.

"Hey, Seth, shut off the TV."

He half expected Jenna to stalk out and tear into him, but Sam reaching out to him instead of her seemed to have broken her. Plus, Brad's call had obviously shaken her to her core. She'd become comfortable with the idea of running. She'd trusted him to help her disappear, but that was it. "I don't think Jenna believes we can stop Brad Walters."

"She's wrong," Luke said. "She'll come out when she's ready. She probably just needs to process."

"Process? Seriously?" Seth laughed. "Where the hell did you learn that?"

"Army shrinks," Luke muttered.

"Yeah, well, Jenna doesn't process," Zach said. "She stands her ground...or runs."

A flash of insight hit him. "Damn it, she runs." He rose from the chair so fast it clattered to the floor behind him. He should have recognized that look on her face. The same resigned determination he'd witnessed after she'd hot-wired his damned truck.

"You think she's gone?" Seth said, following at his heels.

"God, I hope not."

His hand gripped the last bedroom's doorknob. Locked.

He knocked on the door. "Jenna?"

No answer.

He knocked harder. "Jenna!"

"Shh. You'll wake the kid," Luke said.

A dark, horrifying feeling enveloped Zach. She wouldn't have run without her son.

"Check Sam," he shouted at his brothers, then kicked in the door. The room was empty. The curtains fluttered in the window.

"The kid's gone," Luke yelled from down the hall.

Zach stuck his head out of the window and his blood froze at the stain of crimson on the windowsill. The screen lay in pieces on the ground.

No. He cupped his hands. "Jenna!"

His heart raced as he waited, focusing, praying to hear the sound of her voice above laughter from the bar.

Seth ran in. "They're both gone."

Zach turned and his foot slipped on a piece of paper. He glanced down at the floor and scooped up the file folder and the small locket he'd caught her fondling. It didn't take a second to scan her father's mug shot, record, and date of death. Jenna had told Zach her father died when she was fourteen. The same year her father had gone to prison. *Oh God.* Had this been the final straw for her? Had it sent her into the night? *That made no sense.*

"Zach," Luke said, pocketing the necklace. "We've got a problem. My phone was on the bed. She called Walters."

"Oh, Jenna," Zach rubbed his face. He cursed himself for not forcing himself into this room and making her talk to him. "There's blood on the window."

"She could still have left voluntarily," Luke said.

"You're right," Zach muttered. "Check the cars. She might have hot-wired one or stolen the keys. She's resourceful."

They burst out the front door. All the vehicles were there. Zach yelled her name again, his desperation growing.

She'd left on foot? *But the blood...*

Zach scanned the parking lot. The spotlights had been dimmed after the basketball game ended, but something unusual caught his attention. An area of torn-up grass to the side of the house. He knelt down. Wet, sticky. Blood. And two tiny hands had dug into the earth.

Sam.

"Seth, get over here," he said quietly, his fist clenched to tamp down the foreboding.

His brother crouched beside him and let out a curse. He spanned his hand across the smaller handprint. "Sam didn't go willingly."

"Brad's taken them." Zach bit down.

"It doesn't mean he'll kill her." Seth studied the ground more closely. "There was a car here."

"Brad wants the evidence," Luke said. "He needs her until he gets it. We have time."

"The evidence is still in California in a safety deposit box. She mentioned La Jolla. There are hundreds of possibilities."

"Then we'll start searching," Seth said.

Luke let out a slow, deep breath. "She'll buy us time. She's already proven she can think on her feet."

Zach rubbed his chin. "Yeah, but she's afraid of him."

"Jenna had the courage to leave," Luke reminded him. "She called him. She faces her fears."

"She might tell him the evidence is in California and only she can retrieve it. That might give her an escape opportunity. She's smart that way," Zach said.

"We need a watch on the airports. Walters won't want to take sixteen hours to get that evidence. He'll try to hire a private plane."

"I'm on it," Luke said.

Zach followed his brothers inside. Within seconds, Luke had opened his computer, and Seth pulled out his phone to hit up his own contacts.

An overwhelming fear paralyzed Zach. "We've got to find her," he choked. "I don't think I can live without her."

Darkness and cold metal surrounded her. The smell of exhaust and rubber filled the air. A bounce shifted Jenna hard against a mound under her shoulder. The roar of a vehicle rumbled around her. *Oh God.* She was in the trunk of a car.

She groaned, then blinked, but she still couldn't see anything.

The pain splitting her skull pounded incessantly where she'd been struck. She tried to move, but her hands had been secured behind her back. The metal cuffs bit into her skin.

A small, trembling body pressed against her back.

Sam. Oh, God, help them.

The vehicle took a hard left, fast. The movement slammed them against the cold metal.

A whimper sounded from behind her. She squirmed, desperate to touch Sam, but she couldn't budge.

She felt for him and finally caught his little hand in hers. His wrists were bound with rope. He wiggled his hand against hers.

"Baby, are you hurt?" Her husky words filtered through the black.

"No. Scared," he mumbled, as if something were stuffed into his mouth.

The vehicle jerked, slamming Jenna into the ceiling of their prison. They were moving slower now, and bouncing like they'd turned onto a back road.

Brad. It had to be. But why treat them this way? She'd promised him she would bring the evidence. And why hurt Sam? She couldn't believe he'd be this cruel to their son.

The rumbling of the car stopped. Jenna tensed.

The trunk opened.

A bright light pierced the darkness, blinding her. She blinked, but she couldn't see the figure behind the beam.

"Brad?" she choked. "Why are you doing this?"

"Silence," a voice said.

Not Brad's voice. A voice with an accent.

The man grabbed her arm and tugged Jenna from the trunk. She fell to the ground then turned her head to get a view of her attacker. A mask covered his face. He pulled her up by the handcuffs, nearly dislocating her shoulders. She stumbled to her feet. He slammed the trunk closed with her son still inside.

"Sam!" she screamed.

He backhanded her. "Shut up."

He shoved her toward a small, boarded-up dwelling. No streetlights. Trees all around. She had no idea where she was. Or how far from Gabe's house they'd traveled.

How would Zach find her?

The man opened the door. "Sit."

He pointed to a lone chair in the middle of a small, sparse room. The fetid smell of trash and mold overwhelmed her. She didn't want to walk inside. Her entire body trembled.

The dilapidated shack—and it was a shack—screamed at her not to enter. She swallowed, looking right, then left.

"Sit."

He slugged her again and forced her inside. Pain shot through her cheek. She fell to the ground.

He kicked her in the belly. "Chair. Now."

She curled up into a ball. He grabbed her hair and dragged her across the room. She cried out in pain.

"No one can hear you," he said, "but scream again and I will cut out your tongue."

He lifted her onto the chair and yanked her arms behind her. She couldn't prevent the yelp, but bit down hard to stop the sound. He unlocked the handcuffs and threaded them through the back of the chair. He then attached each of her legs by the ankle to the wooden chair. When he'd finished, she couldn't move anything except her head and a slight bend of her wrists.

He stood, his breathing harsh. "Do you know why you are here?" he asked, his accent thick but clearly Middle Eastern.

"Brad?" she whispered, her voice questioning.

"Zane Morgan," he spat. "Or, should I say Zach Montgomery?"

"I don't understand."

"You will," he said, and trained the flashlight in her eyes. She could see nothing behind him, and then a large shadow shifted toward the door, a stick in his hand.

"You will understand an eye for an eye."

Brad stared across the street at Sammy's, the bar Gabe Montgomery had purchased using a fairly mundane dummy corporation.

It had been simple enough for Brad to triangulate Jenna's cell signal to a tower not too far away. She had to be here.

His phone rang. He glanced at the screen. *Damn it.* He couldn't avoid the call again.

"I feel as if we're having the same conversation over and over again, Mr. Walters," the annoying voice droned. "Garrison is *still* alive."

Brad cursed under his breath. He didn't need this. Not now. "He won't be for long."

"So you've promised. Another job has come up, and I'm out of time or I wouldn't be giving you *another* opportunity to fail. And Mr. Walters. Your payment will be half the usual rate until you prove yourself to me again. Screw this up and I'll see that your reputation is worthless."

Brad gripped the phone. They both knew his identity had been compromised. His life as Brad Walters was over—what was his client playing at?

He had to maintain control to keep her guessing.

"Location?" he said, through gritted teeth.

"The outskirts of Denver, very near where you are. This job should make you feel like a patriot. An Afghani terrorist has infiltrated the country. He will be in Golden, Colorado, sometime in the next twenty-four hours." The specific coordinates came through as a text. "I want you to kill him, but I need an identifiable body for the authorities. Do you understand? You may have to get up close and personal."

Brad sat stunned, watching the light that showed the conversation successfully recording and logging the number. *A government number that wasn't blocked.*

For the first time, his client had made a very big mistake. Elated, Brad watched the seconds tick by. No longer was he the puppet. Very soon he would become the puppeteer.

"I understand."

"Notify me when it's done."

The call ended.

Brad drummed his fingers against the steering wheel, planning payback.

Suddenly, the door flew open and a gun pressed against his temple.

"Where's Jenna?"

———————————

Zach's finger twitched against the 1911's trigger. He wanted nothing more than to kill this bastard. Instead, Zach tapped his earpiece. "I've got Walters. Keep searching. Jenna's got to be nearby."

The Chameleon stilled, his hands unmoving. The yellow streetlight illuminated the car. Denver and its suburbs never truly went dark. The nondescript man had kept the CIA, FBI, Interpol, and every other international spy agency completely baffled for a decade.

"Lost your edge, Walters?" Zach asked.

The assassin said nothing.

"Get out," Zach ordered. "On the ground, arms and legs spread. You so much as twitch, you're dead."

Slowly, with deliberation, Brad eased out of the vehicle and lay next to the car.

Zach pressed the heel of his boot against the back of the guy's neck. One wrong move and Zach *would* end him.

"Don't kill him yet, big brother," Seth said, striding across the street. He sidled up to Zach. "We can't find her."

Oh God. Bile slammed into his throat. He briefly closed his eyes, praying he was wrong. He reached into the car for the keys and tossed them to his brother. "Check the trunk. Carefully."

Zach pressed harder on Brad's neck. If Brad had hurt Jenna or Sam...the bastard wouldn't live another thirty seconds.

Seth checked for wires then flicked open the trunk. He looked inside, paused, and met Zach's gaze.

Zach couldn't breathe.

"Empty," Seth said.

Zach yanked Walters off the ground and slammed him into the car's side. "Where is she?"

The assassin blinked. "Last I heard she was with you."

"We better take this inside," Seth said, glancing around. "Too many eyes. Especially if we're planning on encouraging him to talk. Accidents do happen."

Knowing his brother was right, Zach shoved Brad forward. "Walk straight ahead. You so much as look in one direction or another, your brain splatters all over the parking lot and I won't bother to clean it up."

Brad raised his chin. "You clearly believe I have Jenna. You're wrong. She wants to come back to me. She called about starting over. Be a family. She's had her fling with you. It's over."

"Liar," Zach said, his conviction unwavering. He knew his Jenna. Whatever love she'd felt for her husband, Brad had destroyed.

"Sucker," the assassin laughed. "You're in love with my wife. She reeled you in, too."

"She's not your wife, Walters...or should I call you Bobby Swinton?"

Brad stumbled slightly, and Zach got the satisfaction of surprising the Chameleon.

Just as they reached Gabe's house, Luke shot through the door. "Zach, get in here. Now!"

Zach pressed the gun at the base of Brad's neck. "Move it."

Seth opened the door and snagged his duffel. He pulled out some zip ties to secure Brad's hands and feet. "Sit down and shut up."

"What do you have, Luke?" Zach could barely get the words out as he studied his brother's pale features.

"I just received this," Luke said, pointing to an e-mail on the laptop's screen.

"A message for Zane Morgan, aka Zach Montgomery. An eye for an eye."

Seth stared at Zach, in awe. "*You're* Zane Morgan. Holy shit. You're a freakin' legend."

"Most of it's just rumor."

"Bro, that dog don't hunt no more," Seth said. "But I understand why you chose to be a hero in disguise."

"What I've done doesn't matter. Click the link," Zach ordered, his stomach roiling.

A fuzzy image showed on the screen. A Middle Eastern man stood in front of the camera. A man Zach knew.

"What the hell?" Zach shouted.

"Zane Morgan?" The man raised a photograph into the camera. "Remember these people?"

Zach squinted at the grainy picture. Two bodies. *Oh God.* Pendar and his wife, Setara, riddled with bullets.

"You recognize? Pendar was guilty. His wife...they k... killed her because she belonged to him. She was my sister and *you* killed her."

The man stepped to the side. "An eye for an eye."

Zach's knees shook.

Jenna was strapped to a chair. Blood trickled from her mouth.

"You want your woman returned, Zane Morgan? Then you wait for my message. You come to me. Alone."

The screen went black.

Chapter Sixteen

ZACH HEARD NOTHING, ONLY TERROR ROARING THROUGH HIS mind. He reached out a hand and touched the black screen of Luke's laptop.

The room was silent.

Zach struggled to breathe against the clamp of emotion squeezing his chest. Jenna's desperate fear nearly stopped his heart. He had to save her.

With a shaking hand, he reclicked the link. The feed was gone. Jenna was gone.

He rounded on Luke. "Tell me you can track the signal."

His brother's agonized expression shredded Zach's hope.

"I won't give up until I do." Luke pounded on the keyboard for a few seconds, then muttered a curse. "Zach, you have to know…if he's smart enough, I may need another feed before I can hone in."

Zach's eyes closed and he raised his head to heaven. That meant Jenna would be at the madman's mercy. "Pendar was *executed*, Luke. I refuse to watch Jenna and Sam being gunned down over the damned Internet by the guy's brother-in-law."

Brad cut in. "What do you mean Sam? He wasn't there." The assassin stood, his face had gone pale. His hands tugged against the bindings.

"Tie him to the damn chair," Zach growled, pressing the gun into Brad's temple, "or I swear to God I'll shoot him. For all I know the asshole that kidnapped her is working for Walters."

"Think what you want, Montgomery, but I'd *never* put my son in danger like that."

"Yeah, you'd only beat the crap out of his mother so he thinks that's normal."

Seth pushed Zach aside and grabbed Brad's collar. "If Zach doesn't kill you," Seth said, smiling, "I'll enjoy taking a wife abuser like you apart piece by piece." The soldier slapped duct tape over Brad's mouth. "I should let Zach kill you now. Be thankful we have more important business." Seth glanced at his watch. "She disappeared less than two hours ago. They're still in Colorado. He'd be hard-pressed to get her out of the Denver area and to another location, even via plane." He looked at Luke. "We need more help."

"I already sent texts to Gabe and Jazz. Once we locate this guy—" Luke sent a quizzical look to Zach.

"Farzam," Zach replied. "His name is Farzam."

"Right. Once we locate the asshole, we'll need support."

"What about SWAT?" Seth asked.

Zach paced back and forth. He shoved his hand through his hair. "I can't risk it. I don't know who in law enforcement we can trust. Not after the FBI involvement. We're on our own to find them."

He forced his mind to calm and replayed the scene in his head, frame by frame, using every observation skill he'd ever learned—as an actor and an operative. "The walls were void of anything personal. The room was small, abandoned. I only saw the one chair."

Luke pressed a button and leaned in.

The video played on his computer.

"You recorded it?" Zach bit, wanting to look away, but unable to stop staring. He pushed Jenna's beautiful, pained eyes away and studied the surroundings. "Loop it. Turn the sound up."

Luke complied. For several minutes they stared at the screen. It wasn't long before Jazz and Gabe joined them.

She went directly to Zach and hugged him tight. "I'm so sorry."

"Tell me what you see," he said to the woman whose sniper eyes took in more details than Zach could fathom.

The video played again.

"I recognize the sound in the background," Jazz said. "Train. I grew up not far from a set of tracks in New Mexico."

Luke pulled up a Denver map on the laptop, clicking an icon to reveal the railroad lines crisscrossing the area.

"We need to narrow it down more. We can never cover that many square miles of territory," Gabe said.

"Small house. Boarded up, abandoned," Seth commented. "Wood. On the inside anyway."

"Not enough to go on." Zach's gut ached. He rubbed his temples. This couldn't be happening. *Not again*. Was he about to lose someone else he…loved?

Yes, damn it, he loved Jenna. And Sam.

And now, his life—his own actions—had come back to destroy everything.

First his father, now Jenna.

Zach straightened and thrust his hands through his hair. No. Not this time.

"We have to find them," he said to his family. "We have to find a way."

Seth placed a hand on his shoulder. "We will." Gabe, Luke, and Jazz nodded in agreement. "We'll get them back for you," they vowed.

Zach clung to the long shot. He refused to accept he'd found Jenna and Sam only to lose them now.

———————

The small room closed in on Jenna, and she couldn't stop the chill invading her body.

Her captor closed the phone. "The fool will come. You are his weakness."

The man was going to kill Zach. Of that Jenna had no doubt. Unless she got away.

"Why are you doing this?"

Her kidnapper didn't respond. He left the house and returned with a squirming Sam in his arms. "Be quiet or I'll stuff the rag back in her mouth," their captor warned. He turned to Jenna. "You love your son?"

Jenna's heart stuttered. "Of course."

"You would do anything for him? Even kill?"

Jenna swallowed.

"Well, so would I."

Sam whimpered.

The man's phone rang. He stared at the screen, his mouth screwing in disgust. "Yes."

He listened, then laughed. "I will not give you Khalid's location, not until I return to my home...and my son." He glanced at Jenna. "I will have completed my part of our bargain very soon."

Oh God. She had to warn Zach. She worked her wrists against the handcuffs, but they were too tight and cut into her flesh.

"Wait!" Dread laced the man's voice. "What aren't you telling me?"

Jenna froze.

Something had gone wrong.

He began pacing the room, back and forth, his movements jerky.

"Tell me," he said, his voice low.

He dropped the phone to the floor and fell to his knees.

"Noooo!"

The tortured scream ricocheted through the room. Jenna shrank away from his crazed motions.

"It cannot be true. My son, my Hamed!" The man howled in torment, banging his head against the floor.

Sam sobbed, his little body rocking against the restraints that bound him to his chair. Jenna strained against the handcuffs, but it was no use. She couldn't help her son.

"Shut up, you sniveling American brat!" he screeched. He threw the phone at Sam's head.

He ducked. The device smashed against the wall.

Jenna's entire body stilled in dread. Until now, her captor had been calm, businesslike. Now, his eyes were wild with pain. He shook, muttering and pacing the floor like a caged animal.

"My son can't be dead. He can't be. Have to call. Learn if it's true."

Wailing he picked up the pieces of the shattered phone, cradling them next to his face. "Hamed? Setara, what do I do?"

Their captor circled through the room, prowling. He slammed his fist into the wall, digging a hole into the flimsy wood. Finally he rounded on Jenna.

"Zane Morgan did this!"

Hatred flared in the man's eyes. "The American must pay. He will feel my pain."

The man gripped the stick at his side and pointed it at Jenna.

"You. He loves *you*. You must die as my sister did. As my son did."

He crossed toward her and lifted the wood.

She shrank back as far as she could into her seat.

"Don't hurt my Mommy!" Sam yelled.

The man whirled on her son. "Shut up, shut up, shut up."

"Sam, be quiet. It will be OK," Jenna whispered, praying she spoke the truth.

"That's what I told Hamed. I lied," her captor said. "Hamed *will* be avenged. Zane Morgan *will* know my pain."

Her captor raised the stick. Jenna stared up at him. Frantic, she twisted her wrists in the handcuffs. The wood slammed down on her arm and she cried out.

He raised the wood again. "The liar will know my pain!"

––––––––––––––

Anna's tears refused to dry. Even when she couldn't cry more of them, they burned behind her eyes. John Garrison lay pale and still in the bed next to her chair.

He hadn't so much as shifted since she'd convinced Caleb to wheel her to the hospital room over an hour ago. She squinted at the sketch of John's attacker on her lap. She shaded in the man's hair. He seemed so unremarkable, but he'd almost killed John.

She clenched the pencil in her hand. If she'd even been a moment later...

The door swished open. "Mom," Caleb said, his voice soft. "You need your rest. Let me take you to your room. You won't do him any good here."

She straightened and glanced over at her son, the doctor. "You're wrong. We're both calmer when we're together." She made a last few adjustments to the sketch, then smiled. It was him. "Get Nick. I've finished the sketch."

Caleb hesitated.

"Right now, I don't need a doctor as much as I need law enforcement. Your time will come again soon enough."

Caleb nodded, leaving, then when he reentered the room with his twin, she handed Nick the drawing. "This is the man who tried to kill John."

Nick glanced at the sketch and let out a soft whistle. "I'd forgotten how good an artist you are. I'll make sure the cops get this right away."

"Send Zach a copy, too," Anna said. "I have a feeling—"

Caleb groaned. "Those feelings always get you into trouble, Mom."

"No. Most of the time, my feelings tell me when you boys are in trouble."

"I'll send it right now." Nick hurried from the room.

Caleb knelt by her chair. "Please. You need to rest. We thought we lost you," he said softly. He examined her face. "None of us could stand that."

"I need to be here." Anna glanced over at John. "Medicine has done all it can for him. So have you. Now, I wait for John and God's decision to be made." She pulled the rosary beads from her pocket and worried them in her hands. "Please understand. I can't leave yet."

Caleb kissed her hair. "I know that stubborn expression all too well. I'll give you another half hour, then you have to sleep. Doctor's orders. You were hurt, too."

She smiled at her son. "Yes, Doctor Montgomery."

"Nick and I won't leave either one of you alone. You're safe," he said. "I promise."

"I know—and thank you."

The door softly clicked closed. Anna clutched John's hand. His eyes were closed, but his face had lost that grayish tinge that had terrified her when Caleb had first brought her into the room after she'd regained consciousness.

The heart monitor beeped steadily, its regular sound soothing.

She laid her head against his chest, feeling the sturdy thud of his heartbeat. "I thought I'd lost you. I was so scared. Please don't leave me. Not when we just found each other."

Fingertips fluttered against hers, the slightest of movements.

She stilled, holding her breath.

Please God, let it be.

He sighed and his hand squeezed hers. "Anna."

She lifted her head and looked into his eyes. His open, beautiful hazel eyes.

"John?" Her voice was choked through the emotions welling inside her throat. "John!"

She hugged him tight. He grunted in pain and she pulled back. "Sorry."

He licked his lips. "Water," he croaked.

She reached over to a cup of ice chips and fed him a spoonful.

John swallowed, then reached his hand to her face. "I'm sorry, Anna. I asked too many questions. Patrick. Something strange about his death. Didn't...protect you..."

His halting words nearly broke her heart. Closing her eyes, she leaned into John's warm touch, a touch she'd been afraid she'd never feel again. She turned his hand and kissed his palm. "I almost lost you. Do you remember what happened?"

"Bomb."

"You saved my life," she said. "I won't leave you again, John Garrison." She pressed the call button. "We're going to be all right now, and I'm going to wrap you up so tightly and care for you so much..." Her voice broke.

His eyes fluttered opened.

"Love you," he whispered. "My Anna."

He squeezed her hand and closed his eyes, his breathing slow and steady.

"Oh, John. I think I could love you, too."

Icy water splashed against Jenna's face. She sputtered and immediately groaned. Pain, agony seared through her body. *The crazy man...oh God...where was Sam?*

She heard no crying, no whimpering. She forced her eyes open.

Her son stared at her, tears streaming down his face, utterly silent, his body frozen. She blinked at him, but he didn't move.

Her captor chuckled. "The boy knows when to be quiet, like my Hamed. He doesn't want to die."

Jenna tried to smile at her son, to give him comfort from across the room. She had to get Sam out of here.

She struggled to think past the pain. Her captor had hit her and hit her and hit her, again and again and again. Each time he struck he invoked the name Setara, his murdered sister.

"Wake up!" he yelled, throwing more water in her face. "We are not finished." He grabbed her hair and yanked it back. "You have no courage. Not like Setara. She went through the fires of hell on earth before they killed her. So shall you."

Jenna swallowed and licked her cracked lips, swollen from his fists. "Please," she whispered. "Don't."

"Yes. Beg. Like my sister begged. To no avail."

The man leaned in and grabbed her chin. "Beg me," he said. "Me, Farzam. Beg me for your life."

He ran his palm across her face, then pulled his bloodstained hand away. He walked to Sam and smeared her blood across her son's cheek. "Beg for your son's life—as I couldn't beg for mine."

"Farzam, let my son live. Please. I'll do anything you want."

"Say it again. Louder."

She heard a small clicking noise.

God, was that a gun?

She wrenched her wrists against the cuffs and moaned as they cut deeper into her open wounds. The pain was nothing compared to her inability to help Sam. She hated being power-less. Brad had made her feel that way for far too long, but this madman evoked a terror like she'd never known. He could kill them both, at any moment.

She could only plead.

"Please. Please," she begged, sobbing. "Kill me. I don't care, just let my son live."

————————

Brad couldn't look away from the laptop screen.

Sam's face, covered in blood. Jenna pleading for his life.

Farzam struck her again.

Brad's mind swirled with memories.

"You went to the cops!" his father screamed at his mother. She bent over, coughing up blood. Streams ran down her face. "You're as weak and stupid as your son."

He raised the belt. "You." Smack. "Will." Slap. "Not. Talk. To. Them. Again."

With a cry, Bobby ran to his mother and hugged her tight. Wet dampened his face, but not tears. Never tears. Bobby wiped his cheek. His hands turned red. He looked at his mother. Her eyes were swollen closed. Blood dripped from a cut on her forehead. She whimpered even as she held him close, trying to protect him from his father's wrath.

Martin Swinton grabbed Bobby by the waist and threw him against the closet door. His father's huge hand gripped Bobby's throat. "You listen and listen good, boy. There is no room for mistakes. No room for talking too much."

His father threw Bobby into the closet. He locked the door.

Bobby hated the dark. He threw himself against the old oak. "Mommy! Mommy!"

"You won't be talking to the cops again, will you?" A loud smack. A thud. Again and again.

Then silence.

Bobby curled into a ball. Alone.

"Mommy. I'm sorry I told him," he whispered.

Brad's horror still filled his head, screams banging through his skull. His father. Farzam. Brad shook his head to force away the past—a past he'd worked so long to bury. A past that had roared back. A past that he'd repeated with his son.

"Silence!" Farzam dug into Sam's arm, then slapped him across the face. "Be silent and look at the camera, boy. Or I kill your mother."

Sam went completely still.

Brad's nails bit into his palm. His heart racing, his own bloody, tearstained features superimposed on his son's ravaged face.

Nausea rose in Brad's throat.

"Tell Zach Montgomery," Farzam spat, twisting Sam's arm. "Tell him you want his help."

"P...please, D...D...Dark Avenger. Save us."

The camera went dark.

Brad grunted and glared at his captors. He rocked the chair back and forth.

Zach whirled on him, then his eyes widened. He stalked over to Brad and ripped off the duct tape. "You better be making noise over something important."

"I know where that bastard is," Brad spat, "and I want him dead."

Chapter Seventeen

GABE'S KITCHEN WENT SILENT.

"Dear God," Jazz whispered though a strangled voice, speaking the words with the choked sob Zach couldn't afford. She reached out for Luke's hand.

Seth and Gabe erupted with a string of curses through gritted teeth.

Zach didn't know about his brothers, but he couldn't wipe the image of Jenna's bruised face or Sam's stark terror out of his mind. Yet he couldn't let his heart linger on anything but resolve to have them both in his arms again. They didn't need the man who loved them, they needed a warrior.

He grabbed Brad and squeezed the bastard's windpipe. Fury like Zach had never known exploded. "Tell me where they are, you son of a bitch, or die now. We're done with games." He squeezed tighter.

Brad gasped, blinking, sucking in puffs of air. "Safe house. I know the location. I was ordered to kill Farzam."

He released the assassin and shoved him hard against the chair. "So help me, Walters, if this is a trick to save your sorry hide, I'll kill you now and won't ever regret it."

"Sam is my son," Brad choked. "I have to save him."

"And I'm supposed to trust you?" Zach leaned over Brad, placing his hand strategically across his throat. The Chameleon's eyes widened. He had to know one flick of Zach's wrist would end his life. "You helped your son a lot when you beat his mother."

Brad paled, then cursed. "We don't have time for bullshit. They gave me the coordinates for Farzam so I could kill him. It's in that ten square miles you pointed out on the map. Do you want to save my son or not?"

Zach didn't move. Brad didn't shrink away. *The idiot.* Zach's hand twitched. Brad had no idea how close Zach was to—

But the bastard was right. There was no time. "Give me the address."

"I'm not a fool." Brad shook his head. "My contract's been broken. I'm dead anyway. I know too much. Take me with you. I'll help you save Sam and Jenna, then let me disappear. I won't contact you again."

"Dream on. *If* you help us find Jenna and Sam, and *if* they're..." He couldn't say alive. *If they were alive.* No. He refused to consider the possibility aloud. "I *might* put in a good word with the federal prosecutors. That's as far as I'll go. But...I *will* save your son."

Brad stared at Zach for several seconds.

"Take your time, asshole," Zach bit out. "You say you care about your son. Then why are you even hesitating?"

"Agreed. Once Sam is safe, I plan to stay alive...and free."

Zach's gaze burned into his brother Seth. "He so much as twitches in the wrong direction, end it. Get him in the car."

Seth gave a quick nod.

"If anyone wants out—?" Zach began.

"Shut up," Gabe muttered. "Just shut the hell up, Zach. We're all in."

At that moment, Jazz's beeper went off. She cursed and stared at the message. "There's a hostage situation at a day care center." She bit her lip, clearly torn.

"Go," Zach said. As much as he admired Jazz's skills, he didn't want the love of Luke's life anywhere near Brad or Farzam. This fight would be up close and personal. "Those kids need you."

Luke looked at Zach, and he knew he'd done right. Relief flared in Luke's eyes. He gave Zach a slight nod then cupped his wife's cheek. He twisted the strand of long blonde hair that had pulled away from her French braid. "Just be careful. We can handle this. Four against two."

Jazz gave Zach, Seth, and Gabe a stern stare. "Find that little boy and his mother, but I'm warning you. If my husband returns with one scratch, I'll come after you. And I'm handy with more than just my rifle."

She gave them a nod and raced out of the house, leaving Zach and his brothers facing each other. Zach could barely breathe. He hadn't been there for them in five years, and they'd stepped in. Just like his father would have. They accepted the challenge; they accepted him. How could he have doubted them—but he knew his own guilt had driven his actions. He'd hurt not only himself, but his family. "Let's move."

They stashed the gear into the back of the SUV then jumped into the vehicle. Seth held his Sig on a handcuffed Brad as Gabe gunned the SUV. The motor roared and the car raced through the Denver streets.

Zach palmed his father's 1911 and stared at Brad. He wanted to kill the bastard. He couldn't believe he sat a few feet away from him and the man still breathed. But he'd do anything to save Jenna's life, even make a deal with the devil.

Brad sucked in a shuddering breath. "I loved her the only way I knew."

"You had a choice. We all have a choice on how we treat the people we love."

He stared at each of his brothers.

Seth's brow rose. Luke blinked in acknowledgment.

"Damn straight," Gabe muttered. He twisted the steering wheel. The tires barely hugged the street on the tight turn. The vehicle leapt forward.

Zach nodded his own agreement. He hadn't understood the truth of his words until today. His choices had been selfish, protecting himself and his emotions. He'd been afraid to love Jenna and Sam. He'd never even told them. What a fool.

Seth grabbed Zach's shoulder. "Glad to have you back, brother."

"I'm at the edge of the grid," Gabe interrupted. "Which way?"

"Go west of Golden, into the hills."

"Damn. On the very border of our grid. We would never have found them in time."

A beeping noise sounded in the vehicle. Luke cursed. "Link just went live again."

Zach stilled. The third showing of a prisoner. He met Seth's gaze, and his brother's eyes had gone deadly. They both knew what this could mean.

"Open it," Zach said, his entire body rigid. "I have to know."

Luke clicked the link and gasped.

Jenna couldn't breathe. Pain speared through her side with every small movement. He'd broken her ribs. Her arms ached, her wrists were on fire, and her hands had gone numb from the cuffs.

Blood streamed down her face, warm against her cold skin. She couldn't see, but she heard Sam's quiet sobs.

"Silence!" her captor yelled. "You shame yourself."

A sharp slap sounded and Sam cried out.

She struggled but couldn't help her son.

A door slammed opened, then closed, leaving her doused in the dark. *Oh, God, had he taken Sam?*

A small whimper brought her heart back to life.

"Mommy?" Sam whispered. "Can you hear me?"

"Yes," she said through swollen lips.

"The man left," Sam cried. "I'm scared. I want Zach."

"Me too, baby. Can you run away?"

"I'm tied up."

Jenna shifted her hands and the cuffs clinked together. If only she could get at the lock, she might—

The paperclip. The one from her father's file. She'd shoved it in her pants. Her father's lies might come in handy after all.

She bent her wrists, working to reach her back pocket. She bit her lip against the agony.

"Mommy?"

"Quiet, honey."

Success.

She dug into the jeans. She felt for the small bit of metal and used her fingernail to scrape it closer. Seconds later, she grasped it in her hand. She bent the metal and went to work on the lock. She had no idea how much time she had.

"Come on, come on." Every lesson from her life on the streets after her father had left her returned in a rush. The lock clicked. Her hand slipped free. Jenna let out a sob. Should she thank her father for letting her fend for herself? If it saved her son, no question. Yes.

She worked the ropes free from her legs and staggered over to Sam, feeling her way around the ties. He latched onto her. "He hit you, Mommy. I couldn't stop him. I'm sorry."

"It's not your fault, baby. He's a bad man."

Jenna kissed Sam's cheek. "We have to hurry."

She took his hand and stumbled to the door, trying desperately not to cry out. She grabbed the latch, but before she could open it, Farzam pushed in.

His eyes widened, then narrowed in fury. "I will kill you."

Jenna's heart raced. She folded her hand at the second knuckle. She could do this. One blow to the throat.

"You're bad," Sam yelled. He slugged the guy in the crotch. Farzam doubled over. Jenna struck, but the terrorist knocked her off balance and they crashed to the ground. The man clutched her throat, squeezing.

"Run. Get help," she gasped.

Sam didn't hesitate—just like Zach had taught him. He raced out the door.

She sagged with relief. *Thank God.*

Her captor dragged her to her feet. "Your son doesn't matter. All I want is Zane Morgan. We finish this now," Farzam said. He shoved her into the chair and secured a rope tight around her bloody wrists down to her ankles. "You won't get away this time,"

She moaned, tears burned her eyes, but she didn't care. Sam was free.

With an evil smile Farzam picked up the bent paperclip. "You're more worthy a warrior than I expected an American woman to be, but this will soon be over. Your fate is decided. You wish to say a last prayer?"

Jenna sucked in a deep breath, not resigned, never resigned. She'd fight until her heart stopped beating and her lungs stopped breathing. She'd learned one thing from Zach. There was always a way. She gritted her teeth and tested her wrists through the pain. With Sam out of this hell, she could take the risk. She would take the risk, because unlike before, she had Zach to back her up. No matter what happened to her, Sam had escaped. Zach would take care of her son. She had faith in Zach Montgomery. He loved Sam. He would protect him.

He would find her.

"You might want to save yourself. Zach will come after you," Jenna taunted. "Whether I'm dead or not."

Farzam smiled. "Yes. He will. I want him to. Zane Morgan will pay for his crimes today."

Several clicks sounded. The video camera whirred.

"You will give him your last words. Speak."

"It's a trap," she screamed. "Save Sam."

The man slapped her face. Hard. She couldn't stop the cry. Metal pressed against her temple.

"She's dead, Montgomery. An eye for an eye."

The camera went dark.

"How far are we?" Zach asked, leaning forward, studying the streetlights that whizzed past the vehicle.

A beep sounded from the laptop. Luke snatched it. "Got him," his brother said. "Two blocks down." He glared at Brad. "That's a half mile away from where you told us."

Zach pointed his 1911 at the assassin's temple.

"Don't believe the signal," Brad said. "It's a decoy."

Zach met Luke's gaze and could see the uncertainty in his brother's eyes. Zach knew it was his call.

"We're one block away from the triangulated position," Gabe added, from the driver's seat. "Where do I go?"

"How far from Walters's location?"

"Two minutes."

"My son could be dead in two minutes," Brad spat. "Trust me. You guys think I'd lie to you with Sam's life at stake?"

Zach's gut twisted. "If you're wrong, Walters—"

"I'm dead. I know, but so is my son." Brad glared at Gabe. "Don't stop. I'm telling you, I'm right."

The beeping grew louder. They passed an abandoned house. The windows looked very similar to the video. Nausea rose within Zach. If he was wrong, Jenna and Sam could pay the ultimate price.

He couldn't lose them, not like this. Not because of his choices, his decisions, his life.

Thirty seconds.

One minute.

The only sound within the car were magazines snapping into Seth's Sig and Luke's Glock. Zach checked his father's 1911. The .45 caliber had never let him down. *Help me, Dad.* He sent up a silent prayer. *Help me save them.*

Ninety seconds.

The tires squealed as Gabe rounded the corner.

"We're one block away," Luke said.

"Pull over, out of sight," Zach ordered.

In seconds, Gabe maneuvered the car behind a group of pines trees.

Zach turned to Brad. "You're staying here."

"I can help. I'm better than good with a weapon."

Zach ignored him. "Seth, Luke, cuff each hand to a different door, then zip-tie his ankles apart. Make it quick."

In seconds the brothers had Brad spread-eagled in the backseat.

"You'll die for this."

"Heard that before," Zach said, and closed the door on the assassin, flicking the key fob to lock the vehicle. "Let's move."

The four of them peered through the trees at the foreclosed house, its windows boarded up.

"You want Farzam alive?" Seth asked. "For interrogation?"

Zach's expression went cold. "I don't give a shit as long as Jenna and Sam get out alive. Do what you have to." With a scan of the layout, Zach let out a stream of air. The plan could work. "Seth, you and Gabe round to the back. Grab whoever's the closest—Jenna or Sam. Luke and I will hit the front and do the same."

"No way," Seth shook his head. "Farzam wants you dead."

"If—" Zach's throat choked. "If Sam and Jenna are still alive, he wants me to watch them die. Otherwise he wouldn't have hurt them the way he did. Besides, he hates me the most. I go in the front. I'm the distraction." Zach grabbed Seth's collar. "You make sure they stay alive. I won't let anyone else die because of me. You understand?"

"None of us is dying today," Luke said quietly. "Mom would be really pissed."

A small smile tugged at the corner of Zach's mouth. "That she would." His smile faded. "Let's do this."

Brad couldn't hear or see a thing after the Montgomerys filtered through the trees. He tugged against the restraints. *Damn them.* They'd beat him. He had no more tricks. He peered through the front window, but he couldn't see the house. Dark pressed in around the car. He hated the dark.

Bobby buried his face under his arms. He shook. Too quiet out there. Mommy wasn't even crying now.

Quickly, he wiped his tears away. He couldn't let Daddy see them.

The closet door slammed open. Bright light blinded him. He closed his eyes and shrank from the opening.

His father grabbed Bobby's injured arm. He couldn't stop the whimper.

"Weakling," his father growled. "Get out here."

His mother lay crumpled in the corner, unmoving.

"Mommy!"

"Leave her," his father ordered. "We're out of here."

"But I have to help her," Bobby pleaded.

His father backhanded his cheek. Bobby crashed to the ground.

His mother still didn't move.

"You weren't man enough to help her. Weak, pathetic little bastard. You're probably not even mine. You don't want to go? Fine. Stay in the dark."

He kicked Bobby, then shoved him into the closet and slammed the door closed. The lock turned.

Through the cheap pine he thought he heard a very faint groan.

"Mommy!" Bobby banged on the door. "I'll get out. I'll help you."

Brad stared in the darkness. He'd failed that day. Just like he'd failed his son.

A shadowy figure appeared at the door. He heard several clicks, then the car door swung open.

Theresa Banyon shook her head in disappointment. "Damn it, Walters. I set them up. Do I have to shoot them for you, too?"

Brad looked at the face of the woman who had pulled his strings the last few years. He recognized the cold eyes. She was a mirror of his soul. "I can turn this around, Theresa. I'll finish the job for you. Just let me loose and give me time to get my son."

"This is your last chance. Kill everyone else and you can take your brat and leave."

He would kill everyone in that house if it meant having his son. "I'll succeed this time. I'll even finish Garrison off when I'm done."

Theresa weighed a familiar and deadly device in her hand. Brad knew the weapon's power—and its impact. The heat created from the unique explosion burned so hot, the trace evidence was useless, but just like its creator, the bomb was vicious and unpredictable. He'd used it in Stockholm, and the stupid thing had almost killed him.

Crap. She really had gone over the edge if she'd produced more of the unstable explosive.

She smiled. "I'm a forgiving woman." She tugged out a knife and slid it into his palm, then stood back, a gun on him. "Consider this a life-or-death test, because if you fail again, you and your son die tonight."

Brad would succeed. His father had been his first kill. Well, Sam would be his first save—the first time since his mother had died that he cared about someone besides himself.

Just outside the dilapidated building Zach and three of his brothers eased around the trees edging the property. Zach signaled to them. His brothers nodded, then Seth and Gabe headed around the corner toward the back entrance.

Seth stopped abruptly and pointed to a nearly invisible wire spread across the lawn.

Booby traps.

Great.

Zach communicated the information silently to Luke while Seth warned Gabe. He acknowledged the signal. They'd have to be very careful. No storming in. Farzam might be crazy wanting revenge, but he obviously wasn't stupid.

They stepped carefully toward the front door. Zach eased around some misplaced dirt, then flicked a bit away.

A makeshift mine.

After uncovering yet another explosive device, Zach's heart sped up. This was taking too long, but he couldn't help Jenna and Sam if a terrorist bomb took out the rescue team.

A birdcall sounded from around back. Seth. Crazy guy had gotten where he could imitate almost any bird that existed.

Everyone was in place and ready.

Zach looked at Luke.

His brother met his gaze, calm, certain, and deadly. Zach held up his hand and counted down.

Five, four, three, two...

Go!

Zach shoved his good shoulder through the door. The wood exploded into the room. Seth and Gabe slammed through the back at the same time.

Farzam whirled around, momentarily stunned, his back to Jenna.

Zach didn't hesitate. Thanks to the video, he and his brothers knew the layout of the room. He raced to a bruised and battered Jenna, gun raised. "Get down," he yelled.

Simultaneously, his peripheral vision scanned the room. Where was Sam?

Her poor face screwed up in effort. Straining against the ropes binding her, Jenna rocked the chair, knocking Farzam off balance. The furniture tilted on two legs. Her shoulder slammed into the floor. The wood broke under the impact.

Farzam fell back and rolled to Jenna. Time slowed. He whipped the barrel of the submachine gun at Zach. Bullets thwacked against the wood, ripping through the walls. Zach leapt out of the way. Luke dove to the side. Seth and Gabe followed.

The bastard grabbed Jenna, shoving the broken chair aside, and used her as his shield. He scooted toward the corner.

"Don't move or she dies now." Farzam shoved the gun into Jenna's side and opened his jacket.

Everyone stilled.

The guy had strapped what looked like blocks of C4 to his chest. He held a small detonator. His fingers shook as they gripped the device.

Zach faced the man he had met only once at a civilized university tea. He bore no resemblance to the man Zach had known. Farzam's eyes were wild, determined—and totally insane.

Seth eased to the side slightly; Luke and Gabe shifted, too, but none of them had a good angle. Seth gave a slight shake of his head. If they tried it, Jenna was dead.

"Khalid killed my son, Zane Morgan," Farzam said. "I have nothing to lose."

"What about your wife?"

"I am no longer a man to her. You ruined me. You and Pendar and your stupid, grandiose dreams. You don't care who suffers for your selfishness."

Zach shut his eyes against the truth in Farzam's words. "I didn't want Pendar to pay. He wanted freedom for his wife and daughters. He came to me."

"And all he found was death." Farzam's expression grew cold. "An eye for an eye."

He shifted, his finger tightening over the detonator.

A branch crunched outside the open front door. Farzam looked up.

Zach took advantage of the distraction. He tackled Farzam, stripping the detonator from his hand. Seth grabbed the semi-automatic from Farzam's other hand.

Jenna scrambled away, shoving free of the loosened ropes, only to collapse near the back door.

"No!" Farzam slipped a knife from its sheath and slashed at Zach's face. They staggered to their feet. "You die!"

"Not today." Zach spun around and shoved the heel of his hand up and back into Farzam's nose. Bones shattered and drove into the man's brain. Farzam crumbled to the ground. Dead.

"Not today?" Theresa's voice came in through the doorway. "I wouldn't bet on that, Zach."

He turned. *Damn it*. He hated being proved right.

Theresa.

The woman he'd trusted with his life for five years stood in the doorway, a very familiar, very deadly weapon in her hand, her eyes lifeless, cold, and vicious. "You know I always have a backup plan." Smiling, she pressed the timer down. "Sorry about the collateral damage. You should have just died on the road outside Istanbul, Zach. It would have been so much cleaner."

She tossed the device into a pile of trash in the corner.

"Bomb!" Zach yelled at his brothers. "Get out! Now!"

He scooped Jenna into his arms. His legs pumped across the floor.

A whirring noise whined, then went silent.

God, no. They wouldn't make it.

Chapter Eighteen

WHAT THE HELL ARE YOU DOING?" BRAD TACKLED THERESA to the ground. "My son is in there!"

The house burst into a fireball, and flaming debris catapulted around them. An inferno erupted into the sky, secondary explosions discharging like deadly munitions.

"Too late, you fool." She smashed her elbow into his windpipe, then rolled to her feet.

Brad fell to his knees. He clutched his throat and lay choking in the dirt, barely able to hear over the roaring fire. Waves of heat pelted his face, but he couldn't move. Sam was gone. He'd failed again.

She aimed an Afghani-made weapon at his head. "I don't do loose ends."

Fury consumed Brad as he stared up at the woman who had pulled his strings for the last eighteen months. That day, she'd left a not-so-subtle message on his doorstep—a blood-covered baseball glove. The meaning had been clear. She could get to his son. He'd wanted to end their association. Too many jobs for one client wasn't smart business. But somehow she'd uncovered his identity.

He'd agreed to continue their association but he hadn't liked it. Unfortunately, she was smart, and soulless. Raging fire highlighted her eyes—the pupils glowing red, like pure evil. Even he had rules. He didn't murder children, for one. Theresa had no boundaries. Never had.

"You've made a mistake, bitch."

"I know. You're alive. You'd have made my life a lot simpler if you'd been in the house, too, but the gun ought to take care of it. Farzam's body will be unidentifiable, but I'll get the same credit for bringing down the Chameleon."

She stepped closer. "I'd hoped I could salvage you as an asset. I even confiscated your wife's evidence. She hid it under her father's name, ironically enough." Theresa held up a small folder. "Too bad you're useless."

Jenna's folder. There it was. What Brad needed to start a new life. Like he cared anymore. He wanted one thing now—Theresa Banyon dead.

"This made interesting reading. Does Montgomery know you killed his father?"

All Brad wanted to do was to get his hands around her neck and squeeze, but he had to play it smart to kill her. "We can work this out, Theresa."

"Not happening, Walters. Maybe I'll tap your contacts myself. You won't be needing them."

A loud shuffling erupted from the nearby trees.

"Daddy!" Sam bolted out of a thicket of pine and aspen and skidded over to Brad. "Mommy's in the house!" He pointed to the fire. "Save her!"

"Sam, no! Get out of here. Run!"

Theresa turned the gun on the boy. "Not another step, brat."

Sam froze in place, only a couple of feet from the madwoman.

She glanced at Brad and chuckled. "Your son, Chameleon. He picked a really bad time to return. The fire department and cops will be here soon. I don't have time to stay and chat anymore."

She aimed the weapon at Sam.

"No!" Brad lurched from the ground and heaved himself in front of her just as the weapon discharged. The bullet struck his chest, then exploded inside him. He knocked Sam down, covering his son with his body. Blood poured from the gaping chest wound, but there was nothing Brad could do.

He was dying.

Sam was alive.

Jenna lay half-pinned beneath Zach, fire and debris raining over them. Scarlet flames and plumes of smoke obliterated the sky. She looked to her left.

Gabe lay on the ground, unconscious and unmoving, pinned under several large, smoldering logs. Luke groaned and crawled to his brother, tugging at the wood. "Gabe," he rasped. "Hang in there."

Seth sat up just beyond his brothers, holding his bleeding head.

"Help me, Seth," Luke said, tugging at the heavy wood. "They're burning him."

"Daddy!"

"Sam?" The sound of her son's scream and a gunshot had her up and running, then staggering as the pain in her cracked ribs hit.

Gritting her teeth, she bolted around the corner. A woman bent over a bloody body on the ground. *Oh God. Brad.* She recognized his hair, the figure. Sam was struggling to pull himself free of the weight of his father's legs.

"Shut up, brat." The woman took a bead on Sam's head.

"Theresa, stop!"

At Zach's command, the woman whirled around. Jenna didn't pause to think. She dove at Theresa. The woman screamed. Bullets whizzed by Jenna's head, but she hit Theresa in the gut with a full tackle and took her down. Jenna cried out in agony. Pain exploded in her chest, more ribs cracking. Theresa lifted her gun. Jenna didn't hesitate. She slammed her knuckle into the woman's throat.

A crack sounded. Theresa choked, then tightened her hand on the trigger.

She fired.

At that exact second, Zach's bullet shattered her skull.

Jenna lay panting on the ground. Theresa was dead, her brains splattered on the ground. Sam was safe.

"Mommy...help..."

Her son's bubbling rasp terrified Jenna. She rolled clear of Theresa's body, horrified to see blood spreading from a blackened hole in her son's shirt.

"Sam!" She lurched to him.

Her son looked at her, tears in his eyes. He stared at his chest. "It hurts, Mommy."

His eyelids flickered.

She clutched him and lifted the material. Blood flowed from the wound. This couldn't be happening. "No, baby. You're going to be fine. Mommy's here. Zach!" she screamed. "Sam's hit!"

"Shit!" Zack raced over, tore off his shirt, then pressed the cleanest side against Sam's wound. "Luke," he shouted. "Call an ambulance. Seth, get over here and help me staunch the flow. Gabe, make sure that bitch is dead."

No one responded.

Jenna looked up. Luke and Seth carried a groggy Gabe, but Luke still had a phone to his ear.

"Help's coming, baby," Jenna said, touching his forehead. "It'll be OK."

"I'm...sorry, Mommy..." Sam's voice was weak.

Jenna bent down and whispered in his ear. "No way, Junior Avenger. You're not leaving me."

She couldn't stop the tears.

"I love you, Mommy."

He whimpered then went limp in her arms.

Zach paced the hospital room, hating the beeping of the machines hooked up to Sam's frail body. Surgery had taken hours, and Sam had barely moved since they'd brought him to this room.

"Sit down, Zach." Jenna, her eyes swollen and her face bruised and mottled, patted the hospital chair beside her, right next to Sam's bed.

Zach sat and gently took her hand, wincing at the bandaged wrists. He cupped her injured cheek, his gaze tender. "I'm so sorry. This is all my fault."

She shook her head. "You saved me. Another few seconds and he would have killed me."

Jenna bit her lip and stroked her son's hand. "Sam's going to be fine. I know he is." She shifted in her chair, but groaned at the slight movement.

"You need to see the doctor? You need more pain pills?"

"No, Zach, I need you," she said hoarsely, leaning into him. "Stay with me until Sam opens his eyes."

"I'm not going anywhere," he whispered, feeling like his heart would shatter at the faith in her eyes. He tucked her close and stroked her hair. He wouldn't leave her until Sam woke up.

And he had to wake up.

A man pushed aside the curtain and peered into the room. The suit gave the guy away. Zach palmed his father's 1911 and held his finger over the trigger.

Caleb, Nick, Luke, and a bandaged Seth followed the Company rep in.

The visitor's gaze swept the occupants, then stopped on Zach, a flash of pity showing before the businesslike demeanor slipped into place, disguising the man's emotions. "Zachariah Montgomery?"

Zach rose and stood protectively in front of Sam and Jenna. He made his weapon visible. "Who's asking?" he said in challenge.

The man backed off. He didn't attack, just cocked his brow at Zach.

Interesting.

"Stand down. Gavin Sterling. I'm your new boss."

Zach tensed and raised the weapon. "Prove it. *Sir.* ID?"

"He's legit," Seth interrupted. "We wouldn't have let him in otherwise."

Zach pocketed his weapon.

Sterling shoved his identification holder back into his inside jacket. "I should start with a thank-you. Taking Theresa Banyon out tonight solves a potentially embarrassing problem for us.

Evidently, she's been working her own game for the last year and a half. We just caught on to it, thanks to you."

"That's not why you flew from DC to Colorado, though, is it?"

Sterling studied Zach. "You're better than I expected, to be honest. Cards on the table, I need to find out what I can do to keep this situation quiet. Whatever you and your family want, Zach. If it's in my power, you've got it."

Zach stared at Sam, then Jenna. He looked one by one at his brothers. As hard as he'd tried to push them away, now they almost thought as a unit. Even more so than when they'd been kids. No longer did Zach feel apart and different. He was the same. He was a Montgomery.

"The family doesn't need anything," Zach said. With that, his brothers nodded their agreement and disappeared into the hallway.

"But I want Jenna to receive all of Brad Walters's assets and a new identity. Too many people could know about their relationship to me after tonight. I want them safe."

Jenna stood and grabbed Zach's arm. "What about you?"

He turned to her and toyed with the wayward hair near her temple. "This is what we planned. To make sure you're safe. It's the best way, honey."

Sterling cleared his throat. "Not necessarily. Theresa lied about your cover being blown. She put together a sophisticated paper trail, but it fell apart after we tugged a few strings. You could go back to the Middle East tomorrow. If you chose to."

Zach stilled. "Why would she do this? Why did she want me dead?"

"We don't know yet. We're looking into it. We can tell you she put in for my job about eighteen months ago."

"That's crazy. Do all of this for a promotion?"

"There's also the several million dollars in offshore accounts. So far."

Zach rubbed his temple. "I thought I knew her. She trained me. I trusted her."

"We all did."

He searched his mind for signs, or clues. He faced Sterling. "I did some unauthorized research on my father's military career not long ago," he admitted. "She mentioned it as a reason I was being targeted. She was smart. The more lies, the more you have to remember. Review the files. You might find something."

"Thanks for the tip. You didn't have to tell me that," Sterling said, his expression contemplative. "Are you certain you don't want to continue working for the Company?"

Jenna laced her fingers through Zach's hand. He looked over at the woman who had changed his life. In her eyes he saw complete support, complete faith, complete trust. Sterling had just offered Zach everything he'd wanted when this entire mess began. And she stood by him.

Now, though, he simply didn't want his old life. He wanted a new life. With her.

Sterling looked from Zach to Jenna and then at Sam. "I suspect I know your answer."

"Not to be ungrateful, sir, but I've found something infinitely more interesting than taking out bad guys." Careful of her injuries, Zach gently tucked Jenna against him.

She leaned over to him. "Are you sure?" she whispered.

He lowered his head. "I wanted to prove myself. To my father. To my family. Maybe even to you, Jenna. I don't have to do that anymore. There are other ways to help people, and to help my country."

She gave him a bright smile and he kissed her lips gently.

"No, sir. I think I'm done."

"Then good luck. I envy you what you've found," Sterling said, his expression strangely enigmatic. "Hold on to her."

"I hope I can."

Sterling cleared his throat. "Very well. I accept your resignation as an undercover operative. All trace of your identity will be expunged from the records and database. You should be able to live a normal life." He tossed a file on the bedside table. "One last piece of business. You might want to read this over. It's a copy of the evidence file found near Theresa's body. I'm sorry to tell you, but Brad Walters, aka. the Chameleon, was the hired gunman in your father's assassination. It's on page twenty-three, at the top. Street. Time. Date. Your father's initials. Million-dollar hit. It took me a while to confirm everything, but all the travel records and the Chameleon's aliases match up."

Jenna's gasp broke through Zach's numbness. "Brad killed Patrick Montgomery?" she asked, pleading for it not to be true.

"I'm sorry." The man cleared his throat.

Assassinated. How? Why?

Suddenly, the world had tilted.

Lies. Patrick's last word. Zach had believed his father had referred to Zach's failures. He hadn't. His father hadn't been killed in a robbery. The kid convicted hadn't done it. It was all lies.

He replayed the most painful moment in his life—up until Jenna had been taken from him. He understood his father's expression now. Patrick had looked at him the way Zach hoped he looked at Sam. *With hope.*

Not disappointment.

His father had believed in him.

More than Zach had ever believed in himself.

He met Jenna's gaze. The way he would always have faith in her and in Sam. He lifted her hands to his and kissed her palms.

"You were right, Jenna," he said softly. "About my father, about me, about everything."

Sterling cleared his throat. "If you change your mind about coming back, Montgomery, give me a call. I hate to lose a good operative."

"You heard him. He's not interested." Gabe rolled his way into the room, his leg immobilized on the wheelchair. "Besides, Zach and Jenna already have new jobs lined up, so you can leave."

"We do?" Zach stared at Gabe like he'd lost it.

"Sure you have new jobs. Jenna's my new cook and you're my hardworking busboy. Treat me right and I may promote you to bouncer."

"And that's my cue to leave. Good luck, Zach. Thank you for your service. You'll be missed."

Sterling exited the room, his footsteps stealth.

Zach threw a pillow at Gabe's head. "You're an idiot, but thanks for getting rid of him." He looked over at Jenna, his smile vanishing. "Now, get out, Gabe."

His brother studied Zach's face. "I've seen that look before. Don't screw this up, big brother." He wheeled out and let the door close.

"Are you going to mess up, Zach?" Jenna asked softly.

He turned to her. Zach stared down at Sam in misery. "I caused this to happen to your son, and to you." He ran a gentle finger over her cuts and bruises. "How can you forgive me?"

"I'm still here, Zach," she said. "And unless you tell me you don't want me, I'll always be here."

"You really think this will work? We met under crazy circumstances. Are you sure it's real, that I'm real, because I have to admit, sometimes I don't know."

"I'm not on the rebound. What I feel isn't gratitude. Everything within me was destroyed, Zach. I thought my faith was gone. But every action you took, every decision you made, you did it for me, and for Sam. When Farzam…" She swallowed. "When I thought he would kill me, I knew if anything happened, you would love my son. You're the best man I know, Zach."

"Zach?" Sam was beyond groggy. He blinked his eyes. "Mommy?" he whispered.

"Oh, my God. You're awake." Jenna sat down and nuzzled Sam's cheek. Tears streamed down her cheeks. "Are you all right, baby?"

Sam squirmed a little. "I'm not a baby anymore, Mommy." He looked up at Zach. "I hit the bad man who hurt Mommy, Zach. Right where you told me to. Just like you showed me."

"You did a good job, buddy." Zach felt the sting of tears in his own eyes. "I'm proud of you."

"I ran to find help, but the house blew up. When I came back, I saw that bad lady with Daddy. She wanted to hurt me, but he protected me from her." Sam's eyes filled up. "Is it OK if I'm not mad at Daddy anymore?"

Jenna held him tighter. "Of course. Your daddy saved you. He…loved you."

Sam turned slowly in Jenna's arms. He nodded and motioned to Zach.

He sat beside Jenna and leaned in. "You were very brave, Sam."

"I wanted to tell Daddy that you don't hit people you love," Sam whispered, "but the bad lady shot him first. He kept bleeding on me and saying he was sorry. Then he stopped talking. Is my daddy dead?"

Zach's throat closed against the building emotions.

Jenna rubbed Sam's back. "Yes, honey. Daddy's gone."

Sam bit his lip. He placed his small hand on Zach's face. "You saved my mommy. Didn't you? You brought her back to me?" he asked.

"We kind of saved each other, buddy. She saved me inside." Zach pointed to his heart.

Sam's lips quivered. "I'm glad you're both still here."

Zach clutched Jenna's hand. "Me too, buddy. I'm glad we're all here."

"I'm really sad and tired right now." Sam yawned. "Zach, will you be in my family?" Sam closed his eyes. "Mine's all broken."

Zach watched Jenna's son drift off to sleep.

She brushed her son's hair away from his face, her palm cupping Sam's cheek. Tears of relief and joy brimmed from her eyes when she looked up at Zach. "See, Sam chose you," she said, gripping his hand with hers. "Sam loves you. You showed him how a real man treats his family—with love, strength, and patience. As long as we're together, we'll be all right." She hesitated. "I love you. I want to be with you. And Zach, my love *is* real."

Jenna took in a deep breath. "But I do have one condition. No more lies. None. Can you live with that?"

"I'm a very good liar," he said. "My life depended on it. How will you know?"

"Because I saw you lie to your brothers without blinking, but when you lied to me…let's just say, I can tell."

Zach frowned, then recognized the glint in her eyes. He smiled. "I don't believe you. Prove it."

"Oh." She drew back and smiled. "Is that a challenge, Mr. Montgomery? Just try me. Tell me something untrue."

Zach stepped forward and framed her face with his hands. "How about this…" His heated gaze captured hers. "I don't love you with everything I am," Zach whispered and kissed her cheek. "I don't love your son, Sam, as if he were my own, and I don't want us to be a real family." His lips touched her forehead. "I don't want to make love to you for the rest of my life, or to give Sam a baby brother or sister, as soon as possible." He pressed his mouth against hers, gently, reverently. "Most of all, I don't want us to be together. Loving each other. Forever."

He lifted his head and stared into her green eyes. The love shining there warmed his very core. Jenna had healed his soul and filled his heart.

"How'd I do?" he said.

"Wow," she whispered. "You are an excellent liar. Thank God, you're all mine."

Epilogue

The voices over the airport's public address system droned on and on. Jenna stood just outside of security, searching for Zach's distinct ginger hair. Sam held on to his mother's hand and danced at her side.

"Where is he? Is he here yet?"

She tightened her grip as Sam became even more energetic. "Not yet..."

Then she saw a very familiar, very tall, strong figure striding toward her, a duffel thrown over his shoulder. She smiled. "There he is."

Sam let out a whoop and started running.

By the time Jenna reached Zach, her son had already leapt into her new husband's arms. Husband. The husband she'd dreamed of, the one she now called hers. Three months of wedded bliss down and fifty years to go.

"Did you take care of your mom?" Zach asked Sam.

"Yep, and I didn't even have to hit anybody in the *you-know-where*," he whispered way too loudly.

"Whoa," Zach said, laughing. "Speaking from experience, I'm glad about that, buddy." Zach grabbed Jenna by the waist and plastered her against him. "Hey, there. I missed you, wife." He pressed his mouth against hers, his lips warm, wonderful, and oh-so-full of promise. "And I love you. Two weeks is much too long to be away from my family."

"Did you bring me a present?" Sam asked, shoving between them.

Zach smiled at the boy's eagerness. "Didn't I promise?" He knelt down and pulled a small *tabla* drum from his bag. "I love you, buddy. I missed you."

"I love you, too." Sam grinned and pounded his hands on his new toy.

"A real drum?" Jenna groaned. "You're kidding."

"I couldn't resist."

Jenna sighed with resignation. "Then *you* get to tell him to quit pounding on it when he gives us all a headache."

Zach tugged out a vibrant pashmina scarf and let the soft cashmere flutter around her head and shoulders. "Emerald green to match your eyes." He kissed her temple above the red scar from one of the knife wounds. "You've almost healed."

Self-conscious, Jenna covered the injury. "Does it look terrible?"

"No, sweetheart, I see that scar as a badge of honor. To me, you've never looked more beautiful."

"Flatterer," she scoffed, but couldn't stop the smile, knowing he told her the truth—even if he was wrong.

His warm eyes met her gaze, revealing the heat that always burned just beneath the surface, and she shivered in anticipation.

Zach clasped her hand, then kissed it. "By the way, the movie director was ecstatic to have Matt back as the lead on the film. Sterling and I explained what we could and sort of paid off any other questions. As a thank-you, the director introduced me to a contact in Bollywood, who offered to send me an authentic

Indian belly dancing costume for nighttime entertainment. I accepted," he said with a grin.

Jenna slapped her hand over Zach's mouth and tilted her head in Sam's direction. "Small ears. He's embarrassed me enough recently. Your brothers all know about our favorite morning pastime."

"I hate to tell you it probably didn't surprise them all that much," Zach chuckled, taking her hand as they strode through the airport and into the parking lot. "Except maybe your penchant for whipped cream."

He tossed his duffel into the back end of the car. "Do you mind if we make a quick stop first?" he said. "I need to see Mom, and I asked my brothers to stop by."

Sam started pounding on his drum.

"I told you," Jenna yelled over the racket.

"That's all right. I like that he's happy. It was touch and go for a while there."

Zach's eyes went solemn and Jenna reached out her hand to him. "Did you get everything done…over there? Is it over?"

He fiddled with his phone, then passed it to her. The screen showed a news flash that a terrorist camp had been destroyed in Afghanistan. Khalid, the man responsible for hundreds of deaths, was among those killed by a smart bomb.

She squeezed Zach's hand. "You did it."

"Actually, Farzam's wife and son did. Hamed hid a small GPS in his cloak when he was taken. He smuggled out the coordinates to his mother. She gave them to me. I got her son out before the strike."

"Hamed's alive?" Jenna was shocked, remembering Farzam's grief.

ROBIN PERINI

"Sterling found records of several of Theresa's last phone conversations. She'd gotten desperate and careless. She lied to Farzam to push him over the edge to justify killing him."

"It worked," Jenna shuddered, trying to block the memories. "So, where is the family now?"

"I used my Bollywood contact to help them relocate to India. It's one of the more progressive countries in that part of the world for women's rights. Setara and Pendar's daughters will have an opportunity for a good life—and Farzam's son might have a shot at living without a constant threat. I just hope he stays on our side. He's an amazing kid."

Jenna kissed Zack's cheek. "You're a good man, Zach Montgomery. Not everyone would have helped them."

"They didn't deserve the life they inherited because of their parents' beliefs." Zach swallowed hard. "It was my fault Pendar was killed. I could have stopped him."

"Pendar made a choice to try to change things. Farzam made a choice to destroy lives. Theresa made her choices, too. You can't own every mistake, Zach."

He couldn't let the doubts go, but when Jenna looked up at him with such trust in her eyes, he knew whatever had happened in the past, he'd do everything in his power to keep her faith in him strong.

"What about the debrief? Are you still OK with resigning?" Jenna asked quietly.

"No regrets." He took her hand in his. "Sterling confirmed they've found all Theresa's moles. There's nothing left to tie Zach Montgomery to Zane Morgan. And Zane Morgan was officially killed in the blast that took out Khalid. I'm through. Now I get to be an annoying ex-movie-star and house-husband."

"And busboy," Jenna snorted. "I doubt that lasts long." Her smile faded. "What about Theresa?"

"She had ten million dollars in offshore accounts, but that's not the worst of it. She was more than greedy and power hungry. She'd turned traitor. She'd begun to put together a network of buyers and sellers of technology. Somewhere along the line she lost her soul."

Zach pulled into Captain Garrison's driveway. His mom had moved in with John to take care of him during his rehabilitation and never left.

"Do you think you'll miss the excitement?" Jenna asked quietly. "You've had three months to get bored."

He turned and pulled Jenna into his arms. "I don't need any more thrills, except maybe when I'm chasing after *that* guy." He tilted his head toward their little drummer boy.

"Uh, Zach?" Jenna took his hand and pressed it to her belly. "Sam's not the only little one you'll be chasing around in about seven months."

"What?" Amazement and delight filled his voice. "Are you sure?"

She nodded happily. "I just found out this morning."

Zach pulled her close and held her for a moment. "I couldn't love you more if I tried."

A hard rap on the window and a loud cough broke them apart.

"Get a room," Gabe said with a wink, leaning on his crutches.

"Looks like we'll need more than one room. Jenna's pregnant!" Zach exited the vehicle, then strode to his brother and grabbed him in a fierce bear hug. "I'm going to be a father... again. Sam and a new bambino!"

"Damn," Gabe shook his head in disgust. "I guess they let just anybody do that job nowadays. Good thing I'll be the favorite uncle, so I can straighten those poor kids out."

Zach and Jenna laughed as they walked into Captain Garrison's home, Sam trotting at their heels.

Zach's mother sat next to the man who had saved her life.

John rose to his feet slowly and held out his hand to Zach. "Welcome back. Did you find out anything more? Did my digging into Patrick's death stir up these snakes?"

"You and me both, John," Zach muttered. "Dad's past drew a huge red flag for Theresa. Sterling discovered an uncategorized file that I accessed. It recorded a payoff. Five million dollars. Sterling tied the transaction to her. When you started asking questions about Dad, she panicked even more. We think that's why she hired Brad to kill you."

"Makes you wonder what else we don't know," John mused. "Patrick had more secrets than even I realized."

He looked down at Anna with a sympathetic and loving gaze. For the first time Zach recognized the strain in his mother's eyes.

"Mama—"

"I'll be fine, Zach. I have faith in Patrick. Whatever he did, he had good reason. Someday we'll know why."

Before Zach could respond, Sam let out a loud huff. "You guys talk too much about grown-up stuff." He raced over to Luke. "Is Joy here?"

"She's in the den, watching a movie."

"Can I go see her, Mommy? Can I?"

Jenna smiled then nodded, and Sam hurried out the door.

"Sam and Joy have become the best of friends," Jazz said. "He informed me yesterday that he's going to marry Joy someday."

Luke frowned. "Wait a minute. He'd better keep his hands to himself. He's older than she is."

"He's *five*," Zach said. "I don't think you need to start worrying yet."

"Yeah, well, never too early to be careful. I've got a nice convent picked out for her, with high walls and broken glass embedded in the top."

Jenna looked at Zach and laughed. "Neither the high wall nor the embedded glass stopped me—or Sam—from climbing into Zach's backyard."

"That's different," Zach said softly. "You both were coming home...to me."

Zach drew her in for a passionate kiss and Jenna returned it in full measure.

"That's it," growled Luke. "If Sam is going to be hanging around these two lovebirds, I'm packing Joy's bags for the convent today."

Zach turned to Luke and grinned. "Liar."

Jenna laughed and Zach kissed her again. "Guess that trait runs in my family."

Smiling, she looked around the room at her new family. The Montgomery clan. "Just like love."

He held her close and kissed her temple. "Exactly like love."

THE END

Acknowledgments

I am blessed with the most amazing support system imaginable. So many held my hand and propped me up along the way. I wouldn't be here without them.

Kelli Martin – you took a chance on the Montgomery Justice novels, and I can't thank you enough. I am blessed to have an editor with such faith in me.

Jill Marsal, my amazing literary agent – your belief in me and in this book kept me going in more ways than you can possibly know. Jill, I couldn't do this without you.

Charlotte Herscher, editor extraordinaire – your patience on this one astounds me. Your insight and skill made the book what it is. Thank you.

Tammy Baumann, Louise Bergin, and Sherri Buerkle – my talented, honest, and insightful critique group who are always there for me. Not many are blessed with not only great friends but giving critique partners. You are my rock!

Claire Cavanaugh – how many people are blessed enough to have a best friend who can read their heart and mind? You have a gift for story and for brainstorming that is unparalleled. You know me and what I intend sometimes before I do. Thank you for once again navigating with me through the strange world of my imagination. You remain the wind beneath my wings. Always.

Jenn Stark, Jen Fitzgerald, and Jo Anne Banker – for duty above and beyond the call. I can't tell you how much I appreciate you coming to my rescue.

Finally, Stephen Perini, my brother and coach for all things sky bound. Any errors are mine, little brother. You rock!

About the Author

National Bestselling and award-winning author Robin Perini sold seven titles to publishers in one year after winning the prestigious Romance Writers of America® Golden Heart® award in 2011. Her writing's motto: "When danger and romance collide, no heart is safe." An analyst for an advanced technology corporation, Perini is also a nationally acclaimed writing instructor and enjoys competitive small-bore rifle silhouette shooting. She makes her home in the American Southwest.